BANJO
LESSONS

BANJO
LESSONS

DAVID CARPENTER

COTEAU BOOKS

Edited by Geoffrey Ursell.

Cover painting by Ward Schell, 1996.
Cover design, book design, and typesetting by Duncan Campbell.
Printed and bound in Canada.

Grateful acknowledgement is made for permission to reprint from the following:

"Broad Old River," music by Pete Seeger, words by Pete Seeger and Dan Einbender; TRO © Copyright 1993 Melody Trails Inc., New York, NY. Used by permission.

"It Was a Very Good Year," written by Ervin Drake; Lindabet Music c/o The Singwriters Guild of America. All rights reserved

"Blue Skies," words and music by Irving Berlin © 1927 Irving Berlin Music Corp. Used by permission

"Singin' in the Rain," by Arthur Freed and Nacio Herb Brown; Warner Brothers Publications c/o EMI Music Publishers (Canada).

The publisher gratefully acknowledges the financial assistance of the Saskatchewan Arts Board, the Canada Council, the Department of Canadian Heritage, and the City of Regina Arts Commission.

Canadian Cataloguing in Publication Data

Carpenter, David, 1941–
Banjo lessons
ISBN 1-55050-108-9
I. Title.

PS8555.A76158B35 1997   C813'.54   C97-920030-X
PR9199.3.C355B35 1997

COTEAU BOOKS
401 - 2206 Dewdney Ave.
Regina, SK Canada S4R 1H3

Come fish with me (come fish with me)
Out on this broad broad old river
Come fish with me (come fish with me)
Out on this broad old river
And we will see (and we will see)
What we can hook (what we can hook)

—*from* Broad Old River
Music by Pete Seeger, words by Pete Seeger
and Dan Einbender

This novel is for Albert Purkess:
teacher, confidant, friend for life.

BANJO LESSONS

1
SMALL
WORLD

SOMETIMES ALL IT TAKES IS THE RIGHT WORD. When it comes it's like the first trout in a pool of Uncatchables, the first kiss from that special person. It comes to Tim around five in the morning when he and a very special person are ready to collapse from too much talk. She is gazing down at him with a mildly censorious look, as though about to revisit a question she had laid aside a long time ago. His mind is off somewhere, dipping down into dreams and up again to feed on the surface when she asks....

What did you *say*?

When?

On the road, grooving under the stars.

Tim shifts his weight beneath the sleeping bag, yawns, and thinks for a moment.

I said something like...Thank you for the stars and for the fishing trips I've had, and for all my friends, and for... You really want to hear this crap?

Yes.

Well, it's embarrassing, but I felt so *blessed* all of a sudden. I felt so full. All I could do was extol everything I've ever loved in some way or another. I thanked God, for godsake!

What else for?

Smiling, she rises and comes toward him. As she steps over his banjo, the edge of her nightie brushes across the strings, faintly strumming a chord in G major.

What else did you say?

He wants to tell her, but he senses that a forgotten idea, some magic, is somewhere close by, tailing in the current.

ONNA DONNA TINER WAS A BOY NAME TIMMY hes in a canoe now he paddo paddo up dyamazon he sees a big fiss he goes chop chop wif his paddo an he eats it yum.

NOW MUMMYS AT HOME and Daddys at work and Dereks at school and Timmys in the sandbox. Listen to the carpenters. Everywhere in the air they are hammering they go pink pink punk punk pwak pwak pwak. Across the alley down the street. Listen to the tractors the beautiful smell of them. Timmy has a block of wood with a nail this is a tractor it goes jrrn jrrn *jrrn.* Its big and tough its bigger than anything.

NOW TIMMYS IN THE STROLLER GOING DOWN THE STREET. He was sick but he's getting better. Here comes Mrs. Fuller with Nancy shes in her pram she has hair of gold. Shes all in pink even her carriage is pink. Nice if he could climb in there they could be together. They could have their nap together.

NOW MUMMYS IN THE GARDEN SINGING. She sings *blue skies smiling at me.* She is doing the flowers.
    Feebeebee, sings the chickadee so sad.
    Whyou doing that? says Timmy.
    Its to make them grow, says Mummy.
    Whats that?
    Growing is when you get bigger. You grow into a grownup.

Whats that?

Bedding plants. I am putting the plants to bed. Just like you and Derek.

He stands in the shade of a big popular while she digs with a thing in the dirt. She sings away and pats the dirt down pat pat pat like when she makes the beds. The chickadee now hes mad he says *chickadeedeedee!*

Whats that? he says.

Thats a trowel.

A towel.

A trowel. Say it? A trrrowel.

The wind blows through the bedding plants and it blows through her hair. She wipes her hair back with her hand and now theres a dot of mud on her cheek. *Blue skies....*

He makes a song too.

> *The wind blows Mummy the wind blows me*
> *I'm a liddo flower off to see the milkman*
> *Clipclop clipclop toweling and toweling*
> *Smiling at me clipclop clipclop*
> *Off to see the chickadee.*

HE CAN HEAR THE MILKMANS HORSE COMING UP THE LANE. That means its morning. Its all dark outside but its morning. Sometimes hes up in time to see the milkman. His name is Charlie Bream that rhymes with dream. He smells nice. He has a leather apron with lots of money he has more money than anyone. He smells like horses and milk. His horse goes grunt in the lane. Timmy would love to ride in Charlies milk wagon. Timmy says every day, Please Mummy, but she is ascared he will wander off and the tramps will get him. Please Mummy, please. Finally she says, Okay, but just this once. He does it again and again and again.

NOW ITS NANCY AT THE DOOR. She lives down the street. She is Benny Fullers sister. She says, Can Timmy come out and play in the snow? She has some long sticks she says, You take these ones an I will take these ones.

Its cold out its too cold for Benny. Timmy has his Eskimo parka on, in case he could get a chill. So does Nancy. She says that they will pretend to be married and make a house.

I am a tractor, he says.

No you arent.

I am a carpenter.

No you arent either, she says. Whose yard is this? Is this my yard? Right or wrong?

This is your yard.

Was it my idea? Right or wrong?

It's your idea.

She lays the sticks in a big square on the snow. This is our kitchen, she says. You do the grazh.

Okay.

Dont make it too big.

Thats sure a big kitchen, he says.

Its gotta be we got lots of babies.

Oh.

Now we gotta feed em. You go get some money.

He just goes home. He goes home and he doesnt come back. He thinks he will probly not marry Nancy.

NOW TIMMY IS A WHOLE LOT BIGGER he does not grunt his pants any more he uses the toilet he doesnt get sick like he did when he was a baby he doesnt even eat sand or mud he comes in clean from play hes almost as big as Derek he gets along with all the kids even Nancy and its not true he stuck his toes in Benny Fullers picture of lemonade. Derek made him do it. So there.

Derek shoots everybody with his pistol. He goes *kgh kgh* your dead. He scares the dickens out of Timmy.

Mummy? Derek shoots me.

You shoot him back.

Pkshr pkshr your dead!

You dont go *pkshr pkshr* you go *kgh! kgh!*

He tries it. He tries it all day long. He gets a sore throat.

He has a song it goes

> *Blue skies smilin at me*
> *Nothin but blue skies by the sea.*
> *Blue skies singin a song*
> *I love you dearly Rider Wrong.*

He has lots of songs, he sings em and forgets em theres lots more. He sings for Mummy and sometimes for Mrs. Fuller but hes never going to sing for Derek hed just laugh his head off.

Derek comes home from school he goes *kgh! kgh! kgh!* your dead!

I am not.

You are too. I shot you.

I dont wanna be dead. When an honour guy shoots you ydont just stand there, you go *augh* an fall down.

Whats a honour guy.

You know. A guy who knows whats what. Shoot me.

Timmy shoots him.

Derek falls on his bed and holds his belly.

Timmy tries it all day when Derek is at school. He dies regular he shoots the lady who runs the orphanage and then she dies and then he shoots a tramp going by then Timmy he gets it *augh!* right in the middle of the living room he rolls over and over he goes *yarrgh!* because his guts are coming out. Then he is dead hes gone to Heaven its all very sad hes gone and thats all there is to it. Granny Mullen comes all the way from Saskatoon to be there. *Hes given up the ghost,* she says. They all agree, Timmy has given up the ghost. Mummys sad and Nancys sad and old Derek he is so sad he says I am sorry I told you to stick your toes in Benny Fullers lemonade. Nancy says O how much I will miss him. Everyones so sorry they sing a song over his grave it goes

For what we are about to reseed
Make us truly thankful amen.

Everybodys crying even Daddy. Mummy comes in she says, What are you doing on the floor are you crying?

No.

Whats the matter then?

Shes mad. She's got her curlers on.

ONNA DONNA TINE, SAYS TIMMY.

Onna donna tine, says Daddy, there was a nice family. And their names were Mummy, Daddy, Derek, and Timmy.

Thats my name.

Yes, and one day they jumped into their canoe and this time they paddled all the way up the North Saskatchewan—

I dont wanna go up the skachewon, I wanna go up the yamazon.

Well, we went up the Amazon last time.

I wanna go up the yamazon tonight. I wanna go fishing.

Okay, they all got in their canoe—

Onna donna tine.

Onna donna tine, they got into their canoe and went up the Amazon, all the way up the Amazon to dig for diamonds. And one night while they were sleeping in the canoe, who should swim their way?

A fish.

No.

A bear.

No.

A big eagle?

No, a great big anaconda. Thats a great big huge snake. And he is very very hungry and he wants a big meal. He goes hisss, like that.

Sssss.

Yes, he goes hissss.

Mummy comes in she sits on the bed she kisses him goodnight.

Shes got cream on her cheeks all slippery smelling like oranges. Now his lips slide smooth back and forth.

Have you said your prayers?

Yep.

He hasnt said his prayers he always waits till later. She goes out and closes the door. Its all dark in his room. He can see a orange square of light from the hallway thats his door. He can hear Daddy hockling in the bathroom. He can hear the wind blowing outside It says hisss like the Nanaconda. He whispers, Dear Lord in Heaven godbless Mummy and Daddy and Derek and me, make Derek not so bad all the time and make me safe all night long amen.

He waits. The Wind has no lips It just moans around your backyard like a hole with big old dirty teeth. The Wind blows louder It whispers through the cracks in the storm window It says, *Sssss hey Mister, come an show me yer belly.*

Timmy hides so far under his blanket It couldnt never see him. It might come and sniff around for him but It would not find him in the dark It would think maybe he took off when It was moaning down the lane. It might think maybe he was safe in bed with his mummy and daddy It might just slink home.

The sheets were cold but now they're getting warmer and warmer it gets all toasty snuggly down there he could play with his peepee.

The Wind roars away into the dark black sky.

DADDY HE WORKS FOR HATCH COOPER and Strang he prackly runs the place himself. Today Daddy is home early from work.

Derek and Timmy they ask Mummy howcome Daddys home, its only four aclock.

Dads a bit excited today, says Mummy.

Something has just happened, says Daddy. You boys should remember. Atlantic Richfield Number Two blew in today. Ive just been out there.

Where? says Derek.

Leduc. You boys come outside.

He places three lawn chairs down by the flower beds they are in the backyard they are underneath the big poplar. The big poplar is just getting its leaves back. They can hear the kids across the street at the orphanage yelling like crazy.

You go with your father, says Mummy. She waits by the shadow of the house. Derek and Timmy sit side by side, Daddy faces them.

If you boys ever remember one thing in your life you remember this. Atlantic Richfield Number One and Number Two.

What are those? says Derek.

They are two wildcat oilwells and the second one just blew in.

Is that all? says Derek.

Is that all? Do you boys realize what this means? To all of us right here in the province? This could be the richest find since Spindletop.

Derek starts to pay attention. When he is like this he is not so much fun because you can't *do* anything with him. It is a beautiful day. The leaves rattle in the breeze. Mummy brings out a tray of lemonade with icecubes in the glasses she goes clink clink clink.

We could all benefit from this.

Howcome? says Derek.

I am talking about untold riches, millions of dollars. We are sitting on a treasure trove. It means—

Aren't we rich now? says Derek.

No, right now we're in the planning stages. But some day maybe we could move to a real nice neighbourhood and own a house instead of always renting.

A treasure trove. Right under the ground right where their chairs are, right under the big tree. You wait until dark and then you dig and dig away down deep you bring a lamburn. You go down into the hole and there it is in the middle of the cave. The trove is all locked up so you get the key and lift the lid and all the gold and jewels glow in the light of the lamburn. You close up the trove and drag it to your bedroom. No, you leave it down there and say to everybody your just building another house this is the basement we are doing the spindletop next. They say, Can I help? You say, No thanks. You cover up the hole with a green blanket same colour as the grass and whistle when anyone comes near. Wutcha doin, somebody says. Just whistlin, you say.

You boys could get in on the ground floor of this, says Daddy. You could *make* something of yourselves, you could *be* somebody. I am telling you, this is the time and this is the place....

You get in on the ground floor and maybe you pry up the floorboards and down you go. Every night. And there it is your treasure trove. Theres gold gabloons and jewels, marbles and pearls that glow pink and blue like the bubbles in the dishpan...

...came from Saskatchewan in the Depression. You think we had opportunities like this? We never had two nickels to rub together—unless we earned it. We got up at five in the morning. Pitch dark. And we went out and did our paper routes. Every morning we could see our breath in the bedroom. Sometimes outside, it was forty below....

When Daddy calls his name, Timmy is a long way away. I said, Timmy, I would like to hear what you think about all this.

Daddy is waiting, Derek is giving Timmy his older brother look. Hes done it again. Timmy, where have you *been* all this time?

Onna donna tine.

No, onceta ponta time, says Timmy.

Onceta ponta time there was a boy named Timmy.

Timmy on a horse.

Timmy on a horse. And he was going on a long journey up the Amazon to find the treasure of the Onkabonkas. And there was another boy named Derek—

Not Derek!

Shhh!

I dont see why it always has to be Derek.

Okay, Timmy was all alone. So one day he trotted along and he spied a big...

Nanaconda!

Right you are, a Nanaconda and this big fella was very very hungry. He swam up to Timmy and coiled right at his feet because he was about to strike. And do you know what Timmy did?

What?

He took that snake by the tail and stuffed the tail into the mouth of the snake and the Nanaconda went *chomp!* Then he started to swallow his own tail, and Timmy watched nice and safe on shore while the big Nanaconda ate more and more of his own body and got smaller...and smaller...and smaller....

Now Timmy snuggles in his bed. He puts his thumb in his mouth and curls up and he begins to make a story. Onceta ponta time there was a boy name Timmy he was in a canoe he was with Nancy. Him and Nancy they went up the Amazon paddle paddle paddle. They come to a Nanaconda Timmy wasnt afraid he says, Stay. You stay. And the Nanaconda stays, so Nancy she says heres a island lets have lunch they have bananas and cream they have angel cake. Then they have their nap.

No?

Nancy doesnt want to have her nap. She says, You have your nap, Timmy. Me, I wanna go poke around this island.

Okay, he says.

Timmy squirms until the sheets are twisted around his body. Hes too hot, he cant sleep, his story is all going wrong.

Finally it is dark on the island. Timmy hes been asleep he wakes up. He calls out, Nancy! Nancy, she doesnt say nothing she just giggles off in the woods somewhere. Timmy goes out to find her its dark. And theres Nancy shes talking to the Nanaconda. Timmy hes ascared he says, Nancy I wanna go home. Nancy and the Nanaconda they just smile.

NOW THEY ARE AT THIS BEAUTIFUL LAKE its Daddys holidays. Mountie Lake has got everything. Its got a stream that runs in and another that runs out, its got fish in the lake. Its got ponies you can ride around in a circle. Its near the woods, you can see the woods from your tent and you can go swimming. You can run off the end of the pier and jump in and get dried off in the sun and go jump in again. Its got rowboats but not even Derek can go in a boat. Daddy says you could drownd in a boat. You get to sleep in a tent all night long and you go grunt in a hole behind the tent. You can walk to the other beach it has the Cottages. Its for doctors and Nancy Fullers family and Mr. Fuller hes got a motor boat.

The boats are all for fishing. The men go out and catch fish with a rod and pole. They go all morning past the weeds. Back and forth they go. Sometimes they yell out loud *I got one!* Sometimes the fish tastes boney. They are long and very big and green with spots like on snakes. They got real big mouths like a ducks bill but bigger and they bite your line thats how they get caught. When your just little you cant go out with the men and catch fish. But when your big, thats when you can catch them. Some day Derek and Timmy they will be big enough to go fishing and that will be the best thing you can do in the whole world.

Mummy says, you boys go off and play. Daddys going to take a snooze.

Derek, lets go ask if we can ride a pony at the stable.

Derek says, Na. Youd just get allergic.

I would not.

Would so.

Then lets go catch a snake by the rockpile. I betcha we could.

Na.

Whadya wanna do?

Lets go feed Grunty.

You feed Grunty. I aint gunna touch Grunty.

Not *aint gunna* , says Mummy.

Derek, whatll we feed Grunty?

Same as always.

They go each catch a grasshopper. Derek says not to squish it. Its got to be alive or its no fun.

Grunty is the biggest spider Timmy has ever seen. Grunty has a web on the branch of an old stump, the web is shaped like a bike wheel. There it is, sitting right in the middle where all the spokes come together. Grunty looks big and fat and lazy.

Go ahead, says Derek.

You go ahead.

Your ascared.

I am not.

Derek holds his grasshopper in his fingers like a dart. Say bye-bye to the grasshopper.

Bye-bye Grasshopper.

Derek throws it right into the web. It gets stuck and starts to kick like anything. Old Grunty is over there in a second. Grabble grab nip nip and thats all for the grasshopper. Grunty wraps it up and goes back to the centre of the web.

Gimme yours, says Derek.

No, I wanna do it.

Your too scared.

I am not. Bye-bye Grasshopper.

Timmy throws his at the web just like Derek but it lands on the edge of the web and starts to kick and flap its wings. Up comes old Grunty and the grasshopper kicks and flaps so hard it falls down to the ground. The grasshopper is free, it flies away click click click so Grunty goes back to the centre of the web, grumble grumble growl.

That was a lousy throw, says Derek. Go get a nother one. Hurry.

Timmy goes out into the meadow, its got big yellow flowers right up to your waist, its got all sorts of grasshoppers. Timmy runs through the flowers, he flies like a bird, like a plane.

He stops. He does not know why, he just stops right in his tracks. Then he sees it, swaying like a flower back and forth in the breeze. Its got a body like the top of a mushroom. Its legs are striped and hairy and there are many packages in the web. Its big, even bigger than Grunty. One more step and he would of run into it in his bare skin. He backs up slow. He backs up and turns around and walks right out of the meadow.

Get one? says Derek.

No.

Well, hurry up. Gruntys gonna take off.

I dont feel like it. Lets go back.

Your ascared.

I am not. I just dont wanta.

Timmy walks back to the tent.

Scaredy cat, scaredy cat.

Derek! Your brother does not want to play, says Mummy.

If Timmy tells Derek hes afraid of big spiders, Derek will chase him with a spider and catch him and put it down his shirt. You cant always tell the truth. You could get caught if you always told the truth. Bad guys could get you and hold you down. Youd be just like a grasshopper in a web.

Timmy has an idea what a grasshopper in a web feels like.

Derek says, All we were doing was feeding Grunty.

Timmy yells so Mummy can hear too: *Thats cruel!*

He yells it so loud he gets excited. All day he keeps wondering if God was awake and heard him.

LATE IN FEBRUARY, late at night, with the wind pounding the house and rattling the eaves, the phone rings. Timmy's mum answers it. All she says is yes, yes, of course, yes, I will, yes, then she hangs up the phone and whispers to Dad. Back and forth they whisper, and then Dad phones somewhere, and instead of going to bed, his mum begins to move around the bedroom in her shoes, and someone comes upstairs and peeks in his door and he pretends to be asleep.

When he wakes up, it's just his dad and Derek. His mum is on the train to Saskatoon.

Howcome?

Granny is sick.

First I ever heard of it, says Derek.

Well, says Dad, this was sudden.

Granny's always sick.

Well, now your Granny's in the hospital.

In the hospital!

What's the matter? says Derek.

They're not sure. Now you boys eat your porridge. You can't go off to school without porridge.

What about lunch? says Derek.

You'll have to take your lunch.

Only the kids from the orphanage take their lunch, says Derek.

Well, this time you will too. Now don't argue.

My porridge is cold, says Timmy.

Dad gives Timmy a look and Timmy goes quiet and eats more of his porridge. His dad has made it too thin and the milk is smushing into the porridge. The brown sugar is all melted into the milk and the porridge is glunky like that paste you make for the posters in Mrs. Bond's art class.

I still don't see why we have to take our lunch, says Derek.

Because, Mr. Wiseguy, no one will be home at noon, that's why.

When's Mum coming home? says Derek.

In a couple of days.

She wouldn't make us take our lunch. She—

You sit down, young man, and eat your porridge.

They both take a brown paper bag to school. Each bag contains a banana, a roast beef sandwich, a piece of raisin pie, all wrapped up in wax paper and tied with string. Their mum made the lunches before she went to the train station at six o'clock in the morning.

Timmy eats his lunch with all the kids from the orphanage. Big tall Hunch Douglas is their leader. He talks funny. When he sees Timmy he always says, *Hey Timmy Fisho, whenya gunna take me fishin?* Today he keeps looking at Timmy's sandwiches and his piece of raisin pie.

Timmy's mummy she tie up his lunch with little stwings.

Timmy doesn't say anything. Hunch rummages through his own lunch pail. It's black and clunky and made of tin. Some of the orphanage boys have lunch pails. They are rounded on top like treasure chests. Timmy decides that he will ask his dad for a lunch pail.

Leola Hildebrandt leans back in her desk and breaks into an egg sandwich sort of a smile.

She says, Timmy he's got pie. I wish Mrs. Gonner give me pie.

I wun't want your lunch, says Hunch Douglas. You got fleas.

You got fleas your own self, says Leola.

Up my wosy wed, says Hunch Douglas.

He says that a lot. Timmy wonders what a rosy red is but he doesn't ask. Hunch's brother Louie might say, Gimme a smoke, Hunch, and Hunch would say, Kiss my wosy wed. Orville, the smallest kid in the orphanage, might say, Hunch, lemme see your scar, and Hunch would say, I'll show you my wosy wed. As far as Timmy knows, no one has ever seen his scar. Or his rosy red either. Maybe he just shows them to the girls.

Hey, Hunch, who you takin to Noreen's place? Howcome you don't ast Hilda?

She ugly. She got fleas. I get a disease from Hilda.

Louie says, Hey, Hunch, why not you ast Leola?

Augh! Leola worse. She uglier than Hilda. She got fleas an lice too. She awful.

You shut up, says Leola.

Up my wosy wed.

That night Timmy's dad is already at home when they get there. He says, How was lunch today?

Derek has gone to Mole Sharp's for lunch, so he says it was fine.

Timmy says, I dunno.

How was school today?

Derek says, Okay.

Timmy says, When's Mum coming home?

Well, I was going to bring that up with you boys. You see, something happened this afternoon and Mum's going to have to stay in Saskatoon for a while longer.

Awww.

Your mother's had a hard day today. She told me so on the phone. She sends her love.

Why can't she come home now? Timmy says.

Well, I was coming to that.

Dad tells Derek and Timmy a lot of things about time coming and races run and how it happens to everybody sooner or later and for them not to grieve which means bawling your eyes out and how Derek and Timmy should write notes to Aunty Meg and Uncle Randy and maybe also tell Mum how sorry you are, that sort of thing—

But howcome Mum's still in Saskatoon? says Timmy.

Where have you been for the last five minutes? Because she has to be at the funeral.

But that's for dead people! cries Timmy.

Derek gives him his older brother look.

What I'm trying to say is that Granny Mullen has passed away.

Passed away. Like Jesus and leaves in the wind. Granny Mullen, she has passed away. He will never see her again. She will never come to Edmonton for Christmas, she will lie in her grave and never move from her place in the frozen earth. Preserved, that's what she will be. Frozen in a grave in Saskatoon and no one will ever see her again.

He wishes his mum were home.

If that's what happened to Granny Mullen it will also happen to Granny Fisher and then Grandad Fisher. And then it will happen to his dad and mum and Mrs. Fuller. And if it happens to them it will happen to Derek. And if it happens to Derek, it will happen it will happen. It will happen to Timmy. They'll put him in a hole in the frozen earth and he'll be just like Sam McGee from Tennessee. He will never be warm again.

He wishes that he didn't have to eat in the lunchroom. He wishes his mum would come home.

Derek, do you think Granny's gone to Heaven? Derek?

Derek is reading. He is always reading. He says, I dunno. Why don't you go ask Dad?

So he does. His father looks at his watch and says, Yes, likely she's gone to Heaven by now.

What's Heaven like?

Oh, some people believe it's a place where you see all your loved ones again. I sometimes think that when I die my family will be there, that we'll all go there some day and be together as a family again.

How can you go there if they throw your body in a big hole in the ground?

Timmy.

I'm serious.

It's not your body that goes to Heaven. When you're dead, you're not in your body any more.

Then what part goes to Heaven?

Your soul.

What's that?

It's like a ghost. Everybody has a soul that looks like a ghost, and that's the part that goes to Heaven. Your body is drained of all its strength. It just lies there empty.

Timmy remembers Granny Mullen's old saying for when you die: *he's given up the ghost*. All at once the words are thrilling.

He wanders into the playroom and searches through a stack of comic books until he finds the one about ghosts. It's called *The Crypt of the Pharaoh*. In the crypt there's three dead men. They have been murdered and their bodies have all turned green. But their bodies still have muscles. If you're dead and your body is empty and drained of all its strength, howcome you still have muscles?

He crawls in behind the playroom sofa where the wooden frame is studded with little plasticine dials and knobs. He has attached these himself to the frame in the back of the sofa. This is the cockpit of his submarine.

Timmy?

It's Nancy Fuller.

Timmy Fisher, I know you're back there. Mummy says she's real sorry. Me too. I'm really really sorry about your granny. What did she look like? Did you see her? Timmy?

What Nancy doesn't know is that: when you are underwater you can't talk normal. You have to blow bubbles like the fish. How can he tell her that?

Timmy Fisher, says Nancy, you come out this minute.

Bloop. Blup blup.

Let's go outside and play, she says. We made a snow fort. We got spears. We can hunt some polar bears. You should see our fort, it's real neat.

It's cold outside, says Timmy, and then he remembers he can't talk.

It isn't either.

It is too.

How would you know? You've bin inside all day. Am I right or wrong?

It is cold outside, it is cold as a crypt. It's as cold as the place they put Granny Mullen into. But it's warm in the playroom. Down behind the sofa there's warm air blowing through the vent.

You come in here, he says. I made a submarine. We could go fishing and you could be a sailor.

She crawls in behind the sofa. It's not dark enough for a submarine, she says.

Let's pull the curtains and the blinds, he says.

Kay.

They darken the room. A few rays of light come into the room but down in the submarine it's dark.

We're goin down, says Timmy. They curl up on the rug.

This is neat, says Nancy.

Jrrn jrrn jrrn, we're goin through a bunch of seaweed.

I can see a great big giant monster.

Wherebouts?

Over there, a octopus. It's comin this way. Get it!

Kgh! Kgh!

You got it.

Jrrn jrrn.

Timmy's father finds them fast asleep behind the sofa. He says they should never hide like that again, Nancy's mum was worried sick.

Derek says, That was real stupid. Nancy's mum was gonna call the police an everything.

The boys are sitting in the living room. They are waiting for their dad to get off the phone. All we did was play this game, says Timmy.

Well, Dad's all upset, Mrs. Fuller's all upset, now Dad's tellin Mum. That was real stupid. You had the whole neighbourhood out lookin.

Big deal, says Timmy. He misses his mum.

That was a real dumb stunt.

Shutup.

You wanna make me?

Up my rosy red.

It slips out so easily. Derek is on him and pounding and Timmy is holding his hands to his face, wondering one more time about what a rosy red is and why it means such a beating on his head. Then their father is pulling them apart.

A couple of hoodlums, he yells. Just like a couple of hoodlums.

He started it!

No, he did!

Picking on your little brother. Derek, you should be ashamed of yourself.

He asked for it. He swore dirty at me.

I did not!

You did so!

Shutup, both of you! I'm on the phone talking to your mother and I can't even have two minutes' conversation. Now pipe down, do you hear?

They glare at each other. When their father returns, he is pale and shaking. Your mother is coming home tomorrow, and when she finds out you've been acting like a couple of ruffians, what is she going to think? Timmy, what did you say to your brother? Now tell the truth.

I told him I wasn't stupid. I told him me and Nancy were just playing.

His Father turns to Derek. Is that all?

He swore at me.

I did not!

What did you say then?

I only said... Up your rosy red, that's all I said.

What?

The words are wonderful. Timmy repeats them just a little louder.

He thinks and thinks for a long long time. *Rosy red.* His thoughts are more important than his tears and the sting he feels on his rear end. *Rosy red. Rosy red.* That's a dirty word because it's the name of something dirty—like piss or shit or maybe like an infection with pus and like that, and if you said it to Louie or Hunch they wouldn't bat an eye, but if you said it to the teacher or your dad or even Derek... If you said it to Derek, he'd beat you up. If you said it to Dad, he'd hide you. So Timmy has a weapon now. All he has to do is wait till someone makes him angry, and he can say, *Up my rosy red!* and *kgh! kgh!* that guy will crumple up and fall down with shock. And *Up my rosy red!* that's what an honour guy says over at the rink to show tough guys he isn't scared. Timmy could be an honour guy just like nothing.

He grows sleepy tasting the words and wondering about their meaning. And then he has another thought: if you tell a bunch of guys up your rosy red, does that mean you don't get to go to Heaven? He is fairly sure the happy dead people his mum and dad talk about from time to time are not the swearing type. Maybe he should pray to God to ask about swear words, but the flannelette sheet that covers his body begins to feel snuggly all over...and that's why ghosts wear sheets...because a ghost doesn't have a body any more and if you wear a sheet...if Granny Mullen wears a sheet, no one will see she doesn't have her body any more....

He pulls his sheet over his head so he'll know what it's like but the flannelette begins to cover his mind as well and fuzzes his mind and fuzzes his ghost asleep.

THE FIRST ONES TO GO FOR IT ARE MOLE SHARP'S FOLKS. Dr. Sharp gets this great big 24-incher one week before the big day.

Howcome Mole Sharp's parents can afford one and we can't?

Derek and Timmy ask this question at breakfast and at supper and on weekends and just about any time they think of it. Each time they ask, Mum says, You boys go ask your father. Then Dad says, We can't afford it and that's all there is to it.

The Sharps can afford lots of things we can't, says Mum, later, when Dad is outside.

Howcome? says Derek.

He's a doctor and doctors earn lots more money than salesmen. That's why the Sharps can live over on the circle in their big old house and we rent this one.

Yah, but—

You don't go buying expensive little gimmicks when you're just renting.

I'll bet we're gunna be the very last people of all my friends to get one.

Now wouldn't that just be the world's greatest tragedy.

On the big day Mole Sharp invites Derek, and Derek has to bring Tim along, and Sissy Sharp invites Nancy Fuller, and the word spreads. By the time they all arrive, Dr. and Mrs. Sharp's den is crammed with half the kids in the neighbourhood. The signal is set to come on at seven-thirty, it's in the papers and everything. Mrs. Sharp passes out popcorn and that disappears pretty fast, and then she passes out peanut butter cookies and they all disappear, so all she has left is a boughten cake.

She says, if you kids want any of this, you better promise not to tell your mothers I didn't make it myself. Is that a fair deal?

Yes! everyone cries, and before it's even seven-thirty the cake is all gone. It has hard funny white icing that's real sweet.

Mole reminds his dad that it's a quarter past, and he tells Mole that if he needs lessons in telling the time he'll hire a goddam schoolmarm. They all like Dr. Sharp because he swears, and besides, he has a pegleg. He dims the lights and snaps the thing on and nothing happens.

Did you plug it in? says Mrs. Sharp.

Dr. Sharp swears, mostly at the knobs and dials he is turning. He swears but he never says up your rosy red or stuff like that.

A square of bluish light begins to crackle into view and they all see before them a geometry pattern. Shhh, says Sissy Sharp and everyone is quiet.

Did you turn on the sound? says Mrs. Sharp, and again Dr. Sharp swears a blue streak. Timmy's mum says he cusses like that because he has red hair. Mole Sharp has red hair and he swears a lot too. Mrs. Sharp doesn't have red hair and she doesn't swear, and Sissy's hair is only a bit red and she only swears a bit, so Timmy's mum is probably right. About the hair and the swearing.

What's that? says Derek.

That's the test pattern, says Mole.

What time is it?

Shhh.

Still no sound, except a louder crackling as the geometry pattern fades.

What's that?

Innerference, says Mole. Same as the goddam short wave, eh? Static electricity all over hell.

He likes to swear, says Sissy. Makes him feel like a real he-man.

Don't you two get started, says Mrs. Sharp.

He's just showing off, says Sissy. He's always showing off.

That's enough from you, Miss Know-it-all, says Mrs. Sharp, and

Dr. Sharp curses in several different ways including shit and other stuff that he doesn't usually use (he usually swears about God and Jesus and stuff like that). He tells everyone to pipe down and everyone pipes down. By now he is puffing and snorting like a redheaded bull, and that is not such a good sign with Dr. Sharp.

At last they hear the sound of a violin and a tambourine. The static crackles louder than ever, but they can sort of make out the tune. It's obviously a foreign tune, they've never heard anything like it.

Try the knob for dark, says Mole.

Sissy says, *Try the knob for dark* through her nose, as though she has hair lips.

Dr. Sharp tries the knob for dark.

Like a ghost from some other time, drifting out of a storm, comes the shape of a woman. She is very plump and dolled up all frowzy with lipstick and wild black hair, bangles and big earrings, a billowy skirt and blouse. She smiles in a sleepy sort of way and bangs on her tambourine. Across the screen appear the letters, one at a time, T-Z-I-G-N-E. Tzigne.

What's a tzigne? says Nancy Fuller.

Search me, says Derek. He asks Mole.

Damned if I know. Looks like they got some word bass ackwards.

A tzigne is an engizt backwards, says Tim.

Big hairy deal, says Derek, and everyone laughs.

The plump woman begins to sway very slowly and fade on the screen.

We're gonna lose her! cries Sissy.

Don't get your girdle in a knot, says Dr. Sharp. He stands before the screen, hikes up his pants, snorts, and goes back at the knobs. Presently the plump woman returns and begins to dance to the music and bang even more on her tambourine. Sometimes you can see her whole body and sometimes you can see just her face, smiling real sly, the way you'd expect a foreign lady to smile in such a getup.

And then it's all over.

Is that all? says Benny Fuller.

Dr. Sharp smiles and beckons at the set. You can have some more test pattern or I can turn it off.

Test pattern! Test pattern!

That was neat, says Derek.

Yeah, they all agree. That was real neat.

I don't care how neat it was, Dad says next day to Derek and Timmy. You boys can't expect us to go for every fad in the market place.

In the following year, the Fullers get one, and then almost everybody gets one, even the folks at the orphanage. Just when Derek and Tim start threatening never to return home, a little 16-incher appears in their den. So Derek and Timmy begin to spend more time at home.

Whether it's any good for you, Tim's mum and dad just don't say, because they are not sure. But then the Edmonton Eskimos get into the Grey Cup, and they see that on a delayed broadcast. And there is boxing Friday nights for Mr. Fisher, and NHL hockey for Derek. And there is the circus on Ed Sullivan. And there isn't any girlie shows or swearing, and once in a while the CBC does a drama from Toronto and Mum and Timmy like that, and on Walt Disney they learn all about history, like the bravery of those Texans at the Alamo, and what cowardly soldiers the Mexicans are, and isn't that educational after all? You bet.

Timmy's parents have put the television on the table where a nice old walnut radio used to sit. That means that this radio has to go somewhere else. It's a bit bigger than a toaster and real old and classy, but Derek doesn't want it, so Tim gets the walnut radio for his room. At night he turns it on and it glows orange from the dial. It looks like a person with a wide square head and with knobs for eyes. There's all kinds of music at night and you'd think it should look happy playing such nice music, but from Timmy's pillow when he looks over at the radio, it looks like it's frowning. It probably looks that way because it got kicked out by a television.

One night they all get to watch a movie, and this time it's not one of those real old ones but a pretty new one. The movie is called *It's a Wonderful Life*. It starts out funny because you can't see the picture only the sound, and these guys up in the stars are going to see a guy on the Earth, only he's just a kid, so they watch him play and stuff like that. He's a real nice kid named George Bailey and he saves people like his little brother from a hole in the ice only he's not like Derek. Old Derek he'd say swim out of the ice and save your own self. Everybody in the whole family likes this movie, so they watch it till past Timmy's bedtime, and Timmy falls asleep but later he wakes up and there's Donna Reed, she's real nice and pretty, and some guy loses 8,000 bucks and no one is happy any more because they're all worried and then this real cute little kid goes up to his dad who is George Bailey, but now he's a grownup starring James Stewart and he says

Daddy I burped! Derek laughs and Timmy laughs and everybody laughs and then George Bailey he goes and jumps into the river to save this old guy and everyone comes to his home to give him all this money so they sing a song because everyone's happy again.

It was a real good movie. So now Mum and Dad they say it's okay to have a television just so long as you don't watch it too much because it's bad for your eyes.

THE DRUM OF RAIN LIKE A SWEET REFRAIN ON THE COTTAGE ROOF. The CNR from Jasper chug chug chugs him out of his dreams and sings a song along the shore of the lake.

A boner has found its way through the fly in his pyjamas.

He smells woodsmoke, coffee, bacon from the kitchen. His nose is cold, his body warm, his boner....

The word Mrs. Fuller uses to describe the upright piano in the cottage is heavenly. Could his boner be heavenly?

It will rain all day like it did yesterday, like it did the day before. Derek will dash out of the cottage after breakfast and hang around at the Rec Hall. When Tim has done breakfast dishes with his mother, she will grab a book and curl up by the fire. Later, if he is lucky, she will grab an umbrella and go visiting down the beach. But while they dry the dishes, she will probably ask him, is he all right? Yes, he will say, I am fine. Will he join Derek and the other kids at the Rec Hall? Yes, eventually. It's not fair, she always says. All this rain and nowhere to go. I wish your father were here.

He will assure her that there are lots of things to do and that Dad will be out before too long, and Tim will be fine all day in the rain, and yes, he will go to the Rec Hall and join Derek and all the other kids, but not right away. His mother always looks at him as if to wonder.

Sometimes she is gone for two hours or more, and when she goes, a fluttering of joy rushes all through him. Alone with the piano and the old walnut radio. First he turns on the radio and rotates the dial. It has to be the right music, something that dances around in his head afterwards, a song with lots of melody. When he finds the right song he listens carefully, turns off the radio, and walks the song around the cottage, trying to sing its words, sing the low harmony, sing the high, possess the song in a secret way no one in the family, no one at the beach can ever know about. And then he sits down at the piano bench and slowly picks out the melody and adds the harmonies, and before lunch time, before his mother can return, he has enough of it that he can improve it the next time the cottage is empty.

In ten days of steady rain at Mountie Lake he has learned *Blue Skies* (because it's the first song he ever learned), *The Man in the Raincoat* (because it's a sad song about love), and *St. James Infirmary* (because it's a sad song about death).

On this the rainiest day of all, he stops his routine after a couple of hours. His mother might return and wonder about him if he stays home all morning, so off he scampers to the Rec Hall. Everyone's there, even some of the older kids. Margo Godween (or Godwine) says to him, Aren't you Derek's little brother?

Yep.

Well, there's a dance tonight and you should come. What's your name?

Tim.

Do you know how to dance, Tim?

A bit, he says. He hasn't the faintest idea.

Margo darts from boy to boy telling each one about the dance. There will be lots of girls, she says. It's boys we need. She has a nice way about her, for an older girl. She is tall and straight and her hair is black and glossy. She doesn't seem to mind that Tim is only twelve.

No one seems to know where she came from. Benny Fuller says she stays at the Coulsons'. Does that mean she has no mum and dad? Where will she go in the winter time? Is she a poor girl? She doesn't look like a poor girl. She dresses very nicely, he thinks. When it's sunny she tans on the beach in a blue bathing suit. It's the same blue as the sky. She wears a tiny silver ring on her little finger with a pale blue stone, and her eyes are blue. Tim closes his eyes and sees black for her hair, blue for her eyes and her bathing suit, and silver for her ring and the water.

He sneaks another look at her. She has sad eyes. She is smiling but he imagines her to be crying. It's easy, she would cry just like the lady in *Man in the Raincoat* when she sings that he's taken her money and skipped out of town. It's like she is haunted. She has a haunted face.

He stands at the edge of the room and all its commotion and watches her until she goes out the door with two of the older girls.

How wonderful if he could make a song for her! His own song and just for her. It would have to be in a minor key, a ballad, and very sad like Barbara Allan. A melody comes to him and a vision of Margo standing on the public pier at sun-up. Facing out toward the lake, alone and haunted.

As I went out one early morn
To walk along the...

He asks an older boy if he has a pencil. The boy's name is Arthur Locke.

The boy looks down at him and says, Who are you, Pooface?

He says he is Derek's brother.

Arthur seizes him by the shoulders and points him toward the confectionery. That way, Pooface. Pencils. There.

Amber Bole skulks behind the cash register. She has huge breasts. Everybody says that her dad is no good and that's why she and her mum have to work at the store. Her mother makes Amber mind the store whenever she gets sick and takes to her bed. Amber gives Tim a pencil and an old receipt book. He writes

As I went out one early morn
To walk upon the beach,
I spied a fair young mai-aiden
Whose name I could not reach...

He looks up. Amber Bole is peering at him. She cracks her chewing gum and leans on the counter.

That Arthur Locke, she says. Know what I think? I think he's really stuck on himself.

Yeah, he says. Probably.

He begins again.

As I went out one early morn
To look upon the birds
I heard a maiden we-eeping
But couldn't hear her words...

He tries to hum the melody in his head, but now it sounds like *God Rest Ye Merry, Gentlemen.* Can you use a Christmas tune for a love song? Will that spoil it?

Yeah, says Amber, that's his big problem. He's real stuck on himself. He comes in here every day, right? I say gmornin or somethin like that, you know what? He looks at me. You'd think I was the garbage can. Jeez, he could at least say hi. Timmy?

Yep.

Whatcha writin?

Oh, just....

I know. None of my beeswax.

He walks home in the rain, well behind Derek and two older boys. He makes a wish that they will all have lunch and leave, and that his mother will somehow disappear, and the afternoon could be his with the piano. He could finish his song in time for the dance tonight. Maybe he won't actually show his song to Margo, but he'll have it finished. It will be there, finished and perfect in his heart, and somehow she will know.

> *As I went out one early morn*
> *To listen for the birds,*
> *I heard a fair maid weeping*
> *But I couldn't hear her words.*

That's better, and maybe it doesn't sound like a Christmas carol if you think about the girl. What would her voice sound like? Was she actually crying or was she maybe just talking to herself? Her words of sorrow would float across the water and she wouldn't know he was listening because she was looking out at the lake, watching the sun's first pale flush in the east. Her voice is like...her voice is like, well, it isn't like anything when you really think about it....

There's no older boys at the dance. They're all off somewhere together. Several of the girls wonder out loud if the older boys will arrive eventually, and Nancy Fuller says if they never show up ever it's fine by her. Nancy puts on some music. It's nice and slow and mushy, it's Frank Sinatra. Bother on boys, she says, and frowns at everyone.

Well, let's not all sit around.

Tim's biggest fear is that he will have to spend the whole evening dancing with Nancy, but Nancy starts dancing with someone's little brother, and someone else starts dancing with Nancy's brother Benny, and some of the girls start dancing with each other. It doesn't look so hard. You just sort of hang on and slide your feet around the floor.

Someone turns off the main light and all he can see is shadows passing before the little lamps on the tables. He wonders if there will be any smooching, but no one seems to be smooching.

Margo comes up to him.

C'mon, Timmy. You know how to do this?

Off they go, drifting through the dark. She's almost a whole head taller, so he stares at the heartshaped locket that hangs on a chain between her small breasts. Maybe it doesn't matter that she is so much taller, because she has *chosen* him. He is her first dance partner. That has to mean something.

Okay, now, listen to the music, she says. Are you listening? It goes, *you* and the *night* and the *mu* sic, see? *One* anda *two* anda *dee* dee, that's it.

Around they go again and no one's mum and dad is there, it's just kids. He begins to feel older. He begins to feel like Jimmy Stewart dancing with Donna Reed in that movie about old George Bailey.

You like that song? she says.

Yep.

He wants to tell her that Frank Sinatra has a pretty good voice but it isn't really his kind of singing. And that he can sing a song or two himself. She would say, You're a singer? She'd see he could sing and play like a wizard, then she'd call him Tim without being told. Then he would perform her song, except she wouldn't know it was her song until he told her. Then she'd say, Oh, Tim, that's a swell piece of music. She would say it just like Donna Reed. *It's a Wonderful Life*, that's what the movie is called.

Look, Timmy, I'll lead and you follow, okay?

Okay.

They begin again. *You* and the *night* and the *mu* sic....

The doors to the Rec Hall burst open. In comes Arthur Locke, prancing through the crowd like royalty. He's wearing something floppy on his head. In come the other guys, one by one. A girl squeals. They all form a circle around the boys.

Oh, my God, says Margo, that's a girdle! That's a lady's girdle! Where'd you get it?

That's for me to know and you to find out, says Arthur.

Everyone starts talking at once. They all like Arthur Locke, you can tell. Even Derek likes Arthur. Tim thinks he is a smart Alec. Whenever his mother and all the other mothers talk about Arthur Locke, they lower their voices.

Tim walks home alone in the rain. His mum is waiting. She's in a state.

If Derek is out there with those galoots, I will have his head.

Tim says he doesn't think so.

Well, if he's not at the Rec Hall and he's not at home, where is he? Will you tell me that?

Why are you so mad?

Because, one of those pinheads stole my girdle off the line, that's why.

She sends him back to the Rec Hall to get Derek and to get her girdle. He is too tired to argue. Amber Bole tells him they've all gone down to Nancy Fuller's.

See if I care, Amber says. Good riddance to bad rubbish. Are you goin?

I gotta get my mum's girdle. He goes off down the path in the rain, slowly, because it's as dark as it can be. As he goes he knocks down the spiderwebs with a stick, and his misery settles into him like a cold or a fever. Margo will be there at Nancy Fuller's, and all the older boys will be there, and no one will talk to him. Maybe he could grab his mum's girdle when no one's looking and run off down the path.

He knocks on Fullers' door.

Nancy opens it and says, Fishy, you look like a drowned rat!

Her mother comes to the door. She has on a Hawaiian costume. Timothy Fisher, you will catch your death. Come in!

He asks if Derek is there, and she tells him the older kids have gone on to Arthur Locke's parents' cottage but that Timmy should go straight home. He is chilly, even his feet are cold. His socks have both run down his ankles and bunched in sodden lumps at the bottom of his rubber boots. He plods on, striking down the cobwebs.

> *She cried, My house is empty*
> *And I have no place to go,*
> *My lover does not love me*
> *And my heart is full of woe...*

Farther up the beach he hears laughter, but when he arrives at the Lockes' cottage, it's dark. He knocks lightly on the door and waits. He thinks he can hear a girl snicker, but whether her voice comes from the Lockes' cottage, from the beach house down below in the pitch black, or from one of the cottages further down, he can't tell.

At last, with the rain seeping slowly through his cloth jacket and his jeans, he turns for home. When he arrives, he finds a note on the ice box from his mother saying that she has gone down the beach to look in on Mrs. Bole. Derek still has not come home. Tim goes out one more time and listens. Somewhere down the beach, perhaps in the other direction, there is more laughter, but he's too tired to follow the sound.

The new Fisher house is on the circle with a fountain in the middle and rows of faded pansies and snapdragons all around the fountain. It's a quiet old neighbourhood with lots of big trees but not so many kids. They are either Derek's age or too young for Tim. He misses the lake, he misses the fishing. (He has caught seven perch, one sucker, and a jackfish that got away.) He misses his friends in the old neighbourhood, he even misses the rough kids from the orphanage. There aren't any rough kids on Tim's new block or tramps shuffling by with reddened eyeballs and bottles in paper bags. There's no sound of bulldozers, no construction sites. The houses around here, like Mole Sharp's, have all been built a long time ago. The neighbourhood is so quiet that the very trees seem to sleep, and the lawns and gardens and the houses. There are no rowdy parties, no patrol cars or noises in the night. On a Saturday morning after breakfast, Tim can sit out by the fountain and listen to the hissing of sprinklers on the lawns and the chatter of birds all around the circle, but everything else, the houses included, seems to sleep the sleep of the decent.

According to his father the neighbours are decent, their children respectful, and their homes tasteful. Decent, respectful, tasteful. These words begin to appear more and more often in suppertime conversations. More and more, Tim and Derek are given little talks about table manners. If Mr. Strang and his wife came to dinner, what would they think of you two? his father would say. Or, Don't just grab the salt and pepper, say Can I please have the salt and pepper.

Tim is told that the new house is like a reward for Dad's promotion. But with it comes these new manners, and nobody told him whose reward *they* were supposed to be.

His mum and Mrs. Fuller are sitting on the front veranda having a sip of tea and looking out onto the circle. He slouches in the shade of the carraganas where he can hear every word they say. Every day is sunny and warm. And boring. In three days, school will begin. The carragana pods tick all around him, one after the other. *Tick tick tick tick... Three days till school.*

Mrs. Fuller says to his mum, Jenny, I was going to tell you and I kept forgetting. You remember the night at the lake during the last of that rain? The night Derek came in so late?

Oh, that night. Don't remind me.

Well, your Timmy came to our door to ask if Derek was there? I was teaching the girls how to hula and Derek wasn't at our place, and I started to wonder if Timmy would get lost or catch a cold or something—you know how sick he gets—so I slipped out the back door to see if he'd gotten home.

You mean you went out in that rain? Reenie, you *angel*.

Well, it was only a minute's walk and I knew you'd gone down to see how Minnie Bole was doing. Anyway, I came up to your place and all I could see was the faintest light coming from your little sitting room, and Jenny, what should I hear but the loveliest music. Someone singing in a beautiful high voice? Like those Irish tenors?

From *our* cottage?

Well, yes. I thought it was the radio, but I listened. And do you know, it stopped, and then it started in again? Like someone was rehearsing for a Christmas concert? Jenny, you are going to think I'm some sort of a snoop, peering into your cottage at some ungodly hour in a rainstorm, but I could not, absolutely could not—

My God, don't tell me it was Timmy.

Your Timmy. You never told me he was so talented.

Well, just lately, he's had this thing about the piano, but—

Your Timmy was crouched over that piano playing and singing away, it was heavenly, Jenny.

Well, that little sneak. And all along I thought he was so....

Just *heavenly*.

He seemed *sad* about something.

Sad nothing, says Mrs. Fuller. That was the loveliest singing I've heard in a month of Sundays. That's good enough for Broadway. If Nancy or Benny could sing and play like that I think we'd all retire on the proceeds.

Timmy's mum laughs lightly.

Oh, Jenny, sighs Mrs. Fuller, it's a wonderful life.

It's a cockeyed world, his mum says.

TIM'S MOTHER SITS ON THE EDGE OF HIS BED IN HER KIMONO. She feels his forehead and sighs while he rolls the thermometer in his teeth.

Tim can hear Derek in the next room rifle through his desk drawer. A pen, a geometry set. Frantic to be on time. Every minute or so the storm window in Tim's room shudders from the blasts of the wind. It's dark outside.

His mother takes the thermometer from his mouth and rotates it under the light of the bedside lamp, shaking her head. This gesture of hers means, Where do you *find* these things? Mumps, whooping cough, measles, chicken pox, pneumonia, amoebic dysentery, scarlet fever, strep throat, shingles, exotic forms of influenza. Always in the middle of the school term.

Dr. Sharp hobbles in around midmorning with his black leather bag. He grunts and puffs through his usual routine, prodding and feeling, getting Tim to say ah, listening to his lungs and his heartbeat through a cold stethoscope. As always, Doctor Sharp hums the first two lines from *The Sheik of Araby*. He never seems to make it to the third line.

Howdya feel, Timmy?

Achy.

Achy. What else?

Tim goes through the list. He feels punk, he has a fever, his head aches, his joints ache, his skin is sensitive to the touch. No, he isn't nauseous. Yes, he's regular. He sweats bad sometimes. Yes, the aspirins helped a bit. As usual his mother asks about polio.

After a few of the usual tests, Dr. Sharp returns with a diagnosis. This time it's something no one knows very much about. He says that Timmy should get lots of sleep and lots of liquid, and that this goddam thing could last all winter or just a few more days.

Day after day he lies in bed. At night he awakens in a clammy sweat and towels himself off, then returns shivering to bed and damp sheets. All night long the old kettle rocks on the burner in his room, blowing out fumes of Friar's Balsam. Timmy eats little and turns pale and thin, waking and sleeping throughout the day, rarely speaking unless spoken to. He keeps the old walnut radio on. He wakes up or falls asleep to *The Road of Life* or *Pepper Young's Family* or *Fibber McGee and Molly* or *Burt Pearl and the Happy Gang*. Each day his mother brings in and takes out the tray. He accepts her labours like a sickly heir to the throne.

One day Dr. Sharp drops in to see him and to talk to his mother. Tim turns his radio off to hear their voices floating up the stairwell, but only a few words at a time manage to drift through the sighing of the kettle. *On the mend...no medicine anywhere for what he's....*

What if I'm dying, he wonders, without alarm. I am me and when I die, I won't be me any more.

...got to get the little gink off his ass....

No one else is me. No one else is Tim Fisher because no one else is exactly like me. No one has my thoughts. No one else has *this* thought. I'm the very centre of...the very centre of....

Start from the beginning. He is lying in bed in one spot. No one else can lie right now in that same spot because no one else in the whole world is him. He's the only one who can be him. If that's true, he is the centre of the Earth, the centre of all the constellations in the whole Universe, and if he dies and stops thinking, then maybe nothing out there will exist any more. Nothing will exist...because if he stops thinking about things in the world, if he stops seeing them, how can they exist? How can they exist without his constant...his constant...being there to watch everything?

That's it, right?

No, not quite. But this thought he keeps having...this thought...it should have a special name. Tim's Thought, that's what he will call it. Now he can tell it to someone. But who? If he tells it to his mother she might tell him he is just tired and to get more sleep; and if he tells his dad, he might tell Tim why doesn't he get this serious about mathematics; and if he tells Derek, Derek will say, Big hairy deal.

He wishes he could tell Tim's Thought to an older person who would understand. A real old guy but just like himself in every other way. This old guy would be Tim when he's an old man. That's it! He will tell it to himself away in the future. He is older than Santa Claus, older than Old Man Potts from *It's a Wonderful Life*. He is about fifty-five, and he's taller than Derek and just as smart as George Bailey. He's married to Donna Reed or a lady who looks just like her and they are so rich that he can go fishing or take a trip around the world any day of the week. And he really understands kids when they say something.

Timmy begins to write all this down. He tries to imagine what he will look like when he is old and grey, but that's too hard. He creeps into the bathroom, squinches up his eyes to dim his sight, and looks at himself in the mirror. He still looks too young, so he turns off the bathroom light and shuts the blind and squinches up his eyes again, and there...a spooky man is looking back at him.

Timmy writes it all down with an H-B pencil. Maybe after he dies, people can read it. Then it will be like he didn't totally die.

Because what if he really *is* dying? Then if he doesn't write down his thought, no one except his family and a few other people will know he was ever alive. And then *they* will die, and he will be forgotten like Granny Mullen. That's scary, when you really think about it.

Dr. Sharp's voice rises once more above the sigh of the kettle. *You've got to get him interested in things...going again...thinks lying in bed is goddam normal.*

How will his mother manage to get him going? Will they buy him a puppy? Will they give him the same kind of medicine Benny Fuller's parents gave him?

That night and the next night he hears his parents whispering, but nothing seems to come of it.

One evening he is having Tim's Thought again when his dad comes into his bedroom holding a magazine. Here, Son, he says, handing it to Tim. This should keep you busy for a while.

It's a copy of *Fin & Feather* from Dr. Sharp's office. On the cover a man in waders and a plaid shirt smokes a pipe and holds up a string of pickerel. In the background is his tent, and leaning out the flap of the tent is a lady. You can see her smiling face, her lovely neck, and one bare shoulder. Tim is supposed to be looking at the pickerel, but his eyes keep going back to the smiling lady. She has very curly red hair and freckles, and she probably has on nothing at all inside the tent. Why would she be bare naked in the middle of the day? Maybe her husband has just called to her, *Honey, hurry up and get changed! The pickerel are biting!* Maybe that's why he is facing away from the tent, so she can get dressed in privacy. But if that's so, why does she have to change in the first place? Maybe she has slept in, and the reason she's bare naked in the tent is that she has just been changing out of her pyjamas... She takes them off slowly, sliding them down over her legs.

Boner time.

It never fails. He can be waiting for a bus or waking up in the morning and having to pee or just taking notes in class, and boioioing, he's got this stupid boner. It's real embarrassing, except of course when he's in bed and the door is closed. Then he can stroke it like a pet snake until the pleasure is almost too much to bear, all the time gloating as the Gypsy Lady pulls off her veils and her skirt, or the Pirate Lady who is always swimming in the sea and always forgetting where she leaves her clothes, or Liana the Jungle Queen who hardly wears anything at all or Miss Melnychuk his grade eight English teacher, or all of them all at once and Nancy Fuller too, and sploosh into the old kleenex until—it always happens—he feels goatish and empty and so ashamed to have thought such things about nice ladies who didn't even know they were being watched, and it's not the Pirate Lady's fault if she can't remember where she put her clothes.

The whitish fluid is a mystery. It smells like Javex bleach. He's fairly sure that it's premature urine. That's just another reason for feeling shameful. He is tampering with what his mother calls Nature's Processes, and besides, anything that feels that terrific has to be bad for you, and no one in the house or anyone he knows ever talks about it. Not even Gump Lowney talks about it, so it has to be a queer thing he is doing. He will just have to quit. Soon he will quit altogether, and then he will only think nice thoughts.

A day later he picks up his copy of *Fin & Feather* and looks again at the lady peeking out from the tent. He can no longer be sure she is bare naked. Only her neck and one freckled shoulder are bare for sure. Perhaps she has on a sun suit or something. What got into him?

The cover sketch is signed R.J. Stufflebeam. He thumbs through the pages *of Fin & Feather*. There are all kinds of hunting and fishing stories. Some, like a piece entitled "Oh, Those Michigan White-tails!", have photos of the authors standing on dead animals. A couple of stories are illustrated by colour sketches. "Spinning for Specs" is set in Northern Quebec. It's about fishing for speckled trout, and one of the illustrations features an angler who bears a strong resemblance to the one on the cover. But this one has a Frenchy sort of pencil mustache and wears a red mackinaw shirt. Still, he clenches his pipe and smiles in the same way. There is no sign of the redhaired lady, but again, the same signature in the lower right corner, R.J. Stufflebeam. Tim reads every article, and although he finds no mention of the redhaired lady in any one of them, the fishing stories are real good. They all start about the same. *There was a riffle on the pool as I tied a spentwing mayfly onto a 5x tippet. Next to a sunken log the lunker brownie rose again, and I knew this was the moment I'd been dreaming of all winter long....*

You know, Timmy, his father says the next evening, you're getting a little colour in those cheeks.

Yep.

You know what your mum and I are going to do? If you're healthy in the spring, and if you're all caught up in school, we're going to take you fishing.

Where bouts?

Ochi Creek.

Is the fishing any good?

Doctor Sharp says it has some real good trout in it.

Wow! Could I bring a friend?

I don't see why not.

Timmy senses something, an advantage of some kind. He thinks for a moment. Me and my friend, could we camp out in the woods somewhere?

You mean all by yourselves? I don't know, Timmy.

Please, Dad? We could maybe camp right by the creek. If there was *three* of us, we'd maybe be safer, and—

Son, hold on. Let's not run away with this thing. All I promise you is a fishing trip, and you can bring a friend. You think about that now.

His mother comes for his tray and stands by the door. She is smiling.

Did he tell you?

Yep.

Isn't that a nice idea?

He says we could try Ochi Creek. He says I can bring a friend, maybe even two friends. He says maybe we can even camp out in the woods all by ourselves.

His mother frowns. Well, he didn't tell *me* that.

It's a great idea, Mum. We'd be okay. We wouldn't go far.

It's a wonderful idea. He thinks it's just about the most perfect idea he has ever heard. He goes back to his homework with renewed energy. Every time he finishes an assignment he re-reads one of the articles in *Fin & Feather* as a reward.

The following week, around the end of February, another copy of the magazine arrives. This time it comes in the mail, and with his name and address on a small label. First he looks for the redhaired lady. There's another illustration by R.J. Stufflebeam but it's a picture of a man treed by a grizzly bear. He's pointing his revolver at the creature. The caption reads, *I aimed for the space between his gleaming little eyes and squeezed off a round.*

So he turns to the fishing stories. They are by men who fish for trout. They use fly rods and come from New York State or Pennsylvania or maybe Montana. Their streams are as clear as tap water and have names like the Beaverkill, the Battenkill, the Willowemoc. In

every stream there are wily browns (brown trout) or specs (bro
or bows (rainbow trout). The men who write the articles stu
insect life so carefully they can tie their own flies to look like the
ral ones the trout eat. He reads and re-reads these articles, and dre.
his way up the streams. He learns that beaver dams are good for brook
trout; that brown trout feed most actively in the evening, and the big
ones at night; that a dry fly should fall as softly on the water as a petal;
that only hicks use worms; and that if you have to use a spinning rod
and a bunch of gaudy spoons to catch a trout, you don't announce it to
the world. He learns that you try to place your fly close to a bank or an
overhanging tree; that you play a big fish by keeping your rod tip high;
and you never net it when it's still full of fight (they say when it's still
green). He learns that you always cast upstream, because that's how
you sneak up on the fish. Hungry trout always face upstream, the
direction their food floats down from. He learns that wet flies catch
more fish but that dry flies are more fun. And much, much more.

It comes to him one night that Derek knows none of this. Derek
does everything well. He plays hockey well. He belongs to a real team.
In baseball he has a fast glove and usually hits the ball squarely. He can
catch a football over his shoulders with his back to the passer, he can
shoot seven out of ten foul shots or dribble past Tim any time he
wants. He has already shot ducks with Dad and caught a jackfish from
Mountie Lake that weighed seven pounds.

But he caught it on the *bottom*. No one in *Fin & Feather* would be
caught dead fishing with bait on the bottom. And Derek doesn't know
how to catch trout with flies. According to the authors of *Fin & Feather*,
any fool can catch a jackfish, and pickerel get boring after the first thousand. But it takes a real artist with a fly rod to catch a trout. You don't have
to work out with dumbells like Mole Sharp does every day, or have big
shoulders and muscles like Hunch Douglas, or be a real fancy-dan on
skates like Derek. You have to be an artist with the fly rod.

Tim goes back to school in mid-March. He feels weak, tires easily.
He is given a note signed by Doctor Sharp that says he has had a
disease known as mononucleosis. In place of physical education they
allow him to have a library period, and he keeps pace with assignments. At night in bed he reads and re-reads his copies of *Fin & Feather*.

That month his father enrols him in a flyfishing class with his
own fly rod. He assembles the rod. When he is alone in his bedroom, he holds it like a sword. One night a week, after fly-tying,
he and some other boys practice their casting in a gym. Their in-

structor is an old Scot who gives them flies without hooks and teaches them how to false cast back and forth and land these flies on cloth targets on the floor.

The only fellow in this class from Tim's school is Elliott Crystal, an owly looking Jewish boy Tim's age who has skipped a grade. He walks with small purposeful steps and carries a large black briefcase. He has dark hair with tight curls, glasses with thick lenses, and almost no neck at all. He never wears jeans and rarely wears running shoes. He seems to prefer grey flannel pants, white cotton shirts, and oxfords. He always gets the highest marks in his grade, and the kids at school refer to him as The Owl.

Tim and Elliott always go together to the fly-tying classes on a bus that travels to the east end of the city. They never talk about school, rarely about girls or sports. Mostly they talk about fishing: where they want to go when the snow melts, whether their dads will take them, what you can catch and how. Tim decides that he will ask Elliott to come on his spring fishing trip to Ochi Creek.

His other friend is Gump Lowney. He is also a good student, though no match for The Owl. Gump Lowney gets his name from Gump Worsley, the famous goalie who once played in Saskatoon against the Edmonton Flyers. Gump Lowney has a very long nose and a nasal voice. He is big for his age and as gentle as a milkhorse. He likes to go fishing with his dad for northern pike. Gump Lowney, Tim has decided, is his best friend, so even though Gump doesn't know beans about flyfishing, he will also ask Gump to go along.

At supper one night he announces that he has invited Gump and Elliott.

Now just one minute, his father says. I don't recall saying you can bring two friends.

You said so. Remember? When I asked you if we could camp out in the woods? Remember?

Camping out in the woods? his mother says. In *springtime?*

He turns fiercely to his mother. There's nothing wrong with camping out in the woods. As long as you know what you're doing. He tries to catch Derek's eye.

This whole thing is getting out of hand, says his father. I don't remember once promising—

Any idiot can put up a tent, says Derek. It's no big deal.

Let me get this straight, says his father. You have already asked Gump and Elliott without—

You said! You promised!

Boys? says Mrs. Fisher.

I said no such thing.

Boys?

You did so. I told Derek and he wouldn't forget, would you Derek?

Boys! his mother yells. This whole trip has gotten entirely out of control. It started off as a nice little family thing, and suddenly, she cries, embracing the air as though she is trying to catch a canary...suddenly....

Tim knows all about *nice little family things*. Drives in the country with someone droning on about the good old days, and drinking tea after church on Sundays and doing sissy things all afternoon and not making any noise. The tears rush to his eyes, and suddenly he is yelling.

Any time *Derek* wants to do something, great, all he has to do is ask but when I only ask for this one little thing *oh no* Timmy's too little Timmy's too delicate I can't have anything I can't even have a map of the world like Derek he gets to practice driving the car he gets to go to Red Deer for the hockey tournament all of my friends get to do things but when I ask for one measly little trip in a tent it's like I'm askin for a million dollars I don't even get a decent allowance I don't even....

He stops for breath. His father, his mother, and his brother all gape at him.

All through April and early May he reads *Fin & Feather*. It even cuts into his television time. He dreams at night that he is moving upstream along the gravelly shoals of Ochi Creek, or somewhere like it. The water is pure and clear, gravel solid underfoot, mist heavy on the water at dawn, and the trout magnificent. Sometimes he is gliding up the stream in a canoe. Sometimes he meets the Nanaconda or Donna Reed in her dancing gown.

In his best dreams, the trout are everywhere, slapping the surface with their tails or spawning in the gravel like trout in pictures. It's all like pictures, only better, it's like nowhere he has ever seen.

Sometimes, on top of a beaver house or on the far shore, naked or nearly so, the redheaded lady sits combing her hair. He approaches her and then wakes up, aching with desire for her, but angry that he has missed his big chance to catch a fish. Once he calls to the lady as she eases herself out of the water and up onto the bank to sit on a bed of moss. She has wings like a mayfly and she is completely naked. *Please*, he cries, *don't go*. She turns and faces him, the water streaming off her body. Again, the exquisite ache to be with her, but he can't think of what to say. Any instant she might fly away and leave the Earth behind.

Finally he thinks of something.

Do you know the work of R.J. Stufflebeam? I'm just asking!

THE BLUE CHEVY HEADS WEST ALONG THE HIGHWAY towards the village of Mountie Lake. Now the farm country has turned hilly. Tim sits wedged between Elliott Crystal and Gump Lowney in the back seat, the only one in the car without a window of his own. The sky is grey and turning dark purple in the west. His dad says there might be heavy rain coming and that they can still turn back. The car pokes along the two-lane highway and the sky grows darker. The clouds mass from the northwest and move slowly across the road ahead. Finally Tim spots the foot-hills due west, rising between his mum and dad. The car comes to a bridge over the river and turns onto it. The river is swollen and grey with silt.

Doesn't look too good, his dad says.

We're not fishing in this river, Tim says.

I know, his father says wearily.

Where's the creek from here, Mr. Fisher? says Elliott.

Upper end of Mountie Lake. The wild end.

Gump Lowney's head comes up from a doze.

The wild end?

There's no cottages where you boys are going.

Tim's mother turns to Tim's dad but she is silent.

Tim knows that if they don't hurry, it will start to rain and they'll have to put up the tent on the wet ground. His dad will say, That's it, boys, we're all going to stay in a rented cabin.

Across the river is a little store and a B/A gas pump. Mr. Fisher goes into the store while the rest of them wait.

Tim's mum says, Are you guys sure—

Yes! cries Tim.

Young man, don't you yell at your mother.

Sorry.

I was concerned about the weather because I know what happens to you when you get soaked and get a chill. You always come—

Mum.

Gump Lowney and Elliott Crystal stare out opposite windows.

Tim's dad comes out of the store. He is looking grey like the weather. It won't take much to set him off. A few drops of rain will do it. They say the road's passable, he says.

As the clouds grow darker the blue Chev takes them west around Mountie Lake. It goes slow—deliberately, Tim thinks. Tim's dad has never driven this slow in his entire life. But at last they spot the site. A sign says *Ochi Campground Welcome*. They go over a bridge across a tiny stream and through a grove of spruce and aspen to a field.

Tim's father says that was it.

What?

The stream, he says. That was Ochi Creek.

Back there? Tim squirms around to see, but already it has disappeared behind him.

You mean there's fish in that tiny little thing? says Tim's mother.

There is no one parked in the campground. They leave the car at the edge of the meadow next to an old fire pit beneath some big pine trees, and after a bit of hesitation on Mr. Fisher's part, they begin to unload the gear. Gump Lowney gives cautious instructions about his tent, and every time a blast of wind breaks through the trees, he looks up at the sky. The tent is an old canvas affair the colour of floorwax with a wonderfully stale smell. They peg the floor down and push some metal rods through sleeves in the canvas and a big wooden pole up the middle. The musty heap of canvas rises into the shape of a real tent. At his mother's urging, Tim and the boys begin to throw in their sleeping bags and their gear so that things will stay dry.

His dad remains grave throughout the unpacking. From time to time his mum gives the woods a disapproving look. Tim's father offers his advice to the boys about open fires and staying warm and how to prime the pump. No one seems to hear. Elliott collects wood and paper for a fire from a nearby cook shelter. The wind begins to rise.

The five of them stand around with worried looks. Finally Tim's mum says, Look, Pug, if we're going to get on that road again, we've got to go now. They say goodbye to the boys. His mother hugs Tim several seconds too long and says *Now remember, be careful* several times too many, and climbs reluctantly into the blue Chev. His dad starts the car, but clearly he has only begun to give his advice and instructions.

Like I say, Timmy, we'll be down at the cabins, and if you need to walk back, stick to the—

Dad, we're gunna be okay!

Not *gunna*, says his mother.

Let's go, Jenny, his dad says.

The blue Chev moves off down the trail and across the meadow. Then it crosses the bridge over Ochi Creek and reappears on the gravel road. His dad honks the horn, the boys wave, and the car disappears in a trail of brown dust. The boys are alone. Tim jumps up onto a picnic table, facing his friends. At the top of his lungs he yells, Yeeeeehaw!

As if on cue, the first drops of rain begin to fall.

Tim wakes up shivering. He can hear Elliott snore and Gump's teeth chatter. Something out there is not quite right. He unties one of the flaps and peeks out into the dark. Everything is covered with snow. The woods and the meadow seem to glow with it. About ten feet away their campfire smoulders.

Jeez!

What's out there? Gump whispers.

It's snowing like anything!

Gump groans from the depths of his sleeping bag.

I'm freezing, says Tim.

Yeah, tell me about it.

Maybe we can start the fire up. I bet there's some coals.

What time is it? Elliott?

Elliott has a watch with numbers that glow in the dark, but all he mutters is something about feeding liver to the kitty.

Gump and Tim wait in their bags a few moments more, then they seem to move to the same command. They pull on their clothes, toques, and boots and go outside. They try to start the fire but their newspapers have disappeared beneath several inches of snow. Tim piles on some twigs and runs back to the tent in search of paper and matches. He comes out with a handful of kleenex, the map, and some candy wrappers. They dump the paper on the coals and a few more twigs and some bark scrounged from under the picnic bench. They can't find the matches, so Gump kneels on the ground and blows and blows. Finally it catches and a tiny flame bursts out of the twigs. Like hungry ants the two boys dart back and forth in search of dry wood. Gump breaks off some branches from a standing dead aspen and feeds them slowly to the fire. He's smart that way. The little flames begin to crackle. The boys find more and the fire grows. Even the wet branches begin to sizzle and burn and the smoke drifts up in thick choking clouds and follows them all around the fire. Tim throws on some small logs from outside the cook shelter and nearly puts out the fire. But Gump rebuilds the sticks into a little teepee, blows at the coals, and carefully adds the logs. Finally they catch. The two boys stand around warming their bodies by turning slowly around and around, shivering out loud. They sound like frogs. They lay larger and wetter logs around the edge of the fire and balance a couple of these over the flames so that the flames leap through them and around them.

Fantastic, says Gump, and farts.

They spread out various articles from the tent on opposite sides of the fire: Elliott's big rain cape, a small groundsheet, Gump's rubber mattress, a couple of jackets. They lay their sleeping bags on top of these articles, take their boots off, and crawl in. Each boy has several logs beside him, and when the fire gets a bit low, one of them throws a log on. Gump holds his own watch up to the fire.

It's a quarter to three.

Cripes.

Gump wonders out loud what will happen if they run out of logs.

No sweat, Tim says. Don't worry.

He closes his eyes.

They run out of logs a little after four o'clock. It's still dark and snowing lightly. Tim wakes up on his side. His lower hip is cold and damp, the fire out and smoking. He can hear Elliott snoring in the tent. He smells something burning that isn't wood. He raises himself up just enough to see that Gump's sleeping bag is smoldering.

Gump!

Gump seems to leap out of his bag even before he awakens, swearing and dancing and slapping at the sparks.

Throw snow on it!

Gump prances around on the ground in his socks and heaps piles of snow on the smoking bag. Then he pulls his boots on and stomps on it some more. The bag is just like Tim's, a cheap cloth bedroll. It has burned all along the side and turned soggy from the melted snow. Tim leaps out of his own bag, pulls on his boots, and runs for more wood in the cook shelter. He comes back with an armful of logs that seem dry enough. Gump has crawled into Tim's bag and resumes his froggy chatter. Tim builds up the fire the way Gump has done it, and after a while it's leaping high and hot again. He carries back several more loads and this time he has enough for a bonfire.

How in God's name did you burn your sleeping bag?

That's the way the cookie crumbles, says Gump.

This is his favourite saying. In the cold air Gump's voice seems all the more nasal. Sadly he relates the details of his burnt sleeping bag through the opening in Tim's bag. Only his very long nose is visible and all of his words seem to come out like notes from an oboe. This strikes Tim as funny and he begins to laugh, then Gump joins in. Gump's laughter becomes so frantic he can't finish his story. Elliott snores on blissfully.

They take shifts sleeping in the one remaining bag. One falls asleep while the other sits by the fire. They both admit to envying Elliott *his* bag, which is, according to Elliott, a three-star eiderdown for northern camping, one his father has given him from the stock of sleeping bags in his sporting goods store. They consider waking up Elliott and begging him to let one of them trade off with his bag, but neither boy wants to move away from the fire. Tim is first on wood detail, so he sits on a stump where it's nice and warm. Slowly he rotates, like a wiener on a stick, warming first his legs and hands and front, then his back and bum. This time the wood lasts.

By first light Tim is in the bag. He sees Gump rotating himself on the big log by the fire. Tim is falling back into a dream about Miss Melnychuk, who is reading one of Tim's compositions to the whole class in a voice so soft, so soft, so soft, he hears the crash of an animal pounding through the classroom, no, pounding through the bushes near enough to caress, no, near enough to....

Gump?

Jesus!

Gump is standing like a batter at the plate, holding a log in both hands.

What was it? Gump?

Search me. I was dozing.

Maybe it was a horse.

A horse? says Gump. What would a horse be doin away out here?

Maybe it was a deer.

Kinda loud for a deer, Gump whispers. He places the log down by his feet.

They speculate a bit farther on such things as moose and coyotes, but neither mentions the possibility of a bear. Tim thinks that likely Gump will not want to be talking about bears at this time. Gump takes the sleeping bag for the last half hour, and Tim watches the light trickle into the morning, awakening the chickadees and robins in the nearby aspens. By six-thirty it is more than half daylight and the snow has stopped falling. Tim goes looking for utensils, carrying a hatchet just in case. He finds a bag of Mrs. Crystal's home-made doughnuts. He begins at first just to nibble one. Before he's even found the skillet he has eaten two. He feels bad about this, because he hasn't even asked Elliott, who is still snoring in the tent. Well, whose fault is that? Not Tim's. So he brings one over for Gump, who gobbles it down. They sit chewing doughnuts with hands blackened by firewood until the sun has broken through the last of the storm clouds. Gump makes some postum and Tim finds the cornflakes and the milk. They've forgotten to bring bowls, so they use their postum mugs.

From inside the tent comes a mighty yawn. A minute or two later, Elliott Crystal pokes his head out, squinting into the morning sun.

Oyoyoy, he cries. Snow awready!

The boys head upstream from the little wooden bridge by the meadow and tramp into the bush. It's midmorning, the sun almost warm. At first the Ochi is a clear trickle rarely more than five feet wide and six inches deep. They come upon a beaver dam, recently worked on, and this is the reason that the stream has become so small. But the pond is big, and when Gump sees how big it has become, he begins at once to set up his fishing rod. Elliott and Tim go on up the stream. Elliott spots a nice grassy run where an upper beaver dam spills over into Gump's lower one. Here he begins to set up his fly rod. Tim goes even farther upstream and stops in the snow beside a quiet stretch of bubbly water that runs from pool to pool. It isn't like the Willowemoc and it isn't the streams of the Lake District like the picture on his bedroom wall. The trees are wrong and the colour of the water is a very dark amber. Many things are wrong, but the stream holds his attention. It is perfect in some other way.

Almost at once a trout rises. With this little glurp on the water, something in *him* goes glurp. He could call to Elliott. Elliott's just a shout away, and both he and Gump could be right there in a couple of minutes. But Tim doesn't call. This is *his* trout. He begins to piece his fly rod together and fumble the reel into place. A trout rises again in almost the same spot. There are dozens of small black flies in the air. He can see them clearly when they hop on the melted snow. Perhaps the sun has brought them out. He ties on a small black gnat.

To avoid spooking the trout, Tim creeps up to the side of the stream and remains on his knees to cast. A trout rises again, this time below the long grass on the far bank scarcely fifteen feet away. He begins his false cast then lays his line down a few feet above where the trout has broken the surface. His fly drifts slowly downstream along the amber water. Exactly where the last fish has risen, an explosion, and his fly disappears. He rips his line out of the water a second too late and snags it in the willows behind him.

Jesus! O, Jesus Jesus Jesus!

Suddenly weak, he begins to untangle his line from the trees, shaking the branches so that a rain of pussywillows scatters over the pool. He looks back at the stream. Nothing more is rising. He snaps off his leader. His fly remains caught in the willows at the end of a high branch. He grapples it to the ground and retrieves his fly. Kneeling well back from the stream, he ties on his fly again. Nothing rises. Perhaps he has spooked all the trout in the pool. He'll have to try upstream.

He goes up the left side of the bank and climbs a grassy hill with a sparse grove of birches. The sun has already melted the snow here, and he makes his way along a small rocky trail. He looks down on the creek. It's too shallow for trout to lie in, but up ahead there's another small dam. He continues to pick his way along the path, pointing his fly rod through the breaks in the trees. If he's not careful his line will catch. Like the old Scotchman said, when you're flyfishing, anything in the bush that *can* snag your fly *will* snag your fly.

He makes it to the edge of a clearing overlooking the new dam and scans the glassy surface of the pool. Right in the middle a trout rises, and by the cattails, a second trout. But this pool is different. It seems to have no source. The water appears to bubble up from beneath the willows at the side of the bank. Then he realizes that he is standing by the very source of the stream.

He pulls out his leader to prepare for the first cast. He flicks his fly out into the strange pool. Something grabs his fly at once and he strikes back. He is fast to a fish. It dives to the bottom and he eases it back up to the surface. It darts down again, frantically, and he pulls it back up. A small trout, his first ever. He can see it as he draws it through the shallows, up onto the grass, a brown trout, flipping madly. He pounces on his fish.

Hey, Boy!

Tim freezes.

On the other side of the pool a man rises to his feet. He is short and powerfully built, and he wears green coveralls. Hey, whad you doing for dat fish?

Tim gawks at the man. He has a foreign accent.

You kedgit fish good, yass? The stocky man laughs. Fish too...too...too...fast for the hands. He makes a wobbly sign with his hands. Dad's dway she goes, hah?

Tim reels in his fly as the the fish struggles on the bank.

Hey, boy, you give-it dat fish to me. I eat.

The man's arms are wet up beyond his elbows. He has probably been trying to scoop up fish in the shallows. He looks like he could be dangerous, or else hungry. Tim reaches down and picks up the trout in both hands.

You give-it, I eating dat fish, yass?

Tim can see that if he doesn't do as the man says, the man might come over to his side of the pool. And the man looks hungry. Not like the tramps where he used to live. More desperate than that, more tense. Tim tosses the trout across the pool and it lands at the man's feet. The man breaks out in a brilliant smile.

You try water, the man says. Tim shrugs his shoulders at the man. The man shouts to explain. Look look look, he says, scooping out the water and slurping it from his thick hand. You try.

Tim leans his fly rod against a willow branch, kneels down by the pool, and scoops up some water. He sips the water. It is sweet and cold. It's even better than Edmonton tap water.

Good, yass?

Yeah.

The man sits down heavily by the edge of the pool. He breaks the neck of the small brown trout. He pulls out a small kitchen knife. This water wery good. Bast water in world.

Yep.

No one should touching this water. Just leave-it so like this, not touching.

Yep.

Leave-it this water, don't touching like this like that, everything okay cowboy.

As Tim speaks, the young constable takes notes. His father sits in the only other chair in the kitchen while the fire crackles in the stove.

And how tall would you say this man was?

He was real short. He was maybe just a bit taller than me.

And how tall are you?

Five foot four, Tim says.

And stocky, you said?

Yeah, real stocky. Like Mole Sharp only tougher looking. Real tough look—

Mole Sharp?

He's Derek's friend. He's real short but he can even flip Derek.

The young constable stops writing. You mentioned something about his clothing. Would you repeat that again please?

He wore green coveralls like the guys who dig ditches. They were baggy enough for a concealed weapon too.

Do you think the man could have been a fisherman?

Nope.

Why do you say that?

He didn't have a fishing rod. All he had was an old sack. And he talked funny. He talked like a foreigner spy or something.

He had an accent? A heavy accent, would you say?

Tim shrugged. He tries to imitate the man's voice: *Hey, boy, you come here I beat you to pulp.*

Is that what he said to you?

Well, not exactly, but—

What did this man say to you?

Not much. He said he wanted my fish, and about the water and all that.

About the water? What about the water?

That I should drink it. So I did, I tried some. And he said that if people left it alone everything would be...would be okay cowboy.

Again, the young constable stops writing and goes out into the main room of the old cabin where he addresses the others.

Well, the man your son spoke with appears to be the one we're looking for. He left a work camp near Entwistle. Everyone at the camp calls him the Mad Russian. I wouldn't let the name bother you. Minimum security. But he is a wanted man, so if I were you....

The boys try to cross-examine the constable. What's his crime? Could he have a gun? Is he dangerous? The young officer seems to know very little, except to say that they needn't worry about running into him again. When the mountie has gone, Gump and Elliott sag in their chairs. Gump reads an old comic book and Elliott writes between yawns in a scribbler. Tim takes a short stroll down to the spot where the Lower Ochi flows out of Mountie Lake. He has had a bath

in an old tub in the middle of the cabin and he is warm, full of s
and weary like Gump and Elliott. But he is drawn to the strea
spite of the dark.

He sits down on a stone so that he can let his adventure sweep
through him one more time. He watches for trout rising in the last
of the sun's reflection but he can see none. He sits there for several
minutes, staring at the dark water, and he waits for the Mad Russian to rise up again in his mind. Where is he now? What if he
runs into the bear that ran through their camp? What if it wasn't a
bear at all but the Mad Russian who ran through there? Will Tim
get to talk to the newspaper reporters as soon as he gets back home?
How will he tell his story to them? What if they ask him to talk all
about his life? He can maybe tell them about Tim's Thought and
all kinds of other stuff that his family thinks is silly. Then they will
all see how thoughtful he is.

At last, he whispers, something has happened to me. Something important too, and he didn't get sick, and he didn't get scared,
and Derek wasn't there to steal all the glory. Something important,
a real adventure. He will write it all down for his *True Adventures*
assignment and Miss Melnychuk will be amazed. And the main
point is—he can see himself reading this up in front of the class—
the main point is I stood my ground while a *dangerous criminal* was
shouting stuff at me.

That is the main point, isn't it?

Tim closes his eyes again, hoping to shock himself with the
sight of The Mad Russian chasing him through the woods with
the kitchen knife. But all he sees behind his closed eyes are little
glimpses of the water he has noticed all morning dimpled by rising
trout. He can almost see his own first trout, the way it took his fly,
the way it flopped and flipped on the grass. Something makes him
glance up, a sound above him.

A chickadee is calling for its mate. In fact he has been hearing
this call throughout the trip, but only now has it claimed his attention. It's not the scolding cry he is used to hearing in the winter
when the bird seems to call its own name, but a high clear whistle
from somewhere close by. It says *fee-bee, fee-bee, fee-bee*, the first
note higher than the second. Then from the upstream thicket, what
seems almost a perfect echo of the first: *fee-beebee*.

Or maybe from farther away. He listens intently for a long moment, aware only of the stream's rippling music. Then the bird-

calls: formal, yearning, like the voices of shy lovers, like something from when he was a little boy, a sound brought along by the stream all the way from his mum's flower garden. Their cries seem to throb in the air above him again and again until at last they pierce his heart.

Look here, says Miss Melnychuk, leafing through his scribbler. You've got the snowstorm and you boys keeping the fire going. You've got the dangerous animal that turns out to be...what? You've got the fishing stuff. You've got all that conversation with the Mad Russian. Was he the dangerous animal? You never say.

Timmy shrugs.

Anyway, you've got all this....

Miss Melnychuk pauses and looks up at the back of the empty classroom so that her light brown eyes seem to glaze over. She wears a lovely new cashmere sweater the same colour as her eyes and a....

...description. You've got the parents attempting to exert their controls over the youngsters. Then there's this action scene on the beaver dam where the Mad Russian goes after you with his knife... I don't know, Timmy....

He looks over her shoulder and smells her perfume and she turns to look up at him. Miss Melnychuk smiles, and her eyes disappear entirely behind her black eyelashes so that she looks like an Eskimo princess. Now she stops smiling. She seems puzzled. As though she is going to work something out for herself and then for him. When she teaches their class, she never looks this uncertain or this relaxed.

You're not to get discouraged, all right? I mean, I appreciate all the effort you must have gone through to fill all these pages, but....

There are twenty-seven pages in all, including the title page. Gump Lowney's story had only four and a half pages and he writes real big.

...there's just altogether too much to make one story. Besides, you've turned your true adventure into a sort of a boy's tale of courage and daring. I mean, Timmy, I'd rather read what *really* happened.

But all this stuff *did* happen.

All of it?

Ummm. Well....

Timmy, I read the newspaper account, but nowhere did I read of a young boy flipping a dangerous killer over his back into the water and then rescuing him from drowning.

Oh. That. Yeah. I just.

Do you see what I'm saying? I like all these details, but when you try to turn yourself into this movie hero, the whole thing starts to change for me.

You don't like the hero part, eh?

That is very strange, because the hero part is the part he's written for *her*. He was sure she would like it the most. That's the part he's been telling to certain special friends in the schoolyard.

I don't like the hero part, because after all, it just doesn't ring true.

But if I didn't put in the hero part, like, it wouldn't be a true adventure.

Aha, says Miss Melnychuk, and her famous smile begins to crinkle up her dark eyes. Again they disappear.

Ordinary life is full of adventure, but as soon as you put in the heroics, it stops being true. That's what I think. It stops being realistic.

Realistic?

You know. True to how things go.

True to how things go. He thinks of Gump's expression *that's how the cookie crumbles* and how the Mad Russian said *dad's dway she goes, hah?*

Well, yes. True in such a way that...Miss Melnychuk begins to flip through her pile of true adventures until she comes to the one by Elliott Crystal. Like I say, Timmy, there's too much going on in your story. There's enough for a bookful. But in this one by Elliott, there's just the snowstorm. There's you and Gump and Elliott just stumbling through the night trying to keep the fire going. His title, "Night of the Storm," says it all.

But Miss Melnychuk, Elliott slept through the whole thing! It was me an Gump who kept the fire going.

Miss Melnychuk breaks into a merry laugh and he wonders how she can see at all when her eyes disappear like that.

Oh, my! He sleeps through the whole thing! You know, Timmy, I'm glad you dropped in for this talk. Because I want to drive home a point that I know you'll understand. The fact that Elliott slept through the whole thing but tells the story as though he was awake and enduring the storm with you two, that makes his story even better. Do you see? He's used his imagination to tell the whole thing.

But I thought you said I wasn't supposed to make things up.

I didn't say you couldn't make things up. I said you had to write an experience that was believable.

Something that tells how things go.

Exactly. How things go. If you could just pick one action, the part where Timmy, you, that is, catches that fish so skillfully, for example, that would be a wonderful true adventure. If you'd written just that, you might have gotten an A.

An A. He might have gotten an A.

He walks home with that thought and cherishes it like a hero's medal. He might have gotten an A. He tells this to his mother, who is too busy preparing supper to listen. He tells it to Derek, who says Big hairy deal. He tells his dad, who says Better luck next time. And so they all missed the main point. And the point is that he's so talented that he is probably as smart at some things as the Owl except for math and science and reading old-fashioned books. It's just that Tim has too much to say, he has more to say than probably anyone in his class and he can't be bothered writing little piddling things that are okay for average guys like Gump or Benny Fuller. Anyway, how can you just write five pages and stop? There's too much going on all the time, and if you don't write it all down you'll forget it. It would sound like that newspaper story.

He goes quietly up to his room and pulls it out again. *BOY IDENTIFIES ESCAPEE*. He looks at his picture, which is one his mother gave to the reporter. It was taken last year when he was twelve and he didn't smile right for the camera. He looks like about seven years old and there's this ginky stupid smile. He reads the article several times, but the only part he likes is the sentence that mentions his name.

DURING THE WINTER Tim walks to school in the dark and comes home in the dark. The only light he sees buzzes out of fluorescent bulbs. The only weather he knows is cold. Albion Comp is a big, brand new high school that vibrates with buzzers, P.A. announcers, and banging locker doors. Derek has already learned how to fit in. He strides down the halls with a hearty gang of grade twelve guys who go everywhere together. They look so cool they don't even have to smoke.

Tim has joined the drama club. Rehearsals for the year play are held before the first class in the morning or after the last class in the day. Mrs. Elly the drama teacher decides on *A Midsummer Night's Dream*. She is six feet tall and very bossy and everyone likes her. The roles of Theseus and Oberon are combined and given to Alistair Vaughan, a sturdy blond fellow whose parents sound English. Tim is his understudy for both roles and is told by Mrs. Elly that should Alistair God forbid get sick at curtain time, Tim will take his place.

At night he memorizes his lines in the little bathroom in the basement of his house. There is rust around the drain of the tub from a constantly dripping faucet and the linoleum curls like the pages of an old paperback. The bathroom mirror is cracked in two places and framed like an old picture. There each night before the cracked mirror Tim whispers the words of Theseus.

> *Go, Philostrate,*
> *Stir up the Athenian youth to merriments;*
> *Awake the pert and nimble spirit of mirth;*
> *Turn melancholy forth to funerals;*
> *The pale companion is not for our pomp.*

He wonders if he isn't perhaps a bit like this pale companion Theseus speaks of. He tries for a look that is regal and masterful.

> *Hippolyta, I woo'd thee with my sword,*
> *And won thy love by doing thee injuries;*
> *But I will wed thee in another key,*
> *With pomp, with triumph, and with revelling.*

The plot is sort of hard to follow. Theseus is the king and he's going to marry Hippolyta, who's already a queen from somewheres else. Oberon is the king of the fairies and he's married to Titania, who is the fairy queen, and she is really frosted at him for some reason. Then there's these four teenagers. Helena is in love with Demetrius, but Demetrius is in love with Hermia, and Hermia is in love with Lysander who just like Demetrius has the hots for Hermia. These four teenagers all run off into the woods together one summer night, and it gets pretty complicated. Then, if that wasn't enough, there's these six tradesmen led by Peter Quince who are trying to rehearse a play all about love called "Pyramus and Thisbe," and one of them, Bottom the Weaver, gets bewitched by a fairy named Robin Goodfellow and falls head over heels for the fairy queen and he has to wear a donkey's head for his trouble, but everything works out okay.

Nancy Fuller is Hippolyta, and try as he might, he can't imagine himself wooing her with his sword. He blushes at the thought of it. Her boyfriend is Willie Speidel, who plays tackle for the Albion Knights, and Nancy has Willie eating from her hand. Even if a jocky guy like Willie got any fancy notions about pushing her around, he'd learn fast enough.

Tim repeats these lines in a low voice with the tap water running so no one in the house can hear him.

Hippolyta, I woo'd thee with my sword.

Alistair Vaughan complimented him on his English accent. Tim learned it from listening to episodes of *The Scarlet Pimpernel* on the old walnut radio. (*They seek him here, they seek him there, those Frenchies seek him everywhere. Is he in Heaven, or is he in Hell? That darned elusive...Pimpernell!*) Alistair is a pretty good actor. He can say the lines to Nancy Fuller about wooing her with his sword without the slightest hesitation, then be Oberon and command the fairies, and after rehearsal launch one witty remark after another, and everyone laughs, even Mrs. Elly. Nancy looks at him long after the joke is over. They are all beginning to wonder about Nancy and Alistair.

Early one winter morning Tim stands alone and sleepy on the stage. Someone has turned on the theme music for the play. It is piped through the vast darkened gymnasium on the P.A. system, an arrangement of *Song of a Summer Night* with lots of cymbals and soaring violins. The music flows into the gym walls and floods back over the dark stage. He loses himself in the music. Entranced, he wanders by the darkened floodlights. The figure of a girl drifts up to him. She looks like Nancy Fuller.

Hello, Fisher.

It isn't Nancy Fuller.

It's one of the fairies, Moth or Peaseblossom. She takes his hand in hers, places her other hand on his shoulder, and begins to waltz him around the floor. It's like that time with Margo Godween (or Godwine), except this dance is more delicious because he's taller than she. Slowly they waltz across the stage until the other fairies and the stage hands begin to clap. Finally the music stops, and he stops.

He releases her.

She seems to want to continue.

Oh, Fisher, she says. You're so impulsive.

Impulsive. And she is gone. Somewhere. Behind a curtain, behind a prop. Impulsive. No one he knows has ever used that word. She is small and sprightly and forthright. She might have long hair, worn in a way that is somehow special—he's losing her—small, with...something about the eyes, the mouth. Throughout the rehearsal he keeps watching for her. At last she appears. She darts on with the other fairies and cries *Ready!* or *Hail, mortal!* and darts off into the wings. But who is she? How could she know his last name is Fisher? Nancy Fuller would know who she is, but he can't ask her. And Alistair Vaughan is so formal you can't even call him Al, so he can't ask Alistair. Gump Lowney is shy with girls, but he has just been asked to play Bottom, so he might have talked to her once or twice. He asks Gump Lowney.

That's Rita Symington.

Oh.

She lives up north of us.

That night in the basement bathroom he looks up Rita Symington's address. There is a Symington in the Grassmere Apartments. Grassmere. What a lovely name. Would they be ritzy apartments? Not likely. If she lives north of Gump's place, her apartment might be plain but not shabby.

Her best friend is Amber Bole, and Amber is doing makeup. He will find out more from Amber. He contrives an interest in the techniques of makeup, and at just the right moment, he expresses a casual curiosity about Rita. Amber tells him that Slimy wants to be a singer; she lives with her mother and little sister; she too is an understudy (for Hippolyta and Titania); she swears a blue streak and she's lazy as an old dog—but if she *weren't*, she would be an honour student.

Rita Symington calls Amber, Bolski; Amber Bole calls Rita, Slimy. Bolski heaves her big body from room to room; Slimy flutters, lights and flies. She is never still. The two girls go everywhere together, Slimy walking backwards to act out each day's events, Bolski trudging along with her head down, laughing raucously or cynically at all her friend's antics. They will never welcome Tim's presence because it will change things between them. He knows this because whenever they see him approaching during their walks together, they clean up their language or they stop laughing or they go all silent. But there has to be a way.

A plan begins to form, more dream than plan. Alistair Vaughan and Nancy Fuller will have an accident. It will be just serious enough to send them both to hospital for a week or two, Alistair with a broken nose and Nancy with a wrenched neck. Mrs. Elly will phone Rita and Tim and beg them to take the lead roles. They will be thrown together in a fever of collaboration. They will spend their weekends rehearsing in Rita's mum's flat while she feeds them and keeps the kettle boiling and applauds their marvellous delivery. On opening night they will look like a king and a queen, and the whole school, their parents and everyone, will see that they belong together. He will teach her how to play the piano and she will teach him how to jive and maybe even do the Charleston. She will lead him up the fire-escape to the roof of their flat and show him the northern lights. She will shiver in the cold air and he will warm her in his arms. It never gets farther than that.

He works so feverishly on Theseus and Oberon's lines that he learns others' lines as well. After many rehearsals, he's able to prompt Bottom, Demetrius, and Lysander without a script. He can do all the parts for Pyramus and Thisbe and leap about with Robin Goodfellow and the fairies. He falls in love with all the fairies because they prance around in leotards. Mrs. Elly appoints him prompter and assistant director. He grows pale and thin and sleeps fitfully. His father says Derek should take him over to the rink now and then, and don't they ever need a spare goalie or something? His mother urges food on him and hot chocolate at nights. She wonders out loud if he isn't taking this acting thing just a bit too far.

He reminds her that she was once a dancer with Miss Slick's ballet in Saskatoon and sang with Aunty Meg and Uncle Randy over the radio. And what about Granny Mullen? She could have been a great pianist.

Yes, his mother says, but things were different back then.

One week in February Alistair Vaughan *does* get sick. Nancy Fuller says it's the mumps. Tim steps in and plays Theseus and Oberon at rehearsals. Not only does he stare regally at Nancy Fuller and tell her that he has won her love by doing her injuries, but later that week he gets to do the speech about the lunatic, the lover and the poet and tell Bottom in a very superior voice that his palpable-gross play was veddy newtably dischawged. All this without a script and Rita is watching and everyone says what a good job he has done.

But later in February Alistair is back and he does an even better job.

Nancy falls sick with some kind of flu and Rita takes her place in rehearsal. Opening night is three days off and no one knows who will play the combined roles of Titania and Hippolyta. Rita is okay as Hippolyta. She plays her much like a housewife. But as Titania, she's much better than Nancy. Her break with Oberon is full of fire and resentment, her passion for Bottom is tender and funny, and when she and Oberon are re-united in love in Act IV, she casts off her droopy passion for Bottom and seems to surge with renewed love for Oberon. It's disturbing. It's like Rita and Alistair have already lived together as man and wife.

Tim yearns for Alistair to have a relapse or for Nancy to regain her health. But by dress rehearsal Nancy still has what people are calling the Asian flu and Alistair seems healthy as ever. And then just as the makeup girls are filing into the dressing rooms, it's announced that Gump Lowney has come down with the same flu. Mrs. Elly begs Tim to take his place as Bottom. Bottom the weaver. Bottom the ham. Pyramus with a donkey's head. For a few dreamlike hours, Titania's beloved. Bottom and Titania, Tim and Rita. Or as Bolski would say, Fishy and Slimy.

Yes, he tells Mrs. Elly, he will do his best.

Mrs. Elly hustles Tim and Rita into the only convenient space available, the student newspaper room. She hands them their scripts and orders them to do a read-through. Very quickly.

Rita looks grim and pale. She sits on a cushion. Tim sits across the floor on a wooden box. His stomach is in an uproar and his mouth is dry.

Are you scared?

Yes.

Same here.

You'll be fine, she says. You'll get all the laughs. Gump is all wrong for Bottom. He sounds too demented.

He so loves her choice of words, he forgets his loyalty to Gump, who after all is still his fishing buddy.

I think you're the greatest Titania ever.

That's easy, she says. I could do that in my sleep. It's Hippolyta. Cripes.

Ah, she's nothing. All you have to do is look—

He stops himself. He doesn't want her to look all mushy for Theseus. He'd rather she look all mushy for him.

Let's go, she says. Why not start with your song?

He tries singing it the way Gump does, but Gump never could sing, and it sounds even worse when Tim does it Gump's way.

Try it different. Try another tune.

He tries it as a sad ballad. He sings it sweet and sober.

> *The ousel cock so black of hue*
> *With orange-tawny bill...*

Rita cracks up. Yes, yes, it's perfect. Keep on singing. It's the same tune as *God Rest Ye Merry, Gentlemen.* They'll love it!

He sings it again.

What angel wakes me from my flowery bed? she says, and breaks into a fit of giggles.

Mrs. Elly pokes her head in through the doorway. How's it coming? she says.

We're hysterical, says Rita.

Ten minutes. Makeup in ten minutes.

Rita slumps on the cushion, closes her eyes till her breath comes more slowly. Okay, she says. Shit. Okay, okay. She fixes Tim with a grave look.

> *I pray, gentle mortal, sing again.*
> *Mine ear is much enamour'd of thy note;*
> *So is mine eye enthralled to thy shape;*
> *And thy fair virtue's force perforce doth move me*
> *On the first view to say, to swear, I love thee.*

For a moment the gravity holds in her face and he notices how her jaw squares off at the corners of her cheeks and how her hair is swept back along the top of her head and how it goes from dark brown to light brown, and then they both crack up.

He says, Methinks, mistress, you should have little reason for that—

I'm gonna piss my pants, she says.

To say the truth, he goes on, reason and love keep little company together nowadays.

You can say that again, she says, gasping for breath.

Five minutes! cries Mrs. Elly from outside the door.

Nay, says Tim, I can gleek upon occasion! and collapses on the floor.

Shhh, says Rita, weak and gasping.

Do you gleek very often? he says.

Shhh.

Does your mother know?
Shhh!

In no time at all they are made up and pacing back and forth behind the curtains in their costumes, muttering their lines or giggling in whispers. Mrs. Elly is everywhere, handing out encouragement and fussing with pins and belts. Mr. Poulet the vice-principal announces the last minute changes in characters, and the school band begins to play the Queen. The girl who plays Hermia peeks through the crack in the curtains and says it's a full house and Mrs. Elly bustles her away from the curtains and says that was a hicky thing to do. Tim pores over his lines until he can rattle them off in his head at high speed. Across the darkened stage, he can see Rita, now dressed as Hippolyta, doing the same thing. He prays neither of them will crack up during the donkey's head scenes. Before he can wish Rita break a leg, Bolski grabs him and drags him off to the makeup room to try on the donkey's head one more time. It smells of Gump's hair tonic.

The curtain rises on Act I.

The audience is full of students and English teachers from all over the city, all of whom are reading *A Midsummer Night's Dream* for the Shakespeare Unit, as they call it in school. Hundreds of students and their teachers bring identical texts *of A Midsummer Night's Dream* to the play, and when Egeus reports that Lysander has bewitched the bosom of his child, hundreds of pages turn all at once, making a loud crackling flap. Egeus is so frightened by this noise that he loses track of his lines.

Thou, thou Lysander, Tim whispers to him, and Egeus seems to recover.

Before he knows it, Tim is on, urging Peter Quince (as he had said to Mrs. Elly) to name what part he was for, and proceed. They like him. He hams it up and they laugh. It's easy. And when he cries out, *Take pains, be perfect, adieu,* and a thousand more pages crackle, he and Peter Quince do not so much as blink.

The fairies dash out and do a little dance in tights and wingy costumes, and race squealing off the stage. They are so beautiful. Bottom loves them on and off the stage, and they love Bottom. Demetrius and Helena race out and have their quarrel and race backstage to find Helena's sash. They are frantic onstage and off. Everyone becomes wonderfully frantic.

In Act III Tim muffs his lines once, but so does everyone else in

Peter Quince's rough little band of players. The Pyramus and Thisbe rehearsal is a bit like one of their own rehearsals, so they muddle through and it seems to go all right. Then Bottom exits to get his donkey's head. Amber straps it on while Mrs. Elly reads him his lines. The head smells so badly of hair tonic and glue and sweat it smells worse than Derek's football helmet. When he goes back on again he is nauseous. He can't see, so one by one the men in Quince's troupe bump into him and flee from him and the little kids in the audience laugh and squeal. And when he sings his song about the ousel cock and throstle, he can hear even the older people laughing. Then Titania awakens and he hears her before he sees her. Finally she has to pull him over to centre stage to tell him that she loves him, and everybody laughs at that too.

He waits for the laughter to die down.

> *Methinks, mistress, you should have little reason for that; and yet, to say the truth, reason and love keep little company together nowadays....*

He stops at this, struck by it, and loses a line. If the assistant prompter is prompting, Tim doesn't hear her. He shrugs.

> *Nay, I can gleek upon occasion.*

Rita never even blinks at his lapse.

Thou art wise as thou art beautiful, she says, and kisses him on his donkey's nose.

The kiss is unrehearsed, but it's perfect, and for an instant he holds her as he did when they waltzed that first morning, his left hand on her shoulder, his right on her hip. He feels her bones sharp and delicate beneath his hands and he loses another line, but again, she doesn't falter. When the fairies lead him from the stage, the audience gives them all a warm applause.

It all goes by too fast. His turn comes again, and he speaks about the marvellous vision he's had without a mistake. He garners more than his share of laughs. Too soon the curtain comes down. They go out to the apron for a bow, Mr. Poulet calls out Mrs. Elly, and one of the fairies presents her with a bouquet. She calls out to Rita and Tim and tells the audience how they had to step in at the last moment, and while Tim and Rita hold hands, the audience gives them a special round of applause, and someone with a flash attachment for their camera takes a picture. Rita's thin hand in his: almost unbearably blissful. When the curtain comes down he's still holding her hand, and finally she withdraws it.

Oh, Slimy, he says, you're so impulsive.

She just looks at him. She hasn't gotten his joke. After a while, after thinking about it, he isn't sure if he got it either. In fact, it's probably just about the stupidest thing he could ever have said.

Nancy comes back for the next performance. She is fine as Hippolyta but lacks the fire of Titania. The applause is polite for her, but enthusiastic for Bottom. Rita returns to being a fairy and helps Amber Bole with the makeup. Then, on the third night, Gump Lowney is back to take over Bottom's role, and he is all right. He gets some laughs. Rita is nowhere and everywhere backstage. She won't sit still. He can't talk to her. He remains just inside the downstage curtain and prompts while Alistair charms every well-read girl in the audience and every girl's mother besides. Such a bright boy, he hears Elliott Crystal's mother say at intermission.

After the last performance there is a cast party at Mrs. Elly's. Tim goes with Gump Lowney. It's a subdued gathering with Alistair Vaughan and Mrs. Elly trading witticisms across the living room while Mr. Elly mans the grape juice bowl. Then Nancy arrives with Willy Speidel in tow, and Willy hulks in the corner of the room while Nancy does the rounds. Bolski arrives without Slimy and follows Tim around as he paces from room to room, waiting for Rita to arrive. Mrs. Elly has some jokey gifts for the cast. She asks Nancy if she and Alistair Vaughan will hand out the prizes. Nancy drifts from room to room looking for Alistair, but no one can find him. He seems to have gone home without telling anyone.

Finally Tim gets up the nerve to ask Bolski very casually where Slimy has gotten to. She says Slimy had to go out somewhere.

Slimy's kind of in demand these days. You wanna sit next to me? says Bolski. Her wide face twitches with eagerness.

He walks home with Gump and does the last mile alone. It's a clear night in early March. As his galoshes crunch over the icy roads, he tries to count his blessings. He has the memory of Rita's laughter on the floor of the student newspaper room. The memory of holding her hand, and twice, briefly, her small body. The memory of all that applause, the love he felt for the beautiful fairies and for everyone in the play. Even Alistair, who still makes him feel jealous. Even poor

Amber. And Rita's hand in his. How perfect it felt. And how she had laughed!

As he approaches the skating rink he hears the faint slice and rasp of a skater. He stops and squints. There are no lights on. Over the ice a girl seems to float in a slow figure eight. As light as a fairy—as though she has leapt over the stars directly from the brain of the great Shakespeare.

He can scarcely see her, but somehow she becomes Rita Symington. Twirling now and leaping, perfect on the ice.

He passes like a shadow from the rinkside. He takes his vision of Rita home with him and speaks to her and adores her and watches her fly from his to someone else's embrace. He nurses his anguish until it begins to gratify him, and then at last he sleeps.

THERE IS A DANCE IN APRIL, A SOCK HOP. Loud, terrifying rock n roll. He wants to flee but he's paid three dollars to get in. Rita is there, dancing with a big wild looking fellow from Grade XII who plays football with Derek and Willie Speidel. At the intermission she speaks to Tim.

Hi, Fisher.

Hi, Slimy.

Well, Fisher....

Well indeed.

We were stars.

What?

You and me. You were a great Bottom.

Aw.

And I was a sizzling Titania.

You bet.

Isn't there a saying about fleeting fame?

Fame fleets, eh?

That's how the cookie crumbles, Rita replies.

That's the way she goes, eh?

Do you see what I see?

Rita nods in the direction of the stage. Alistair Vaughan is holding hands with Nancy Fuller. What will wee Willie say about this development, Fisher?

Willie Speidel or Willie Shakespeare?

That's a good question, Fisher.

Alistair and Nancy...hmm. Our friend the bard would say forsooth. That's the first thing he would say. Then he'd say that Alistair's eye is enthrall'd to her shape.

Reason and love, says Rita, much older now than she has ever sounded. Reason and love. They keep little company together nowadays.

Tim thinks briefly about asking her for the first dance after the break. Perhaps he will be lucky and they'll play a slow one. Without warning his throat begins to swell and tears begin to prickle his adenoids.

Slimy?

Yes.

That first day, when we waltzed across the stage. How did you know I was named Fisher? Did you think I was Derek?

Derek? she says and looks with some concern at Tim, as though she can see the beginnings of his tears before they have even begun to gather.

My big brother, he says.

Everyone knows who you are, she says. You're the guy who got his picture in the newspaper.

The Mad Russian strikes again.

What's the matter? Timmy?

He tries to speak, but the words will not come and the music finally starts. It's fast and jivy. He looks away from Rita as though to scan the bleachers. The first person he recognizes in the blink of tears is Amber Bole giving him a long sad look.

The big fellow from Grade XII grabs Rita by the arm and pulls her onto the dance floor.

Rita waves goodbye to Tim, and her eyes for a second seem to focus on him and soften, as though she understands something. As though she is going somewhere and he can't go. As though that's just how the cookie crumbles.

WHEN HE HEARD ABOUT TIM'S CHRISTMAS MARKS Derek showed no mercy.

Don't be so easy on yourself, he said.

Fine for Derek. He has never gotten anything lower than a B in his entire life.

When you miss a night's studying, *you make it up the next night.*

When you go upstairs to study, *you go about it with a sense of purpose.*

Some brother. Tim gets depressed. As usual, this is followed by a head cold. It comes at the start of the Easter holiday. He talks things over with Gump Lowney on the phone. Gump says if you don't study you'll end up like all those guys who spend their weekends *under a car.* If there's one thing more boring than math, physics and chemistry, it's working on cars. Maybe Gump has a point.

He decides he will make up his mind after church, because maybe something will happen there that will influence his decision. If old Reverend Ross says Beware ye the evils of sloth, he will take that as a sign. But if he says something like Come ye now and rejoice, and like that, Tim will just know it's time he sat down and smelled the flowers. Tim's mum likes to stress the importance of stopping to smell the flowers whenever he's real busy with something. But when he's lounging in front of the TV set without a care in the world, she's the first to say, For Heaven's sake, Timmy, get up and *do* something.

He sits in church between his dad and Derek, trying not to sniffle too loud. In front of them are the Fullers. Nancy has Alistair Vaughan in tow, and Benny as usual is looking very ill at ease. Mr. Fuller is in his Sunday mood, which means looking calm and slightly bored and not cracking jokes about travelling salesmen. Mrs. Fuller as usual is all in pink and mink and waving and smiling in everybody's general direction.

Every time Nancy glances to the side or turns around to whisper hi to someone, he notices her. She has somehow become cute just over the past year or so. She knows it too, you can tell. Her hair is darker than her mother's; it has tresses here and there the colour of...corn syrup? Varnished hardwood? Benny's hair is the same shade of light brown, almost blond, but on Nancy it looks *like perfection itself.* That's how his mother would say it. But how do you describe Nancy's hair without sounding dumb?

Reverend Ross doesn't give the sermon. Instead, he introduces the New Man, as Tim's mother refers to him. Reverend Mountjoy is his name, a chubby fellow with a beautiful shiny bald dome, a friendly smile, and a melodious voice. Many people are curious about him. According to Tim's mother, he is said to have new ideas—especially for a minister. He has written his own pamphlets about his missionary work in Kenya when he was young, and he often refers to new books about things like the H-bomb and the Cold War. Perhaps the New Man will say something about scholastic achievement or smelling the flowers. Tim isn't sure what you're supposed to talk about on Palm Sunday.

Reverend Mountjoy chooses to talk about doubt. Doubt, he says, is not such a bad thing. It's a sign of our times, he claims, and out of doubt came great discoveries and great faith. Look at Job, he says. Look at Jesus on the cross. Look at Copernicus.

Pretty good stuff for a sermon. It makes Tim feel a bit better about flunking math and physics at Christmas time. In fact, Tim is probably the best doubter in his family. He doesn't have a clue what he wants to be when he leaves the nest, as his mum puts it. His dad says maybe he ought to think about a commerce degree, and his mum says maybe he ought to look at teaching. So all he can do is doubt their wisdom.

Derek never has any doubts, you can just tell. He's headed straight for the top of the ladder. He'll get his honours in economics, then he'll fire into law at Osgood or somewhere, then he'll become a big corporation lawyer and that's the end of that. Come to think of it, Derek is just about the lousiest doubter Tim has ever seen. He even walks to university in a non-doubtful way. No more slumping along. He strides purposefully, shoulders back, swinging his arms several inches out from his body. Of course, he probably walks like that so he can show off his chest and his biceps, but you can just tell, the last doubt he had about anything was probably when to switch from diapers to pants.

One look at Nancy Fuller and you can see she doesn't have much doubt in her mind. She's going to snag Alistair Vaughan and raise a bunch of blond-haired kids. And old Alistair, he's heading fast up the highway of success. He's probably never had a moment of uncertainty in his entire life. You just need to watch him recite the Apostle's Creed. *I believe in God the Father Almighty, Maker of Heaven and Earth...* The neighbourhood mothers say he's a born leader. Doubters don't have blond hair like Alistair Vaughan. They don't play English rugby or marry the school princess. All doubters can do is doubt. They never get their pictures in the Albion High School yearbook because there isn't a School Doubting Team. If there were, Tim would be captain of the squad.

He decides that the New Man up there is okay. He decides he would like to stop in and talk with him some time.

One night when Derek is out, his dad is curling, and Tim lounging before the TV set, his mother asks him up for a cup of postum. She sits across from him at the kitchen table in her blue kimono stirring her postum. Her hand is veiny and freckled, and as it goes stirring

ɔund, his mind goes around and around with the spoon.
hinking about the strangest things, she says. I've been
ɔur birth, of all things. Did you know, Timmy, you
lifficult birth a mother could ever imagine?

Howcome?

Well, stop me if I've told you this, but you seemed to fight it every inch of the way. It's like I almost had to bribe you to come out. Did you know you were almost two weeks late?

Yek.

It's like you were perfectly content to stay snuggled up in there for the rest of your life.

Well, he says, that's one way of avoiding grade twelve math.

She smiles and then she turns serious. Something else has been on my mind, she says. Your Grandfather Fisher was an upstanding man, and so is your father, and your brother Derek will probably do just fine in that department. But my dad, your Grandfather Mullen, he was a different story. He was Irish. He was a dreamer, an eccentric, and he always found excuses not to do his job. He had all the brains a man could want but not one ounce of common sense. In that one way, I suppose, he and my mother were a pretty good match. If he ever got some money together he'd squander it on his dogs or his boats or some prospector up north who said he'd strike it rich. And not a penny to show for any of his schemes and dreams. I guess what I'm saying is that you have two fellows inside of you, Timmy, and the time has come to choose which one you'll be. I don't care what you choose. I don't care if you decide that university isn't for you. But to see you...

Like a pair of pigeons her hands fly up from her postum mug

...throw away all your choices and go through your life dreaming, Timmy, that would just destroy me. If you want to be a Mullen then God help you. But if you want to be a Fisher, you've got to pull up your socks and try a little harder. Derek is right. He was right all along and I didn't see it. He knows you can do better. This math thing is your problem and you've got to do your very best to lick it. You're too young to just give up on math and science. You're a fighter, Timmy Fisher, and it's time you went to battle.

She takes a deep breath, stands up slowly from the table, and gives a long sigh.

Whew. This speechmaking is downright exhausting.

According to Derek, the way you pass the chemistry

departmentals is to memorize everything. The way you pass physics is to do all the problems at the end of the chapters and check them with Mr. Gooder after school. The way you pass math, however, is a bit more involved. There's this young teacher named Mr. Huculak who gives early morning math classes for all the dumbbells. According to Derek, who has sailed through math, Mr. Huculak is lots of fun, and he explains things in real simple terms. Go see this guy every morning at seven-thirty, Derek recommends. That's how the dumbbells did it last year.

Seven-thirty! I'll have to get out of bed at six o'clock!

Derek combs his hair in front of the hall mirror in a new shirt. It's a white buttondown with red vertical stripes and the label on the shirt reads *Ivy League*. He pauses to admire his handywork with the comb. Greatness, he proclaims in an Ivy League sort of voice, doesn't come easy.

This pronouncement is at least an advance on his grade five hockey motto: *Either you got it or you ain't.*

Departmentals, they are called. One hundred per cent of each final grade rides on just one final exam set by the province. What a terrifying word for final exams: Departmentals. If you split the word in two, it conjures up an image of nervous breakdowns. The approach of departmentals ushers in a conspiracy against idleness. First it was Derek, then Gump Lowney, then his mum, and finally now it's his dad. Tim knows this the moment he knocks on Tim's bedroom door one night in early April. A dog, he thinks. Dad will bribe me with the promise of a dog.

This Mr. Huculak. Sounds like quite a guy. I hear he even runs in marathons.

How did you know?

I have my spies. Tell you what, Son. You give this fellow a try for six weeks, and I will—are you ready for this? How would you and Gump or Elliott or anyone else like to do a little fishing up at Mountie Lake around the May long weekend? You could have the same cabin we rented last year all to yourselves and I'd pay the shot. You could drive up in Gump's car.

He leans against Tim's door with a jaunty look. Tim wonders if his dad has ever been a doubter. It seems unlikely. Some boys are born knowing where they want to go. Life for them is just a straight highway from childhood to manhood with no side roads. By the time you graduate you're supposed to know where you're going. But how can you know when no one has given you the road map?

His dad is waiting by the door. What do you say, young fisherman? Do we have a deal?

Mr. Huculak likes to wear red. One morning it will be a bright red vest. The next it will be red socks or even red trousers. He is definitely not cool. No one dares imitate his style. He slicks his hair down and combs the front part into a round little curl above his forehead. He calls Nancy Fuller Nanny, and when finally Tim starts to get a few right answers, he calls him Fishy. Mr. Huculak's first name is Dennis, and in the yearbook they call him Dennis the Menace, but everyone in class calls him Mr. Huculak. He only preaches one sermon and it's brief, the thing all the neighbourhood fathers and future employers have been trying to teach Derek and Tim and all their friends from their earliest years: *If you can't cut 'er you can't stay.* Mr. Huculak is never still, always pacing, always cheering his students on. A wrong answer brings on a loud and theatrical moan of despair; a right answer always brings the brightest of smiles and a cry of *Cha!* All the grade twelves begin using the word. It becomes cool to say *Cha!* The early morning class grows from one dozen around Easter time to more than sixty in May. The dark cloud *Departmentals* looms closer, and Mr. Huculak has become the most popular teacher in the school. At any time of the day some guy can be heard shouting the phrase in the hallways, *If you can't cut 'er you can't stay.*

Mr. Huculak is maybe a bit like the new minister, Reverend Mountjoy. Neither man is considered to be cool in the way that pop singers or athletes or movie stars are cool. Reverend Mountjoy is too grand and proper to be cool. His voice is too warbly and genteel for coolness. And especially, Reverend Mountjoy is too *bald* to be cool. If you painted the top of a hardboiled egg pink, that is Reverend Mountjoy's dome, as though inside of his head there is a mind equally pink and shiny and wholesome. But as soon as he begins to speak, his voice is so rich and musical you never notice his lack of coolness.

One evening he asks Tim, What do you believe in?

I dunno.

I'm not asking for anything profound, do you see? Maybe you believe in progress, or maybe you believe in Jackie Parker or Dief the Chief.

This'll sound real dumb, Reverend Mountjoy, but I guess I believe in trout streams. I've got some ideas about trout streams.

What do you like about these streams?

Trout, mostly.

Did you ever think about where these wonderful streams came from?

You mean like underground springs, or glaciers?

I'm asking you to wonder a bit. These streams you like, they have trout in them that spawn every spring?

Sometimes in the fall too.

And did it ever occur to you that these streams are part of a scheme? Part of an unfolding miracle?

I guess so. Yeah. Maybe.

Think about the smallest trickles feeding into the rivulets that come down from the glaciers. Then think about the network of rivulets that feed the small streams. And the small streams that feed the larger streams. Before long you have a river. And what amazing things they are, these rivers. On a map they're coloured blue. That always used to fascinate me when I was a boy.

The man is obviously warming up to his subject. He stands and begins to pace back and forth behind his desk. He stops, stares at the messy bookshelf by his window, covers his chin with his large hands, almost as though he is praying.

These rivers and streams. Let's colour them red. What would they be like then?

Blood veins, you mean?

Well, yes. And if we painted them brown, what would they look like then?

I dunno. Tree branches maybe.

Yes, exactly. And if we inverted these things that look like the branches of trees, what would we have?

Roots, I guess.

Exactly. Exactly. We would have roots. And all from rivers, the shape of rivers. Even *highways* have the shape of rivers. Thoreau had this notion that God must labour constantly with the idea of rivers.

That's neat, Tim allows. When you really think about it.

Would you like to read this man? Here, he says, fumbling through some books on a shelf nearby. He hands Tim a copy of Thoreau's *Walden*.

Tim can't quite escape the feeling that any idea from the mouth of Reverend Mountjoy could become a fantastically good idea because is so beautiful. Each syllable comes out as clear and limpid as from a soloist in the choir, and each word has exactly the right asis. No wonder he makes doubt sound so interesting.

Each time Tim returns one of Reverend Mountjoy's books they have one of their talks. These take place in the minister's office on Sunday nights when the weather begins to warm in May. The office is always messy, the desk heaped with correspondence and books.

One night the minister asks Tim what he wants to do with his life. He tells Reverend Mountjoy that he would like to do a B.A. in something, until he's made up his mind. Maybe something to do with foreign languages so that he could travel all over the world.

What languages would you like to study?

Well, I like French, and I'd like to be able to speak Russian too, or maybe German if Russian's too hard. Maybe Spanish too. I dunno.

Have you ever thought about the ministry?

Well, I've *thought* about it.

Well, Tim, perhaps it's worth thinking about.

Yeah.

Do you know where your name Timothy came from?

My Grandad Fisher. He was a surveyor up in the mountains and places like that.

But do you know who the first great Timothy was?

The guy with the stores, he's the earliest one I ever heard of.

Well, you'll find a better one than Timothy Eaton in the Bible. This Timothy was one of Paul's first converts, and he spread the word of God in the early years of Christianity. That's what your name means: Honouring God.

These days, thanks to Mr. Huculak, his name once more is Fishy—like it was in his old neighbourhood a long time ago when Hunch Douglas and his brother in the schoolyard used to yell, *Hey, Fishy. Whenya gunna take me fishin?* Tim wants to say something that will please Reverend Mountjoy, something devout and full of enthusiasm, but all he can think of is that he isn't sure he believes in God, and besides, he isn't *good* enough to be a minister. Whenever he's on a good streak, he wakes up one morning with a boner on, and one thing leads to another, and a few minutes later, all that shame. The merest thought of Rita Symington, the tiniest conjuring of her, makes him feel like a fiend. He even feels that way sometimes about Nancy Fuller. And even if this fiend isn't really *him*, you can't be a minister and have thoughts like that. It just isn't right.

Maybe he'll end up being a teacher.

Okay, Nanny, simplify.

What do you mean?

Simplify! $7(y-1) -2y = 13$. You can't work with that. Einstein couldn't work with that.

I still don't see what you mean.

Anybody! Fishy!

$7y -7 -2y$?

Yes? Don't stop, Fishy.

$5y -7 = 13$?

Yesyesyesyesyes! Nanny, do you see what Fishy is doing? Do you see?

Nancy smiles at Tim. She used to smile like that years and years ago when she got an idea. *I know! Your wagon's a ambliance and we're goin to the hostipal!*

$5y =20$? she says.

Mr. Huculak waves his chalk in the air. Yes, Nanny? Don't stop.

$Y = 4$?

Mr. Huculak wheels away from Nancy's desk, and from a distance of more than twenty feet, flings the chalk into the wastepaper basket. He spins around with a smile on his face and points a finger right at Nancy. *Cha!*

The problem with talking to Nancy these days is that she is undeniably cute. He can't stop blushing, and the more he blushes, the more tongue-tied he becomes. She never used to have that effect on him. Nancy has lead Tim over to a bench on the grass outside the main door of the school. She bids him to sit down beside her. The air has turned warm. Only a few piles of grimy ice remain unmelted on the ground.

Timmy, she begins, when's the last time we had a good heart to heart?

Grade two when my granny died.

Be serious.

Nancy rearranges her skirt beneath her, points her nose up at the sun, and closes her eyes.

I hear you're going fishing up at the lake.

How did you know?

Little bird.

It must have been the mums around the Circle, Tim is sure. They hit the telephones around midmorning and by noon everyone in the neighbourhood knows. It's faster than his dad's wire service.

You're lucky, she says. Boys are lucky. They have so much fun.

You used to say, Bother on boys. That was your favourite expression.

She favours him with a smile.

Did I say that?

All the students are streaming out of the school, heading for the lawns and the new shopping centre. One guy after another gives Nancy the eye.

Tim tries to look real casual.

I don't suppose Benny would ever go fishing.

Your Benny?

My Benny. I'm worried about him. He's got the weirdest friends. And he frets so much.

What about?

Same old stuff.

The same old stuff means germs and allergies. Benny is the school hypochondriac. He keeps a dusting rag in his briefcase to wipe off the seat of his desk whenever anyone else has sat in it.

Nancy leans back into the bench and stretches out her legs, taking the sun as directly as she can.

I don't suppose you and your friends could snap him out of it.

You and your friends has an unpleasant ring. Nancy moves around in different circles these days. All her friends look so perfect. They always wear the right clothes and they always have such a good time. Tim's friends all seem to have pimples or carry briefcases and slide rules. Derek claims that Tim's friends are ginky. This appears to be another word for *square*. When a gink throws a football it never has a real spiral. Girls never go out with ginks; they just borrow their homework. Tim doesn't think of himself as one hundred per cent gink. It's just that he doesn't seem to fit anywhere else.

Nancy is waiting.

How could me and my friends help Benny?

With two feet of bench between them they squint at one another. Squinting, Nancy is easier to talk to because this way she doesn't look quite so cute.

You could take him fishing sometime.

Hmm. Tim looks away.

Well, no harm in asking.

I don't know, says Tim. Maybe. Sometime.

It's just that...Benny doesn't like Alistair and his friends. He says they're all too....

Too what?

She wrinkles up her nose the way she used to a long time ago when anyone mentioned parsnips or lima beans. Oh, one of his *expressions*. He says they're all too hiddy-eye-booboo.

They're *what*?

I think he means hideous. But he thinks you're okay. You and Elliott and old Gump. Guys tease Benny, you know.

Yeah?

Willie Speidel called him a homo. I don't know how some guys can be so cruel. Anyway, she sighs, I thought that maybe if he got out now and then with some *normal* guys, then maybe he'd....

Nancy puts her hand on Tim's arm. Would you guys take my brother fishing on the long weekend? For me? Please?

Nothing Benny wears ever seems to get dirty. He has on galoshes, the kind Tim used to wear in junior high school. Benny's are shiny and black like patent leather. And brown corduroys. They seem a bit formal for this occasion. His car-coat is buttoned right up to the neck. So is his shirt. In fact, even his galoshes are zipped up tight as though Benny is afraid of letting something in or out.

They go onto the pier but the wind and the whitecaps are still too high for rowing.

Maybe we can cast from the pier, says Tim.

You go ahead, says Benny.

Benny stands with hands in pockets and presses his lips together in such a way that they disappear inside his mouth. This is his tucked-in zipped-up look. He always does this when he's uncomfortable with things.

Tim makes a short cast, but the wind is so strong it almost throws the line back into their faces. He tries again.

We need to get to the other side, he says. We need to get out of the wind.

Can we drive in Gump's car? says Benny.

We could drive part way, but when we came to Ochi Creek we'd have to cross and walk about half a mile.

Benny resumes his zipped-up look. The wind ruffles his hair the same colour as Nancy's.

I don't think that would be very good for me, says Benny. It's the spring, mostly. My allergies get bad when I go outside. I get all stuffed up and when I blow my nose, my sinuses get all blocked. Then I get these headaches?

The four of them sit in deck chairs at the end of the dock. Benny Fuller is on the far left, then Gump, then Tim, and Elliott on the far right. This is an interesting arrangement because they're also sitting from oldest to youngest. Benny is oldest by almost a year, Gump is next, then Tim, and then Elliott, who has just turned sixteen today. This event also seems odd to Tim, because on the Albion High School scale of academic certainty, Elliott, the youngest, is bound to graduate from Grade Twelve this June with all A's. On the other end of things, Benny is doomed to flunk his year. He claims that math and physics are so demanding they give him stomach cramps and rashes. The Fullers will send Benny off to the States somewhere, but not to a university with high academic standards. He will get a mickey-mouse degree in hotel management or building golf courses or something.

They are all drinking cokes, munching on peanuts and sunflower seeds. The evening is warm and quiet. They can see the Fullers' cabin across the bay on the Doctors' side of Mountie Lake.

Nancy is there with her hiddy-eye-booboo friends, says Benny. She told my parents that she wanted the cottage to herself so she could study all weekend. Sometimes I think she goes a bit overboard. With the partying, I mean.

The fabled Fuller cottage has all the lights on, and occasionally the music from Mr. Fuller's big new record player reaches across the bay. The water is perfectly calm. Even Benny is calm. There is no one here to call him a homo, no diseases in his immediate vicinity. The whitefish are swirling out beyond the shallows, but the boys are all fished out.

Well, Crystal, Gump yawns, happy birthday to yiz.

They raise their cokes. Elliott yawns back.

Tim says, I want to thank Elliott on behalf of all of us for not telling us it was his birthday until today.

You think you fellas are off the hook yet?

No stores around here, says Tim. It's his turn to yawn. You see any stores around here, Gump?

Gump shakes his head.

That's the way the cookie crumbles.

Benny?

Benny shakes his head.

That's okay. I don't want you fellas to buy me anything. I just want you to *give* me something.

I got an old pair of boxer shorts, says Gump.

If you guys are really my friends you'd give me your most valued possession. Whatever. Gump would give me his fishing hat.

Gump's old hat is part of his Gump uniform. He is never without it on weekends. To everyone's surprise, he takes off the old hat and gives it to Elliott, who holds it as though it were yesterday's fish guts.

Benny would give me his antihistamines, Elliott continues.

Benny pulls the little vial out of his pocket and gives it to Elliott.

And Fishy would give me his biggest fish.

I knew you were going to say that. Not a chance. You'd tell everyone you caught it.

Elliott is rocking in his chair like a demented old man. It's my birthday, Fisher, and I want a present.

I'll give you a fishing lesson free of charge.

Wow, says Gump, will you listen to this guy?

The Ray Coniff Singers send out a chorus from Nancy's side of the lake, announcing to all and sundry that someone's broken love affair is all over town.

It strikes Tim at this moment that the reason Nancy inveigled him into taking Benny fishing for the long weekend is that she wanted to have one of her exclusive parties without her brother hanging around, and maybe she wanted to make out with Alistair. Tim doesn't give a damn. Why should he? He is glad to be on this side of the lake in what brother Derek would call gink paradise.

Gump begins to sing in a falsetto voice better suited to calling dogs, *My love affair is all over town....*

They all join in.

At the end of August, Elliott, Gump and Tim see a movie starring Tony Perkins and Jane Fonda entitled *Tall Story*. It's about a cheerleader and a college basketball star. There's a scene where all the young people gather around the fire and do one of the songs his mum used to sing on a Saskatoon radio station. It begins, *Come a little closer to the fire.* The young people around the fire are perfect in every way. Perfectly groomed, popular. They worry only about dates and parents and winning the next game. A fellow who is slightly ginky accompanies the singalong on his ukulele. Tim can strum this song, it's easy. His mother has taught him.

He wonders if the ukulele player ever ends up with a girl. Not in this movie. It concludes with the cheerleader and the basketball star kissing under the shower. The cheerleader is like Nancy, and the basketball star is a tall dark-haired version of Alistair. They are comfortable in every room they enter. Alistair and his friends can look at you as if you weren't even there. Their eyes are trained from early age to exclude ginks. These days Nancy won't even say hi to Tim. He might complain to Benny about his sister, but Benny has already left for the States.

I brought you something, says Gump, handing Tim a small envelope.

What's this?

Graduation present. Open it, Gump says.

Tim looks at Elliott.

Elliott says, It's a token of our esteem like. I mean, how often does a guy with your mental capacity pass grade twelve math?

Unless it's your most valued possesion, I don't want it.

Inside the envelope is a large snapshot in black and white. Elliott looks bored and self-conscious. Benny Fuller smiles sweetly as though he's proud to be one of the ginks. Tim holds a jackfish by the gills. His smile hasn't quite got there. A hint of something troubling him.

Whadya think? says Gump. I blew it up myself.

When Gump set up the snapshot, Tim was thinking, *I am glad I am staying on this side of the lake. I wouldn't go to a party with Nancy and Alistair Vaughan if they paid me by the hour.* So why is his smile so unsure?

Staring down at the viewfinder of his camera, Gump had said something like, Fisher! Wakey wakey!

Gump snapped the picture.

I like it fine, he says to Gump.

But? says Gump.

His mind is wandering again. Back to the lake. He remembers now. He was *also* thinking wouldn't it be terrific if he could just once do a slow dance with Nancy Fuller all alone in the dark.

❷
UPSTREAM

I NEVER THOUGHT I'D SEE A SON OF MINE DRIVE OFF IN A THING LIKE THAT.

She never really looks at Derek's car. She always seems to avert her gaze, like women do at the drive-in when guys come out of the men's can pulling up their flies. In her arms she holds a puppy named Pepper, an English springer spaniel. She is only three months old, and when Tim's mother frets, the puppy whimpers.

Well, says Dad, he bought it with his own money. He's a man now, Jenny.

If he's a man he should drive a man's car, not some hot rod straight out of a Hollywood movie. He just got it to pick up girls, that's all he got it for.

Our eldest isn't just a ladies' man, says Dad. He respects girls. We brought him up to respect girls.

It's not a hot rod, says Tim. It's a sports car.

Sports car, she snorts.

She still won't look at it. Derek's first car is a secondhand MG as red as a fire engine. It has a convertible top stored in the trunk because the top won't stay on right. Derek has confided this fact to Tim because Tim will be riding in the car all the way to Lake Louise. Then Derek is on his own, off to Vancouver and his first big job. It's quite a day for Derek. He's doing the last-minute packing. His shaving kit, his tennis racket, a bag of sandwiches and cookies Mum made after breakfast, some bottles of pop.

If he starts to go over the speed limit, she says to Tim, you tell him for me to slow down.

He doesn't speed.

Oh? That's news to me. If he doesn't speed, why does he buy a car that looks like a rocket ship?

He won't speed.

Promise me?

I promise.

What if it rains, for Heaven's sake?

He'll put the top on, says Dad.

If it *rains?* Derek said to Tim, aghast. Since when did a little *rain* ever hurt anyone?

And you, she says to Tim, you're the last of my boys, you take care of yourself and don't go....

Her voice trails off, as though she is trying to imagine the most frequent causes of death for cab drivers in the Rockies. That's Tim's job for the whole summer. He can hardly wait to get a cab assigned to him. He can hardly wait to get the hell out of here, actually.

Little Pepper begins to whimper again.

You're getting upset, Jenny, Dad says.

If anything, Dad looks worse off than Mum. His job always makes him tense, but this morning his face seems to hang from his ears like a rubber mask.

Derek's got a job in Vancouver, she says, as though it were North Korea. Timmy's off to the mountains, we won't see him till September. *You're* never home. I'm about to lose my family. Who wouldn't be upset?

They offered Derek five hundred bucks a month, says Tim.

He probably can't wait to see the last of us.

Oh, Jenny.

That thing was built for racing. It wasn't built for people like us. He has no idea who owned it. Do the *brakes* even work?

When Derek buys a big enough place, we can visit him in Vancouver, says Tim.

Answer me that, Timmy. You just got your chauffeur's license. Has anyone even *tried* the brakes?

I got one question, Tim says, as they blast past an old dump truck on Highway 16 west of Edmonton. Can we just once in a while listen to one of *my* radio stations or do we have to listen all the way to Lake Louise to *your* radio stations?

What's wrong with my radio stations?

What's wrong? All that *white* rock n roll?

Whadya mean, *white* rock n roll?

Pat Boone.

Pat Boone? No one listens to Pat Boone.

Fabian. You like *Fabian?*

Not particularly.

How about all those Bobbies?

What Bobbies?

Bobby Vinton. Bobby Vee. Bobby Darrin. Bobby Curtola.

I've never hearda half those guys. You seem to be really up on your *white* rock n roll. I suppose you want to listen to classical music all the way to Lake Louise.

CKUA.

Oh, gimme a break.

It's got lots of good stuff. It's got folk music.

So has CJCA. So has CHED.

That's not folk music. That's college boy picking. That's about as authentic as white rock n roll. Rich kids singing about poor people.

What's so great about *your* stuff? Old farts who can't carry a tune groaning into a five dollar tape recorder. I mean does *musical talent* figure into your scheme here?

Pete Seeger's a great instrumentalist. He plays a fabulous banjo.

He's white.

Leadbelly's got a great voice. Blind Lemon Jefferson.

Who?

Blind Lemon Jefferson.

Say, isn't he the guy who does white cane benefits with Crumbling Cedric Vomit?

Hardy har. Don't knock it till you tried it. Besides, CKUA plays jazz.

I got nothing against jazz, just as long as it's not that progressive crap.

What's wrong with progressive jazz?

It's I dunno it's *vague.* You listen to that junk long enough, your mind goes foggy. You forget the day of the week. I like jazz you can hum to.

Jazz you can *hum* to?

Yeah. I figure a jazz musician should at least be able to carry a tune. It's only the lazy, no-talent guys who play this progressive crap. You think Louis Armstrong would get hooked up with a progressive jazz band? Can you see Louis Armstrong wearing a beard and a beret accompanying a poet?

Sure.

Get outa here.

Besides, he's good. I've got nothing against Satchmo.

Satchmo? You two are real good pals, I take it?

I call him Satchmo, he calls me Pops. We write occasionally. I told him in my last letter that I'm trying to wean my big brother off *white* rock n roll by pretty boys like *Fabian*.

I told you, I don't like Fabian.

Then who do you like?

Brook Benton.

He's black.

Chuck Berry.

He's black.

Jerry Lee Lewis.

He *sounds* black.

Comeon, howdya *sound* black? Do you take black voice lessons?

It's a natural born thing. To quote Albert Einstein, "Either you got it or you ain't."

Albert Einstein never said that. What are you laughing at?

You said that, ya bozo.

I never said that.

You used to say it all the time. I got you this time.

Did not.

Did.

Did not.

Once they are past Mountie Lake and into the foothills, the radio isn't much good. By the time they head south along the Banff-Jasper Highway, the sound is mostly static with the odd crackling surge from a thunderstorm moving in slowly from the west. Massive blue clouds descend from the peaks; forks of lightning scribble above the highway.

Uh oh.

Jeez.

What about we try to get that top on?

Nah, let's just make a run for it.

They meet the storm head-on just south of Bow Lake by the Crowfoot Glacier. At first, rain, then hail, then big sodden snow-flakes lash out at the speeding car and they howl back at the storm until the snowflakes turn back into rain and they both turn blue with the damp and cold as the night comes on. Derek fiddles with the dial and curses until, at last, on a dry road again, they hear the voice of a CBC announcer. Suddenly the reception on the radio is so clear it's like they've passed through the wilderness and out the other end.

> *When I was seventeen, it was a very good year*
> *It was a very good year for small town girls*
> *And soft summer nights...*

That's Bob Shane.

Shhh.

They listen without a sound, converts to a new religion. The voice wavers a bit off key, it's husky and hoarse, perhaps from too many whiskeys, but the poetry and the voice ring true.

Great stuff, eh? Fantastic.

Pretty good for a white guy.

Take off.

Pretty good for a college boy picker? Wouldn't you say?

Thanks for the insight, Derek.

Dear Mum and Dad, he writes. *All is well in Lake Louise. Nancy's up here with Alistair (or is it without Alistair? nobody knows). I have a bunk in the drivers' quarters. The mountains are magnif, and so are the guys I work with. A great place for recovering from first year university. Derek took off for his big job this morning. You don't have to worry about his car, it rides real good. I'm glad we drove up here together. Gave us a chance for a visit. Love, Tim.*

PS If my German grade is as bad as I think it will be, I might just have to forget about university in the fall. Will see. Fingers crossed.

Sometimes his mind wanders so much that he may as well go back to bed. Asleep, however, especially in the last drift before awakening, he is strangely awake. This morning as a pilgrim. Fleeing a mob. Running for the river up ahead. The river, to find the secret cave or the secret spring, the secret thing. Running to get away. The river ahead. Concentrate.

Behind him a great clamour. The pilgrim turns from his flight and sees them nearing...with bodies of men but the aspects of mandrills and ravens. From their mouths, laughter and groaning and weeping. Their eyes rolling white in their heads. And the pilgrim enters his rowrowyerboat and gently up the stream goes he. The river is broad and muddy with offal and muck from the bodies of the creatures. They do not follow.

Throughout the seventh day the river is foul and shapeless, and the pilgrim grows weary. He rows upstream backwards against the night, and on the morning of the sixth day he is faint with fatigue. But on the fifth day he sees that the river is narrower. And the curves of its banks are rounded and firm and the water grows clear, so he rows on until evening.

At dusk on the fourth day the sun seems nearer and its light brighter and it retires in a blush of a thousand hues. The curves of the river are sinuous, it is slender, a stream abounding in clear water, gurgling riffles, maidenhair and mossy rills on boulders brown and slippery. The pilgrim no longer feels his limbs, but still he continues on through the night of the third day and of the second. *When I was just sixteen*, he sings, *it was a very good year....*

He rows on. The brook flows as though it were issuing from the bowels of night. The boat glides into a wide slow pool and the pilgrim hears the splashing of fish.

The sun rises pink and blood rich on this wide pool. Mist. Sound of birds. Sunlight and white clouds and a forest carved in gardens, animals grazing between clearings and trees. He raises his hand in salutation, and the animals move in a company near the shore. The little dog Pepper is there, the orange eyes and diagonal stride. The pilgrim greets Pepper and all the animals, and he does rejoice in them.

Haben-Sie schon gehört das Frau Pabst ein Kindt bekommen hat? cries Alph the Mad Russian.

Ja, gewiss.

The sign reads, Beginning The In. Ochi Campground Welcome. Everywhere trout. Arcing through the water clear as a mirror. The pilgrim takes a rod, a snappy fibreglass flyrod with a Shakespeare reel and double- tapered line and a size 14 black tickler he has just tied on himself. He casts for many a trout on that first day. His eyes flash in the sun, his arms begin to return to life.

When lo, on the bank, who should he see but the brownhaired virgin whose name is Slimy whose name is Tit whose name is Titania whose name is never the same. His fly alights by the far side of the bank to an explosion of water and his rod comes up whipping stiff.

We're closed, cries the maiden. No more slipp'ry blisses.

There is a swishing like fly rod or willow trees. Windsweep. A drumming in rhythm as from a huge heart.

Heart-thump. Windswish. Hand on the old stufflebeam. Other arm still no feel. *Jabberjabber jay.* Heart-thump. Swisssh. Wummmp. Heartspin.

Jabberjabber.

He opens his eyes and frowns out at the world.

A chilly fragrance from the fir trees whispers through a crack in his window.

Through the same crack comes the bickering of whiskeyjacks.

From two floors below next to the grease pit, up the stairwell and through the cracks in his ill-fitting door, comes the rhythmic groan of the wringer washer. It says, *Heart throb, heart throb, heart throb.*

A sweep of rain on the window refracts the trees.

He levers himself to a sitting position on the bunk. Why, this morning, does the wringer washer say heart throb? It's like the last word of a tedious dream where lovers search and wait for each other and never meet.

He yawns, closing his eyes, and sees a trout rise.

Fisher! Fisha-a-a-ar!

The voice below rumbles like an avalanche. It seethes through the cracks in his attic door. The voice belongs to Biggs Altrogge the winter dispatcher, who apparently sleeps as rarely as he shaves.

Tim opens the door and stands shivering in his undershorts by the stairwell. Mental note: adjust door somehow so that it fits the frame, then he can shut out all that noise. He can shut out Altrogge.

The mornings are getting chilly. This late in September the rain could easily turn to snow. The mountains seem to beckon the storms.

I'm up here.

Clean your goddam limo!

I've gotta fix this door. Besides, I don't have to pick up my people till after lunch.

Sandy MacDonald needs the ramp. Move it, Fisher.

Sandy MacDonald is here ? Tim bounds back into his room,

...t the morning rain, raises his arms as though where the ...acks jabber outside his gable window a big band awaits ...ection. One two three and a one two three....

I'm singin in the rain...

Since coming up to Lake Louise in May with Derek, Tim has lived in what everyone at Lake Louise calls the Garage. It's an old frame building, vaguely alpine, huddled in a thick stand of fir trees on the slope of Paradise Mountain. Owing to these trees, tourists on their way to the Chateau are spared the sight of the Garage. It has the dispatcher's office, a grease pit and a laundry facility on the main floor where the mechanic and Dispatcher Altrogge nurse their hangovers and their beleaguered opinions about women with cups of instant coffee. On the second floor, now empty, is a large dorm for the summer drivers. Next to the empty dorm are Altrogge's and the mechanic's quarters, which Tim has never entered. These two rooms give off a perpetually rancid bouquet of rye whiskey. On the top floor is an L-shaped attic with its own tiny bathroom. When the drivers left at the end of the tourist season, Tim took over this attic from Sandy MacDonald, who was supposed to be in Edmonton taking another shot at his B.A.

Since Sandy's departure at the end of the season, the Garage has become a place of ghosts, a sort of moldering monument to the summer of 1961. Tim can almost hear snatches of Bob Shane singing about when he was twenty-one it was a very good year. He can almost see the women that might have inspired that song, the ghosts of the women.

He can almost see the girls from the Chateau, the summer ones who have all come and gone.

Sandy's former garret retains a hint of perfume. Scented soap, perhaps? Familiar, but he can't place it. On one long wall above the bed Tim has hung his fly rod, and against the other he has stacked several apple cartons for his book shelves. Next to the little bathroom and right above his dresser he hangs his five-string banjo. Beside his cot he has installed a small table and lamp borrowed one night from the lobby of the Chateau.

This garret is where he will study. And do a bit of writing. And fix up his badly fitting door. And grow worldly. But mostly he will study. To be re-admitted to university next year he must write two supplemental exams in October, one for German and one for English. None of his grades has been distinguished, and these two courses he has failed outright, German with a high enough grade that they're giving him a second try at it. He dislikes memorizing vocabulary, but here in the mountains with little to do but trips to the station and one or two tours per week, he will buckle down. *Haben-Sie schon gehört das Frau Pabst ein Kindt bekommen hat?* (Have you heard that Frau Pabst has just had a baby?) Every driver in the Garage has endured that one. His English is a different story. He has failed it because he went to the examination hall on the wrong day.

Occasionally a driver coming down from Jasper bunks in the big fetid dorm beneath Tim's attic. Otherwise the dorm remains empty. When he enters this big room it proclaims itself in a cold and abandoned yawn that reminds him of a curling rink after a game. Everything echoes. And from the empty bunks, all those man smells. Cigarettes, spilled wine and beer, sweaty clothes, deodorant. The wraith of each smell has settled in the dorm, stale and pungent with memory like the ghosts of old drivers. Tim's own former bunk in the dorm retains a trace of rum and vomit. Mattresses never forget.

Ah, but in his new bunk in the attic, this strange and almost familiar perfume.

He has time for fishing now, time for hikes into the mountains above Lake Louise, time to master his German vocabulary and bone up on the English. He's just finished a whole wad of Shakespeare, some poems by Dylan Thomas, all of *Pilgrim's Progress*, and is inching through Keats and Coleridge. More and more, however, he finds himself hanging around Biggs Altrogge's office, which is attached to the Garage. The Night Dispatcher's conversation is taciturn at best; he seems to put more concentration into smoking cigarettes.

Near the top of the treeline the clouds hang in sullen tatters, obscuring the mountains above, raining on the valley below. Tim trudges over to the stretch limo, spattered now with three days of slate grey mud and looking as desolate as the weather and Biggs Altrogge.

Sandy MacDonald (Old Wire to his intimates) emerges from the grease pit holding one of Altrogge's cups of instant coffee with both hands as though it were a urine specimen.

Old Wire, back in uniform. His version of the Brewster Grayline uniform. Rather than regulation grey pants and black shoes, Sandy has opted for blue jeans and cowboy boots, a ski sweater from one of his Scandinavian shopping trips, company jacket bearing his fraternity pin on the breast pocket, and positively no cap, thank you. The cap left a ring around his brushcut which he claimed induced baldness. Sandy's Flex is parked by the open doors of the Garage. He is all smiles again, as though the summer has just begun. He ambles over to the ramp to watch Tim hose down the limo.

Hi, guy. How the hell are ya?

Hello, Old Wire. You're supposed to be in Edmonton.

I am, he says. At least technically. You look hungover, Fishy.

I just have to breathe the air from Altrogge's room. It seeps into the attic, remember? What are you doing up here?

You won't believe it, Fishy.

Wait wait wait wait. You've dropped out. You want to be a bus driver when you grow up.

Guess again, he says, breaking into his customary laugh, a nervous high quacking that shakes his entire torso. A banker's laugh, Tim has decided.

Wait. No wait wait. You've been chosen to be tour-guide and chief *masseur* for the Miss Canada Pageant.

How do you pronounce that?

Masseur?

MacDonald screws up his pudgy face and gives it a try.

Never mind. Phone our good friend Rita. She would say it correctly, and she would say it sexy.

Sandy looks as though he's about to announce something, but he remains silent. He glances over at the Garage and flings the coffee into the bushes. Tim turns off the hose and backs his limo off the ramp. Sandy ambles along beside him, pauses.

You will not believe this. The boys in Banff phoned me in Edmonton to ask me—beg me, Fisher—to do a Car-Tan Tour for a nice bundle.

I knew I should have learned to drive a bus.

Wait, Fishy. Here's the juicy part. My people are from France this time, a group of vineyard people. MacDonald pauses. *And they needed a bilingual tour guide!*

Tim and Sandy roar.

MacDonald's aptitude for French has become legendary around the University of Alberta. First year French seems to be the only dark spot on his horizon. He has tried cramming, brown nosing, hypnotism with a young Edmonton psychiatrist, even studying, but every time he hears the words spoken by his profs (there have been five, not including tutors), every time he hears the French voices on the tapes in the language lab, he has the hardest time relating them to the words he has seen on paper. If the French people wrote *Oui, Monsieur* they should say it that way: oo-ee monsyer. Or if they went around saying things like *Weem sur*, they should spell it that way. Fair was fair. Each successive encounter with French has plunged MacDonald into the worst kind of boredom, and he's never even come close to a passing grade. His mother in Calgary, who in spite of prodigious wealth has kept Sandy on a strict allowance, arranged for the special tutors, but the tutorials cut into Sandy's sporting activities so severely that he paid his last tutor even more than his mother had paid the man not to return.

Dispatcher Altrogge is glaring at them from beside the grease pit through booze-reddened eyes. Sandy strolls toward Altrogge, towering over him, claps an arm around his shoulder, and walks him towards the front of his bus. Side by side, the Good Humour Man and the Bad Tumor Man.

Two weeks, Biggsy. Just two weeks, and I've missed you. That's because you're such a sweetheart of a guy.

Fuck you, MacDonald.

I rest my case.

With a short chopping jab Sandy pops open the door of the big Flex. Fishy! he calls. Come to the Nose Bowl.

What's a Nose Bowl?

We do this annual football game with a Jewish fraternity. It's an all-out paralytic blast. Bring your banjo. Bring the limo. Bring Altrogge.

Aren't you staying here tonight?

Maybe, calls MacDonald, looking off down the road. No. I think I'll go to Calgary and see Mum.

He climbs up into his bus, pumps away on his brakes, honks his horn, and drives off down the hill.

The whiskeyjacks resume their bickering in the trees. As Tim approaches the laundry room, the wringer washer is rumbling *humour tumour humour tumor....*

When Tim brings his own laundry down, the machine is saying something else.

Boombar boombar?

He isn't sure. When at last the machine is free, he dumps in his load, fills the tub with water and a mugful of soapflakes, pulls the lever to start the rotors, and collapses into the only chair in the room.

There's a full-length mirror on the opposite wall, little more than a speckled sheet of glass left there from the days when the mechanic had a wife. Now the mirror holds his attention. He sees a young man in tennis sneakers, coarse wool socks, jeans, Norwegian sweater with a black and white snowflake design. The socks and sweater are hand-me-downs from MacDonald, the young man's style somehow MacDonald's too. The brushcut, for instance. The brown sad Irish eyes are Tim's mother's. The brooding expression, that is also his mother's. The thin beaky nose, the jutting chin, the shy quick smile are his father's. The habit of squinting at horizons for planes or birds, the tense carriage, the restless look of a salesman with more hope than money, these too are his father's. Or so everyone who knows them both seems to think. He has two incisors that protrude just enough to catch on his lower lip every time he closes his mouth. Not even his brother has these. His beaver teeth. Keep pushing them back in, and some day they'll look normal, his mother has told him. He's tried it from elementary school to first year university, and they remain in their stubbornly beaverish stance as though eager to proclaim something twitty in his veins.

The young man in the mirror is depressed. You can tell by the way he drifts off. Where is he drifting? He is drifting away with the wringer washer, and the washer, as usual, is churning back into summer.

Boombar boombar

Or is it *roombar roombar?* Sometimes you have to listen carefully. He learned that the night he drank all that rum.

Of course! That's it.

Rumbarf rumbarf rumbarf...

The depressed young man is drifting back through September, August, July, June, early June. His first bunk was a lower, third on your left as you entered the dorm. It was good to remember this if you were coming in drunk for the very first time.

The offending liquor was Captain Morgan Dark Rum, purchased with MacDonald's ID. The drivers said you mixed it with Coke but no one had any Coke, so he got one in the café just before it closed, and they all went at it. Tim, MacDonald, Altrogge, who seemed less taciturn in the spring, and someone else. Alistair, of course. Alistair Vaughan, still in his agent's blue blazer, company tie and crest, gray flannels, and an old cowboy hat Altrogge had insisted that he wear that evening. Tim Fisher did the honours.

More, Fisher. Great. Hold it. More Coke. That's it.

Squirt some lemon in there. Ah!

Hit me up. Good.

A toast, said Vaughan, who always got English after his first drink. To John George Diefenbaker.

Piss up a rope.

Why then, chaps, what about a small libation to Ernest C. Manning, praymyer of the glawrious praaa-vince of Alberta.

Boooo!

How about a toast to the Dominion of Canada?

Siddown!

Well, then, something truly elevating, like the legs, the long legs, the leggy legs on the girl at the teahouse.

The legs!

Which teahouse?

Lake Agnes. She hasn't yet had the pleasure of sharing my bed.

Howdya know about the gams?

I saw them, both of them. Brown and shapely and cool in the wind. Went clear up to her body. I've known them for years, actually. So has Timmy. Gentlemen, once again, to the incomparable legs of the teahouse maid.

The legs!

They ran out of coke on the second round. Tim discovered, however, that if you squirted in a bit of lemon, the rum went down easy enough. Straight down, the way the sailors drank in movies. Not bad at all. After two or three of those, he didn't really feel much of anything. His tongue and the back of his throat went sort of numb. But he wasn't what you'd call drunk. He'd show these frat rats. He'd show Altrogge too. He'd put away a couple more and walk the straightest line they ever seen. Saw? Seen.

They all seemed to be *watching* him. As though he were about to take off and fly over the Victoria Glacier.

He would settle for Lake Agnes. Perhaps he would re-acquaint himself with the teahouse maid. Alistair said Tim had known her for some time. The only woman up here that he'd known for some time was Nancy, and it wasn't Nancy. Who could she be? He rose to his feet. Vaughan and MacDonald rose too. The three stormed down the stairs and into the chill night air, and that's when it struck. The legs went first, kneebones turned to lemon jello. He had to lean on his friends to cross the little bridge over Louise Creek.

And where are you heading, Captain Morgan? Alistair asked him.

He told them.

Well, Fishy, we think you should come with us to Lakeside Rez. It's full of chars and waitresses, and they'd fancy meeting you. Besides, it's closer, and we think you'll be a real hit.

Fine with me. What shall we say to the girls of Lakeside? he said, either to himself or to Alistair. Wait. Shall we give them a demonstration of our....

Sandy and Alistair seemed to be well ahead of him on the path. He stumbled up to them. Our social prowess?

Careful, Fishy.

Poppy beds. On your right.

Did you know that my Grandfather Fisher marched with a survey crew into these majestic mountains?

His friends chuckled.

No, wait, seriously. My Grandfather Fisher was a sort of a surveyor. I wonder if the girls of Lakeside Rez would be impressed to hear—

For some reason he was flat on his face. Sandy and Alistair helped him up.

Dint feel a thing.

Steady.

Haben-Sie schon gehört das Frau Pabst ein Kindt bekommen hat?

Again, laughter. Tim had no *idea* he could be so comical.

They approached Lakeside. There were still a few lights on, including a lamp or two in the common room.

Alistair, who are you going to be when you walk through that door, eh? I mean, like, to meet the faces that you meet?

Well, Timmy, what are my choices?

Tim stopped so they would wait for him.

You can be Theseus and I will be Oberon. Howzat?

Tim turned to Sandy. Thass the whole situation. You can be Theseus or you can be Oberon.

The enormity of this idea was staggering. His friends dragged him along the path and he stared up at the stars. Dazzling.

Then he was inside, surrounded by girls in their pyjamas. A number were sitting by the fire in the common room, so he introduced Sandy as the Good Humour Man and Alistair as Bob Shane, lead singer for the Kingston Trio.

Oh, cried Nancy. A celebrity in our midst.

She and Alistair did a formal kiss like the one they had to do several years ago in the year play. Everyone applauded. The girls were up and clapping and then they were all around Tim, crying *speech speech speech* in their pyjamas and very fetching they were so Tim did a recitation, that thing about the lunatic, the lover and the poet and a fine frenzy something-or-other. Everyone clapped. One girl said that he should hold onto one foot and give them a song. How vulgar, he said in his best home counties accent, and did another recitation, this time something about how he might see young Cupid's fiery shaft quenched in the chaste beams of the watery moon.

Fiery shaft, eh?

Is *that* what they call it now?

Sounds fun to me.

They clapped and laughed and the matron came in to make a special presentation.

But wait, where were Nancy and Alistair? Where was Sandy MacDonald? Where on Earth did they get to?

Thank you, Ben Hur, said the matron, and clamped onto his arm. He was propelled toward the door with alarming speed.

Wait wait wait wait.

If the matron wasn't careful he would find himself outside again. He confided this to the matron, whose limbs were made of stronger stuff than lemon jello. A difficult message to convey. But he tried, and found himself nevertheless sitting on the path beneath a glittering host of galaxies. How they spun! Where were the girls? Where were Alistair and Sandy? Where was Tim?

Where the golden poppies are blowing by the banks of Lake Louise. Where the deer and the antelope play. On his bum. He would stand up, that's exactly *precisely* what he would do.

With an exaggerated rolling motion that left him some forward momentum, he got to his feet and wobbled like an old tire down the path. The moon had risen. He found himself marching with elaborate care in front of the Chateau. Around the side of the Chateau. Past the parking lot. He found the little wooden bridge. Or thought he did. He tripped and plunged headfirst into the creek.

The water was fast and icy and it carried him downstream some distance before he discovered he had a mouthful of pebbles and difficulty breathing. For some reason, however, he was not drowning. Rather, he was going backward up the bank on his belly, his beaver teeth cleaving a nice furrow in the gravel. This is what ploughs do, he thought.

Someone let go of his legs, someone laughing. He found himself on his feet, more or less. He spat out some gravel and beheld MacDonald and Vaughan. They were holding him up by the armpits.

Have you ever viewed the canvasses of R.J. Stufflebeam? he said. His women are reproduced in the pages of *Fin & Feather* for your delight and oedipucation.

They got him inside and made him undress, but as soon as they turned out the lights on him, the ceiling began to spin and the mansmell stench of the drivers' dorm began to move like warm smog up his nasal cavity. On its way past his uvula it blew essense of stale sock on his pharynx, and he responded with a volcanic projectile of vomit. All over the bed and everywhere else too.

Someone else, who wasn't quite so pleasant, helped him into the can. A hot shower awaited him. And that was okay. Better by far than Louise Creek. After the shower, a bit of midnight laundry detail. That had been Vaughan's idea. Tim was as pliable of will as he was of body, so he found himself staggering down the stairs of the Garage, dressed once more, and holding an armful of vomitty sheets and blankets.

He puked again, this time outside beneath a sympathetic gathering of pines.

Get out there and walk it off, said Vaughan from the doorway of the Garage. He seemed to know something about drinking. They *all* seemed to know something about drinking.

The wringer washer ground out a sententious little song.

Rumbarf rumbarf...

After a while it changed to something else. He had to listen very carefully, and leaned his forehead against the machine and it was saying it was saying lemme see....

Upstream upstream upstream...

One moment he was down on his knees, the next he was stumbling past Lakeside to a chorus of frogsong and up the broad path that lead to the Lake Agnes teahouse. He was not really going all the way to the top. Surely not. That would be romantic horseshit. (This last he said out loud.) He was going just far enough upstream to work the booze out of his system, as Alistair said he should. The bridge across the upper creek would do fine thank you very much.

When he reached the bridge, he drank the glacial waters from the stream. He could see the Chateau below him like a castle, tinted silver by the moonlight, and he made up his mind to go on a little farther up the hill. He decided that he was probably a little more sober than drunk. He kept up a steady pace until the path wound into a series of hairpin turns. He could see all of Lake Louise below and galaxies like luminous clouds above. Presently he heard a sound, and listened, puffing, on a bench. More frogs. This time from a large pond. He had arrived at a place called Mirror Lake. A wooden sign on a tree indicated that Lake Agnes was only half a mile farther up.

Frogsong and something else, a bonka-bonka sound.

He followed the trail up a steep grade. He had to go slowly. The trees were large and thick near the pond and cast well-defined moonshadows over the path. The tresses of black moss on the firs and larches looked like witches' hair, the larger boulders like animals. And the sound, that other sound. It had a melody, a bonka-bonka metal twang. He made his way along the trail to the edge of a steep rockface and looked up to see a cataract that seemed to spill out of the stars. To his right there was a staircase almost as steep as a ladder, and fashioned from rough boards and logs. He made a stealthy ascent. He had no idea what awaited him at the top of the stairs, but he wanted to see it before he was spotted. The first thing he saw was Lake Agnes: silvery, still, surrounded by a cirque with a small glacier that seemed to glow at the upper end. Beside him was the stream plunging out of the little lake and a crude bridge leading into an alpine meadow that went all the way up to the glacier. This was the source of Louise Creek, which fed the Bow which fed the Saskatchewan which....

He left the waterfall behind and once again heard the music. He sat on a log and peered through the trees, smaller and sparser now above the rockface. A larch-scented breath of wind greeted his nostrils.

If only the drivers' quarters could smell like this.

He went closer and spotted a large log and stone cabin with a big veranda about a hundred paces up the slope. This was the teahouse. Someone sat on the steps. A girl in pyjamas and an open parka. She was playing a banjo in her lap, her head and her long hair bowed over the instrument. Tim moved closer.

The girl was playing some sort of hillbilly tune in a minor key. Her right hand bounced up and down from the wrist, striking the strings in a doorknocking motion. The song had a little chorus. Her left hand went up and down the neck, and the fingers of her left hand hammered and slid through each lick. In a major key, the song might have sounded happy, but in the minor key, the fifth string droning with every stroke, the melody was oh, so haunting. She sang,

> *Wish I had a banjo string made of silver twine,*
> *And every tune I played on it meant that boy would be mine...*

The moon left a glaze on her long hair. She sang in a low clear voice. The banjo rang bold and metallic with every lick. It went bonk tiddy bonka tiddy bonk tiddy bonka tiddy. It filled him with a throbbing sensation that was different from getting a hard-on, a rapture he had felt only in dreams. He thought, *This is the meaning of heart throb.* Alistair Vaughan would have clapped in a gentlemanly fashion like someone in an opera box. *Well done, well done,* he would have shouted. Sandy MacDonald would have called to her. *Miss? Miss? Do you need a manager?* He would have risen to his feet and walked up to her without so much as a blush. Alistair Vaughan would have done the same. Holding her banjo by the neck, she stood and flung her long mane of hair back over her shoulder. She stretched and yawned like a pagan priestess up at the raging moon. Then she tripped up the steps and slipped inside the door.

When he returned to the Garage in the half-light around three o'clock, his vision of her still before him, the wringer washer was groaning away. He listened, half asleep. It sounded at first like gottem, gottem, gottem. Which meant what? That she had got him? By the heart? Who was she? Hadn't Alistair said that they both knew her? The more he wondered at the vision he had seen, the more he realized what the old machine had been saying all along.

Bottom Bottom Bottom

If you got drunk and threw up all over your bunk, you were Bottom. If you fell in love with moonlit visions, you were Bottom. If you were the butt of the other guys' laughter, you were Bottom. If you had to wash barf off your sheets and blankets at three in the morning, you were definitely Bottom.

So what you needed to do, said Sandy MacDonald the following afternoon, when Tim's hangover had passed into melancholy, was *assert yourself*. Walk up there again. No more hiding in the bushes. Tell her you liked her music. Tell her you want to see her. Take her to a roast this Friday. That's it. Tell her about our roast down at the campground.

What roast?

We'll organize one.

Just for me?

Of course. Great excuse for a party.

He walked up the trail to Lake Agnes after supper. It was a vigorous half-hour hike, and when he reached the top of the cataract he was puffing.

The evening was clear and the sun was just sinking beneath the mountains. The sunset left little daubs of orange light on the rocks of the alpine meadow. Pikas piped their messages in nervous whistles from their nests among the boulders of the scree. Nighthawks swooped and roared down on humming clouds of mosquitoes.

The teahouse maid was watching him from an upper veranda. She was moving a tray with one hand and sucking on the straw of a milkshake. Before he could call to her, she called something to him. The noise from the waterfall drowned out her voice. He would always try to remember her that way, straining to hear her, with a tumbling waterfall like the River Alph between them.

As he approached, she came down to meet him. She wore a large straw hat so that her face remained in shadow. She didn't look much like the girl he had seen the night before, and yet in another way she *did* look like her.

We're closed, she said. She had laid her tray down on one of the outside tables and began once more to suck at the straw of her milkshake.

Oh, I don't want anything, he said. Well....

Well?

He noticed that she wore her hair in long braids. Her arms were nicely tanned for June. There was something about the way her chin squared off and the frank manner in which she smiled at him, waiting for him to say what was—*My God!*

Slimy?

Timmy Fisher? Timmy? Whadya know.

She looked a bit taller. Her old scrawniness had somehow turned elegant, but she was different in some other way, as though all the gestures, all the lines she had delivered with such ready wit in high school had become polished and rehearsed and even more fetching. The girl in the apartment with a mother and no father had somehow been replaced by this worldly one. This lovely one.

I heard you last night, he said. You sounded terrific.

She smiled.

You saw me up there? she said, pointing to the steps. You saw me and you said sweet buggerall?

I didn't know it was you. Besides, if I said something, that would've ruined it.

Jesus Murphy.

I gotta know how you do that stuff. With the banjo.

Jesus H. Christ. She reached for a pack of cigarettes in her apron pocket. I know, she murmured, don't tell me. I swear too much.

Just say furschlugginer.

What does that mean?

It doesn't mean anything.

Halfway through the banjo lesson, he held his fingers over the strings to silence them.

I hope I'm not stretching my luck here....

Yes? she said, looking sideways at him, her knee bouncing up and down with impatience like a bored and restless Titania.

He seemed to gather his will for a mighty leap over an even mightier chasm.

The drivers are having a roast in a few days.

Yes?

And I was wondering if you'd like to go there. With me, like. Maybe you could bring your banjo. I could come up here. We could walk down around suppertime. Or after your shift. If you like.

All this he said without swallowing.

Sure, she said, as though he had merely asked if he could taste her milkshake. Okay.

He strode down the mountain singing one of her songs, a southern mountain tune that went *Goin up to Cripple Creek, goin in a whirl, goin up to Cripple Creek to see my girl.* After a while, the footpath converged with the horse trail. Here he met Johnny Aubichon, a halfbreed guide who worked with Buddy Brewster. Johnny was leading a string of ponies to the corral.

Don't you mean goin *down* to Cripple Creek?

Didn't think anyone could hear me. Nice evening.

Don't think I can complain.

Johnny brought his horse to a halt and the ponies joggled past. A big woman on a dark mare brought up the rear.

Timmy? she said. Timmy Fisher?

Her voice was familiar. Who's that?

Amber.

Amber Bole? I don't believe my eyes. What are you doing up here?

I'm a cowboy, she said. Talk about a coincidence. Not an hour ago I was tellin Johnny about that awful school we went to. Whoa there, I'm talkin, you bitch!

I just had my first conversation in ages with Slimy not fifteen minutes ago, he said.

And she let you call her that?

Sure. Are you heading up there?

Yes we are, said Johnny. It's a small world an that's the God's truth. Johnny touched his hat with his fingers and his horse plodded behind Amber's up the slope.

Keep on with the singin there, Tim, she cried. You're about set to be a cowboy yourself.

Rita Symington. She was starting education at the university in Edmonton. Her program would be designed to teach French to kids in elementary schools, but what she really wanted was to sing folk songs in coffee houses.

You mean like the Kingston Trio?

Are you outa your bloody mind? Gimme a break. You don't mind if I swear, do you, God, I gotta watch that. At least I'm not as bad as Bolski, Scuse me, Amber. You have to call her Amber now. The Kingston Trio, Jesus, I can't believe you'd say that.

Who do you like?

I like the real stuff, I like Wobbly songs, I like the Weavers, I like Joan Baez.

Who?

She spoke so rapidly that sometimes he could hardly keep up with her. She had learned to speak French like a native, she read Karl Marx and D.H. Lawrence, she smoked Peter Stuyvesant filter tips and always sat down-wind, and she blew the smoke out of the corner of her mouth. But it was her banjo playing that haunted him most of all. She could have done anything; he would resolutely adore her banjory. He vowed he would buy his own five-string banjo the next time he was in Calgary.

By the time the drivers held their roast, Tim could strum almost any simple folksong in G or C. He could do a bit of frailing (old-timey, Rita called it), and he could pick out all the notes to *Red River Valley* and *The Banks of the Ohio*. He could even play one or two plaintive things in C minor, and this was by far the neatest key to work in. C minor was made for songs of unrequited love.

Say what you will about unrequited love, it is much less terrifying than the real thing. This thought comes to Tim during the rinsing of his wash. It comes with the full weight of his late September gloom. He rejects the thought with a little twist of anger.

Altrogge slouches through the door that opens from the grease pit.

Goin to see his mum in Calgary. Sure. An I'm the King of Siam.

Huh?

Altrogge glares at Tim and begins to nod his head.

Do I have to spell it out? MacDonald's got some pussy down at Paradise Lodge. I seen that MG of his.

There's lots of MGs around, says Tim.

He's only half listening. He is still revolving on the stuck record of unrequited love; it's like the sadness of autumn. Altrogge walks into his line of vision.

Fisher, you ever had a good piece a ass?

Tim gives one of his stock evasions: Depends what you mean by good. Altrogge swears softly and slouches out of the laundromat.

Tim seems mesmerized by the motion of the rotors. A banjo plays wildly in his head. It isn't Rita Symington playing or even Pete Seeger. It is just the song, exuberant, mournful, frailing away in mountain minor. He checks the young man in the mirror. Is he admiring himself?

Yes.

Is he still depressed?

Yes.

Is he maybe enjoying his depression a little bit?

Maybe.

Is he going to spend the whole godforsaken winter in this godforsaken garage with the unbearable Altrogge?

Yes.

Why?

Why not?

That's no answer.

The pay isn't bad. He hasn't become an alcoholic, not yet. And besides, it's only September 29. A little more than a week ago, it was still summer. In six months or so he will have paid back his dad for tuition and books. By then he will have passed his English and German. He'll be a wizard on the banjo. He will learn how to ski like an Austrian. In his attic he will rise above the muckiness of the world. He will fill his notebooks with brilliant writing.

Horseshit horseshit horseshit

He decides the place needs some music, so he bounds up the stairs to his attic and gets his banjo. He brings it down to the laundry room and begins to play. The rain is back. The roof trembles with its pelting. In a few minutes it is more sleet than rain. He plays as loud as he can, and it seems to work. *Goin up to Cripple Creek, goin in a whirl, goin up to Cripple Creek to see my girl.* Bonka tiddy bonka tiddy bonka tiddy bonk....

His banjo manages to bring back warmer times. Snuggling around the campfire with Rita Symington. Going down to the creek to get more Crackling Rosé, calling out for a toast. His arm around her shoulders. Smelling the fragrance at the back of her neck. Singing all those songs until he was hoarse, until everyone was hoarse.

Between songs she had reached up and held his face in her hands and whispered, Remember, in front of all these hotsytotsy people, I'm Rita, not Slimy, you got that? Rita. What a weird thing to say, he thought, and soon put it out of his mind.

They had all thrown down their blankets and sleeping bags in a circle around the fire to stay warm and cuddle in the cool night air. Two by two the lovers would disappear as discreetly as possible into the bushes, leaving the rest of them to sing about such things as ill-fated love and hardship in mining communities.

Once, on his way back from peeing, Rita came up to him. They held each other and kissed. She went off into the bushes and he waited for her, watching for bears. He felt chivalrous. Then he had a thought: *I will never be happier than I am right now. I am eighteen years old and I will never be happier.* It staggered him. When she had finished peeing in the bushes, he told her this thought.

What collossal twenty-two carat horseshit, she said, and smiled. You just wait.

He stumbled after her back to the fire.

For what?

Never you mind. You just wait, Timmy.

How could anything be more perfect?

Je ne peux pas dire.

Tell me. You can tell me.

You know what, Timmy? You're an angel. I like you. I think you're an absolute goddam angel.

Alistair Vaughan and Nancy joined them on their blanket.

Isn't he? Rita said to Alistair. Isn't he a goddam angel?

A gentleman and a scholar, said Alistair. Not the best rum drinker I've ever encountered, but a fine fellow. A fine fellow.

We will never be happier than we are right now, Tim proclaimed sadly. How could we ever be happier?

Oh, Timmy, Rita crooned. *Allons donc! Quel tas de merde!*

Nancy said, Listen to this girl, Timmy.

Why did everyone call him Timmy? He didn't call himself Timmy.

The cool guy in the mirror with the banjo in his lap doesn't look like Timmy. He seems too far into the mystery of life. He is definitely Tim, no two ways about that. So what did she mean, *Oh, just wait?*

Wait for what?

Angel angel angel

That was his first date with Rita. There were other dates and banjo lessons and friendly chats up at the teahouse. They made music together, but that was all they made. Obviously she liked him, and if they liked you, Sandy said, that was half the battle. Just as obviously there were things you could not tell angels.

To be more specific, things you could not *do* with angels.

Slipp'ry blisses, he says drowsily, as though he'd gotten the answer too late to put it in the exam. The answer cruises past his face, tails briefly in the current, snaps up a nymph, and drifts downstream into a deeper pool.

Some of Sandy and Alistair's fraternity brothers from the Vancouver chapter paid them a visit. Nancy Fuller said they were top drawer all the way, which meant that they were gentry. Was it just Tim's memory, or did they all groom their hair in such a way that when the wind blew, their forelocks fell unerringly into their eyes?

Sandy threw a roast for the occasion. Nancy had to do a late shift, so she couldn't come. Tim, she said, maybe you and Alistair can keep each other out of trouble.

What do you mean?

Just a thought.

Rita said she would come to the roast, but not as anyone's date. She was going to be the entertainment. For the occasion Sandy also hustled up some waitresses who seemed a bit on the wild side. They all went to a little picnic spot overlooking Johnson Lake a day or two after Labour Day. For some of them it was a sort of farewell party. No tourists around, and the mountain air was cold, the aspen leaves turning bright yellow, the berry shrubs going orange and red all over the lower hills. A small creek with a beaver dam flowed into the lake beside their campsite. It reminded him of Ochi Creek.

Down went the blankets, around went the wine and the snacks. Tim sat next to Rita, hoping to proclaim something territorial to the other guys. Rita sang a few songs and drank some wine and everyone was having a terrific time. Well, almost everyone. Tim kept trying to talk to Rita but she was too intent on trying out her new songs to pay him much attention.

Some fellow asked her, Do you know that one, *It Was a Very Good Year?*

Rita said she didn't like it very much.

But can you sing it? he persisted.

Maybe some other time.

Fishy, said Sandy, get out your banjo. He's fantastic.

He got out his banjo, a lovely old Gibson he'd bought in Calgary. He played, and some of them sang, and everyone was happy. Well, there was the Rita problem. And, as things turned out, Alistair was feeling frisky in Nancy's absence so there was one guy too many. But for a while, at least, they all sang and clapped their hands. Then one by one they stopped singing, but still they exhorted Tim to keep on playing. It wasn't long before Sandy MacDonald was occupying a spot on the blanket next to Rita, who was babbling in French for anyone who would listen. They all extolled Tim's banjory, so on he frailed and strummed while they bantered and joked all through the night. And these people were really all top drawer, hadn't Nancy said so? And she was right. They were all suave and witty and they kind of knew things that only really sophisticated people would know like how Sweden was a really great country because the girls all knew the score and probably, of all the countries on the continent, Switzerland had the most non-assholes, but absolutely *no one* went there for skiing any more because all the wrong sort of people went, and besides, you got better skiing and better service and a better rate of exchange in Austria and he tried to remember the things they said so that he'd know next time (you pronounce it *Van-cue-ver*) but the talk grew softer, they all seemed to know what the other one meant by the smallest gesture and after a while the fire faded, and all around there were slow movements under the blankets.

Tim played on. He played his whole repertoire so that Rita would hear, and then she'd know how good he had become, he played it all to their whispers and sighs. He did a long improvisation on a flamenco piece he'd heard. Someone sighed her approval, so he waited, played some other songs, and then picked up the flamenco number again. Passionately. His fingers flew over the banjo as they had never flown. He was master of his instrument now, better even than Rita.

Where was Rita? She had disappeared beneath a blanket. She was there in front of him, but where? It seemed, at least from the sound, that Sandy MacDonald was with someone else. Did that mean that Rita was with Alistair Vaughan? The fire had fallen in upon itself so that only the embers remained. Peering through the smoke he could see only the vaguest forms moving beneath the blankets. When he stopped to retune his banjo, all he could hear were tiny whispers, some quick breathing, an occasional moan. There was no sign of a person, only a mass of them, moving as one in the dark like a huge coiled worm.

Was this, then, what people called an orgy? In an orgy, wasn't *everyone* welcome? When you went partying with really sophisticated guys like this, you probably couldn't just throw off your clothes and jump in. You had to say the right thing first, you had to know the code.

He was looking at the dark space on the other side of the fire, the space obscured by the smoke and embers. Into this space Rita had disappeared and she would stay somehow out of sight so that he would only be able to imagine her the way pilgrims did. Exalted. Or the way knights errant imagined their ladies when the knights were off in the Holy Land to fight the Saracens. The ladies and their wealthy lords would remain safe in castles with their moats and rose gardens, but they would be locked into loveless marriages.

A space like this he created for Rita Symington. Except she would have mountains instead of castles and someone like Alistair Vaughan hanging around, and in her moments of remorse she would yearn for the day that he would ride back with a banjo on his knee and claim her. She would show him the love songs she had written for him in his absence. Something like that.

It was past two o'clock in the morning. Tim put his banjo back in the case, found someone's half-empty bottle of Crackling Rosé and wandered down to the creek via the main hiking path. The moon was still up. He sat on a rock by the edge of the path and heard little splashes at his feet. He drank slowly. More splashes. Fish, from the sound of it. He spotted a pool that seemed to hold the moon and watched for more splashing. Before long a trout rose, then another. They were rising all over the pool and downstream in the faster water. Huddled in a blanket, perched on a rock by the side of the stream, he watched and dozed. The fish were early-spawning brook trout up from the lake, most of them more than a foot long.

He heard a noise on the path behind him. His first thought was bears, but he was too weary to fear them. He turned around.

It was Nancy. She shone a flashlight on him.

I thought that looked like a human being, she said. What happened to the big party?

Oops.

Does that mean what I think it means?

I'm afraid so. Last time I saw him he was lying in a pile of heaving bodies up the trail.

Nancy looked beseechingly up at the stars and said nothing.

Tim sat hunched over in his blanket, looking down at the stream while Nancy stood beside him with her flashlight off, hugging herself against the chill air.

Show me, she said.

It's just over there, a hundred yards. You can smell the smoke from their campfire.

In a few minutes Nancy returned. Without a word she sat down beside Tim on the blanket and snuggled into it.

Was he there?

Was he ever. I left him snoring into some slut's armpit. He had told me he was going to have a few drinks and come back at the end of my shift. I knew something was up.

You drove all the way down from Lake Louise for this?

Sometimes you have to know, she said.

Who was the girl?

It wasn't Slimy, if that's what you mean.

Who was Slimy with?

I couldn't tell. You like her, don't you. Don't deny it.

He denied it.

He said, You drove all the way down here to find out that Alistair is acting like Oberon.

Looks like you're having a pretty wild time of it too, Fishy. What are you doing down here all alone?

She turned to look at him. She looked at him for a long few intimate seconds as though not a thing in the world could ever surprise her again, and then she looked away. At last they gathered up Tim's things and headed back down the trail to Nancy's car. She glared at the road ahead. She was worried she might fall asleep at the wheel, so she charged Tim with keeping her awake all the way back to Lake Louise.

Howcome girls like you end up with guys like Alistair?

What do you mean girls like me?

You know.

No, she said, I don't know what you mean.

Well, he said, you're a real glamour puss. You could have any guy on the block.

Thank you, she said. You like me, don't you.

At that moment he realized that, yes, she might have a point there. In fact, for a long time, yes, he has been imagining delightful things about her.

Oh, I guess so.

Thank you again. And what do you mean by guys like Alistair?

You know.

No, I *don't* know.

I'm trying to find an acceptable word.

Nancy stared straight ahead and gunned it. She said, How about tail gunner?

Well....

How about meat hound?

Yeah.

Am I shocking you? she said.

No, but I bet you've forgotten my question.

Why do girls like me go for guys like Alistair?

Yeah. Enlighten me.

And not for guys like you?

Well....

Your time will come.

He wasn't sure what she meant. Time for Nancy or time for gals in general? He kept wondering about the change in Rita. From teahouse maid to everyone's favourite girlfriend. They drove past Vermillion Lakes and Nancy's headlights picked up a herd of elk crossing the highway. About a dozen cows and some large calves trotted stiff-legged across the road. Nancy pulled over and they watched them until the last cow had crossed.

Wait, said Tim, and another elk loomed into view, a young drooling bull, weeks ahead of the rut, head raised, sniffing the breeze.

Nancy broke into a desolate smile. She said, Is that who you want to be when you grow up?

In mid-September he returned to the scene of the crime to give the Johnson Lake brook trout a try. All but a few of the summer workers had left. Rita and Nancy would be going back to Edmonton the next day. He asked Rita to come fishing with him, but she couldn't.

He hiked into the stream above Johnson Lake and found the campfire. He found some of their garbage, a shoe and a girl's knickers, one of Alistair Vaughan's empty bottles of Bass Ale, some neat looking wine called Mateus. There was nothing remarkable about the scene of their last party. Johnson Lake, from this angle, was not the stuff of tourist photographs. The real alpine country around Lake Louise was up the Bow River Valley, off in the distance. This was downriver, just a small lake surrounded by gentle hills dotted with aspens and pines. But something about the woods...absolutely still. The evidence of their last little bacchanal, something desolate and resonant. He could almost hear his own banjo frailing beneath the moon. He took his rod down to the pool where he had heard the fish rising. There he found his empty bottle of Crackling Rosé. He took the bottle and heaved it up at the pile of garbage by the campfire.

The brook trout were downstream. Occasionally one would break the surface of a shallow riffle. Tim peered down into the water and saw that they weren't really rising for insects. They were hanging in the current, dozens of them. Some would flirch into the gravel, creating little explosions of silt. They were digging spawning trenches all along a ten-yard stretch. When the trout broke the surface the sun caught their flanks in flashes of the deepest orange. The cold autumn air, the season, the thing that turned the leaves into a saturnalian festival of colour, it was at work among the brook trout in a magic way that made them dance.

He put down his fly rod and watched. Somewhere off in the woods an elk was bugling. After a while, before the sun had reached the horizon, before the moon had had a chance to rise, he climbed the hill to the place where they had partied and he got rid of their garbage. All but his empty bottle of Crackling Rosé. He considered bringing back the bottle as a candle holder or maybe a keepsake.

A keepsake of what?

A shaft of anger passed through him as he stood by the lake. He heaved the bottle out beyond the reeds as far as he could throw.

After his trip in the stretch limo, he returns to check his clothes. They hang from a rope in the empty dorm. Altrogge must have heard him. He shuffles into the big room with a glass in his hand.

Jesus, Fisher, you look like you need a drink.

Altrogge's room is the drivers' summer dorm in miniature. A bare bulb with a brass chain sways from a cord in the ceiling and casts an unclean light on the cement walls of his lair. On one wall is a girlie poster, *circa* 1950, extolling the virtues of Autolite Sparkplugs. Altrogge's clothes are piled on an empty bed and stuffed into cardboard boxes. The air is stale with whiskey and cigarettes. Here and there a whiff of deodorant in abject retreat from the force it was sent to conquer.

Altrogge pours Tim three fingers of warm rye.

Who died?

Tim shrugs.

Summer's gone, MacDonald and Vaughan and all their college boy buddies have pissed off, all that fancy pussy gone back east. Hey? Hey, Fish? No more weeny bakes? Hey? Fuck off with that, Fish. Fuck right off.

The only time Altrogge's voice ever approaches tenderness is when he says *Fuck right off.* He raises his glass to the big poster and they drink.

That's what happens, says Altrogge. That's what always happens. In summer it's a la-di-da parade, you get pissed. In winter it's a funeral, you get pissed even more. After a while, you don't know the difference. Hey? Drink up.

Tim drinks up. Altrogge sloshes more rye into Tim's glass.

Altrogge, a while ago you asked me if I'd ever gotten laid. What if I told you, no, I have never ever gotten laid.

Knock me over with a feather, Fish.

Let me ask you a question. Have you ever been in love?

Altrogge roars. It sounds like pain.

Fuck *off*, Fish.

Just asking.

Fall in *love?* I have seen a whole decade of fancy pussy come up here.

Anything as nice as Rita Symington?

Nice?

Altrogge seems as though he wants to say something. He rolls his eyeballs toward the ceiling in an all-knowing gesture, as though the obvious answer was up there somewhere.

Yeah, says Tim, I'd say she was pretty nice.

Well, at least she's not stuck on herself like some of those friggin frat girls from down east.

Altrogge smirks at Tim.

Fall in love. I don't know about you, Fish.

Tim assumes that the conversation is over. He gazes around at the squalor of Altrogge's room until once again he sees the girlie poster. Something familiar about it, something about the girl stepping out of the bubble bath. Like someone he knows. She is very attractive.

Fall in love. Wow. Yeah.

Altrogge mumbles these words like a stuck record, nodding all the while.

They come in here every spring. All dolled up. The French bitches come in here lookin for some nice all-Canadian Anglo stud, and if they speak English they want a *frog* to put it to them, and they all get what they're lookin for. Except for you an me, Fishy. You because you are still in the goddam cradle, an me because I...just...say...wank it. Hahah! Wank it! That's the answer!

Altrogge has suddenly gone deranged. He is Tim's first full-blown cynic. The very word makes Altrogge easier to take. You can file him away under C and forget him. Forget him and return to the mysterious girl still easing one leg out of her bubble bath. The poster is from an illustration, perhaps an oil painting. The bob of her jet black hair calls to mind movies made just after the war.

Drink up, Fish, for chrissakes.

Tim swallows some warm rye.

You know what your problem is, Fishy? You don't see what they're tryin to do. They walk into the driver's café with their bermuda shorts, they come in swayin, tits first. Oh, Biggsy, when are ya gonna show me your bus! Oh, Biggsy, take me up to the crystal caves!

Take me up to what crystal caves?

Altrogge swears absentmindedly. Eyes glazed over, he slumps in his chair. He speaks as though he is coming back from far away.

This broad, he says. Candy.

Huh?

Candy, her name was Candy. That was ten goddam years ago. She had this thing about seein the crystal caves. No one knows about them. They're up the hill past our dump about five hundred yards. Big deal. Altrogge's voice goes into cartoon falsetto. *Oh, Biggsy, show me the crystal caves.*

I don't get it.

Have a drink.

She wanted to see these caves. So?

Altrogge rises stiffly to his feet. He mumbles something about taking a leak and ambles from the room.

Tim has another look at the poster. The girl is a dark-haired beauty. The hair is bobbed and sheeny, blue-black. All she wears is bubbles. She smiles in an unfocussed way, as though she has just remembered her name. The smile...no, she's not smiling, she's just not closing her mouth.

He takes a closer look. The illustration is signed R.J. Stufflebeam. Aha, the immortal Stufflebeam! Illustrator of nubile virgins and other clueless beauties in such engaging tracts as *Fin & Feather* and *Man to Man*.

What the hell are you lookin at? says Altrogge, swaying in the doorway.

Where'd you get your poster?

Mabel? She's been hangin around the Garage since day one. She's belonged to every Night Dispatcher since the dawn a time.

Thought it might be Candy, says Tim with a smile.

Only one similarity. They was both brunettes from stem to gudgeon.

Tim looks at the poster for a long moment.

Altrogge, you're some kind of a weird romantic!

A veil seems to lift from Altrogge's bloodshot eyes.

Takes one to know one.

He follows his pronouncement with a fierce belch.

The morning sky is overcast, the mountains once more obscured by floating banks of low lying clouds. Occasional tiny flakes feather down through the trees like ashes. On his way to the station, Tim stops off at the Paradise Bungalows.

Altrogge was right about MacDonald. His white MG is parked next to a small log cabin. Tim almost knocks. He half wants to pay his respects. He needs to return Sandy's borrowed ID, a valid driver's license for buying liquor that he has kept all summer in his wallet. He also needs to know who Sandy is with. He hears voices from inside the cabin, so he waits outside the screen window. Sandy is enunciating something Tim can't understand. A woman's voice responds with a trill of laughter.

Non, non, she says. *Pas Voulez-vous. Veux-tu. Veux-tu.*

Vutchew cooshy avec ma?

Again, her laughter.

Veux-tu couchez avec moi?

Vutchew cooshy avec moi?

Coo-shay. Coo-shay.

Coo-shay.

The other voice is Rita Symington's.

In fact, isn't that also her face in the calendar? That's why it was so familiar! But no, wait, not her real face, maybe just her expression. Or maybe not exactly her expression, but smiling the way Tim likes to remember her in those unguarded moments when she was back in grade ten and suddenly she had to play Titania. And those recent moments when they were together, alone, at a banjo lesson, and she doesn't quite close her mouth.

Tim slouches back to the limo. He doesn't want the two of them to know he is here, to know that he's upset. He eases the gear into neutral, floats the big limo into the stream of traffic, and glides down the hill.

In mid-October Tim gets a ride down to Edmonton from Lake Louise to write his supplemental exams. His English sup comes first. He sits alone in an office in the old Arts Building while a storm blows outside. He goes cautiously through the first two essays and runs wild on the third one, a question on *Romeo and Juliet*. He even gives his essay a title, "The Vanities of Profane Love." His recall of the play is good.

In a spirit of expansiveness he goes on to compare the tragedy of Romeo and Juliet to the comedy of Peter Quince's little play of Pyramus and Thisbe from *A Midsummer Night's Dream*. When the three hours are up he has answered all the questions in some detail and has had time to proofread his work.

But when, on the following day, he arrives for the German exam, the idioms seem to swarm in his head. Too much memory work too late in the game. Professor Mahler is explaining something to a grad student when Tim walks in the door. He likes Professor Mahler. The man has a passion for jazz and a good sense of humour.

Herr Fisher, he says, give for yourself lots of time to the last question. It's worse forty per cent of the exam. I put this question in for nice surprise, *nicht*? *Also*....

Also, pronounced Al-zo. Professor Mahler was always saying it as a preliminary to something. Tim once asked him what it meant.

It means nussing, Herr Fisher.

The first section requires a series of short answers based on idioms. The second is a translation from German to English. The third section is Mahler's little surprise. *Schreiben Sie ein Stück um drei bis sechs Seiten über eins von das gefolge: 1) Mein Liebste Deutsche Gedicht, 2) Feuerwehr bei der Arbeit, 3) Schmauss und Strauss, 4) Bei der Zahnartzt.* When Tim reaches this section, he has exhausted himself on the other two, and he has only thirty-five minutes left. A play? Three to six pages? Is *Feuerwehr* fire-power or fire equipment? Who are Schmauss and Strauss, composers? Does it matter? Of course it matters! This is a final exam and everything matters. But *three* pages. Is a *Gedicht* a story? Some kind of diction?

Tim knows two things. That he now has twenty minutes for this, the weightiest of all the questions, and that a *Zahnartzt* is a dentist. Sometimes, in a moment of extremity the Muse is kind. She's up there singing of Mount Abora. Sometimes it's a dulcimer, sometimes a banjo. Something cloacal, hitherto retentive, decides to open.

Bei der Zahnartzt
ein Stück von Tim Fisher

Die Personlichkeit:
Doktor Schmidt, ein Zahnartzt
Hans, ein Patient

Doktor Schmidt	*Also...sagen Sie "ah."*
Hans	*Ah.*
Doktor Schmidt	*Lauter.*
Hans	*Ahhh!*
Doktor Schmidt	*Etwas langsamer bitte?*
Hans	*Ahhhhhh.*
Doktor Schmidt	*Haben-Sie schon gehört das Frau Pabst ein Kindt bekommen hat?*
Hans	*Rngy?*
Doktor Schmidt	*Wieder bitte.*
Hans	*Ahhhhhh.*
Doktor Schmidt	*Ach so!*
Hans	*Was ist los?*
Doktor Schmidt	*Die Zahnen. Die furschlugginer Zahnen.*
Hans	*Was?*
Doktor Schmidt	*Öffnen Sie die Monde. Danke schön. Also... sagen Sie "ah."*
Hans	*Was meint "also"?*
Doktor Schmidt	*Es meint nichts. Sagen Sie "ah."*
Hans	*Ahh.*
Doktor Schmidt	*Fühlen-Sie etwas?*
Hans	*Grrnzss.*
Doktor Schmidt	*Ach so!*

He waits in a dark hallway outside Mahler's office with the grad student while Mahler grades Tim's exam. It is almost too dark to see the other student's face. He or she is blandly dressed in nondescript slacks and sweater. Neither speaks. From the far end of the dark hallway the figure of a large man appears. He lumbers toward them, Sandy MacDonald.

Hi, guy. How the hell are you?

Hi, Sandy.

Sandy sits next to Tim on the long bench.

Why didn't you tell me you were in town? You missed the Nose Bowl. We beat the Sammies by a field goal, it was a real gas.

I must have had a lot on my mind, says Tim, nodding in the direction of Mahler's office.

How'd it go?

He's marking them right now. I should know in a little while.

Sandy pauses a moment before speaking. I have to tell you something, he says, rolling forward on his buttocks, clasping his hands and staring at the floor. You won't believe this, Fishy. It just sort of happened, but Rita, she was here in Edmonton. We were together. For a while we were in pretty hot, I guess. And then she got...she got pregs...and I guess things got a bit crazy.

MacDonald is having difficulty keeping his voice under control. He doesn't sound much like Old Wire, the Good Humour Man. The student across from them releases a disapproving stare. Perhaps s/he has overheard.

I offered her money, I offered to get her in touch with some people Alistair knows, so she could at least have the option, you know, and she...well, the long and the short of it is that she went down to Calgary and had it done and that's the end of that.

My God.

Doesn't that beat everything? Are you pissed off at me?

No.

It just sort of happened and then she got knocked up and then it was over. I mean it was never anything but a roll in the...you know. You can't go getting serious over girls like that.

What do you mean, girls like that?

She's not the girl you thought she was, Tim. I mean, it's not like I was the first. Not by a long shot.

Right.

They sit together until Mahler calls in the other student. MacDonald rises, stretches, and claps Tim on the back.

When you get the good news, Fishy, you come on over to the fraternity house. I'll buy you a beer. The guys would like to meet you.

Thanks. I might just, ah...

Oh, Fishy, do you still have my ID?

Tim picks through his wallet, finds the driver's license, and hands it over to Sandy.

You're not upset? says Sandy. About what I told you?

Tim is feeling like men these days who write country music for a living: magnificently sorry for himself. He is afraid he will lose his grip on this feeling, which confers its own kind of loser's dignity. He doesn't want to seem too forgiving or too easily restored to his usual good spirits. In fact, he is a short brood away from having a nice little cry. He wants Sandy to go, but he doesn't want to lose his audience.

The grad student, probably a her, shuffles out of Mahler's office. On her way past she glares at them.

Sandy shrugs.

For a while, I mean, I kind of *liked* her in a weird sort of way, even after I'd heard about her, ah, adventures, but when she got pregnant and everything, I had to wonder about me going out with—in public, like—with a...well, she's a bolshy, for God's sake, Tim. Can you imagine that? Me with a bolshy? And who's to say *who* the father really is, right? So I guess I started to panic, and one day, all of a sudden, it seemed like nothing I said seemed to help. I guess all along the whole thing was a mistake. I tried to imagine bringing her home to Mum. Maybe just for laughs, but can you imagine...a real R.F. all the way.

A real R.F., eh?

Yeah.

The meaning of R.F. is even more obscure than that of *al-zo* and furschlugginer. According to MacDonald, R.F. is a rat fuck, but he always goes cryptic upon further questioning.

Sandy looks up from the floor and regards Tim for a long moment.

You're a good shit, Fishy.

Aw.

Tim can feel his adenoids prickle, which he believes has much to do with seeing into the heart of life's bitter tangles. He's beginning to move into the role of good loser. If this is what they call tragedy, he's up for it. Several lines from his recent essay on the vanities of profane love are about to glib their way into the conversation when lo—there comes a chuckle from Mahler's office. Thus interrupted, the two of them stare at the door. The chuckle rises to a yodel of laughter then plunges into a long sigh. *Um Gottes Willen!* the voice declares. At length it whimpers out a few last strains of expended laughter.

What's with him?

I think, says Tim, that I just passed my German exam.

Now that's more like it, his father says as they move into the smoking lounge.

He can't believe he's done it. The sports jacket, the good pants, the newly polished shoes, the overcoat. He could almost pass for one of Alistair's horsey friends from Van-cue-ver. There are several reasons for this attire. The event is the annual father-son lunch at the Edmonton Club, but that's not reason enough to go out in public furschlugginer royalty. There are the urgings of his mother, 'he fact that his brother has flown the coop and *someone* ith dad. The fact that they are rumoured to be serving up a ig, now *that's* a reason.

He ... nks of himself in the Edmonton Club as a spy for the other side. He hasn't yet found a name for the other side, but their ranks are beginning to show. 1) People who listen to jazz on CKUA and admit to it. 2) People who refuse to be impressed with Cadillacs or Lincolns or corporate success or movie spectacles on Biblical themes. 3) People who proclaim that curling is boring. 4) People who read poetry surreptitiously behind copies of *The Financial Post*. 5) People who—

You look more like your brother every day. There's Myles Locke. Myles. Pug.

Who's Myles Locke?

President of the Oilmen's Club. President of Carson, Weir & Locke. Civil engineers. He built the Yellowhead Highway.

All by himself?

His son is Arthur Locke.

Oh, *him.*

They move through the thunderous rumble of men's voices and cigar smog into the serving area. Pug Fisher is straining to see ahead.

There's Stew McCosham. Stuart.

Pug. And Derek! My but you've shot up.

Hahaha. This is Timmy, our youngest. Derek's out on the Coast with Fas-con. He's in the construction business. Timmy, Mr. McCosham.

Howdyado, Mr. McCosham. Hi, Dr. Sharp.

Pleased to meet you, Tim. Call me Stuart.

Tim's having a look at the transportation business, says Pug Fisher.

Oh? What side of the business are you looking at, son?

Well, I'm driving up at lake Louise.

He's taking a year off his B.A.

Well, Tim, I've always said a man can be too educated to make any money.

How's it look, Stuart? Rollie?

Not so good, Pug. All those big wheels got in ahead of us.

They're not big wheels, Rollie, they're just taller. Oh, there's our chance. Seeya, Pug.

I'm stayin put, says Dr. Sharp.

McCosham trots up the line about a dozen places and waves back mischievously at Tim's dad and Dr. Sharp. Tim can now smell the suckling pig, he is sure, but they still have a long way to go. They do not return the wave.

Who's Stuart McCosham?

Head of Northern Pacific Transportation. Started as a bush pilot back in the thirties. Now he owns a whole fleet of planes. There's Art Macilvany. Art.

Pug. Rollie.

Howcome all these guys get to jump the line?

Shhh.

I hate line crashers.

Some guys'll do any goddam thing for a chunk of pig, says Rollie Sharp. He is beginning to wheeze like a bulldog.

They pick up their trays at the edge of the stainless steel serving racks. The men ahead of them shuffle into the big dining room holding trays heaped with roast beef, potatoes, gravy, a scattering of peas, diced carrots and corn, and morsels from the coveted suckling pig.

How's it look now, Rollie?

Our friend the chef is having a go at the joints, Pug. Those high rollers up ahead sure got to heap their plates. Maybe if we're nice they'll save the ears and tail for us.

I thought we came early, says Tim.

We did come early, says his father.

Rollie Sharp turns around to face Tim and his dad. If you don't golf with Myles Locke and Fuller and the boys you could line up at six in the goddam morning and still come up short.

Pug Fisher nods and smiles, but Tim can see that he is not happy with the situation.

I'd give our chef a hand with those joints but I left my scalpel in my bag.

Pug Fisher laughs at that one.

So, what kind of future do you see in the transportation business, Timmy?

He's really up there to make contacts, aren't ya, Timmy.

I'm up there to drive a limo, he says.

Rollie gives a brief guffaw and begins to fill his plate.

What are you talking about? Tim's father whispers.

I'm not looking at the transportation business. I'm not up there to make contacts. I'm up there to make some money and take off.

The way you talk.

What do you mean, the way I talk?

You think life was one big excuse for a party.

There's not a lot of partying at a deserted resort, Dad.

You think you're going to make your mark by driving a limo? By driving a limo and then just taking off? Where are you taking off for?

I don't know.

You think this club serves a feast like this to bus drivers?

If I want to line up for a meal like this I'll go to any cafeteria in town.

You don't know what you're talking about. You have no idea what life is about, do you. You think life is just one free meal after another.

Judging from today, I'd say it's more of a lineup at the trough.

When are you going to learn how to make your way in the world?

His father turns to the business at hand. He begins to fill his plate. First vegetables, then potatoes and gravy, then a slice from a big carcass of prime rib. He leans over confidentially to the chef.

Henry, do you think you can dig out some of that pork for me and my son?

Sorry, Mr. Fisher. Looks like we ran out again.

Nothing? Not even a scrap.

See for yourself. Sorry.

Pug Fisher mutters something that could have been intended for Tim or for the chef or for the entire membership of the Edmonton Club and moves off scowling into the dining hall.

Tim is left musing over the suckling pig. The head lies next to the peeled off skin on a massive carving board. A perfect young pig's head with red maraschino cherries for eyes, a crabapple in the mouth. Mouth open in surprise, like a faithful clerk who has just been terminated. *Alas, poor Porik, I knew him well.*

Tim waits a moment longer until he is sure his insolence has run its course, then does a quick interrogation of his soul to be sure he has reaffirmed his unbelief. He holds his tray before him and walks towards his father's table.

His parents have driven him to the train. It is cold and blustery as they walk across the parking lot of the CPR station. Now his mother is restating her theme of the weekend. She addresses his father.

Timmy doesn't have to stay in that awful old garage all win.
long. I know him. He'll get himself all depressed and then he'll g
run down. He's already getting a cold. I can tell.

I don't have a cold.

You can't fool your mother.

Your mother's right, says his father. If you're going back to Lake
Louise because of that nine hundred dollars, forget it. I've already
forgotten it. We can afford to support our youngest.

The way he eats? his mother says.

She is wearing bright red lipstick for the occasion and her muskrat
coat because of the cold fall wind.

Buck up, Son, says his father.

He hates being told to buck up. He hates people assuming he is
depressed.

You've got a full year of university behind you now. You're a second year man. Next fall—

He knows, Pug. He'll be just fine.

No harm in counting his blessings, says Mr. Fisher.

Tim kisses his mother and shakes his father's hand.

I swear, says his mother, you're almost as tall as your brother.

You've been saying that since I was three years old.

Mark my words, he's got a cold coming on, one of his doozers.

She will stand here in the CPR foyer for half an hour and talk about
colds if he lets her.

You might ask yourself one question on your way up there, says his
father. Where is all this restlessness leading to? I thought you went up
there to make contacts, meet the public, figure out where you're going. What do you want to do with your life?

Hunt for emeralds up the Amazon.

His father chuckles ruefully and looks meditative for a moment.

You don't forget much, do you.

Nope.

Always going back to your childhood.

Yep.

Timmy, were you clearing your throat?

Nope.

He has taken the train from Edmonton to Calgary, and now it chugs
westward through the late afternoon, climbing slowly past the foothills and into the mountains. When Tim's coach reaches Banff it's

dark out and the inside lights are on. Because of the reflection from these lights, Tim has to strain to see the mountains. They are covered now with a layer of early snow and seem to glow in the night. He will soon arrive at Lake Louise. He has no idea what he's looking for up there. You finally get to Paradise, you find Altrogge, a smelly garage, and a stretch limousine. You find you would rather be elsewhere. Adventure and love are elsewhere.

His mother was right. He is getting a cold. He blows his nose and looks up. He sees his own face mirrored spectrally in the passenger window, a much older version of himself superimposed upon the mountains like some brooding alpine spirit. He stares at this older self and the mountains all the way to the station. No one is there to meet him, so he catches a ride up to Lake Louise with one of the wardens. There's a light on in the Garage. Tim climbs the stairway slowly past Altrogge's room with its familiar stink. He is about to continue on up to his attic when he hears someone guffaw behind Altrogge's door. It doesn't sound like Altrogge, and the mechanic is gone till next spring.

He knocks on the door.

What's the password?

Scheiz.

Altrogge comes to the door. He looks uneasy about something. He is shaved and he's wearing a rather good ski sweater. One of Tim's, actually. A hand-me-down of Sandy MacDonald's.

Hiya, Fishy.

Timmy Fisher? says the other person in the room. It sounds vaguely female and quite familiar.

Altrogge frowns, mutters something, and invites Tim inside. There on the bed usually reserved for dirty clothes sits Amber Bole.

Siddown before ya fall down, she cries.

How did you meet this little scum? says Altrogge to Amber.

We went to the same crummy high school. Not that you'd know it, she says, glowering briefly at Tim. You never said boo to me the whole summer.

He tries to protest but they yell him down. He tosses his bag on the floor and sits on the other bed. Life keeps running into me, he wants to say.

Shall we tell him? says Amber to Altrogge. Her face is flushed and full of mischief.

Naw. Let him find out.

Biggsey, comeon.

What's the big secret, Altrogge?

We got you somethin for your attic, says Altrogge. Haven't we, Amber.

What?

You mean you can't guess?

I'm too bushed for guessing.

I'll give you a hint. Every night dispatcher needs one.

A better salary?

I'll give you another hint, says Altrogge, but first I gotta bleed the weasel.

He slouches out of the room.

Long time no see, Mr. Bottom, says Amber, raising her glass.

Mr. Bottom, yeah.

You looked quite the sight in them donkey ears. I was your makeup girl, remember that?

Amber Bole has become a big and raucous party gal. Her voice has acquired a hoarseness that seems to suit her. The jeans jacket, the cowboy hat, the cigarettes, they all seem to go nicely with her lumbering gestures. He remembers the twitchy makeup girl at the mirrors of the dressing room—three years ago?

Long time no see, Amber.

You growed up, she said. You got whiskers an everything.

Do you remember the Rec Hall at Mountie Lake?

Don't remind me, she says. All those friggin snobs with their bratty kids.

Do you remember that day when it was raining and I was trying to write a song?

Amber seems to find this amusing, but no, she can't remember.

How about Arthur Locke? He used to call me Pooface. You used to have a crush on him if I'm not mistaken.

What is this, the third degree?

She peels the label off her bottle of beer, rolls it into a little ball, and bounces it off the wall.

I remember you doin all that stuff for the play. You an those others takin your bows. I remember thinkin you must of thought you were pretty hot stuff.

Maybe you're right. Maybe I did.

Ah, you weren't as bad as some of those snobs.

Altrogge returns and makes a few nervous grunts in Tim's direction. Then he nods at the door. Tim gets the picture. He finishes his drink and stands up to go.

Hey, Rita was by.

Tim stares at Altrogge.

Day you took off, Altrogge continues. She wasn't lookin none too hot. She said she wanted to talk to you. Looks like you shoulda stuck around, Fishy.

Where is she now? Did she say?

Altrogge turns to Amber. Where's Rita bunkin?

Amber shrugs.

Well, where's she at?

I've had it up to here with her problems. I'm not her goddam mother.

Welcome to Lake Lowsy, ya little fart, says Altrogge, and closes the door.

Tim climbs the stairs up to the attic. He is tired. His nostrils are beginning to run and his throat is dry and burning. He drags his duffel bag into the centre of the room where the peak of the roof arches high enough so that he can stand straight up. He stays there in the dark for a moment, listening to the commotion below. Altrogge has apparently turned on his radio to drown out his rutting sounds, but over the voice of Johnny Cash comes a variety of grunts and bouncing noises. Tim fumbles for the chain on his bedside lamp, but just before he pulls it, he smells the perfume. A faint little waft moves past him like the ghost of Rita Symington. No doubt about it. So this is where she and Sandy had begun their secret affair. He remembers Altrogge's strange gesture of looking up at the ceiling of his bedroom.

Nice?

Yeah, I'd say she was pretty nice.

Altrogge must have heard them up in the garret. Who else had known about this? Were they all just trying to spare his feelings? This is where Rita and his friend—Old Wire—betrayed him.

Betrayed. It's such a grand word, worthy of an opera. The anger he has been denying finally begins to mount. He stands in the dark and lets it build. On this bed she lay with big Sandy grunting away on top of her. Perhaps occasionally they made light of Tim and his angelic qualities.

Oh, Timmy. Allons donc! Quel tas de merde!

He can see her say this as though she is there in the room.

In June, a day or so after they'd rediscovered each other, she had walked him down the path to the Chateau. It was a warm night and she took his hand. Shyly, the way they had held hands on the stage in high school. At one point she smiled up into his face. Was this the moment when he turned away? From what? An eventual marriage to her? Surely not. Bliss in bed with her? Her dark brown eyes said something terrifying. They said, come with me. Let's have adventures, intimacy. No, not that much. Not even a real flirtation. With her smile she had merely sent out a tiny electrical signal. Promising what? An exchange of delights? A possibility?

And he had turned away. Commitment, is that what he feared? Or did he just remove himself from the race because he knew he could never win? Nothing remained between them after that but jokes and banjory. That was the thing they did instead of love. Love was like plunging into Louise Creek in the dark. You never knew where it would take you. Drowning is always a possibility.

Your time will come.

He gropes for the light bulb chain and pulls. There on the wall is Altrogge's gift. Mabel, companion to all night dispatchers. Still rising from her bubble bath. She gives Tim a familiar look, as though he has been hanging around for a long time.

Jesus Murphy. Did you hear? Amber and Biggsey, they're goin steady. Isn't that swell?

Swell, Mabel.

Amber just took him up to the crystal caves, if you get my meaning.

I get your meaning, Mabel.

Haben-Sie schon gehört das Fräulein Rita ein Kindt bekommen hat?

Ja, Mabel.

Tim keeps his light on while he lies in bed, sniffling, listening to Altrogge's clamour below. Most of the noise comes up the stairwell and through Tim's door. He is reminded for the umpteenth time that it fits the frame much too loosely. He has an idea. He pulls down the big poster and tacks it over the door. He stuffs kleenex into the vertical cracks in the lower part of the frame, the part not covered by the poster. Then he stuffs a towel into the bottom crack between his door and the floor.

There.

He steps backward to admire his handywork, sits on the bed and listens. The sounds from the stairwell are still audible, but much less distinct. He leaves his lamp on, tilts the shade towards the door and lies back on top of the bed for a few moments in his longjohns. It's chilly in his attic, but he's almost past caring. The lamplight allows him to ogle Mabel's soapy little breasts. It may be a trick fostered by the dim lighting, but she looks even more like Rita Symington.

Finally he climbs onto his bunk and pulls the quilt over his head. Sleep is somewhere close by, but that involves a further surrender, and he feels, for reasons too obscure to understand, that he has already surrendered enough territory for the night. For the week. For the summer and fall and all his life. He closes his eyes and opens them, closes them again, opens them again. One of the revellers down below finally turns off the radio, and Tim lets go and feels the grip of a current carry him down down down toward the sound of Altrogge's scoffing laughter.

Someone is tapping on his door. He is almost awake. It's dark out and his table lamp is still on, and Mabel is still emerging from her bubble bath with a guileless and tentative look on her face. He should get up and answer the door, he knows this, but he can't be sure if it's morning now. It gets dark so early these days and stays dark for so long it could still be the middle of the night.

Again, the tapping on his door, louder this time. And what if it's Altrogge in some kind of panic because Amber has passed out or freaked out or something entirely gross?

Come in.

His voice croaks, as though he hasn't used it for months or years. He pulls the blankets up to his nose. Whoever it is, he is going to say, I've got a doozer of a bad cold. I can't get out of bed. As he rehearses these words into the chilly air, aiming them at the sparkplug poster, he hears something rip. Through the poster a woman stumbles into the room. It is just like a circus act.

What in the hell? the woman hisses. They got you up in quarantine or something?

Rita?

Saw your light on. Thought maybe you'd pour me a coffee.

What time is it?

You sound awful. It's just about 7:00 A.M. What's this *great big sheet of paper?*

Oh, God. Look—

Jesus Murphy, Timmy, what is this? A pinup?

A gift from Altrogge. It wasn't my idea. I don't have any coffee.

Let's have a look at her.

Let's not.

Rita kneels on top of the poster and squints at Mabel, whose bubble bath is now almost virtually a thing of the past. Her hair dangles in one long pigtail.

Can you please throw me some pants? he says.

You sound awful. You shouldn't get out of bed.

You can make us some tea. Just put that kettle over there on that hot plate over there. No, Mabel, over there. And I've got a box of Dad's Cookies in a bag somewhere.

Did you just call me *Mabel*?

He groans.

Are you delirious?

She approaches his bed and places her hand on his forehead. Her fingers are chilled and brittle like small icicles. Suddenly she is bustling and solicitous. She fills the kettle and finds a small tea pot. She finds the cookies, rinses out a couple of mugs, makes the tea, pours it, and places the tea and the cookies on the cover of an old LP.

You got any aspirin? Never mind. Here, try one of mine.

He takes the aspirin with the tea. She watches him, nibbling cookies from her end of the bunk.

Guess what? I quit university. I'm never going back. I'm hitching the first ride I can find back to Edmonton tomorrow.

Is that what you came to tell me?

Drink up.

The bustle is gone from her manner and something else has replaced it.

Here's to old times, he says.

You sound awful.

Yeah. You look awful.

Thanks. I probably looked a lot worse last week.

I hear you and Sandy broke up.

Ohhh, shit.

She curls up on the far end of his bunk and holds her head up with her hand.

I spose he told you the whole sorry mess?

Tim nods.

Did he tell you where I went?

You mean....

To get it done.

Maybe it's the way she supports her head on her hand or maybe it's the mood she is caught up in that makes her look so different. Not remotely attractive or frisky. Nothing like the Teahouse Maid. He sits further up in his bunk so that he can look at her.

Sandy didn't tell me much about that. I think he mentioned something about a friend of Alistair's.

A family friend, a doctor in Calgary, a real old fart, I guess he actually delivered Alistair, he doesn't deliver babies anymore though, he lost his license, a real alky. I was in an out of his house in a couple hours, old guy, I don't know, he wasn't all that....

She lies there with a vague smile on her face and her eyes closed until something inside seems to pass through her and out beyond her, and still she lies sideways on the bunk as though she is trying to remember the details of a dream, and all Tim can hear is the sound of the wind and the sound of Altrogge snoring down the stairwell, determined, like a bulldozer.

He wasn't all that bad, really....

And then her lower lip extrudes and begins to quiver and she brings up her other hand with the mug to cover her eyes. He can't actually hear her at first, but then the spasms begin and then the gasping and a great fountain of grief until the whole bed is shaking with her bereavment. He creeps down to her end of the bunk, takes the mug from her hand, places it on top of the album, then places the album onto the floor. It is Pete Seeger's *How to Play the Five-String Banjo, A step-by-step approach for the beginner.* He sits on the bunk hunkered down and close enough to touch her while she wails on and on. He strokes her head as though she were his dog Pepper, as though she has just come home spayed from the vet. He stops after a while, wonders if that was how you were supposed to do it. He crawls back and gets her a pillow for her head and lies down facing her. It seems like an awfully long time.

You sure are stuffed up, she says. Sounds like we're both drowning in snot.

We're a pair all right.

Who the hell is *Mabel?*

She's the gal in the poster.

Wait a minute. That poster is from Biggs? If it's from Biggs, howcome you got it covering your door? *Blocking* your door. Are you getting weird on me?

Probably.

He has to get up and find some kleenex to blow his nose. She takes some as well and they both blow their noses. It is still dark outside.

Rita, I thought you said it was seven A.M.

So what if I did?

It's *still* not seven A.M.

I thought if I told you what time it really was you'd tell me to fuck off.

Daisy Mae, yo shore does have a filthy tongue.

I'm not as bad as Amber.

That poster. You know what? It reminds me of you.

She raises her head from a wadded fist of kleenex as though to dispute the point. But instead she says, a little sadly, That's sweet!

Fisher! Fisher! Fisharrr!

The voice rages like a sudden squall. It shakes the window panes and echoes up and down the stairwell.

Fisher! Station overload! On the doubaaawl!

Tim staggers toward his door, tramping on the fallen poster. He pokes his head out at the stairwell and sees Altrogge on the landing. Altrogge is still wearing Tim's ski sweater.

I've got a cold, Altrogge, and I feel lousy, so fuck off or go back to bed.

This is the day in the mountains, above all days, that he will never forget. He'll remember it like you might remember a popular song soaked through with the nostalgia of a certain time, not word for word, but knowing the tune and the minor key it's set in and all the harmonies. He will remember the way Rita tumbled through the poster over his door, the way her face crumpled from a girl's troubled revery into a woman's ancient sorrow, the way they slept at opposite ends of the bunk and waited on each other all day long and into the next day as well. The way it began, before daylight, and then what happened when daylight arrived.

He has a fever and she has the shakes. Hers is only a temporary condition, she tells him. Something to do with blood loss. By Christmas time she'll be as right as rain.

Without a word, they drift together into a healing mode. The only travelling they do is to the toilet or the sink in the tiny cubicle at the far end of the L. She sleeps covered by his sleeping bag, with her head on a pillow at the far end of his bunk. He sleeps and wakes beneath the covers. When he rolls over or moves his head, he touches her feet inside the sleeping bag. When she moves her feet, she touches his head and shoulder. They face each other between sleeping and waking. One of them makes some tea or later grabs a bowl of cereal. When he wakes up in the afternoon, it is snowing. Rita is rummaging

.ksack for a toothbrush. Later, still shivering, she col-
ed. He gets out of bed and throws a can of soup into the
.r. Then he falls into a doze beside her.
    .bably wonder why I had anything to do with the likes of
bed I mean.

1.

She is standing by the bunk, holding out a mug of soup. He takes the soup and blows on it.

Well, I'm not sure you'd understand.

Try me. At least I'm awake now.

She takes a deep breath and sits down wearily on the side of the bed.

I had to know what made guys like Sandy MacDonald tick. I wanted to know how guys like that could stand around in any situation and sound so *confident*. It's like they had this power.

Wait wait wait wait wait. They had this power, so you just....

I've done this before. Just out of curiosity and maybe just for fun, same with Sandy, but with Sandy, things got serious. I think, for a while anyway, he was all gaga over me, until I told him I was up the stump. Boy, that cooled things off in a hurry. For a while there, I guess I thought I was pretty hot stuff. Like I'd joined the upper classes or something.

I would have been different, you know. I would have been different from those guys.

Woulda been. Hah. That's a great expression.

For what it's worth, you'll always be pretty hot stuff as far as I'm concerned.

Thanks. I am eighteen years old and I have no idea where I'm goin. I used to think it was you who'd screw things up for yourself.

Howcome?

I really wondered about you, Tim. It's like you would of rather been reminiscing about your childhood than havin a good time.

My time will come.

I know. Don't get all resentful at me.

She looks at him out of the corner of her eye as he drinks his soup. She gives him the once over, seems to feign desire.

Too bad I can't hang around for a bit, she says, trying for the small town sultry tone. Maybe I could teach you a thing or two.

PEPPER THE SPRINGER is a spayed black-and-white bitch who chases socks, tennis balls, even rocks in several feet of water. Alistair Vaughan also has a dog, Albert. He is named after Queen Victoria's consort, a lusty male German Shepherd, big even for his breed. Like Alistair, Albert is built like a brick shit-house, and the dog has acquired Alistair's regal manner. At heel he prances. When he sits by his master's left leg, he whimpers for release and surveys the river valley below Wellington Crescent as though his ancestors had conquered it. Then Alistair touches him on the shoulder, and he leaps into the ravine like one of the Queen's footsoldiers intent on glorious victory. Sometimes there is a startled cry from a small animal, but whatever Albert kills, he has learned not to bring back. Alistair does not want to know. He keeps Albert away from other people's dogs on Wellington Crescent because, he says to Tim, Out here, a person's dog is his property.

Out Here means oldish money: houses that some call mansions and occasionally appear in *Better Homes and Gardens*. Sons who go to private school, daughters who take riding lessons on their own horses and finish their schooling in Switzerland.

Alistair has an exquisitely sharp nose that looks as though it were designed to smell only that blessed and narrow range of objects that offer up a bouquet. From his regal bearing and his striking abundance of straw-blond hair, anyone can tell that some day Alistair Vaughan will end up Out Here. He is sturdy and big-boned like a rugby player. He has a military sense of mission: he is going to be a somebody; it is his Godgiven right. Like his big German shepherd Albert, he has breeding. All the mothers say so. It wasn't Mrs. Elly who ordained that Alistair would play Theseus; it was God. God these days looks vaguely like John F. Kennedy, but he speaks with just a tinge of a BBC accent.

Mrs. Vaughan is the source of Alistair's nose and Alistair's politics. She is regally tall and blonde. But her nose is what Tim watches. It is simply the most perfect little nose in all of Alberta.

Tim has heard Mrs. Vaughan's political views on a variety of subjects. Native people in Northern Alberta, for example. Their women are *super fertile*, she says with quiet emphasis. Before we know it they will have populated the entire north and they will swarm down here in the tens of thousands. You mark my words. This province's welfare budget will not support that kind of population.

When Alistair approves of a fellow he uses the word "sharp." *Sandy MacDonald is a sharp guy*. Always, when the word "sharp" is conferred on one of Alistair's annointed, Tim thinks of Alistair's perfect pointed

he two friends are standing on the outer edge of Wellington
it where it overlooks the North Saskatchewan and the Univer-
Alberta campus beyond. Albert is off down the ravine on a raid.
Pepper is digging up a large rock to retrieve.

Alistair points his nose toward the campus on the south side of the
river. This university, he says, could have become an institution to
make us all proud. But instead? Apathy.

Alistair is referring to a Stan Kenton concert on campus that
flopped because only a handful of people showed up. Alistair and Nancy
showed up. So did a few of the younger set from Out Here and a few
dozen bohemians. But the evening was an expensive flop, and the
Students' Union had to pay the bill.

Do you think this would have happened in a real city?

Like where?

London, Alistair says with a brooding look. Toronto, Vancouver.
Even Victoria or Halifax.

What's so hot about those places?

There's more non-assholes there.

Not fewer assholes, but more non-assholes. An interesting dis-
tinction there. Where has Tim heard that expression before? Ah, yes.
The bluebloods from Van-cue-ver.

Up comes Albert, panting, slobbering. Today, no death cries from
the ravine.

Albert! Alistair whispers, and hugs the big dog in a rush of affection. Pepper deposits a chunk of cement at Tim's feet.

Do you know why we can't get anybody out for a Stan Kenton
concert in Edmonton? says Alistair. Do you know why this campus is
a great haven for apathy?

Tim pretends he is going to toss the chunk of cement down into
the ravine. As he winds up to throw, Pepper dashes halfway down the
first big slope. Tim turns and tosses it in the other direction. He doesn't
approve of Pepper's rock chasing. He should have brought one of her
tennis balls.

Why?

Because it's a hodgepodge of Eastern European bohunks, a sprin-
kling of Africans and orientals, and a minority of Anglo-Saxon Prot-
estants, that's why. It's our country, and here we're in a minority for
God's sake.

He gazes at the campus with a doleful intensity that reminds
Tim of Alistair's mother. Her most hateful utterances emerge in

the throes of nostalgic depression when her perfect nose is reddened from sniffling.

Comeon, Alistair. You can't possibly expect—

I mean it! he says. Fiercely. Sometimes I think I should go into politics. Except too many assholes are allowed to vote.

Albert is up on his hind feet with his front paws on Alistair's chest. Alistair holds him and strokes him like a lover on the dance floor.

It's a hodgepodge over there. Ukrainians, Poles, Packies, Japs, Catholics and Jews. And Chinese. The Chinese students, do you know how they *live?* Ten to a room. The rooms are infested with bed bugs and disease and God knows what else. Our entire student population is a hodgepodge, and people wonder why no one shows up at a Stan Kenton concert? It's this....

Alistair lets the breeze ruffle his hair until it falls presidentially over his brow in a moment of perfect dishevelment. He flaps his hand at the distant campus until his word comes out.

Mixture. The races were never meant to be mixed. It's a bad show all around. It's bad for genetics.

There is a word for people like Alistair. Nazi? Surely not. After all, Alistair has become fast friends with Elliott Crystal. But Tim has heard things about Alistair and his fraternity. According to Elliott they wear long white-hooded robes to their meetings and they never pledge blacks, East Indians or Jews. Alistair has decided Tim is a safe audience for his political monologues. As they walk the dogs along the crescent and back towards Tim's more modest neighbourhood, Alistair warms to his topic.

Can you imagine what a mongrel you would be if your parents weren't both white Anglo-Saxons? Can you imagine what you'd look like? Can you imagine what you'd *think* like?

I'd probably be better hung.

Alistair guffaws.

Fisher, you are hopeless.

This guffaw of Alistair's always pleases Tim. Sometimes it reddens Alistair's complexion, brings tears to his eyes, and sends his voice into a high grunting spasm a bit like a bull elk in rut. It's Alistair's only mannerism that doesn't seem to belong Out Here. This guffaw, and the fact that Tim can cause it, are two of the reasons for their rejuvenated friendship.

Pepper walks diagonally and yet straight ahead, her body slanting northwest, her trajectory straight north. She has always walked this way, as though her hind quarters were slightly at odds with her front quarters. Albert comes up behind her and gives her ass a sniff. Pepper's tail goes down. She moves away and looks annoyed. Albert persists with his sniffing.

Call your dog.

No, says Alistair, let's watch.

Albert tries to mount Pepper. She nips at him and he growls.

Call off your goddam dog.

Why? She wants it.

What on *Earth* are you talking about?

It's the way she walks. Look! She's asking for it.

She is not asking for it. She's spayed. That's the way she always walks. Your dog is trying to force her. There he goes again. *Albert!* Tim yells. It's not enough he gets to depopulate the entire ravine of animals. Now he's added rape to his repertoire.

Albert pants up to his master, looking from Alistair to Tim, back and forth. The dog seems confused.

You keep that meat hound away from her.

Fisher, you saw how your dog was walking.

How was she walking?

Well...provocatively. She was wiggling her bum.

That's called tailwagging. It's a thing dogs do when they're not being attacked.

You can call it tailwagging. I call it provocation.

Your dog was just horny and looking for the nearest orifice. You've got to control that hound or someone's gonna do it for you.

You can't control nature. Dogs fucking isn't a question of right and wrong. Fisher, what's got into you?

You said my dog was asking for it and I say your dog was forcing her. It's as simple as that.

Alistair looks as confused as Albert.

Let's just say it's bad for genetics, Tim says. It's racially impure, okay?

This is sex between dogs, for God's sake. Animal pleasure. It's not like they're going to produce a litter.

Right. And your hound is not gonna fuck my dog—and that's that.

Fisher. Jesus.

In spite of occasional disagreements, Tim thinks that Alistair has become his replacement friend for Gump Lowney. This makes Tim feel upwardly mobile. Besides, Gump has fallen. One day single, the next smitten, and suddenly planning marriage to a girl named Sherry Love. No more fishing trips with Gump. No more beers in the Strathcona, phonecalls after midnight.

The engagement party was like a wedding. She is only seventeen and Gump, at twenty, seems even younger. He did a lot of smiling in that conciliatory way you might adopt for your captors if you were manacled to a conveyor belt. And now he is no doubt steeling himself for the one-way walk.

And who should show up at the engagement party but—

How ya doin, Timmy?

Rita Symington. A dishevelled looking bearded fellow stands behind her as though he is timing her conversation. Is he the one? the fellow asks.

Yes, she says, with a friendly, nervous smile, to both of them.

She gives Tim a warm hug. He is still trying to think of what to say to her but he is tongue-tied. All he can do is stand there while she introduces the bearded fellow. Lamont is his name, his *first* name. He is the guitarist for Rita's new band of folksingers, she explains. They do the coffee house circuit between Edmonton, Calgary and the mountain resorts.

You should hear us do our stuff. A lot has happened since you know when. Rita says this as though the sadness of her season at Lake Louise added up to a broken gig.

He is undone by the suddenness of her appearance and by her new-found partner. He waits to see if Lamont the guitarist will drift off into the crowd, and at last he does.

Are you and Lamont, you know, are you two....

Oh, says Rita, backing away with a fetching smile. She shrugs.

And she is suddenly standing with a different group of people.

Tim feels a sweaty attack of exultation and terror. After a stiff belt of rye in the men's can he returns to the reception hall fortified, eager, but she's gone. She is *always* gone when you want her.

Maybe I could teach you a thing or two, eh?

Her honest words hang from the picture frames in Mrs. Love's living room, they dance beneath a bouncing ball on the bathroom mirror, they float above the immaculate beehive that adorns the face of Sherry Love.

Sherry dyes her hair blonde. She wobbles along on pink spike heels, she wears a pink dress and red lipstick. She looks like a strawberry sundae on stilts, and she insists on calling Gump *Clarence.*

No more ogling at Westmount Shoppers' Park, no more cruising along in the Gumper's Studebaker.

Well, Gump.

Well, Fishy.

Think they're bitin?

Damn rights they're bitin. Fishy, she's gonna be a good spring.

A good spring and many more of them.

Here's to the trout to come, and here's to the ones that bit the dust.

Here's to you, Gump, you fast-living old rake.

There is a moment before sunrise when the birds are no longer silent in a dream someone with a flute urges Hilary to cheer up in little bursts he says it again and again Timmy doesn't even know Hilary he has no idea why she needs to cheer up....

But it works, the sun begins to rise to the bait, and Tim opens his left eye.

Cheer up Hilary
Hilary Hilary

A robin out on the Circle at five A.M.

He slides out of bed and checks the sky. Somewhere between the receding dark and the flesh-pink sunrise there is a sweep of aqua that will intensify to cobalt blue all across the parkland and down through the prairie. As the morning progresses everything will be drenched in staggering light: the stucco on the side of the garage, the new buds on the poplars, the squares on the linoleum, the logo on the fridge door, the flower beds out on the circle, even the gravel on the driveway—all things explode with morning light into their primary colours.

To the sleeping houses around the Circle, the daffodils and tulips around the big fountain, he wants to declare

A day of dappled seaborn clouds

but there are no clouds, much less an ocean. How would Stephen Dedalus describe this early morning in May? What would he say about Edmonton?

Quickly Tim dresses, descends to the kitchen, sniffing. Bran muffin and Johnson's Paste Wax. Buttermilk and postum. Sleeping dog. All the things that make a home smell like a home. He grabs a muffin,

and before anyone stirs, he is off on his womble. South f
to 102nd Avenue, then east to the corner of 124th Stre
to be seen.

How could you say anything poetic about 102nd Aven
Street? How could you write a poem about a city that gr   - ~y
crater like a war zone? Everything is so new, there is no room for
ghosts. Jacob Marley wouldn't be caught dead here.

He heads east down 102nd Avenue and passes through the old
district toward his very first home. On the lawn of the old frame house
two robins fly down from the poplar by the carragana. The cock robin
runs and pauses, runs across the dewy grass. The hen hops behind
him, cocks her head, pecks the ground, recoils, a large beetle in her
beak.

Who the hell is Hilary?

The robins regard him, self-important in their brick-red vests.
He watches the two birds, and then, as sudden as desire, it starts to
come back....

> *Let us arise, you and I*
> *In the grey dark hours of the morning*
> *When the robin's gurgle is heavy with sleep*
> *Far ahead of the sun.*

He had written several stanzas on a napkin the night before, thinking
of his encounter with Rita Symington. Thinking about how perfect
she could have been. How perfect she used to be before her abortion
when they all called her Slimy and he danced with her on the stage of
the gymnasium. He is no longer so sure that robins gurgle. The first
line sounds like something he has read, Yeats perhaps. Or Prufrock.
Did that mean that it was a phony beginning? Maybe it just meant
that he was well read and that his verse carried with it the echoes of
great poetry everywhere.

Maybe not.

If only he hadn't left the napkin in the bar.

He walks on. Already the old neighbourhood has that chipped
and broken look about it. The old frame houses seem to lean. Thread-
bare with a touch of gentility, like retired English professors. As a
small boy he had watched the newer houses being built. The bulldozers went jrrnjrrnjrrn. The wonderful smell of diesel fuel, their drivers
like the heroes of sagas, curling back the blueblack waves of clay with

their blades.

He circles around his first home and goes up the alley. The sandbox in the back yard is gone. Lawn and the back fence have almost disappeared. About where his mother's flowerbeds had lain, an old half-ton and a derelict Hudson are sinking slowly into the ground. The flowerbeds. His mother's pure soprano as she puts in the bedding plants. The sadness of that happy song.

Blue skies...

The Fullers' old house has suffered a similar fate. The back yard where he and Nancy had built their first house out of sticks, flat on the ground like a blueprint, is now full of junk, the fence fallen in. To the north the city has eaten up a dozen miles of cow meadow and farmland. It's all suburbs, shopping malls and apartments with scarcely a tree in sight. By the pond where he, Derek and Mole Sharp had caught frogs in the spring, there is now a traffic circle.

How could anyone write a poem about Edmonton? World's largest construction site. Ego capitol of Canada.

His question is taken up by a chickadee calling from somewhere down the laneway, *fee-beebee, fee-bee.* The call is answered by another in the lane ahead of him. Could they still be courting this late in the spring?

> *Let us arise*
> *If only to kick our last stone down the street*
> *Our last round of hide-and-seek*
> *And in our gutter clothes walk*
> *In this unawakened song*
> *Far ahead of the dawn.*

Jesus, that's good.

He leans against a parked car to scribble it down on a tiny notepad. This time he won't lose it. He will show it to Elliott.

He goes south toward the river valley, then turns east past the Lemarchand Mansion, past the Cathedral and the Misericordia Hospital where he was born. The oldest hospital in the city, and soon it too will be gone. The elms are big and old and fold over the street in perfect regiment like a long Gothic archway. Here only is the city old enough to feel like it has a past. A French past haunted by nuns, priests and Métis.

Still no traffic. Birdsong everywhere. You can like Edm
six in the morning, but you cannot write a poem about it. `.
walk the streets from dawn to dusk, but try as you might, yo
even find a sky that resembles a patient etherized upon a table
can't even feel despair properly in this town. It's bad for business.

He has conceived an ambition to go to London or Paris where
people knew about culture and cared about trees and how their city
looked. He has acquired a snobbery on the subject of buildings that
Alistair admires.

He walks east and squints into the sun to peer at the old MacDonald
Hotel and its new annex. The old hotel rises into the morning in all its
chateau glory. Its annex is an earnest cement block of a building. The
MacDonald Hotel and the box it came in.

The MacDonald coffee shop opens early. He will go in there and
read for a while. Reading and writing poetry in coffee shops and bars
has a special savour. People will see him scribbling there and *they will
know.* They might feel derision for him or they might admire him. He
likes to imagine their derision best of all. He courts derision.

The coffee shop is almost empty. He sits by the window at what has
become his morning table. Josie sidles over with a smile. Her father, an
ancient and stooped Cantonese, has run this café from before the war.
Josie has acquired her father's sleepy manner. The mysterious East now
faces him, perfumed like a flower, silent like death, dark like a grave.

Izzin it a nice day.

Sure is.

Beautifo.

She pours him a cup of coffee and moves off toward the glass case
with the butter tarts.

She moves like a fawn, far ahead of the dawn. Well, not really.

> *Far ahead of the dawn*
> *Far ahead of the bells*
> *Far ahead of the vows*
> *Far ahead of the honks*

Far ahead of the honks?

Whad you rideen? You rideen a pome?

He shrugs at Josie, who looks over his shoulder.

Ah.

I know, she says. Nung of my business.

Tim pauses in his scribbling for a *déjà-vu*. But where and when? He resumes his writing, takes down three more lines, scratches them out.

He tries to remember the engagement party where he saw Rita Symington. Gump Lowney and Sherry Love. Sherry's widowed mother: tall, anxious, mouth unaccustomed to smiling. Two plotting succubi, and Gump their plump and willing victim. Gump musters a desperately jolly persona and dances with his future mum-in-law.

Here's to you, Gump, you fast-living old rake.

The Mysterious East returns.

Whad you say?

Talking to myself, Josie.

You wan mo coffee?

Thanks.

> *Let us arise my love*
> *And walk among the sleepy coos of the mourning dove*
> *Far ahead of the life wherein we live out*
> *The slow dance of disenchantment.*

He pauses in mid-adoration. Surely you don't live out a dance. He tosses back his coffee, pulls out his book. He reads,

> *I went out to the hazel wood,*
> *Because a fire was in my head,*
> *And cut and peeled a hazel wand*
> *And hooked a berry to a thread....*

It isn't fair. No one has any right to do it so beautifully. And it all comes out so simply! Maybe you have to be Irish or something. Maybe you have to live in a poetic landscape. Maybe if he lived for the rest of his life at Lake Louise or Mountie Lake, he would become a real poet.

> *I will arise and go now, and go to Mountie Lake.*

Everywhere he looks, a poem dies and curls up like bubblegum on the sidewalk.

> *And when white moths were on the wing,*
> *And moth-like stars were flickering out,*

I dropped the berry in a stream
And caught a little silver trout.

In a few months he will be twenty-one and he hasn't even pul
poem. His university career has been a bit of a drag. He hasn't caught
a brown trout over two pounds. He is still a virgin. Reading Yeats'
lines makes him feel helpless, like when he hears Earl Scruggs play
banjo on *The Beverly Hillbillies*.

A distinguished looking young man in a dark suit is staring his
way, familiar somehow. The bored look, eyelids at half-mast. He wears
his bankerly blue suit as though born to such finery. He draws himself
languidly to his feet and walks over to Tim.

Pooface, is it really you?

Tim blinks.

I'm Arthur Locke. One of your earliest tormentors. Surely you
remember me.

I didn't recognize you without my mother's girdle on your head.

Arthur laughs. His eyelids rise above the half-mast position. For
perhaps one second he looks non-bored.

Is this Yeats? Really, Fisher, he purrs. Poetry at seven A.M.

I haven't seen you for a long time.

I've been in New York. Mostly.

What doing?

Haven't the mothers told you? I'm flogging art to the bourgeoisie.
I own a gallery. Don't tell me. *You're* a fishing guide.

No, not quite.

Do I get another guess?

I'm in charge of recreating the unforged conscience of my race in
the smithy of my soul.

Oh dear. How's the pay?

I've asked my dad to up my allowance.

My my. Pooface, you used to be so serious.

Arthur glances at his watch. I have to go. Look, I'm having some
people over to the Crop. Why don't you tie on a toga and drop in?
And bring your banjo. Elliott Crystal tells me you're pretty good.

Arthur gives him directions to the Crop, which is a few miles west
of Edmonton right on the North Saskatchewan River—indeed, on an
island owned or leased by his parents. They shake hands and Arthur
leaves, walking as he always has with a slow paddling motion of his
hands down the river of life.

Tim waits by the café window, watching the sparse traffic on Jasper Avenue. The sun is too bright for poetry.

You wan mo coffee?

No thanks, Rita.

Who dis Rita jazz?

Sorry. Josie.

Sleepy among the silent birds? Pristine?

He stands up and looks around. A coffee belch and a thought bubble to the surface: Am I taking a step up in the world? Could I be a hit some day with the upper classes? Could you be a hit with the upper classes and still become a great poet? He drops a fifty-cent piece on the table. It wobbles ostentatiously on the formica as he strides from the café.

His mother is dressed smartly in a green suit. She is much too gussied up for a mere shopping trip. He comments on this.

Big interview, she says. Does this look too...you know, too—

Interview? What interview?

They're looking for people at the radio station.

You mean like a job?

Yes sirree. She is looking around for something, distracted.

But you're my mum. You can't have a job.

He means this ironically, but somehow it doesn't sound very ironic.

Oh, can't I.

Can I have the car tonight?

May I have the car tonight.

He sighs.

Ask your father.

Seriously, what's this job all about?

Derek's gone and you'll be next. I can't be looking after you forever and ever. One day I'll look up and you'll have flown the coop and I won't have anything of my own. Besides, we might just need the money?

You do?

Hasn't your father told you? About our declining prospects in the world?

He never talks to me about *real* stuff.

Well, he worries a lot about you.

You mean because I don't fit into his plans for me?

No, I don't mean that. He worries that you might never be able to handle things on your own.

Oh, *that*.

She stares for a blank moment through the living room window at the Circle and the fountain. Your dad and I, we should have had one more.

One more kid? You sound serious.

Yer dern tootin I'm serious. What do you want the car for?

A party at Arthur Locke's.

My my, aren't we the socialite. Going with a gal?

Nope.

She is still staring at the fountain when she says, Do you like girls? Don't go getting all offended. I was just asking. I'm your mother, you know. Mothers are like that.

Of course I like girls.

She looks at him for a long moment. Promise you'll be careful with the car. And promise you won't wear that awful turtleneck. The Lockes will think we've gone and raised a beatnik. Wear something nice. Wear your blue blazer and grey pants.

He has never quite figured her out. She wants him to be involved with girls, but she is uncomfortable with anything that might suggest sexual leanings. His black wool turtleneck, for instance. It is the sexiest sweater ever worn by an Edmonton male, a real Heathcliff special. It proclaims its owner a tortured misunderstood genius, and the second he turns his back, she will give it away to the Salvation Army. In a matter of days some panhandler on 97th Street will be knocking off verse epics.

And now she wants a job. He's not sure he likes this either. All her talk about him flying the coop. He has no plans for flying the coop, at least not yet. He wouldn't know *how* to fly the coop. He likes the house, the view of the circle and the fountain from his room, the meals. He likes the smell of bran muffins, porridge and buttermilk in the kitchen. And especially, he can't *afford* to fly the coop. He wants to do one more year of English so he'll have a degree and a chance of prolonging his life as a....

My life as a what?

Not sure. No use rushing into things.

The Crop, he expected, would have something to do with thoroughbreds or wheat, but he's wrong. It is short for Acropolis, and in the centre of the island is a model of the Parthenon complete with white pillars and marble floor. He comes with his banjo, wearing his deadly black turtleneck, jeans stiff and fresh off the line, and sandals. The effect is mildly bohemian. He is one of a handful of dissidents not wearing a toga.

Elliott Crystal is there. His toga, bowler hat and cigar make him look like a particularly well-fed snowman. Elliott has become, suddenly, a young man about town. He is still The Owl, still a gink. But somehow, among the young set from Out There, the jazz and blues jet set, he has learned to turn his ginkiness to his advantage. Alistair Vaughan is there with Nancy Fuller, which means that it's probably on again. Alistair laughs a lot and flirts and talks football. He seems to be having more fun than Nancy. There are people in togas speaking with foreign accents. Gump Lowney would say that this was just like in the movies.

If so, who is Tim? He is that guy with the banjo. He drinks a goblet of punch, and after a while he is sure that he is that Greenwich Village sort of guy with the banjo and the poems. He is nothing if not that guy.

Nancy sidles up to him. Her toga is slightly askew, just enough to celebrate cleavage in a number of ways, some of them unintended. Nancy is tipsy. She stares at Tim for a long moody moment before she speaks.

Well, how's the bull elk these days?

He laughs so loud that people look their way. Arthur Locke spots him and cries out, Pooface!

What? says Alistair Vaughan.

The poet, Locke says. Here comes our poet.

Locke is always so haughty you never know how to take him. Does he like Tim now? Has Tim passed some sort of inspection for bluebloods?

Pooface? cries Nancy. Is that a nickname or something?

I calls em the way I sees em, says Arthur. Will you ignore this siren and play for us, Timmy?

This has been happening lately. People have seen him perform down at the Yardbird Suite or perhaps heard about his banjory from others, and they cajole him into playing for them. He likes it; or rather, he doesn't dislike it, because he still has the ham instinct and because this act allows him to maintain just the right distance from these people. He never feels this distance with Gump Lowney because Gump is humble by nature. Tonight Tim will be Nero and do some classical picking. He will, of course, this time, hope to inspire an orgy.

There is something magic about the banjo. A happy sound for a happy year, something like that. It feels as though for the first time in his life, like Elliott Crystal, he is *fashionable*. All he has to do is hold the thing and pick out a simple mountain tune and he will have a special aura. They clap and make requests (which Tim refuses), and Vaughan, who is getting bombed, yells out Pooface, and Elliott Crystal, who squats only a few feet away from Tim and who is smoking something suspicious, tells him loudly and repeatedly that his frailing is really dead centre. Nancy Fuller seems unmoved by the carousing and stares past everyone. She looks desolate and magnificent, like someone in a movie or a painting. She looks even better than a Stufflebeam, classier. Surrounded by revellers on the steps of the Parthenon, Tim realizes he wants to be with Nancy Fuller.

He is a hit. Would his mum be proud of him and see a little of herself singing lovesongs down at the Saskatoon radio station *circa* 1930? Or would she shake her head in exasperation to see her youngest son a fool lost in vanity? Is she even capable of appreciating the importance of fiddling while Rome burns?

Arthur Locke stoops over Tim's banjo case. On top of a pile of songsheets is a freshly typed copy of Tim's poem. Arthur picks it up, smirks at Tim, and begins to recite.

> *Let us arise, you and I*
> *In the grey dark hours of the morning*
> *When the robin's warble is heavy with sleep*
> *Far ahead of the sun.*

Everyone seems to be listening to Arthur's languid, purring voice, oddly suited to recitation. The traces of sarcasm that cling to his voice seem to have disappeared.

> *Let us rise*
> *If only to kick our last stone down the street*
> *Do a last round of hide-and-seek*
> *And in our gutter clothes walk*
> *In this unawakened song*
> *Far ahead of the dawn.*

For the first time Nancy is attentive. She tilts her head and listens as though someone in a dream has called her name. The spotlights catch one side of her face, her throat and her arm, and her toga seems to glow. This is delicious. This is even better than having his work read in Miss Melnychuk's English class.

> *Far ahead of the bells*
> *Far ahead of the vows*
> *Far ahead of the honking cars*
> *And the too-sweet smiles of the bridesmaids*
> *Burning from the tips of lighted cigarettes.*
>
> *Let us arise my love*
> *And walk among the sleepy coos of the mourning dove*
> *Far ahead of the life we are to build,*
> *The Golgotha wherein we waltz*
> *The slow dance of disenchantment.*
> *Let us walk in the grey morning*
> *One last naked walk*
> *You and I*
> *And breathe the breath of awe*
> *Silent among the sleepy birds*
> *Pristine among the unawakened trees.*

Arthur drops the pages of Tim's poem back into the banjo case and bows, then gestures to Tim, who receives his applause with the tight look brother Derek used to deploy when he caught a long pass at the stadium.

Nancy smiles, it would seem in the half-light, radiantly. She smiles right at Tim and there is that old friendship returning. That and something else. Yes, definitely there's something else.

Pardon me for saying so, says a woman, but this poem of yours is a load of the worst kind of bourgeois horseshit.

He finds himself nose to nose with a pinchfaced woman in black pants and a black sweater something like his own. She speaks without a trace of irony. *The Golgotha wherein we waltz the slow dance of disenchantment? In our gutter clothes?* Where do you get your words from? By reading all the fashionable poets your professors tell you to read? What do you know about gutter clothes?

Arthur interjects. This lady is Techla Wahrsager. She reads a lot and she hates anything nice.

Techla Wahrsager pays no attention to Arthur Locke. To Tim she says, Don't give me that wounded look. You have your poem in your banjo case at a party, yes? Don't tell me you didn't wai

I don't know what you're talking about, says Tim.

He looks around to see if Nancy Fuller has heard th
seems to have disappeared.

I see I have managed to offend you, but this was not m)

He looks right at her. She has very short hair for a wom. .quiv-
ering intensity in her face, and glasses that make her look even more
severe. He has seen her somewhere before.

What was your intention? he says.

When I look around and see all these people applauding you like
you were God's gift to poetry, I have to speak out. In my opinion you
have not yet sprung to the heights of Parnassus.

I still don't get it.

Of course you don't get it because you are a dilettante, and worse
than that, you are a middle class *Canadian* dilettante.

Meaning?

You like to turn a moment of self-indulgence like puppy love into
a lofty sentiment and extol things that do not deserve to be extolled.

Tim has learned that in a debate to the death, you let your attacker
exhaust himself on his own words, then leap in for the kill. The problem with this attacker is that she seems to know what she's talking
about, a thing he has not yet learned to admire in women. Worse still,
she has a slight accent, which probably means she is truly cultured and
well read. She would likely use words like *Weltanschauung* as though
she knew what they meant. Back up, bob and weave, wait for a chance
to counterpunch.

What do you mean, extol things that do not deserve to be extolled?

Innocence, she says, without hesitation.

Innocence?

Unawakened trees, sleeping creatures. The whole thing is presexual.

Tim's ears begin to burn. Again he checks the crowd for Nancy,
but thank God, she has truly disappeared.

Don't you see? says Techla Wahrsager. You're playing right into
their hands.

Whose hands?

Into the hands of the bourgeoisie.

She explains herself, but he has heard this line somewhere before,
though not from one of *his* friends. The people who talk like this
drink coffee on the other side of the student cafeteria. They wear old

ercoats and ban the bomb buttons and hang around with philoso-
phy profs. Joyless outcasts. Alistair Vaughan says these people might
just as well draw salaries from Moscow because they're all just a flaming bunch of reds. Not that Tim believes everything Alistair says.

Complacency, Techla repeats. Complacency. Of course they want
you to extol your innocence. Sleep is what they desire most of all. The
sleep of the conscience.

If he is to counterattack, he must be able to call his enemy something.

What are you anyway? he says.

What do you mean what am I?

What's your label? What do you call yourself?

Alistair strolls up to them, pats Tim on the back, and says, Fishy,
that was damn fine.

Techla looks at Alistair as though he were some sort of infection,
but Alistair can't seem to see her. He has a way of dismissing any data
he can't turn into compliments.

I suppose if one must resort to labels, says Techla Wahrsager, I am
an anarchist.

What is this, says Alistair, a serious conversation?

She turns to him with icy candor.

It is a conversation that would not take place in your fraternity house.

She strides off darkly into a crowd of togas.

Side by side in brotherly solidarity, Tim and Alistair pee into a
thicket of wild rosebushes.

I'm not sure, Alistair, but I think I just met my first intellectual.

Alistair considers this comment. Finally he says, I'll bet Techla
Wahrsager wishes she could do this.

Tim wanders away from the Parthenon and farther into the woods.
He wields a dry branch for knocking down spider webs. The trees are
enormous. He hears an owl hoot at the far end of the island, and the
farther he goes from the party's noise, the louder comes the hooting.
Alistair's joke, like the booze, is beginning to wear off, and Techla's
voice returns. He remembers now: she was the grad student outside
Mahler's office when he was waiting for the results of his German
sup. She must have overheard them talking about Rita's abortion. Could
she have been right about his poem? Is it possible his virginity is showing? A large flat cloud passes in front of the moon.

Uh who who who?

His heart lurches. The owl is right above him, huge, horned,
vulching on the branch of a dead cottonwood. Tim steps back and

looks up, and hears the cracking of a twig. Someone in a toga is coming his way. He can't see her face clearly, but from the way she walks along the path, the way she holds her head, the way her arms move to part the branches, he knows that this is Nancy. She is tipsy.

It's beautiful, she says.

Tell that to Techla Wahrsager.

Who the hell is Techla Wahrsager?

She tore my poem to shreds.

I was talking about the owl, says Nancy. What are you doing out here so far from your adoring public?

I didn't know I had one.

Well, she says, you've got one fan. I guess I should feel honoured.

Something in her tone tells him not to ask why.

Well, I do, she says, coming up to him, much too close. Thanks. I loved your poem.

He shrugs.

But there's one thing I've got to ask you. Did you write it after you heard about Alistair and me or before?

About Alistair and you?

Our engagement, she says.

The wide cloud obscuring the moon passes, and suddenly he can see the plains of her face, its serious tilt, the profusion of light brown hair that falls around her shoulders.

I wrote it just this morning.

Well, she says, slurring her words slightly, I must admit, I never knew you felt this way. I mean, I had my suspicions up at Lake Louise of course, but....

Uh who who?

The owl moves on its perch above them, ruffling its feathers like a judge in a wig. *The defendant will answer all questions as unambiguously as he can. Proceed.*

Let's walk over there, says Tim. He might think we're a couple of big rabbits.

What do you think about Alistair? she says. I mean really. You've never told me.

Oh....

And don't try to be *nice*. You're always trying to be so bloody *nice*.

They stop for a moment. He looks back to see if they are out of the owl's immediate range. Its head swivels in their direction. Elliott Crystal in a bird suit.

I've never been that close to Alistair, he says. The only thing we do is walk dogs, and he travels in—

Does the word sonofabitch ever come to mind? she says.

They walk through a grove of poplars and out onto a beach by the river. Suspended between two large clouds, one silver and one black, a gibbous moon begins to throb.

I'm sorry, she says. I'm being awful.

She stands directly in front of him, swaying, so there is no choice but to hold her in his arms. A strange thing to do with the girl he abandoned during the construction of their stick house, *circa* 1946. A disagreement over money he now recalls. She feels very good in his arms. In fact, she feels terrific in his arms, right up there with Rita Symington, and maybe after all Vaughan *is* a sonofabitch.

So? she says into his chest. What do I mean to you? Tell me what I mean to you.

In the absence of ready words, he kisses her. It is meant to be a firm kiss, not long or lingering, but nonetheless assertive. Something takes over. He can't say what, exactly, more in her than in him? But the kiss goes on and on, and before he can wonder who is kissing whom, they are rolling over slowly back and forth on the sand. His hands are beginning to discover what a flimsy thing a toga is when at last she stops him.

Seriously, she says, what am I to you?

You're the muse in the pink carriage.

The what?

A muse is a beautiful woman you see on a mountaintop, he says. It helps if she sings of Mount Abora.

I know what a muse is. What's this pink carriage bit?

Your mum used to take you out in a pink carriage when we were three years old. I can still remember.

Uh who who?

I don't think so, she says. I was walking when I was one.

She begins kissing him again, and stops.

You haven't really answered my question.

I used to make up stories about going up the Amazon with you. I was the hero and you were the heroine.

Was I in a pink carriage then too?

Nope. You were in the bow.

Boy, are you weird.

Didn't you ever make up stories about me? Once upon a time there was a handsome prince named Tim?

Nancy adjusts her toga once more, leans back on her elbows, and stares at the moon.

I could give it a try, she says. As long as we're in a storytelling mood. Once upon a time there was a handsome prince who was also a lying sonofabitch. He even lied to his intended, the beautiful and charming princess. She'd had it up to here with his lies and deceit, so she met a handsome court jester with a beaky nose and two beaver teeth right here, who maybe wasn't as ambitious and powerful, but nevertheless he had his virtues.

Name them.

You're not supposed to interrupt. He was great in the stern.

Uh who who?

Timmy! she cries.

The owl ruffles his feathers magisterially.

Stop laughing, Nancy says. This is serious. This other guy, the court jester, he flips for the princess even though she is engaged to be wed. But he is bashful and he could never tell her. He just wrote a bunch of poems, and one day she found one of them and read it and then she knew.

But she had suspected all along?

Yes, he had a way of looking at her. And when the princess found out about his purple passion for the princess... I like that, purple passion for the princess....

I was just getting interested.

When she found out about his passion for her, she went up to him and said....

Yes?

Nancy Fuller holds Tim's head in her hands and kisses him very softly on the mouth. He gives her one back. She returns it. One, long, kiss. As long and deep as the tongue of the nanaconda, the more they kiss, the more they roll over and over on the cool sand, the less toga Nancy seems to be wearing, and he's never had a whole tongue in his mouth other than his own, at last she kneels and tears off the toga altogether, and in not very much underwear at all, whispers, I could get to like this.

Mmnm.

Let's be adulterers!

You mean....

Of course I mean.

I've never really, I mean technically at—

Never mind. I think your time has come.

And maybe Nancy has a point there. Tim has no ambition to be an adulterer, but he has no objection to doing the things they do to become adulterers, so before long, he and Nancy are divesting him of his killer turtleneck and his jeans and his fear, and their hands and skin are sliding everwhere delightful as they move. He closes his eyes upon the image of her luminous arms. And opens them again. In silversided nakedness she eyes him with a look of devout lust. And sad. As sad as she can be. She straddles him and guides him, and in the moment it takes the owl to float across the moon, he feels his entire self drawn up into her and engulfed. Gone. He forgets who he is. Or with whom.

A film is running through his head. He calls it *Slipp'ry Blisses*. Nancy's body in the moonlight. Nancy's legs and arms, Nancy's breasts, Nancy's feet, Nancy's bum, and the resilient nest at the bottom of her belly. Try as he might, he cannot write about Nancy's body. Phrases like elegant limbs and alabaster skin come panting onto his page and are promptly shown the door. He reads his *Let Us Arise* poem over again, he reads his other poems, and he wonders if they are self-indulgent or immature. Having seen Nancy naked, having done that brief amazing thing with her, he is less fond of his poems. Not that he thinks Techla Wahrsager was right. No fuckin way.

One day in the library he comes across a call for poems by new writers from a magazine in California. He likes the format and writes down the address. He scribbles a note to accompany three of his best poems, a message that falls just short of apologizing for even sending them, and drops the bundle into the mail.

He phones Nancy several times. She is never there. He asks Mrs. Fuller to have her phone him. He is terrified she won't return his calls, terrified she will, and then say more than he is prepared to hear. One day he sees her walking along Wellington Crescent with Alistair Vaughan. They are holding hands and both wearing shorts. Together like that they are appallingly beautiful.

He falls into a stubborn melancholy. This mood will persist unless one of two things happens: Nancy returns his call or the magazine accepts his poems. Preferably both. Nancy will speak shyly at first, apologizing for making him wait. She will tell him that her engagement to Alistair is broken and that she and Tim must meet again on the island. They will seek out the owl. He will perform their ceremony and there in the moonlight she will become his pagan bride. It will be just like in D.H. Lawrence.

He mopes around the house. He wants to think that he is dying from a mortal wound to the heart, but the thing that smarts most of all is his pride.

Why don't you and Gump go fishing? his mother says. You've got a long weekend ahead of you.

Nah, he says. I don't feel like fishing.

Well then stop mooning. Do something. Phone up someone. Anything but this lounging around like it was the end of the world. Is it the end of the world?

You wouldn't understand.

You'd be surprised.

His summer job is mowing greens and fairways at the Riverside Golf Club. He likes the work because all day long he doesn't have to talk to anyone. During lunch he listens to Country and Western with the other workers. According to the radio in the mower shed, the song they're all craving is *Let No Man Sunder*, sung by Daisy Duncan and The Boys in the Stable. This is the opening lament.

> *Let no man sunder these vows we've made*
> *Is what the preacher said,*
> *But when I feel my Johnny's touch*
> *I wish I'd never wed...*

It is always Nancy who sings this song, and Alistair she is leaving. Whenever a girl approaches with a golf cart, he thinks it might be Nancy. Whenever he asks his parents if there have been any calls, it is Nancy's he expects. Whenever he checks for his mail, however, he expects news from the magazine in California. Life on the golf course inches by like a night crawler; life at home is full of sullen silences. He sleeps fitfully. When at last the phone rings at two A.M. he knows it will be Nancy.

Fishy, you awake?

Gump Lowney's nasal voice. He wants to go for coffee. We gotta talk, says Gump. Can I come around and meet you by your driveway?

Gump is waiting in the Studebaker as though their old high school capers had never been interrupted.

This is the first time in months I've seen you without Sherry.

To hell with Sherry.

Old Gump never says things like that about Sherry Love. He is usually too much of a gentleman to express strong feelings about anyone. Gump drives through Old Glenora yawning and blinking.

If I didn't know you better, Gump, I'd say you had something on your mind.

Gump shrugs. He can't seem to stop yawning and blinking.

If you were to sum up what was on your mind in one word, Gumper, what would that word be?

Women.

Ah.

They drive slowly through the residential streets and east on Stony Plain, then north on 124th toward the all-night restaurants. A burger place is open near their old high school.

And Gumper, if you could sum up the solution to your problem in a single word, what do you think that word would be?

Fishin.

Laud o' mercy, dey's a God in Hebben.

Where Ochi Creek descends into Mountie Lake, there is a long series of beaver dams, some an acre or more with holes that go seven or eight feet deep. You wade upstream in the gravel. This keeps you down low and hidden so that your head is almost level with the dam. This way the rising trout don't see you coming up on them. You cast from behind the dam, standing in the stream below it with the sun somewhere in front of you and none of your shadow falling on the water. You are not by the water, you are *in* the water—oh, God, he should write this down—you will slip unobtrusively into the great chain of life and predation and live briefly by those ancient terms. Only your arm and your rod are visible to the trout. You never know what you'll get. More than anything you hope for a brown trout, but it might be a brookie or a rainbow. When they're hooked, the brookies go for the snags, and the rainbows leap for the sun. You could get a seven incher or a two pounder or a real lunker. Tim has never hooked a lunker, and Gump (who is still shameless and fishes with worms) has hooked a couple of lunkers but never landed one.

Gump takes a lower dam. Tim can see him swatting mosquitoes and baiting up. Gump casts out into the middle of the dam and leans his rod into the crotch of a forked stick. He has tied on a clear plastic bubble about four feet from his worm and he waits, smoking, for the bubble to be jerked under. He grins at Tim.

Fishy, she's gonna be a good spring.

Perhaps he means next spring, because the summer is more or less underway.

Tim has a size 16 mosquito on the end of a recently greased floating line. He uses an extra long leader and he's spotted several rises less than twenty feet from the edge of the dam. The idea is simply to catch the dumbest trout in the school, slit the fish's belly, and examine the stomach contents for what the trout are feeding on. After the first one, the rest come easier. The only problem is the willows behind him. He is sure to catch these willows on his backcast before he can get out enough line for a decent cast. What to do?

Easy when you know how. You throw out a short line, tempting but not quite reaching the willows behind you, and you lay it down. All they have to do is swim about eight feet his way, and chop chop, dinner is served. Simple, yes? No? They are trout and must be courted by an aggressive suitor. Their rule tonight is *you come to me*. They think this way because, like the women painted by the eminent master Stufflebeam, they are born beautiful.

Approaching the edge of the dam and risking exposure, he draws more line from the reel, pulls his fly slowly back, and rolls it forward with a whipping motion. The roll cast sends the fly about six feet farther into the pool. He has done this a thousand times but once again it's the first time. The fly shifts on the still surface as the leader uncurls. With a *glurp* it disappears. Tim is fast to a fish. He whoops this fact to Gump, who stands there smoking.

The fish cleaves the surface with its tail, but it doesn't actually leap. Therefore, it is probably not a rainbow. It fights well below the surface. Its first run is very strong. Too strong.

Oh, Jesus. Gump, I've got the all-time monster.

Should I get the net?

The trout takes a second run out past the middle of the pond, and then the surface erupts in a golden brown explosion of back and dorsal. Gump is standing there in his waders with the net in one hand and his cigarette in the other.

Think it's a brownie?

Yep. It's gotta go four pounds anyway.

Oh, shit, says Gump, and bounds mooselike down the incline to the lower beaver dam. Tim doesn't have to ask. He knows that Gump also has a fish on and the next few minutes will be chaos. Tim's fish sulks on the bottom until he decides to move it. With his free hand he taps the middle of his rod and the fish takes off on another long run. Once more Tim snubs it before his trout reaches the weeds on the far side. It comes in slowly, but it comes, diving and twisting, a huge brown trout. Like a man on the cover of *Fin and Feather*, Tim eases the trout toward the net. The trout comes belly up and tries to right itself. It is more than two feet long with black spots on the back and sides and bright flecks of red. The fins have an opaque yellowish colour. Five pounds? Six? Seven?

Tim's fly is stuck to the trout's lip by a thin layer of golden skin. The lunker rights itself and tries one last feeble dive just as the net slides underneath. The fly comes out, the rod whips back, the net scoops down and up. Empty. The trout turns slowly away and tails back into the deep water. Tim falls to his knees on the edge of the dam, staring.

Oh, my God.

Gump calls from the lower dam holding a nice foot-long brookie up by the gills. He grins proudly.

How big is yours? he cries.

She says to me maybe we're gettin a little bit hasty. She says maybe we ought to be seein other people. I buy her a big Jesus diamond from Birks and she says maybe we should be seein other people.

At least she gave you back the ring.

So next time I go over there she's with this *Gary* yoyo, fartin around on the chesterfield. Come on in, she says, all smiles. Hell with that noise, I says. I know the score.

Gump throws another fish on the moss. In all there are seven. The largest is a thirteen inch rainbow. A good catch, and there will be more the next day, maybe even a lunker. Only now, it seems, once he has proven himself and caught five of the fish, can Gump talk about his broken engagement to Sherry Love. Or maybe he chooses now to confess because it's almost dark and they can't clearly see each other's faces.

Did you just hear something? Gump says, pausing on the moss. He inserts his knife into the anal canal of the last fish and slices up the belly.

No.

Anyway, I figure I won't die.

Attaboy. You're well out of it. She seemed a bit of a fribble to me.

Fribble, says Gump. Yeah.

Tim likes the word fribble. He got it from *Sons and Lovers*. No one seems to know what a fribble is but no one ever asks what it means. Forever after, Sherry Love will be known as the fribble. She will never live it down.

Gump runs his thumb up the cavity next to the spine of the last gutted fish, takes out the clotted kidney, and tosses the fish into the creel. They rub sand and mud into their hands to remove the slime and wash them in the lake.

The only thing is, Gump continues, I gotta get back into circulation.

At least for a while, says Tim, you've *been* in circulation.

Shhh.

Tim hears it too. A stealthy sound. He motions for Gump to get into the canoe. He tosses in the last of their tackle and the creel. Gump crawls in and Tim pushes off from the rocks. The canoe glides out through the shallow water. The noise comes again, a dragging scraping sound. Tim and Gump paddle through the falling dark away from the cove. They are safe. They have seven trout and the weather tomorrow will be beautiful. Neither Tim nor Gump will die of a broken heart. The bear or whatever it is can eat the entrails of their fish and hope for better luck next time. They will all hope for better luck next time. The lunker got away, so did Sherry Love, so did Nancy Fuller, but they will all rise to fight again.

Gumper, she's gonna be a good spring.

Gump nods. Tim directs the canoe homeward. The tent, the fire pit, their sleeping bags await them. The only sound is the song of frogs and the water curling in little whirlpools behind their paddles.

Row row row your boat
Gently down the stream
Merrily merrily merrily merrily
Life is but a dream...

The flag football women are singing in the corner of the bar. Janey Bream dismisses them with a flapping motion of her hand behind her back. Really, she seems to say with her expressive brows, you can't trust your own friends to behave themselves.

Hey?

You can call me Tim.

Tim. Right. I know. How can you stand to live at home? she says. I just couldn't. I'm not criticizing you... I'm not criticizing anyone.

She wears an orange and white flag football uniform. A grass and mud stain extends the length of one pantleg. Her face glows with a healthy flush. She leans over the table on her elbows toward Tim and Gump to make herself heard.

I just can't see how you can stand to, she says.

Tim asks Janey where she lives.

Basement apartment, she says. I've got a room-mate. It's a nice arrangement.

Another roar goes up at the table behind her, and one of the flag football women calls out her name.

Just a minute! she yells back. Jeez.

My parents are okay, Tim says. Besides, I'll be gone by next spring or summer.

Where to?

Grad school.

Grad school? says Gump. When are you gonna get a job like the rest of us?

Job schmob. Don't rush me, I'm not even a man yet.

They look at their watches.

One hour and ten minutes, says Gump.

See? Lots of time.

Sounds to me like your parents are something else, says Janey. One day at home an my mum starts in on me. I'd say we're maybe good for half an hour in the same house.

She looks behind her at the flag football table. Hey, I've gotta go now. It's been nice meetin you fellas.

Janey returns to her table and the women start up a chorus of *It's Three O'Clock in the Morning*. Tim's parents used to sing this song. He is surprised these gals know it.

What do you think? says Gump.

Not bad. I wouldn't mind being equipment manager for all her friends there, but a guy could do worse than Janey. What do you think?

Could get interesting in the showers all right, says Gump.

But Janey, I mean. Think she's maybe a bit easy or something?

Gump shrugs. I wouldn't kick her out of bed for chewin crackers.

I was trying to find out where she lived. I should have gotten her phone number.

Yeah.

They talk randomly. Either Tim is checking out the football women at the table behind Gump, or Gump's eyes are sliding sideways to watch the flow in and out of the women's can.

Forty-five minutes, says Gump.

Don't tell me, I don't want to know. I don't want to think that suddenly I have to act like a grown-up man.

That's the way the cookie crumbles.

So, you're gonna be twenty-one, is that it?

It's Janey again. She has brought over her own glass of draft.

What's with your friends over there? says Tim.

It's all over, says Janey. I've divorced them.

Here's to the next twenty-one, she says to Tim, and here's to your first apartment before too long.

Gump's twenty-one and *he* still lives with *his* parents.

Then you guys should live together, she says. I don't know how ya do it.

How can you afford living in an apartment?

I got a job, says Janey. I'm a part-time lifeguard.

A lifeguard! says Gump. You're a lifeguard?

Bring em back alive, all sizes.

What are you taking at the uni?

Phys-ed, she says. But I have to take this killer option in soash.

She explains that she has been talking to all sorts of people about their parents. An informal survey, but part of a project for her sociology class. That is the reason she has approached Gump and Tim in the bar. Except she isn't sure, she says, how much she will remember because of the drinking. She turns to Tim.

How would you describe your old man?

Oh, kind of ordinary, he says.

Kind of ordinary? No one's ordinary.

Well, Gump, how would you describe my dad?

Kind of ordinary.

You guys are such a disappointment. What's your dad doin right at this very moment, Timmy?

Tim.

Tim. What's your dad doin right now?

He never tells me what he's doing. He's going through a phase.

Seriously.

He's playing crib with Dr. Sharp and the Cronies.

Doctors? He has doctor friends? Is he a doctor?

Nope. He's a salesman.

Ah. So would you say you guys were both middle class?

Gump and Tim shrug.

I guess so, says Tim. If we actually owned the house we lived in, ere middle class, no question. I never really worried about

our mother. Now don't tell me she's ordinary.

is. She's a typical mum.

Oh, God, I can't stand it.

Fishy, I think you're flunking sociology.

Janey smiles tolerantly at both of them. Another uproar goes off behind her. The football women want her to lead them in another song. But Janey is enjoying herself.

Where is your mother now? she says.

Tonight, says Tim, she's a wahine.

A what?

That's Hawaiian for middle class housewife in a grass skirt.

So?

She's in a big house with a bunch of other Edmonton wahines. She's got this friend named Reenie Fuller who likes to teach people how to do the hula. They're rehearsing it for the Junior Hospital League Follies. A charity thing like.

Well, that doesn't sound very ordinary to me. Why does she want to do that?

She likes it. She's a ham, like me.

So, when you think of your mother, what's the first thing that comes into your mind?

Bran muffins. Blue skies. Singing. Dancing. Playing the ukulele. She's good at that sort of thing.

Now we're getting somewhere. And what's the first thing you think about when you think about your dad?

Football, baseball, hockey, hunting. Haunted by dreams of prosperity. Get organized, son! Right now you could no more make it in the brokerage business than fly to the moon.

Janey shoots Tim a sort of TV advertisement grin. She wears her long hair tied at the back by a rubber band. It is very nice hair. Her flag football game has left her smudged, but she doesn't seem to care.

Thirty-nine minutes, says Gump.

See? Lots of time. I'm still a boy.

Okay, Janey, what about your parents? says Gump. First describe their social class.

Janey closes her eyes. Father: English working class, downwardly mobile, drinks too much, estranged from family. Depressing to think about. Mother: lower middle, social climber, resentful of daughter's freedom, wants daughter to care for her. Depressing to think about.

Wow, says Gump, obviously impressed. What does your dad do?

He's retired. He used to be a milk man. Getcher cream from Charlie Bream.

Tim sits up suddenly. Is your dad tall and lean with this huge grin? A sort of homely toothy grin, and he limps?

For an instant Janey loses her composure. She nods.

Charlie Bream was our milk man! Tim cries. He used to give me rides in the milk wagon!

Janey unties her jacket from around her waist and drapes it entirely over her head. She is just slipping into something more comfortable and she will be out shortly.

The football women are yelling things to Janey that are full of innuendos. Gump and Tim contrive to escape with her into the street. It is raining. The three of them drive down Whyte Avenue in Gump's Studebaker and north on 109th until they find a pizza place. Gump suggests this place because, he confesses, he's never had a pizza. The restaurant is called Giuseppi's. It's nice, quiet, a bit *outré*, with jazz piped in through the sound system. A bearded man and a lean woman in the corner are sitting with Mahler, Tim's former German professor. The men are playing chess. The décor is exactly right: no wallpaper or decorations, just a continuous painting of distorted figures doing a weird dance. The artist has apparently been coming in for weeks to paint the mural right onto the walls. Gump is very impressed with the place. He even likes the mural.

Let's order, Janey says.

The night has begun anew. Tim is a little drunk, but Gump will be driving. In a few minutes, Tim will enter manhood.

No, that's not true. If he concentrates hard, he will make the night last forever. He looks at the clock, the smiley face of a little old man. It serves as the head of a stick man in the mural. The minute hand on this clock will cease inching its way up the wall. With the right kind of attitude, the hands will never reach the top of the old man's forehead, which is midnight. That's why the clock is smiling. Cinderella can dance the night away; her coach will never come for her because the coachman is drunk. He has conceived an immoderate heat for the Fairy Godmother.

Tim pauses to feel for some sort of difference, a hint of what some might call maturity.

Nothing.

So, says Janey, tell me all about your birth. I know, it was sort of ordinary.

I was born twenty-one Octobers ago just before midnight at the Misericordia Hospital, and after that, my parents gave up on begetting. As the story is told, I was a slow and painful birth. Unwilling to leave home, you might say. I was two weeks late.

You're a serpent, says Janey.

Come again? says Gump.

Were you born in nineteen forty-one? she says to Gump. That makes you a serpent too. I was born in forty-two. I think I'm a rabbit.

Tough luck, says Tim. I think serpents eat rabbits, don't they?

Only in uncivilized countries.

She shovels her pizza down, gathering in the strings of mozzarella that stick to her chin. So, she says, if you're not going to be a writer when you grow up, what are you going to be?

I'm going to grad school. In the States, he adds, partly for effect.

What's wrong with being just a writer?

You've got to be different somehow. French or Irish or something. With a name like Winthrop Mackworth Praed. Writers always have great names. You've got to have interesting parents, he says, aiming a smile at Janey.

What do you mean? If you like to do it, you just do it, right?

It helps if you were born during a bloody revolution or maybe grew up in a leper colony. Anyway, you've got to hear yer still sad music of humanity, eh?

Gump plays an imaginary violin.

Does he always go on like this, Gump?

He's worse when he's sober.

Professor Mahler comes over, looking smug. Herr Fisher, I have just defeated Kaufmann. Look at him, crushed. He sulks like a dog in the corner. You must introduce me to your friends.

Tim does the honours. Gump, he announces, is my fishing buddy, and Janey my fiancée.

But you have no ring, says Mahler, when he has kissed Janey's hands.

I never wear it in public, says Janey. There's a dozen ways to crack a diamond, did you know that?

Mahler gives Janey his doubting look. Is this what people in Edmonton do for action? Is this where you make the scene, hm?

They shrug.

Where do people go? says Mahler. Where's the *life* around here?

I go to Vegreville, says Janey. I was last year's koobassa queen.

Seriously, says Mahler. I live out my life here, I pay my taxes here, I want to know what to do wiz myself.

We're doin it, says Gump.

Janey draws an imaginary number one in the air over Gump and pats him on the back.

I try already to read Canadian literature, says Mahler. The high point, it seems to me, is your poem you show to me last year. Is that published now, hm?

No word yet, says Tim.

This is a slight exaggeration. The poem was rejected in August and sits in Tim's desk drawer beneath his new green spiral notebook. He remembers one sentence from his letter of rejection: *Unfortunately, you seem to be striving for high literary effects.*

Techla, she hates your poem.

He looks to where Mahler is indicating. The woman at Mahler's table is Techla Wahrsager. She is deep in discussion with Kaufmann, the sulking dog. She uses both hands for emphasis, as though shaking a large invisible skull.

You must be mistaken, says Tim. She told me it changed her life. She grovelled. She wouldn't meet my eyes. She told me I was a genius.

Perhaps you hide your light under a bushel, Herr Fisher. Anyway, I read this guy Grofe? *Over the Prairie Trail?* You read that *Auswurf?*

No one at the table has heard of this Grofe fellow.

I read other ones too. I read this long, *utterly* long poem called—

He rushes over to his chess partner and mutters something in German, then returns.

It is called *Up to the Last Spike.* Oh, cheese-us, it was boring. A great verse Schlafmittel about building the railway. This great saga of technology conquering the elements. At first, I think to myself he writes this abortion to be funny, ya?

It's almost time, says Janey, pointing to the clock on the wall.

The stick man with the smiling clock head in the mural seems to be gesticulating. He holds a scythe and he is declaring Tim's official minute of birth, eleven fifty-five. But wait, there are still a good fifty seconds to go.

Time for what? says Mahler.

For nothing, says Tim. It's still my unbirthday. The second hand will never reach the top of the dial. This is still an illegal beer I'm drinking. I will never actually become twenty-one. Because before I can become twenty-one, the second hand will have to reach half-way.

It's reached half-way, says Gump.

Why, then, it will have to reach the three quarter point, then the seven eighth point, then the—

Is this your birthday? says Mahler.

Yes! cries Janey.

No! cries Tim. We will never leave this café. We will always play chess and drink in here, and shovel in the pizza, and the pizza will always be only half eaten. Like the lovers on the Grecian urn.

Gump and Janey give each other a bewildered look.

Janey will always be a guard in the swimming pool of life. She'll never grow old and arthritic. She'll always do the *breast* stroke. And Gump will always hook the biggest brown trout in the stream of life, and he will never land it. The incomparable Miss Wahrsager will always admire my genius. And Professor Mahler will always be writing his treatise on Heinrich Mann's debt to Goethe.

Thomas Mann.

Thass what I said. And our waiter, Tim shouts, beckoning to a bald and bearded little man approaching their table, will always be just bringing our drinks and we will never be happier than we are right—

Fishy? says Gump, pointing to his watch. Happy birthday.

Gump raises his hand like a choir master, and he, Janey, and Mahler open their mouths in unison while Tim slumps in his chair at this final act of betrayal.

The song is over. Janey looks Tim's way as though she has noticed something.

What's eatin you?

Somewhere in the cartoon factory that his mind has become, a girl is tuning her banjo among the larches above Lake Louise.

I am, he says.

Some time after two in the morning he has to pee. Pepper follows him into the bathroom, sits and watches. Pepper yawns. Tim yawns. He has the faintest memory of a dream about Janey Bream. Dream a dream of Janey Bream. From Charlie Bream you get your cream. Charlie smelled of milk and horses. Small world.

He goes back to bed and Pepper follows, her nails clicking on the hardwood floors. He climbs into bed and is about to turn out the light when he sees Pepper sitting at his bedside. Pepper looks at him as though Tim is about to do something entertaining.

Tonight Pepper thinks Tim is Mole Sharp's TV set. Any second the Gypsy Woman will leap out of Tim's head, shaking her tambourine.

The house is so quiet he can hear his alarm clock ticking. He can even hear the sound of his father's breathing. Every so often the air whistles past his father's gullet in a slow drawing in of breath. It never quite becomes a snore and it never seems to awaken Tim's mother. *Whenever my head hits the pillow,* she is still fond of saying.

And now Tim is massively awake. Why awake? Is he depressed? No, not very. He is just wakeful. Pepper yawns, her head is sinking, but still she sits by Tim's bedside. Waiting.

Is it Janey Bream then? Is he falling in love with Janey Bream? No, he is in love with Nancy. No? No. With Rita Symington. No, wait wait wait. With the *memory* of Rita Symington. But he will phone Janey Bream before too long. She's as unlike Nancy or Rita as a girl can be. He and Janey might get along pretty good. As long as she doesn't expect him to be a jock, he won't expect her to read his favourite books. *William Faulkner?* she said. *Didn't he star in* Born Yesterday *or something? Well, didn't he?*

No, it's not Janey Bream. His mind is unleashed, roaming fitfully through some sort of jungle. He should probably write this all down. Small world. He should write about his *own* small world. Pepper obviously thinks so. He reaches over and scratches Pepper's head. She allows herself to be petted, but she is obviously not in her sucky mode. And she is not begging to go out. Nor is she hinting to be allowed up on the bed. She is there to watch the action.

What action?

No action around here, Pepper, he whispers to the dog. Pepper looks away. If ever there was a guy born to inaction, he is lying in this bed. Hamlet with a live dad and nothing much rotting in the state of Denmark. Twenty-one years ago he lost a battle to stay forever in his mother's womb. And then he tumbled out into the river of life.

He whispers the phrase to Pepper: *Out into the River of Life.* It was late October when he was born. The river might have been frozen.

Yes? Pepper seems to say.

Once upon a time in the steaming jungles of the Amazon a baby was dropped into the mighty river to swim with all the piranhas. He had to learn how to fight with his brother (who couldn't wait to get into the River of Life, who was still swimming downstream), he had to learn how to hide his fear, how to drag himself off to school each day, how to talk to girls, how to lose his virginity, how to co-exist with the unbearable Altrogge, how to contend with a thousand illnesses, how to write poems to impress women, how to live in a world run by the people Out There, how to keep...how to keep....

He wants to say out loud *how to keep everything from disappearing*, but he doesn't really understand what this means. Maybe he just got it from a book. What is disappearing, after all? The haloed world of his golden youth? Big hairy deal. Except: you don't have to swim with all the piranhas if you can swim somewhere better. You could leap over the nanaconda's lair, you could paddle up to the source of things where the trout were rising. A long time ago the Irish kept trout in their wells because it was said to purify the water.

Pepper extends her nose to the bed, sniffing. A moment ago her nose was dry; now it glistens with moisture.

Pouring out of your mother's womb was like going from a rearing pond to a river. Reverend Mountjoy's miracle. Roderick Haig-Brown's miracle. Thoreau's miracle. Izaak Walton's miracle. God's miracle.

Yeah, says Pepper. Now you're cookin.

Always, in his father's stories, they would go up the Amazon to find the emeralds of the Ucayali warriors or whatever. Always *up*. Because if you went down the Amazon things would get murky? You'd have to contend with *civilization?* Questions you can never ask your father.

But upstream, that's where the action is. Treasure troves, crystal caves, good fishing, clean water, a girl with a banjo singing of Mount Abora, happy endings, Blue Skies, God, the wine of God, Artemis, birdsong, the mountains, no nanacondas, lots of brook trout and brown trout, the women of the great master Stufflebeam, which rhymes with Charlie Bream, from whom you get your cream.

Where you get your cream.

Pepper is all attention. Pepper is lapping it all up. Milk from the tits of the Great Mother Springer.

He should write this all down. There is a pen and his new green spiral notebook in his desk drawer. There's nothing written in it yet, not a word. But where would he start? I was born in the month of the scorpion, in the year of the serpent, 1941, the darkest days of World

War II, and I was christened Timothy. Timothy, son of Pug. Which means Honouring God.

Unfortunately you seem to be striving for high literary effects, says Pepper, lowering her head once more, lowering her body to the rug.

In the beginning God created the trout streams...no?

No, sayeth Pepper, who lyeth on the rug now, sniffeth the air, waiteth patiently for Timothy's overture.

It was the best of times, it was—

No, sayeth the world.

No?

No. No. No.

His novel would be magnificently sad. Something to do with unrequited love, like a song in a minor key.

> *Blue skies, smiling at me,*
> *Nothing but blue skies do I see.*

Such a happy message, such a melancholy tune. Like the courting song of the chickadees. Sad rapture.

> *Blue skies, singing a song,*
> *I love you dearly, Rider Wrong.*

Timmy Fisher, age three, tractor driver and song stylist.

Get on with it, says Pepper. I haven't got all night.

Once upon a time and a very good time it was—

No, says Pepper. Earlier. Go back. Upstream.

Once-ta pon-ta time—

Earlier.

He really should get up out of bed and get a pen and his green spiral notebook and get this all down. All it takes is the right word, the first trout in a pool of Uncatchables, the first... On the other hand, it must be three o'clock in the morning and he's got an eight-thirty class.

Pepper moans, lowers her head onto her paws, yawns mightily.

Her master follows suit. He turns off his bed lamp and curls up into a tight capital G. G is for goodnight. G is for God rest ye. G is for God's wine, G is for G is for G...is for ghosts. G is for gone, with Nancy's pink delights in the owl grove. G is for G is for G is for go to bed. G is for getting up early. G is forgetting. So is Tim. He hears his mother clearing her throat in sleep, his father pause in breathing, his dog sigh, his clock tick. Sleep. That is the only the only answer.

After all. It's three o'clock in the. Morning and he has an eight-thirty. And the clock won't stop. And when that machine goes off goes off when that thing goes off he will. Plunge out of bed he will plunge out of bed and be and be he will have to be wide

❸ DOWNSTREAM

AUGUST 24, 1963. "Dejection: an Ode"

> Best to be teary
> And honestly dreary
> Than teary and dreary in theory.

AUGUST 25. Tick tick tick, say the caraganas. Edmonton bakes in the dusty copper light of late summer. The air is rich with August rot and stubble.

AUGUST 26.   "Forbidden Fruit"

> From Eve did Adam get much woe
> And guilt with which to grapple.
> What profit, then, to lose his rib
> To gain his Adam's apple?

AUGUST 28. Troubling conversation with Mum. Packing car just to see if my junk would all fit in. "But you're not going till Saturday!" she tells me. I tell her that I have to try things out ahead of time. "You're anxious to get going, aren't you," she says.

Didn't know it was so obvious. Like I'm just an open book my mother can read so easily.

This eagerness to hit the trail seems to sadden her. She watches me as I wrestle with the trunk, etc. She tells me (once again) that she and Dad should have had at least one more kid. This confession surprises me. Don't know why. If I were them I'd be damn glad to be rid of me. I've been a moody ungrateful little bugger. But I think Mum would like me to stay here and be her little boy forever.

Derek told me long distance from Vancouver that for my own good I should get the hell out of Edmonton. Departure much overdue. Probably right. It feels very good to be hitting the trail. To do the thing that George Bailey could not do: shake the dust off this crumby little town forever.

Mum says the house won't be the same without me. She says that this is a mother's fate. From the moment a boy comes into the world he spends the rest of his life trying to run away from home.

AUGUST 30. Hot and dry again. Said goodbyes all around town. Gump was flippant, but he will miss me. Tells me *She's gonna be a good spring, eh.* God bless the Gumper. May we fish again before too long.

Had a dream last night. Went down into the basement of our house and into the bathroom to learn my lines for the school play or maybe to look in the mirror. Or maybe I had just taken a bath. The linoleum still as grotty as ever, mirror still cracked, and that secret teenage feeling of original sin still there. I saw my face in the mirror, clearly, with the bathroom light on. My face began to swim before me into a butterscotch pudding with whipped cream or something. Couldn't recognize myself. Woke up feeling hungry for butterscotch pudding.

AUGUST 31. Went to see Mahler to say *Aufw*. Entered Arts Bldg without noticing who was behind me. Heading for elevator when voice behind me says, "Timmy Fisher, I wondered what that bad smell was." I turn around and there is Alistair Vaughan. Was he sneering at me or was this his attempt to be friendly? Asked about Nancy's whereabouts. Vaughan went cryptic, muttered something about travels. We waited for the elevator. A real old creaker, this one. Notoriously slow. Just then, along comes none other than Techla Wahrsager, out for blood.

How do I know she was out for blood? She *always* looks that way. Thin hungry mouth, pointy jutting little canines. I knew I could scarcely take Alistair's sarcasms without vomiting. But Alistair and Techla in the same elevator? I'd rather shove hot needles into my eyes. I pretended to Alistair that I had forgotten something and fled without acknowledging the presence of the vibrant Miss Wahrsager.

Returned in a few minutes and pressed the button. No elevator. Only a bell ringing from somewhere inside the old shaft. That and the muffled sound of voices. And *still* I didn't get it. It took me some minutes to find out that the damn elevator was stuck—with Alistair and Techla inside! There but for the grace of God, etc.

But think about it. I literally could have been stuck inside an elevator with my two greatest pains-in-the-ass at the same time! Stuck, as it turns out, for five bloody hours!

What did they talk about? He sees her as a spy from Moscow bent on destroying western civilization. She sees him as an imperialist traitor to humanity. Would they destroy each other with rhetorical death rays? Would they make love?

Scratch last possibility. I can't imagine Alistair making love with Techla Wahrsager and I can't imagine Techla making love with anything.

According to Mahler's secretary, some French prof managed to pass in some thin volumes of poetry for them to read while they were waiting for the repair guys. I could not have invented a better scenario: two souls come together from the opposite ends of the universe, and to survive, they must read poetry and talk with each other. What happens when you are forced into bed with your opposite?

All of my nemeses contained in that one little room! But what did they say? If I knew that, I'd have a wonderful story.

I must have willed it to happen. I must have known that this was the day the Arts Building elevator was to go on the fritz. Playing the ultimate director of human affairs. God or Ingmar Bergman.

Who can I tell this to? An older version of myself? Old Bugger, old fartmeister, stand me now and ever in good stead.

SEPTEMBER 2.   "CAN-tos"

> Corinna, wake this morning!
> The Muse my loo's adorning.
> The songs of man
> Festoon the can,
> So skip to the loo, my darling.

SEPTEMBER 3. LAKE LOUISE. Ran into Amber Bole and Altrogge! They are *MARRIED!!!* Didn't know what to say. Asked about Slimy. Her latest letter had no return address. She has a new folksinging group and they did a number on the Tommy Hunter Show. She's moved to Toronto or somewhere. Sigh.

SEPTEMBER 3. DEREK'S APT IN VANCOUVER. Had a dream I've had before. Woke up, like always, with sad memory of a stream or some trout. ??? I *think* it's about fishing, or not being able to go fishing. Not sure. When I wake up, this sense of meanings just withheld. Dream is just around corner, in next pool. Must sleep with green spiral notebook right there on bedside table. Next time net it before it gets away.

Today I say goodbye to Derek and cross the border. Seattle for lunch, Oregon for supper. Open your gates, America. Remember, I left the womb for this, so it better be worth the trouble.

Tim has the feeling that he is on television, that a secret documentary is being done on him as drives south in his little red Beetle. A tiny camera mounted on his rear-view mirror records the interview. The host is a fast talking fellow with an engaging smile. Tim's family and all his friends are watching at the other end. Everyone in Canada, everyone in the whole world with a TV is watching to hear what he Tim will say. *He* wonders what he will say.

Okay, for starters, Tim, I hope I can call you Tim.

Yes, by all means, call me Tim.

Why are you heading for Oregon of all places? Good scholarships?

Well, to tell you the truth—

Dapper Dave.

To tell the truth, Dapper Dave, I wasn't such a hot student as an undergraduate, you know how it goes, and Oregon is the only place that'll take me.

Any chance for a scholarship?

Well, no, Dapper Dave. Actually, I'm on probation until I mend my ways. Academically speaking.

I see, and Tim, if we can get out the old crystal ball and look ahead a bit, what do you think you'll be doing around the year 2000?

You got me, Dapper.

Moving now to the world scene, Tim, do you think that Khrushchev or Kennedy might just start something they can't finish?

Nah. Things are looking pretty stable on the American side of things, Dapper Dave. Smooth sailing all the way. Tranquil seas ahead, as they say. If I were Khrushchev, though, I'd be worried about this guy Kennedy. Looks like a comer.

What about your own future, Tim? What sort of job will you have? Teaching English in some ivy-covered college in the mountains? Will you have a wife? A mistress? Several mistresses?

Oh, Dapper, I think that *several mistresses* is a pregnant possibility.

Keep your mind on your goddam driving, says someone else, perhaps the director of the show, an obscure figure on the roof of his car. You can't drive and think about sex.

Tim focuses on the road ahead.

EVERY NIGHT HE LEAVES THE LIBRARY AT CLOSING TIME and walks home through the cemetery on the edge of campus. The graveyard is a tract of ancient forest left untouched by the bulldozers, its graves shrouded in the gloom of dripping fir trees. When the rains came to stay, he bought a black umbrella and he carries it wherever he goes. When he walks through the graveyard at night, the umbrella is his rod and his staff. When it isn't raining, he swings it in a jaunty way through the graveyard like a London banker. It's like reading poetry in the bar; it accentuates his difference.

No one seems to notice.

After a while, in the late fall, the intense reading begins to get to him. He develops a case of nerves and has to force himself to go downtown and see people, because if he doesn't go downtown, he'll have to go straight home to an empty room.

He lives in a big old frame house. His room is really only a cubicle slightly larger than his bed. He can hang a few clothes on nails, but everything else has to stay in his trunk because there is no room for a chest-of-drawers. He lives here to save money. There are five upstairs cubicles all in a row, his next to the kitchen. The second cubicle is occupied by Jarvis, a crippled logger. The third one is occupied by a slow fellow named Al who has recently been in prison for a break-in. Next to Al is Mr. Weatherbum, who is newly divorced and sells meat to retailers. And next to Mr. Weatherbum is a guy named Wally who used to box in the navy. Their landlady and her husband are retired farmers, Baptists from Thayer, Missouri, and no women are allowed upstairs.

Jarvis Larson, the crippled logger, is from Portsmouth, New Hampshire. He pronounces it Jahvis Lahson from Pottsmuth New Hampsha. He has an artificial leg, just like Mole Sharp's dad. One night Tim was on the kitchen phone talking long distance to his parents. He was telling them that he had passed his first exam. Jarvis came in and got an earful. Several days later he entered the kitchen where Tim was heating some canned beans. Jarvis said, You strike me as real close to your folks up in Canada. He hadn't meant it as an insult.

Jarvis is very friendly. He claims to love two things, eatin an fuckin. He is free with his advice on both subjects. He spends his weekends with a widow named Sharon, or else alone up in the hills shooting rattlers and rats and anything else he can pick off with his gun. It is a six-shooter. It looks like a cowboy's revolver. He keeps it loaded under the front seat of his car.

Only once, according to Jarvis, had a woman ever gotten the best of him. This was his girlfriend back in New Hampshire. It happened before he lost his leg. He was real sweet on her but eventually she ran off with another guy. He figured he lost her because he ran out of new ways of doing it. She must of gotten bored, he said. You should always be up on your technique. He gave Tim an old-fashioned man-to-man wink.

One night in winter Tim asked Jarvis why he kept his revolver loaded under the front seat of his car.

Niggers, said Jarvis.

They got into an argument about that, and for a while afterwards Jarvis was silent whenever Tim came into the kitchen. That left the ex-con to talk to, and he read muscle-man comics for a good part of every day. He was offended if you didn't pretend to like his muscle-man comic books. And of course there was Mr. Weatherbum, whose dedication to the meat business was so complete, he scarcely talked about anything else. The sailor fellow was pleasant enough, but he hardly ever spoke to anyone.

At first Tim is amazed at his tenacity as a scholar. Knowing that he's paying his own way makes him study harder, and perhaps it helps that he has no social life. It also helps that he would rather be studying for a master's degree in English than working at a job. It's either study hard down here or take a year of education and go out and teach school like Gump has done. Every night he's in the library stuffing his head full of scholarly facts and critical theory. He compiles a stack of five-by-three index cards that grows until it's six inches high. Each card summarizes a scholarly book or a journal. This is his way of retaining enough for the big final. The course is called Methods of Bibliography and Criticism. The grad students call it the wipeout course. You can flunk it twice and they let you try again, but three strikes and you're out. He is determined to pass it on the first go.

He receives a post card from Slimy, again with no return address.

His green spiral notebook has been abandoned.

He has acquired a bad case of the shakes. He phones home less and less. At night he walks downtown in the rain and all around until the shaking stops. It's not like a physical palsy, more like a shaking of the soul. It starts as a fear in the belly, and it crawls up slowly toward his mind. He never wants it to reach his mind.

He usually ends up in the Willamette Café, an all-night grill in downtown Eugene. He likes to look at the waitresses in their little brown polka dot uniforms and caps. They are all so cute he can't choose a favourite right off.

One night after studying, the shakes are coming on, so he goes on his evening womble. This time he can't walk them off. He goes to a funny movie, *Carry On* something or other, but it's not funny. So as usual he wanders over to the Willamette Café and his favourite booth. He is still shaking somewhere deep down inside. The shakes will soon rise higher. He orders tea because coffee makes his nerves worse. He begins to stir his tea and notes that his hand is shaking. This means the shakes have come all the way up from his belly to his chest and shoulders and travelled outward to his hands. The next stop will be his neck, then his head. God, but he doesn't want them to reach his head.

One of the girls comes over to his table and asks if she can bring him more hot water for his tea.

No thank you, he says.

Excuse me, she says, but are you all right?

She leans over his table and looks into his face. She wears the kind of grave expression you might receive from someone who knows you well, your sister or even your wife. It's a personal look. *Excuse me, but are you all right?*

He could be anything, an escaped criminal, a psychopath or a sex maniac. But to her he is just someone who looks like he needs help. He walks home thinking about her. Her words return to him like a song he is learning. *Excuse me, but are you all right?*

He tells her thanks, that he is all right.

Later, out on the street, he notices that his shakes are all gone. It's like a miracle. The rain has stopped, the clouds have rolled away, and as he crosses the Willamette Bridge he looks back at the downtown and up at the stars. He hasn't seen the stars for a long time.

And then he sees the cross. It sits on top of Signal Hill, a small mountain that rises like a dark mound above the downtown. The cross is a high thin neon sign. Jarvis Larson has said that you can see it from almost anywhere in Eugene. If it weren't raining you could even see it from Springfield. But he has never seen the cross until this November night when he met the Café Madonna.

That is his name for her. He returns to the Willamette Café several times after that, hoping to see her again.

A week or so passes and the envelope comes. A letter from the head of the English Department tells him that he has passed with a bare minimum B-. He goes straight over to Max's bar to tell someone he'll never have to take that damn course again. No one he knows is there, so he waits and has a few beers. He is sure someone from his year will show up.

Something is wrong in the bar. People look gloomy, as though the weather has finally gone too far. But it's not the weather, because some people are actually crying. That's when he spots the girl in the uniform. It's the same kind of uniform the girls wear at the Willamette Café, a brown skirt and blouse with white polka dots and a little maid's cap to match. Her hair is straight, shoulder length, mousey brown, and her eyes seem very large. He can tell from the redness around the eyes that she has been weeping. He goes over to ask if she's all right.

I guess you haven't heard, she says. About the President.

What about him?

Somebody shot him. He's dead.

You mean Kennedy? Shot him dead?

Where have you been all day?

In the library. I've been acting like a hermit, actually.

She fills him in on the details. It feels as though a wake is in progress. He waits until she has told him everything about the assassination, and then he says, Excuse me, but you don't remember me, do you.

No. Sorry.

They talk until closing time and at last he walks her home.

The first time they did it was at her place. After a conversation in bed, he walked home in the rain. He gave himself a B. The second time they did it, also at her place, he lasted longer and they did it twice, and he walked home again. This time he gave himself a B+ but downgraded his first time to a C-.

The fifth time they did it, she said, If I were married I'd do this every night and every morning and three times on Sunday. He didn't know what to say. He tried to think of a joke.

The seventh time they did it was in a motel room they rented just for the afternoon. He reminded her that he would have to return to

Canada when he graduated and look for a job, and she broke down and cried. She said it never failed.

As soon as I think I've found a nice one, he up and takes off, just like that. Yes, this is what you might call a regular occurrence with me. And some of the guys aren't so nice, either. Some of them are real shits. I've had to put up with some awful things. You'd be surprised.

The sixth time they did it, he confessed that the first time they'd done it, technically speaking, was only his second time.

Do tell, she said.

On the occasion of the fourth time, she was about to put her favourite record on the stereo. It was an LP by Peter, Paul and Mary entitled *Blowin' in the Wind*. He asked her not to put on that record. So instead she put on *Days of Wine and Roses* by Andy Williams. He stayed all night and they did it again in the morning.

The third time they did it, he asked her how she liked it and she said, Fine, you did just fine. He compared notes with Jarvis Larson and he agreed that Tim must be right on track with her.

That sixth time he confessed he'd had so much trouble doing it in the past because he felt he was taking advantage of them like.

Maybe you're just a late bloomer, she said.

I don't know, he said. It always seemed to be a question of right or wrong. Having sex with someone, he said, thinking out loud, it's something you can't go back on. You can never undo it.

What do you mean undo it? she said.

He couldn't explain.

Later that night he thanked her.

She said, Don't go thanking me, don't go talking to me like I was your social worker or something. I'm not your damn social worker.

Oh, shit, he said to himself. Oh, shit shit shit shit shit shit, all the way home.

That first time with her, it was almost spring. Somehow the season was important. After it was over he walked home in the rain toying with the notion that the rains were symbolic of fertility. It was a neat feeling. He'd never had that feeling before.

In the evening of the fifth time (but before they had done it), they went to a play. It was Arthur Miller's *After the Fall*, and the production wasn't so good. Or maybe it was just that the theatre didn't have air conditioning and he was too hot. She kept moving her hand up and down his thigh and clutching his arm and sighing. That might have been all right, except for the heat. All they had to do was touch and their skin went moist. Her apartment was a relief because she had a fan.

I've hurt you, he said that last time, the seventh time, when they were in the motel. I really didn't want to hurt you. I guess I thought this whole thing was going to be fun and I hoped it wouldn't get too serious. When it started to get serious I didn't know what to do. I didn't want to just never see you again but I didn't want to go—

Enough! she cried. She held her fists up by her ears, and her face clenched so that the eyes disappeared. She stayed that way for a very long second or two. Enough! All right? I have heard this song before.

The problem with the Peter, Paul and Mary record being played all the time was that it reminded him of Rita Symington, and that made him feel homesick. It started to get to him, so as nice as he could, he said, I wonder if you'd put on a different record this time. She never put on Peter, Paul and Mary again and they never discussed it.

The second time they did it she had removed her girdle and put on a kimono and they lay on the chesterfield. Now you behave yourself, she said. Keep your hands to home. What do you want anyway? He did an imitation of Boris Karloff. Slipp'ry blisses, he said. I would lurch a mile through the forest for slipp'ry blisses. She roared at that one.

Eventually he gave himself an F for that first time, but he has no unhappy memories from it. He remembers going in and out and in and out, and how pleasant that was, then launching a serpent from away down. He knew he hadn't satisfied *her*, but he couldn't get worked up about it. After lying there a while he said he had an exam the next day and he'd better get on home.

But it's raining, she said.

Her name was Ginny Culp. She was doing a degree in psychology. About a week after he met her in Max's, they had their first date. When he showed up, her roommate told him to go down to Max's bar and Ginny would be there. She was in a booth drinking with some guys. When he tried to talk to her, the guys wouldn't let her out of the booth. It was their joke, to keep her trapped in the booth with them. Finally Tim just walked off. He had gone about a block when she caught up with him. She said she was sorry. She was really embarrassed. She said she always hated it when her friends acted like assholes. He wanted to say, Well, if they act like assholes, why are you friends with them? He didn't see her again until well after the Christmas break.

There were a lot of things he wanted to ask, but he wasn't ready to

hear the answers. She seemed to know about things, forbid
She seemed to know he wasn't ready. She always seemed to
ing before she had gone too far.

Ginny quit her job in the Willamette Café in the summer an
work doing research for a guy in the Psych department. She did int
views and collected data on addiction from a group of people in town.
She knew a lot about drugs and alcohol. She'd heard some real horror
stories.

She just couldn't get her life together enough to finish her B.A. She
kept taking incompletes on her last few courses. She blamed men. She
said (after the sixth time), I admit it. I like men. These days they're on
my mind you might say.

After they'd stopped going to bed, they had coffee now and then.
It wasn't much fun. On one of these occasions he showed her his *Let
Us Arise* poem.

When she had read it she said, I don't know, it's so *innocent*.

What do you mean? What's wrong with that?

Well, she began slowly, it's like anyone who gets married in your
poem is phony, and anyone who likes to take these poetic walks in the
morning is wonderful. It's so *presexual*.

A letter arrived from some college in Ontario. It had gone to Tim's
home in Edmonton and been forwarded by his mother. The sender of
the letter was a Mr. Swan, who was editor of *Neoparnassus*, a poetry
quarterly. Mr. Swan wrote to say that *Let Us Arise* had been accepted
with a few small changes. He apologized for writing so long after Tim
had sent the poem, but that their editorial board had experienced an
upheaval and his manuscript had been left by mistake with one of the
ex-editors. By way of apology, Mr. Swan enclosed a cheque for five
dollars, even though the poem wouldn't actually get into print for another year.

Tim showed this letter to Ginny Culp. Presexual, eh? Tell that to
this guy.

What do you mean?

Well, now what do you think about my poem? He read it to
her again.

Breathe the breath of awe? she mused out loud. I just had this
interview with a guy back from Vietnam who's addicted to morphine.
He says he can't go to sleep unless he's in bed with a prostitute on one
side and his service revolver on the other. I don't know why I'm telling
you all this.

She returned her atttention to the poem. Breathe the breath of awe? I dunno.

But that first time, trudging home afterwards in the rain, the woody smell of the graveyard and all those gardens just coming alive again.

Knowing that he and this wonderful sad woman had broken the manacle around his libido. He could do anything. He could be J.D. Salinger or go to Greece or Paris. He was free.

Free. From what. He doesn't know exactly. He comes from a country where nothing bad ever seems to happen to anyone. Or at least this is true in *his* old neighbourhood. Is there anything in his homeland to be free from? The Queen? The Canadian armed forces? The Mounties? The tyranny of the Liberal Party? No one sends him draft notices like down here. No one has ever tried to shoot him or rob him. There are no despots, hardly any causes worth dying for. No one in his right mind would consider assassinating Prime Minister Pearson; it would mean another Royal Commission on assassinations. And not many people from his part of Edmonton could get real excited about those skirmishes over in Vietnam. In fact, maybe if there was a war in Canada, or in the very least, some race riots and civil rights marches, he'd be better able to find himself. There would be allies and enemies. He would know what it was like to be shot at. He would know things Americans were learning about.

He takes his green spiral notebook out of retirement and writes the following declaration:

March 31, 1964.

> I am free from the tyranny of
> a) my monastic morality
> b) being what all the mothers in my neighbourhood
>   refer to as a nice boy
> c) being just a passive asexual guy
> d) a lurking suspicion that I might be queer
> e) innocuousness
> f) none of the above.

Reverend Mountjoy said once in a sermon that if you can't see tyranny anywhere, look inside. Does this mean I am rakish? Unnice? Sexually promiscuous? Nocuous? All of the above?

He walks upstairs to the cubicles. He is damp all over because he has forgotten his umbrella. Jarvis and Mr. Weatherbum are still up drinking. Who's that? cries Jarvis.

Who?

Who! Jarvis yells.

Uh who who! Tim hoots.

It's that goddam canuck, says Mr. Weatherbum.

No, says Tim, I am the nanaconda.

He keeps coming back to that first night when he walked home from Ginny Culp's. There had been a light rain. Somehow, that was important. He walked through the alleys smelling the trees and the ripening gardens as light on his feet as he could ever remember, thinking *I did it. I am free. I have come back from the dead.* He didn't exactly feel like he'd become a man; it wasn't like that. But it did feel as though he were no longer that good little Fisher boy. He was no longer what Rita Symington would have called an angel. And the heavens seemed to open in response. There was no hint of that sulphurous belch from the Weyerhauser plant in Springfield, no evidence at all of burning from the sawdust mills. Only the scent of wet ferns and rotting greenery from the gardens and a soft wind up from the ocean blowing down a spray on the back of his neck.

He phoned Gump long distance around one-thirty in the morning. Gump sounded grumpy at first. He said he had to get up for work in the morning. Work? What's that? Gumper, tonight at this gal's apartment. You guessed it. She took me all the way to the Promised Land.

The following Christmas he returns to Edmonton. He has made it to the end of his last semester but he's broke. He takes a job at a slum school subbing for a woman who teaches English as a second language to new Canadians. In his spare time he tries to return to his green spiral notebook, but there doesn't seem to be anything to write about. He tries to study for his comprehensive, but day after day he finds his mind is wandering off the page.

He and Gump share a cheap and cramped little apartment with only one bedroom. Gump is a cheerful roommate, which is especially good, because Tim is often in need of cheering up. He doesn't know why. He almost has his M.A., only one trip left to go for the big comprehensive; he has his freedom; he is now managing to pay his bills; he will never have to stay with his parents again. But his depressions move in on him capriciously and stay like the Oregon rains.

He tries to locate Rita Symington, but according to her mother, she is always relocating somewhere with her new group. He tries to find Janey Bream, but she has moved. He phones up an acquaintance of Nancy Fuller and hears she has returned to Edmonton and that she is once more going with Alistair Vaughan, but her number isn't in the book and he doesn't feel like phoning up her parents or Alistair.

He misses Ginny Culp. He doesn't miss the rain all winter long or the sodden walks through the graveyard each night coming home from the library. He doesn't miss the marathon studying, but he misses Ginny. The talks they had, the sex. He even misses her bitterness, her occasional sarcasm. 1965 is going to be a trial.

What's she up to now? Gump asks.

He imagines her alone in her apartment, in a state of disarray, listening to Peter, Paul and Mary. Or lonely in a crowd at Max's, surrounded by her asshole boyfriends. Or up in the psych department compiling data on addiction. Love's addict. *I've had to put up with some awful things. You'd be surprised.*

I don't know, he tells Gump. I wasn't really in love with her.

That's the way the cookie crumbles.

Gump is having a last smoke before he turns in. He lies on his bed in the dark, and all Tim can see of him is the big orange nose whenever Gump takes a drag from his cigarette. It is late but they aren't sleepy.

I really took advantage of her, Gump. I really hurt her. I mean, it only hits me now how much I let her down. Either I love them too little or I love them too much. I can never get it just right.

Alistair Vaughan, says Gump. There's a guy who gets what he wants. I never see him when he's not arm in arm with some real knockout.

I thought he was going with Nancy Fuller again.

No kidding.

I can't figure it, says Tim. They never like me when I'm Mister Nice Guy. But just occasionally, when I become the rake, you know?

Yeah.

You know? They can't get enough of me. I mean, why is it the loveliest women get the hots for a prick like Alistair? It can't be just his fucking fallen forelock. I mean, Gump... *they love a guy if he can be a sonofabitch.* That's the only way to fly.

Maybe. I try not to think about it, says Gump.

The last time Tim and Ginny did it, he waited till they were finished and then he reminded her about his plans to return to Canada. It was probably a mistake. But is there ever a good time to tell them? She seemed to fall apart right there before him. It might take her some time to recover, he suspects. He has never done that before and he never wants to do it again. What he wonders is....

He turns in the direction of Gump's glowing cigarette.

If you treat them nice, they tell you you're an angel and go off with some playboy. If you treat them with indifference, they cling to your leg like a bandaid wherever you go. So can't there be a happy medium? I mean, does there always have to be a casualty?

Try not to think about it, Fishy. You think too much.

Tim watches the cigarette come up to Gump's mouth, glow briefly with the intake of Gump's breath, then float like a firefly over to the bedside chair where the ash tray sits and everything goes dark.

It's an apple you can't unbite.

Come again?

Love. Sex. Affairs of the heart, whatever. Once you've tasted it, you can't ever pretend you're...you know...innocent.

Like I say, Gump yawns, and blows out into the darkness the last of his smoke.

Gump often declares that life is one damn thing after another. Tim has been entertaining the proposition that life is one exam after another, and that even when he's shuffled off his mortal Buffalo, it will never end. He will approach St. Peter at the gate, or maybe Reverend Mountjoy, and Tim will say, May I come in now? I worked hard all my life, and I obeyed the law, and I was good to my parents.

Well, Mr. Fisher, entrance is no longer automatic for the righteous. We are now a degree-granting institution. You will have to pass an entrance exam on the morality of trout fishing. I hope you don't mind using a quill and ink pot. We're a little behind the times up here.

The Oregon rains are out to greet him, and all week long, as he crams for the big comprehensive, he remains in a state of stalwart gloom. Jarvis Larsen has arranged things at the rooming house so that Tim can sleep in the cubicle rented out to the ex-con who reads muscle-man comic books. The man has recently disappeared. Each day Jarvis goes out to work apparently secure in the belief that Tim spends his day ogling co-eds on campus.

His routine is to study until he is ready to scream, then he picks up his banjo and frails some of the old Rita Symington songs. The frailing cheers him up somewhat. It almost brings Rita into the room with him. He will have to find her some day and thank her for these sessions with the 5-string. He plays with a mute stuck on the bridge of the resonator so that no one else in the house will hear.

The exam is a gruelling affair. For three hours he goes glib and learned, rolls like a dog in critical clichés, compares and contrasts text after text with an enthusiasm so entirely bogus that by the end of the three hours he wonders what has become of Tim Fisher. (*In a discussion of Henry James's The Ambassadors, it is perhaps not inappropriate to suggest at the outset that...*). He walks out into the rain, turning down the offer of a ride home, so that he might reaffirm his unbelief.

Jarvis Larsen is waiting. He is nervous.

Timmy, I've got a little scheme I'm cooking up here. And I could use your help. I hope you won't mind, but me and my woman, we'd really like to have a bit of quiet time, and—

Quiet time?

Up here like. In there, Timmy. Sack time?

Oh, that! You always used to go to Sharon's place.

Can't. Not this time.

How come?

Ah, it isn't Sharon. We've had a pahtin of the ways.

Oh. But what if Old Man Vickers sees you coming in?

We got that worked out. We're coming up the fire escape.

But those old stairs, I seem to recall they're real noisy.

Well, Timmy my friend, that's where you come in.

Jarvis breaks into a nervous grin. He is full of strategy. He stumps up and down the kitchen floor with an exaggerated limp, whispering.

I see you brought your banjo down here. Can you play that thing any louder? Good. Well, just about nine o'clock on the dot, me and this new gal, we are goin to hit those stairs.

How'll I know you're there?

I'll flash my headlights out back. Besides, if you're listenin, you'll hear my truck. You'll know.

And when I see you out back, you want me to do some serious picking, is that the deal?

That's the deal, Timmy. You game?

Anything for love, he says.

After all, for nearly a week now he's been sleeping in the rooming house free of charge thanks to Jarvis's intercession with the Vickers. He owes Jarvis every chance at a night of passion with this new woman in his life, even if he has to listen to it from the next cubicle.

By nine o'clock, he is ready. The mute is off, capo off, the banjo tuned. He will play something in G, because everything on a 5-string seems louder in G. He will make the old house vibrate. Old Vickers won't mind, surely. His wife might be a bit less tolerant, but she wouldn't be likely to do anything about it. Vickers's wife's name is Dorthy, apparently with only one 'o'. They rarely speak with the men upstairs, but they have always been clear on the woman question. They were kind enough to allow Tim to sleep in the abandoned cubicle for the week of his comprehensive exam, but one whisper of a woman in the upstairs rooming section and the wrath of God will surely descend. Mrs. Vickers especially has a four-square look about her that brooks no arguments on the subject of carnal bliss.

The flash of headlights comes at nine on the nose. A quick peek out the kitchen window confirms it: Jarvis and his woman are heading for the fire escape stairs just below the kitchen.

Tim seats himself on the kitchen stool and lays into a breakdown. The banjo responds; it is amazingly loud. But perhaps not loud enough. So Tim sings along.

He relaxes into it, the way he's always done, the way Rita taught him. In spite of Rita's absence, he finds himself in the midst of an improbably jolly narrative. *Ah've got a gal an she loves me, she's as sweet as she can be. She's got eyes of baby blue. Makes ma gun shoot straight an true.* He frails away in a driving rhythm so loud and exuberant, it's hard to believe that Rita is not right there in the kitchen singing along. It's hard to believe that it's raining outside.

He looks up. Pouring, actually. Heavy driving rain lashes at the kitchen window. The first tropical-style deluge he's seen in Oregon in almost a year.

> *Goin down to Cripple Creek*
> *Goin in a run*
> *Goin down to Cripple Creek*
> *To have some fun.*

He times it so that the very second Jarvis and his woman come in the door, he will be doing his banjo solo. The pickin an grinnin frenzy will be upon them all. They will have no choice but to applaud.

Goin down to Cripple Creek
Goin in a whirl
Goin down to Cripple Creek
To see my girl.

Behind him, there is a noise. He stops playing, turns around, and Old Mr. Vickers walks through the kitchen door. He has a look of absolute delight on his face.

Is that a banjo? he says.

Well, actually—

I haven't heard no one play a banjo like that since we was back in Thayer.

Oh, well, yeah. It's just—

Play, Timmy. You play something. Play what you was playin when I broke in on you. I hope you don't mind.

He is touched by the old man's sincerity. The old man has ceased to be Old Biblebelt and become simply Mr. Vickers. He has come alone, which might mean that his wife is less approving of music than Mr. Vickers.

There is a prolonged creak on the fire escape stairs, but for all Mr. Vickers can tell, it might have been caused by the storm outside. Perhaps, if he plays loud enough, Jarvis and his woman will be able to beat a strategic retreat down the old stairway and into Jarvis's pickup.

He plays "Old Joe Clark."

Mr. Vickers grins with wonder. He claps.

Tim plays "Shady Grove."

Mr. Vickers has lost twenty years on his face. He looks like Father Time on a coffee break. He stomps his boots on the kitchen floor. He slaps his thigh to the rhythm of the banjo.

Tim plays "Ol Dan Tucker."

There is a polite knock on the kitchen door. Mrs. Vickers creeps cautiously inside. Her face is suffused with girlish glee.

Oh, Timmy, don't mind me. You jiss keep on playin.

Tim plays "Pore Ground Hog."

Mr. Vickers is still fascinated. He looks at the resonator of the banjo as though it contained the gift of prophecy. But Mrs. Vickers is simply enchanted. She has become entranced; perhaps she is reliving moments from her Missouri girlhood. She has become utterly human without a trace of the bigotry Tim had often ascribed to her.

He plays a particularly long version of "Sourwood Mountain."

Oh, Timmy, that was so nice, croons Mrs. Vickers. Would you play that one again?

Mr. Vickers gets out a couple of spoons from the cutlery drawer. That's a fine idea, he says.

Tim plays it again.

You better get packed up an outa here real fast.

Mr. Weatherbum the meat salesman is standing at the foot of his bunk.

Am I in your room? Did I get into the wrong bed?

No, says Weatherbum. But he's comin right back. I think he might want to drill you.

Who's coming back? The comic book guy?

No, Jarvis. Jarvis Larsen. Didn't you hear him?

I've been sound asleep.

When I came in from the bar he was blue in the face. His gal was halfway froze to death. And he has a temper. You probably don't know that. But he has one hell of a temper.

Oh, my God.

He was pissed at you. If I was you, Bub, I'd pack up and hit the road. I wouldn't wait till morning.

Oh, Jarvis wouldn't do anything. He's just, he was just a little—

Well, like I say, Tim, he was blue in the face. He was pissed at you. He had to take his gal home, but he's comin back. And he's got some short fuse on him, Bub. I was you, I'd head on down the road. I'd haul ass. I wouldn't wait till morning.

Mr. Weatherbum takes his sad countenance out of the cubicle and heads for the bathroom. Tim falls back on the bunk. He begins to formulate a plan of escape. It involves a quick trip to the bathroom, but Mr. Weatherbum is in the bathroom. Well, anyway, after he goes to the bathroom, Tim's plan involves a quick descent down the stairs. This time Jarvis will use the front stairs, so in order to avoid running into Jarvis, Tim will use the fire escape. Yes. He will have all his things in the duffel, except for the banjo, of course. His plan involves a bit of stealth, but first he has to have a pee. Then he'll just...his plan involves a horse, a fast horse that will know the neighbourhood and knows where the bus depot is because it's still storming outside. The horse will be brown. He will jump on its brown back and ride on out of there. On the back. The back of the brown horse....

Something goes *click*. At first he thinks that it's the lock on the bathroom door, but it's not that.

The wind is blowing hard outside and the rain is falling. Probably not so bad now.

Something metallic. *Click click click*, it goes like clockwork. This is a sound from the movies. This is a familiar sound. In one swift motion he is out of bed and has his pants on. His shirt on. His sweater and his shoes. His watch.

Jarvis Larsen comes in gun first, like a movie bandit, pulls the cord and turns on the light. The gun is bright silver and the barrel is very long.

Give me one good reason I shouldn't blow your brains out.

I'm your friend, Tim cries.

He's your friend! cries Mr. Weatherbum.

He is still in the bathroom. He has locked himself in there.

He *was* my friend.

He's still your friend, Jarvis. He's a good fellow.

What kind of *friend*, Larsen snarls, would leave me out in a rainstahm to freeze off my ass? What kind of a friend is that? Is that your idear of a friend, Garnet?

Jarvis, don't—

Let the *bahstid* answer the question.

He forgot, cries Mr. Weatherbum. He's human, he forgot.

I didn't forget, Jarvis, I just figured you'd go back to the truck when Old Man Vickers came upstairs, that's all.

We couldn't, you stupid little *faht*, because old man Vickahs would've for sure heard us. Them stairs? You already forget about them rickety stairs? You people want me to get kicked outa here, is that it? It won't be the first time some bunch of individuals tried to get me kicked outa some place. So I think I'll just blow your head off and don't think I'm afraid to. I always finish what I start.

We don't want you to get kicked out, Jarvis. We're your friends, cried Mr. Weatherbum. Because of the bathtub, his voice sounds like a man with an echo chamber. We love you, Jarvis, he cries.

Let the *bahstid* answer the question.

I'm sorry, Jarvis, cries Tim, but the Vickers kept after me. They wouldn't let me go. I had to keep on playing.

You were real popular tonight, is that it? Puttin on a real show?

What does Fisher know about how you do things? cries Mr. Weatherbum. He's from up in Canada. He's a good fella. But he's from Canada, that's his basic problem.

I've had enough of this bullshit, someone else bellows.

It's the ex-boxer fellow from the navy.

He walks over and leans against the doorway to the cubicle. Tim can't even remember his name. Jarvis turns to face the man but keeps his revolver trained exactly on Tim's belly. It's uncanny how he can turn and look at the ex-boxer and keep the revolver on Tim's belly.

I gotta get up at six in the morning, the fellow says.

Big deal, says Jarvis. I got goddam pneumonia and I'm gonna blow this little faht's head off and you gotta get up at six in the morning?

What did you say to me? says the fellow. What did you say?

I said big deal. I'm gonna blow—

Who do you think you're talkin to?

Wally, says Jarvis, this has nothin whatever to do with you. Now you just go on back to bed and I'll finish up with this. I always finish what I start.

Don't do it, Jarvis! cries Mr. Weatherbum. We all love you!

Oh, for the love of God, cries Jarvis Larson, lowers his revolver, and fires. Twice. Into the floor.

Oh, for Pete's sake, cries Mr. Weatherbum. Jarvis, why? Why? Your whole life in front of you.

That was a stupid fuck of a thing to do, says Wally.

Who are you sayin that was a stupid thing?

I am tellin you, Larsen, that was the dumbest fuckin thing I ever seen. You coulda plugged old man Vickers. You coulda plugged his goddam wife.

That's ridiculous, they're in the back. I'd have to aim over there.

Over there! cries Wally. Over where?

Oh, sweet Jesus! echoes the voice of Mr. Weatherbum.

Here, right here, says Jarvis. He walks out into the kitchen. Tim and Wally follow him. He aims his revolver at the floor a few inches from the stove.

You're crazy, says Wally. Their bedroom is right under there. Right where Bonehead useta read his comic books. It has to be. It's on the east side.

Jarvis walks past Tim into the bedroom he was using. He points his pistol at one of the holes he has made in the floor. He smiles triumphantly. Now I *know* you're crazy, Wally. Because this is directly above the living room. It has to be! It's on the east side!

Their bedroom is on the east side.

Mr. Weatherbum yells from the bathroom, I'm afraid you're both a bit off on that one, boys. The Vickers's bedroom is right snug up against the southeast corner of the house. Remember that little window by the trellis?

Oh, by Jesus, Garnet, I take it back. You're right, Jarvis just shot the living room.

Jarvis laughs.

That's okay, Wally. I'm just sorry I had to wake you up. This shit-for-brains canuck got my dander up.

Oh, don't let it worry you none.

Garnet! cries Jarvis. Garnet! Come outa there! I gotta use the can.

I'm positive, cries Mr. Weatherbum. It's right snug in the southeast corner.

Will you get the hell outa the can, Garnet? I promise not to shoot you. It's five o'clock in the mahnin. Now can I please get in there before I piss my pants?

Tim also has to pee, but it can't wait, so he creeps downstairs, outside the front door, and around the side of the house. By the trellis he eases his bladder. He is still shaking so badly that his stream goes all over the place.

He hears a voice from inside the house. He looks up at the window in front of him. Because of the gloom outside and because a light is on in the house, he can see inside without being seen. Mr. Vickers is in his pyjamas with a phone in his hand.

I said, I would like to report a disturbance. Oh, I am so sorry. I must of misdialled. Dorthy she has better eyesight than I do but she is down on the floor prayin. So sorry to git you out of bed. Say that again? Is that the police number or your number? I see. I thank you sir, you are very kind. Good night to you.

Mr. Vickers turns away from the window. Dorthy, I do wish you would come over here and just dial this old dial. I'll do the talkin.

THE FALL OF 1965 HAS BEEN MONUMENTALLY GLOOMY. It's either because of the weather or because of Tim's return to graduate school, this time to snag a Ph. D. Or else maybe it's a mood that Tim can't seem to shake. Each day he walks the sidewalks of Edmonton through blasts of sodden wind, gleaning a desolate comfort that Nature is responsive to his gloom. Today his refuge from the weather is Hurtig's bookstore on Jasper.

He is barely inside the door when he sees her browsing among the travel books. He hides from view behind a special display of James Bond paperbacks. For a second her name is lost on its way up. She has an insomniac pallor about her. He follows her unseen up to the till. The clerk is asking her something.

The rain streams down the store window in a wash of grey light turning Jasper Avenue into a mural of suggestive smudges. The rain again. Again, the girl's haunted face. A flood of rainy memory prickles his adenoids and he is the boy knight errant with a song about to be born. The problem, as usual, is the tune, which still sounds like *God Rest Ye Merry, Gentlemen*.

I can't even find my driver's license, she says.

Just a sec, says the clerk.

She turns and gives Tim a blank look. Sorry, she says, without recognizing him. It must be his newly sprouted beard and moustache. She roots about in her handbag.

At last he says, Your name is Nancy Fuller. I will vouch for you.

She turns again. Timmy! she cries. Timmy Fisher! She gazes at him. Her hair is askew.

The little café they go to is steamy with the smell of raincoats and downtown bodies. Nancy pours the tea. She does this skillfully, like her mother at a sorority luncheon. Her voice has slowed down; it is drifting and aimless. The weather is in her voice.

So. Are you a famous poet yet?

Retired, he says.

Edmonton is so boring, she says, for the second time.

It was ever thus.

Was it? she says, apparently to herself. So. Here we are, both back in town.

Never more to roam.

Mom said—when was it, this year some time—they wanted to draft you. How tedious.

That was in 1964. The last I heard about you, you were either going around with Alistair or not going around with Alistair.

That sounds about right.

He squints up from his teacup. Her hairdo has fallen and she tosses her bangs out of her eyes to sip her tea. She does this carelessly, as though today, in all this rain, the rules of vanity have been suspended.

But a bit out of date.

You mean....

She lowers her gaze into her teacup. Must have been a couple of months ago, she says, he wrote me the big letter. He didn't have the courage just to phone me up.

Sorry. I hadn't heard.

She shrugs in reply.

Alistair has certain problems. Certain hangups let's just say. And he now has this big...life's plan, and I am not part of it. So...she yawns again, shakes her head. She looks at Tim as though she has forgotten something, then perks up. Know what he used to do in restaurants? she says. This big Hunkus athleticus?

Nancy perches primly in her seat.

First he sits down. Then he rearranges his cutlery. Like this, see? Knife here, fork here. Spoons just so, just like Mummy does. Everything has to be...sort of...squared off. He adjusts his water glass like if he didn't, he would lose marks for deportment. Then he arranges his nappy just right. Then he picks up his menu and he says, Hmm, hmm. He's so earnest and prissy. He's a worse priss than Benny sometimes.

Your voice sounds funny, says Tim.

Valium, says Nancy. It's the new answer to everything. I must have valium voice.

She returns to the subject of Alistair, speaking in a monotone. Nancy is still the same shape, and with a touch here and there, she would again be pretty. Right now she is not pretty.

Two years ago Alistair and I flew to Montreal to see Arthur Locke. I got a job in one of his galleries. Did you know that's where I was back then?

I'd heard you were travelling or something.

Well, see, that wasn't the whole story, Nancy says, leaning forward, yawning again, her eyes half closed, her voice low and plodding. I got pregs actually and I had a kid.

Oh, my God.

Nancy chirps like a joyless child: And-*then* I-*gave* it-*up*. She waits for Tim to say something. He fiddles with his spoon.

So, everything is just ticketyboo, as Benny might say. Everything is just neat as a pin. The kid got a home, Alistair has decided to piss off, and I'm as free as a bird.

Tim buries his nose in his tea cup.

Do you mind me telling you these things? says Nancy.

No. No. Of course not.

She looks at him for an uncomfortably long second or two.

You don't get it, do you Timmy.

Get what? What don't I get.

Oh, nothing.

What don't I get?

Nancy brushes her hand over the conversation and sweeps it aside. She does the refills.

I bought Benny this copy of *Europe on Five Dollars a Day* for his birthday. Isn't that a riot? He won't set foot on a boat or a plane. And he thinks all foreign food is diseased. When he goes on a trip he takes his own food. I think Mum should have given Benny away at birth. You know what? They never tell you who gets your kid. It's wavewave byebye to Mummy. Probably I should have had an abortion. Or maybe I should have kept the kid.

I'm sorry, Nancy.

With shaking hands Nancy lights a cigarette.

You know what it's like? You want to know what it's like sometimes? I have this dream. There's a little boy...little toddler. Nancy positions her hand a couple of feet above the floor. He's walking down a lane, like the alley in our old neighbourhood? It's...Christmas maybe, there's snow and wind, and he's lost. He can't find his way home, he can't get warm, and he's calling for Mummy. In the dream, of course, I am his mummy.

Nancy puts down her teacup. She looks reprovingly at her shaking hands. Apparently they have betrayed her.

Nancy and Tim walk outside in the rain. Nancy has forgotten where she parked her car. They circle the entire block on foot before she spots it. They stand in the rain beside her car. She is shaking all over now.

Nancy says, Timmy, give us a little hug.

He hesitates.

Wait, she says. Get some body warmth into this. She struggles with the belt on her raincoat. Right out in front of Hurtig's Bookstore they have their hug. They hold each other for a long time. At first her body trembles uncontrollably, but then something happens: a current seems to pass from her to him. She sighs. This is not a lover's sigh. This is not a sigh you could associate with romance. A current passes from Nancy to Tim, and Nancy releases him. She looks at him strangely, as though something has happened and then averts her eyes.

Thanks, she whispers. That felt pretty good.

She belts up her coat without fumbling, smiles an old smile, ironic but with a touch of repose. She has a pretty face now and her rainfallen hair almost becomes her.

Can I call you? she says.

Of course. Yes. Of course you can.

Nancy looks as though she will sleep tonight without sleeping pills or valium. She circles her car in the rain. She turns to look at Tim, who stands stunned in front of Hurtig's. She smiles and turns away. Something has lodged in Tim's midsection. It will soon begin to rise like a kind of nerve gas of the soul. He knows this because his hands are shaking. And this time there is no Café Madonna.

WHAT IS A POET? HE READS. *An unhappy man who in his heart harbours a deep anguish, but whose lips are so fashioned that the moans and cries which pass over them are transformed into ravishing music.*

He stares at the wall, the dent in the plaster. He listens to the moans of the wind rattling his only window and reads on.

His fate is like that of the unfortunate victims whom the tyrant Phalaris imprisoned in a brazen bull, and slowly tortured over a steady fire; their cries could not reach the tyrant's ears so as to strike terror into his heart; when they reached his ears they sounded like sweet music.

He lowers his book and stares once more at the dent in the plaster. It was not this book, but Artaud's *The Theatre and its Double* he had hurled at the wall the week before. It struck so hard it dislodged his framed photo of Gump, Tim, fish, and friends.

What's gotten into you? Gump wanted to know.

Gump should at least be forced to read Kierkegaard. All roommates of guys with artistic temperaments should be forced to read Kierkegaard as part of their training.

I don't know, Gump. What do you think has gotten into me?

Nancy Fuller phoned again. She wanted to know why you haven't returned her calls

Shit.

Gump peered at him down his long nose, honestly baffled.

Jeez, Fishy, who are you waiting for, Elizabeth Taylor?

I don't know what I want. I hate grad school. I'm sorry I came back this fall. I hate the thought of getting another part-time teaching job. And every time I think of going out with Nancy Fuller, I get this feeling of dread.

Dread? Fishy, she's got the hots for you. Tell her *I'll* take her out.

Nah.

Why not?

I want to have my cake and not eat it too.

Gump didn't laugh.

And men crowd about the poet and say to him, "Sing for us soon again"
—which is as much as to say, "May new sufferings torment your soul, but
may your lips be fashioned as before; for the cries would only distress us, but
the music, the music, is delightful."

Right on, Soren.

He rises from his bed and stands in the middle of the room holding the book open, tapping the pages. He is twitchy and buzzing with nervous energy. The night before, he was too tormented to sleep. Sometimes the words burn themselves line by line into his brain and come out the next week in arguments with brother Derek and his friends. Derek has returned to Edmonton to get a law degree. He and the other guys in law have begun to avoid Tim, so Tim drinks his coffee on the alien side of the cafeteria, perilously close to the long overcoats, the ban-the-bomb buttons, the draft dodgers, and Techla Wahrsager.

And the critics come forward and say, "That is perfectly done—just as
it should be, according to the rules of aesthetics." Now it is understood that a
critic resembles a poet to a hair; he only lacks the anguish in his heart and
the music upon his lips. I tell you, I would rather be a swineherd, under-
stood by the swine, than a poet misunderstood by men....

He should jot down these three sentences on a Hallmark card and drop them on Techla Wahrsager's table at coffee. He could send them as a Valentine but it's only November.

He is half-amused, half-alarmed at the thought of this caper. What the hell is happening to me, he wonders day after day.

In the dark they look like clowns, doing a boozy burlesque along the sidewalk: a big one, a little one, a medium-sized one. Their gestures are exaggerated. The big one moves with elaborate attempts to stay on his feet, willing his motion straight ahead, but lurching from side to side. The other two follow the big one, then stop to yell at one another. The big one swings at the next biggest, catching him flush on the face. Down he goes. Now the big one and the little one stand, gesticulating over the fallen man.

A silent movie. The windows of Tim's Beetle are closed to the sound of their voices. His is the only vehicle stopped at the light on

124th and 102nd, an intersection at the east end of his neighbourhood. The three are not clowns, of course, but drunks, the smallest one a woman. She has become the prize. The big one wades toward her and she runs out onto the street. Tim accelerates through the red light. The woman lunges in front of Tim's car and he drives ahead slowly to remain between the drunken man and his prey. Tim opens the passenger side window all the way down. The woman grabs on and clings like some kind of shellfish to the door of the car.

Gun it! she croaks.

The big man puffs in pursuit down the middle of the street, but the Volkswagen with its new attachment outdistances him. The man stops in the middle of the road and shakes his fist.

Stop, for fucksakes! cries the woman.

A block or two away from the big drunk, Tim stops his car. He walks over to the passenger side where she hangs onto the door by one arm, her legs dragging on the road. He helps the woman to her feet. It is two fifteen in the morning and cold.

The woman is dark and dumpy. In the feeble rays of the street lights she could be any age. She stinks of something imbibed, perhaps of several things. Loud enough to be heard blocks away, she curses in a shrill nasal voice. At first he thinks that she is cursing her assailant, then perhaps the man whom he so easily knocked down, then perhaps himself. But the curse is a general sort of utterance, aimed more or less at the genteel shops and apartments lining 124th Street.

Can I give you a lift?

A what?

Can I drop you somewhere? In my car?

In that little christer? A krautwagon? Less go downtown.

Downtown?

I do my bezniss downtown.

He tries to explain. Get in, he says, before that guy catches up to us.

Are you a cop? she says.

No.

Well, what in the fuck's yer angle? I always put my cards on the table, you get my drift? I don't piss around. You wanna go downtown or what?

He climbs into his car and drives away. She remains beneath the street light, swaying and shrieking. His hands shake at the wheel.

Beginning with the clownlike apparitions on the sidewalk, he plays the scene over in his mind, again and again. And he isn't really playing the scene; he's merely allowing the scene to run its course. He tries to

write it funny in his green spiral notebook. He tries to give
the dumpy woman. He never saw her clearly, so he tries all kin
is a gypsy, perhaps, or an Indian woman from a northern reserv
a woman with a tragic past. Or a fiery Calabrian peasant w   ₃
someone's cleaning woman Out There on Wellington Crescent. In all
these attempts he falters, but the film-clip will not stop playing. In
spite of his efforts, it refuses to become television. Who would play
the woman in a Hollywood movie? Who would bother rescuing her?
The scene becomes his microcosm of the world.

He tells this to Nancy. She is not particularly impressed with his story
about the three drunks or with his new-found despair for humanity.

Some day, Timmy, you might discover that I have a few stories
myself.

She is dressed to kill. She wears a black maxi coat, open, over a
hip-riding miniskirt and high leather boots. Her cheeks have regained
their colour and her light brown hair, grown longer now, whips around
in the early November wind. Perhaps she has begun to recover from
breaking up with Alistair and the thing with the baby. She has cer-
tainly begun to turn heads again. Nancy and Tim walk all the way
down to the Rice Street Farmer's Market and the men watch her swift
nervous gestures as she sweeps by. He should feel lucky.

She wants to know why he hasn't returned her calls.

I haven't called you because I've been in a funny mood.

Does it have anything to do with me?

No, nothing.

I thought we had something, Timmy. I thought we could do things
together.

We could, he says, but not now. I'm in this funny mood. I can't do
my grad work any more. I can't write. I don't sleep very well. Gump
tells me I'm getting moody. He's right. I think I might move out and
get a place by myself. I might even drop out of grad school.

Why don't you just finish your year and then decide?

I can't decide anything. Half the time I'm too depressed. I'm kind
of messed up.

She looks piercingly at him. She is once more a fine looking woman,
he can see that, but her good looks have no effect on him. He is afraid
of her, afraid of her turbulence. At the tiniest cue she might get back
into her routine: how much she hates Alistair, how much she misses
her baby. She has developed a cackle like a Disney witch. He fears this

new laugh. He is afraid she will go into the details of her latest solution, a therapist recommended to her by Barb Viner, her roommate. She will probably suggest that *he* try out the same shrink. If you have to see a shrink, then there really *is* something wrong with you. He is afraid she will make him think even more clearly about himself, and any kind of introspection these days is unbearable. He is afraid most of all that she has begun to care for him.

I've got this seminar paper due next week, he tells her. A thing on Joyce's *Portrait*. I've read the book but I can't seem to get down to work. I should be working right now, but I can't seem to open the novel. I haven't opened a book all week.

I've got an idea, she says. Let's both of us go out to the lake. We can stay at our cottage. Mom and Dad are in Maui. You can work on your Joyce thing and I'll bring some books along. It'll be real quiet. No one goes up to the lake this time of year.

I don't know, he says.

She sighs. I *know* you don't know, but I *do*. Let's leave this one up to me, okay?

He looks away from Nancy. She has shifted back into her bossy mode. This time he will not give in.

Once upon a time and a very good time it was there was a moocow coming down along the road and this moocow that was down along the road met a nicens little boy named baby tuckoo....

He steals a glance at Nancy who is curled up on the chesterfield by the fire. Nancy hasn't lost her determined edge. She is determined that Tim will finish his reading and write his paper well within the time limits. She is determined that they will have a lovely weekend. Even the weather is conspiring to cheer Tim up. A chinook has been blowing all morning like a reprieve. The lake is still unfrozen. The sun is up late, but while it is up, the day is almost warm. Wind jostles the ragged branches of the trees around the cabin. Clack and scratch of rutting skeletons.

His father told him that story: his father looked at him through a glass. He had a hairy face.

He was baby tuckoo. The moocow came down the road where Betty Byrne lived: she sold lemon platt.

Nancy sits in front of the big picture window and points at the valley, which rises at the far end of the lake, perfectly, like a picture in a tourist brochure. Ain't nature grand, she says. She is silent for a moment and looks up. I'm distracting you.

He reads more of the first chapter. He doesn't underst
Roddy Kickham has greaves in his number. What are greave
number? He begins to panic. Hamilton Rowan had thrown $
hat on the haha.

What's a haha? He has never known. Why has it never bothered
him until now? Why doesn't Stephen Dedalus go fishing or play with
a six-gun? What kid would go out to play without a six-gun? What is
a seasoned hacking chestnut, conqueror of forty? Is it a nut or a horse?
He reads on. It doesn't seem to have much of a plot. When he read it
five or six years ago, he was sure it had a plot. He'd read the whole
Portrait in a state of prolonged worship. What has happened to his
worshipful ways? Is he beyond salvation in any possible sense of the
word? *Salvation.* It used to be such a boring word.

He looks across the living room at Nancy. A slash of sun has caught
her long hair, a wonderful sheen of dark and pale gold. Her hair is
almost the same colour as the varnished logs in the living room. She
belongs in this living room and will always belong here, a perpetual ad
for gracious living. Why is her beauty incapable of reaching him?

He feels stupefied, as though he is being sucked into some sort of
motion. He shakes his head.

He reaches the end of the chapter and a funny thing happens: he
can't remember what he has just read. He looks at Nancy, asleep now
on the chesterfield. At his suggestion, they have slept in separate beds.
She has complied with this as though it were her suggestion too. Perhaps she has slept badly.

He begins the first chapter again. *Once upon a time and a very good
time it was there was a moocow coming down along the road and this
moocow that was down along the road met a nicens little boy named baby
tuckoo....*

He reads two pages and looks up. He *still* can't remember what he
has read. This is ridiculous. He doesn't have all year; he has only five
days. No one gives a late paper. If you're late the seminar will have to
be cancelled. His seminar is filled with budding geniuses. The in-
structor is a friend of Mahler's, an expatriate Californian with thin-
ning faded blond hair who looks like an aging disc jockey. He swears
by Antonin Artaud and speaks in a compelling voice about the plague
that humanity has become. *An actor's training is not complete until he
has mastered the scream. Ah, yes, the scream.* His grad students all smoke
dope in the basement of the Arts Building. They are mostly budding
revolutionaries. Tim can't figure them out. When he hears them talk

about what they call *straight guys*, he knows they are talking about guys like himself. Tim mentioned to one of these fellows that he liked a certain tale by Conrad and the fellow said that Conrad was a mind fuck. He thinks that is a bad thing, but he's not sure.

Once upon a time and a very good time it was there was a moocow coming down along the down along the yamazon along the and this canoocow that paddo paddo paddo down along the road met a nicens little met a nicens little boy named

Timmy?

He looks up from his book. Nancy is yawning.

Have you reached that part where Stephen hears the sermon?

I haven't the slightest idea.

She frowns at him.

Do you mean that?

Mean what? Yes. No. I don't know.

Nancy makes a lunch for both of them, but Tim can't eat it. He can't generate any saliva. She brings out one of her dad's spinning rods, but he has no desire to go fishing. So Nancy drives them all the way home. She says she doesn't trust Tim driving his own car. He'd forget which road he was on. She is probably right.

Nancy has driven for some time in silence before Tim notices that the sky is dark. She stops at a drive-in somewhere west of Edmonton.

If we got some fried chicken, do you think you could eat it?

Yes, he says.

She comes out with a bucket, and the deep-fried smell fills the Volkswagen.

I got some corn fritters too, she says. Eat up.

What do I owe you?

Just eat up.

He picks out a drumstick and tears off a hunk. The meat becomes a fibrous wad in his mouth. He can't swallow.

What's the matter? she says.

I really thought I was hungry.

Nancy looks straight ahead, pushing hard on the wheel, and sighs.

What are we going to do with you?

They arrive in the dark back in Edmonton and she drives to her apartment. In a listless voice she says, Can you get yourself home all right?

Can I come up?

She shrugs.

She has a big flat in an old mansion on Villa Avenue. They walk up the stairs and Nancy lets him in. He stands with their knapsacks in the dark hallway until she turns on a lamp beside a large sofa. For a moment they sit on the sofa. I have to tell you, he says, I think I'm in trouble.

You mean with that term paper?

Well, yes. I guess I'll have to drop the course, he says. I'll maybe have to drop out entirely.

Good. You'll be happier then.

No, he whispers. I mean, I'm afraid I am going to disappear.

What do you mean? Her voice is suddenly mellow with concern. What on earth are you talking about? Timmy?

I'm afraid to go home alone. I'm afraid I really might go over the edge.

Do you want to stay here for the night? Barb won't mind. She'll probably be in later.

Yeah. Thanks.

Poor baby, she says, and gives him a hug. You must've caught my spook. I'm sure you've caught my spook. Her arms tighten around him, and after a while they lie on the sofa in a tense embrace. He remembers his night with Nancy on the island with the owl. He remembers a time centuries ago when they fell asleep together *behind* a sofa. He remembers Nancy and the nanaconda.

She begins to rub her body up against him, at first gently, until by some small miracle he is aroused, and then with greater urgency until her entire body breaks into a spasm of throbbing. They cling to the remnants of her forlorn pleasure until her spasms have subsided. They remain this way, fully clothed on the sofa.

Whew, says one of them.

Presently she detaches herself and goes off to bed. He hasn't really slept properly for a week, and with Nancy off in her own bed, his fear comes and goes like the November wind that seems to shake the old house. He tries to pray. *Please, God, just get me through this night. Please, God, don't let me lose myself. I just want to wake up sane, please. And protect me all night long, Amen.* Each time his fear begins to ebb, he feels sleepy and dozes off into the Valley of the Shadow of Death, then jerks out of it, awake and sweating. But Nancy is in the next room. If he feels he is losing it entirely, he will go in there. That is the deal, the emergency plan. If his need is less than catastrophic, there is a valium and a glass of water beside the sofa. Nancy takes these all the time, but he has been resisting them. Finally he gulps the pill down, soon it starts to take hold, and in a matter of minutes he feels himself releasing his spook into the windy night.

Well past midnight Nancy's roommate returns. Through the crusty slits in his eyes he sees her looking at him beneath his blanket on the sofa. She takes off her coat and stands over him, a tall robust looking brunette wearing a cocktail dress with a black and white checkerboard pattern. Lots of leotarded leg. On Nancy this outfit would look slinky.

You're Timmy Fisher, right?

He nods beneath his blanket.

You're the guy who talked with the crazy convict away back years ago. You got your picture in the paper.

Yep.

So! she says. You're out here and she's in there. Is *that* how it is.

He wants to tell her that he hopes he is not imposing. He would like to be able to tell her that he is here because he is depressed. He really wishes she would go away.

Isn't this the right psychological moment for us to introduce ourselves, I mean wouldn't you say that this was exactly that moment, given our combined *savoir faire* in these matters? Given our obvious sophistication?

My name is—

I *know* awready! But you haven't asked me *my* name yet. Sheesh.

What is—

Barbara Viner, I thought you'd never ask. She smiles a burlesque of a smile. Now don't get up, I'll pour myself a nightcap. No, really, I'm perfectly capable.

She kicks off her boots and goes into the kitchen. He hears her pouring something. She pokes her head into Nancy's bedroom.

This one's on the sofa. That means he's fair game, right?

Zollyers, mutters Nancy.

Right, says Barb Viner, her voice sliding half an octave down the scale. She brings her drink into the living room and pulls up a chair a foot or two from Tim's face.

Now you just relax, she says. We're going to take good *care* of you. *Heggup!*

I'll be out in the morning, he says.

Barb turns on her chair.

He's not very talkative, she cries. What does he like to talk about?

Tim closes his eyes.

Your hair isn't very long, she says. That's not a value judgement, just an observation. And I like your beard, I really like your beard. If you'd only *grow* it a bit more. Well, on second thought... Do you like extroverts? I mean women who babble on like this to strangers?

You used to take early morning math classes with Mr. Huculak.

Well, Timmy Fisher, you sure got that right. She hiccups again. Charming, she says.

He awakens some time later to hear Barb rummaging once more in the kitchen. He tries to relax under the blanket. He tries to think, relax from head to toe, relax from head to toe. He drifts a little closer to sleep.

Barbara resumes sitting by his head. Again she hiccups. You ever wonder howcome there's never a letter Q on the phone dial? Have you never thought about that? Hey, don't you play the banjo?

Nancy is whispering something. She stands at the foot of the sofa, sounding dopey.

He's had what you might call a hard week, she says.

Well, what did you *do* to the poor fellow?

I think I might have given him my spook.

Well, Nancy, get some *clothes* on, you slut. Look at you in that getup.

Nancy yawns. I'm going to make some Ovaltine, she says.

Tell me something really awful, says Barb. Anything at all. She takes a big breath and holds it.

The anaconda is a South American constrictor, he says, a river snake that attains a length of more than twenty feet at maturity. It swims through the weedy shallows in search of mammals, birds, fish or reptiles. If the prey in question is small, it seizes the animal in its jaws and swallows it. When it finds a larger animal, a wild pig for instance, or a monkey, it throws a coil around the animal and crushes it. The victim dies of suffocation.

Barb Viner laughs.

That's not bad, she says. But my thing is moths. I never could abide them. Moths and those big bats that suck your toes?

She claps her hands.

Wait! she cries. I'm cured! *Nanny, I'm cured!*

His beard won't progress much beyond a stringy oriental affair with bald spots on either side of his chin. The hair on his head grows long and unruly. He buys a war surplus parka for the winter. The lived-in smell of the coat seems in accord with Tim's winter mood. He moves into an attic in an old house across the ravine from Nancy's flat in the mansion. It reminds him of his garret up at Lake Louise. Nice view of

Nancy's house and the ravine below it. The bathroom is slightly bigger and has a shower, and the kitchenette has a real stove.

He writes his graduate supervisor a long letter about the agonies he sees around him, how he must try to do something to right the wrongs of his society. He wants to do *relevant work*.

He drops all but one course so that he can still have coffee in the student cafeteria without feeling a complete fraud.

He and Nancy have agreed to be friends. They have lunch now and then, but Tim rarely eats anything at all. He has a problem with digesting food and a perpetual case of diarrhoea. He is losing a lot of weight. The only thing he can get down is a strawberry milkshake. He has one at noon every day.

As the winter progresses he gets up later each morning. He moves about in a dream, forgetting things. He no longer identifies with Stephen Dedalus or even with George Bailey in *It's a Wonderful Life*. He has pretty much made up his mind that it is not such a wonderful life after all. Now he identifies with Oblimov. He makes duty lists and ignores them. He sleepwalks into the corners of rooms where he stands dumbstruck until someone talks to him. He can't seem to converse for more than a minute or two before he is drawn back into the whirlpool of his own gloom. *What?* he says. *I beg your pardon?*

Well, if you won't go and see a doctor, his mother says, why don't you at least go and see Reverend Mountjoy? He's very fond of you. He asks about you.

Have you told him? About me?

No, of course not. But you should look him up. He'd understand.

Tim's dad has a different approach. I probably have about five years to go, he says. Maybe ten if I'm lucky, and then I'll be gone. There isn't enough *time* left to go about moping.

Derek tells Tim that he should stop brooding so much. He is just not getting his money's worth.

My money's worth, he mutters. I'm not getting my money's worth.

On the cork memo board in his old attic he has pinned the business card of Nancy's therapist. The man is a clinical psychologist downtown who, Nancy claims, is very much *in tune with our generation*. His business card is framed with cartoon flowers like the decals on Tim's Beetle. The man is Joel Black, a draft-dodger from New York.

In spite of the sombre lighting in Tim's attic, Joel Black's little white card draws the light from the snowy street and reflects it like a symbol of hope. Tim doesn't phone the man, but he keeps his card for

the same reason an airplane keeps flotation devices. And for
reasons, he keeps a small, scarcely used bottle of valium in his ̩
cine cabinet. He fears his need to use the valium, but he fears e
more his temptation to call on Joel Black, M.A.

One morning in the student cafeteria, Techla Wahrsager sits down
across from him. She looks paler and even more severe than she did
the last time he saw her.

You look to me as though you have crossed over, says Techla. Welcome to the gutter. You must learn to stop looking so disenchanted with
things. You need to acquire some toughness. What has happened to you?

He tries to explain.

Oh, yes, she says. Graduate student *Weltschmerz*. Don't let it get to
you. I suspect you are dying. Your old self, I mean. The one your parents or your friends want you to become. Like those empire builders
over there, perhaps? A success story, a somebody? And it doesn't quite
fit, hm? So you die at Christmas time, a good time to die. And someone new is heir to your body and takes your place. A brand new Fisher
to confront the world. A thinker or a wanderer. Perhaps even a poet,
she says, and flashes a thin and bitter smile.

It is the first time he has ever seen Techla Wahrsager smile. Her expression says, Now you are one of us. Or perhaps it says, come to my place
and I will take care of you. Techla Wahrsager has seen too much of the
world. She is too thin and hungry looking to be a refuge for anyone. He
wonders what she thinks about in her most private and least political
moments. He wonders how close she might be to her own brand of grad
student *Weltschmerz*. He also wonders if she could help him.

What do you dream about? she asks him suddenly.

Me?

Yes. Tell me one of your recurring dreams.

Tim drifts off for a moment. Sometimes I dream about going fishing, trout fishing. With my parents and maybe my brother. Except we
can never find the stream. We know it's somewhere close by but we
never seem to *get* there.

Hm, says Techla, fiddling with her coffee spoon.

What did you think I would dream about? he asks.

Nothing quite so spiritual, she says. A search for a stream.

What do you dream about, Techla?

Bombs.

Bombs?

In my most beautiful dreams I am the one to detonate them.

At night you dream about bombs?

Waking and sleeping, explosions. They can be like tropical flowers. They can be entirely beautiful.

Again, like punctuation, the bitter smile.

Joel Black has a bushy dark beard, dark Rasputin eyes. He is tall, with hair more than halfway down to his shoulders, and oddly compelling in his jeans and his T-shirt, his lean, well-muscled body. A homely man women would be likely to fall in love with. He sits in a plush old leather chair behind a cluttered desk, fiddling with a hand exerciser used to develop his gripping muscles. He cannot sit still.

Lemme get this straight, he says. Nancy recommended me to you, right?

Right.

That Nancy, says Black. Beautiful girl. A beautiful person. Her old man is loaded, she has it all her own way and then *pow*, man. She really lost it. Nancy is working on—he pauses as though the next word has become his very own. *Will.* She is trying to get back her will. Without will, man, life is one big pain in the butt.

Yeah.

And you are here because—lemme get this right—you feel like you aren't all there? Did I get that right?

Well, says Tim, speaking slowly and deliberately, I feel lately like I hardly exist at all. That I don't exist. I feel like people could almost walk through me...as though I were a ghost or something.

You've lost your will, man. Just like Nancy. What is this? I come up here two years ago. It's like some kinda plague, right?

Nancy just said I should talk with you.

Well, good. I'm glad. You're a grad student, right?

Sort of.

Sort of. Wow.

Joel Black smiles and an astonishing mouthful of bulging teeth emerges from the dark foliage of his beard. A becoming smile: boyish, ironic, accepting, lovingly contemptuous.

I'm depressed. I'm sort of depressed all the time, and I didn't used to be depressed. I'm usually a bit more up.

Are they fuckin you over in grad school? They did a number on me and I hit the road, man, and now I'm makin good bread by talkin to their wives.

Tim allowed it was possible that grad school was one of his problems.

First they tell you you're gonna learn some wonderful stuff. Then you find they want you to skip rope for them. Do courses you haven't got dick-all interest in, right? And *they* just happen to teach these courses, right? They're fuckin wit you, man. They want you to wind up just like them. Just as dead.

Joel changes hands and does a dozen or so presses with the hand exerciser. He appears amused at his own behaviour. So, he says. Some professional type dude, huh? He calls himself a therapist and what does he do all day? Bench presses and sit-ups and works on his vice-like grip. Timmy Fisher, just how fucked-up are you? Can you tell me that?

I don't know. Like I say, Nancy told—

Yeah. Listen, Timmy my man, I want you to come back. I think we can talk. But first, I want you to memorize this one little sentence. Can you do that for me?

Yeah.

One sentence, says Black. He raises his hands as though conducting a singalong. The will invents the world.

The will invents the world, says Tim.

And the irresolute are responsible.

And the irresolute are responsible, says Tim.

For their own losses.

For their own losses, says Tim.

Put it together, man.

The will invents the world and the irresolute are responsible for their own losses.

Great, Timmy Fisher. I think we got a good thing here. Do you think we can talk?

Yeah. Maybe.

Right on, Saigon.

Techla Wahrsager has a whole network of disaffected friends: intellectuals, witches, trans-sexuals, artists, political dissidents, panhandlers, junkies, and a gay foursome she refers to as The Boys. The Boys have a contract to do the window displays downtown in some large department stores. Sometimes before a big sale they work through the entire night. The Boys let Techla in, secretly, so she can do her research. Her work takes her to the toy department. The Boys' only stipulations are that she promise never to steal the toys from the shelves, and that she always leave the store when The Boys go home. Sometimes they all stay till six or seven in the morning. If she gets tired, she sleeps in one of the bridal beds and they wake her when it's time to go. The Boys are fussy about how she makes her bed.

It is difficult for Tim to believe that The Hudson's Bay at midnight is the same store it is in the daytime; the lighting on every floor is lurid, gothic. The mannequins take on their noctambular look; they seem to move at the periphery of Tim's vision as he drifts in a valium dream through the clothing displays. He half-expects the mannequins to do arabesques and pliés in their Christmas outfits when he turns his back on them.

The toys are Techla's true subject matter; they inspire her to rage. Look at these Barbie Dolls, she hisses. Don't wander off on me. Just look. What do you see?

She shines a flashlight on the Barbies.

I see a girl's doll, says Tim. I see that she is pretty, she has a lot of clothes, a boyfriend. Maybe she's from a well-off family.

He stops there. It is the most he has said to anyone in days.

Would the celebrated Stufflebeam girls come under this category? says Techla with great interest.

Good God! How do you know about him?

Why should I not?

Because he's an old neighbourhood joke. No one's ever heard of this guy.

Except for your enemy, that is. Vaughan, is that his name?

You know him?

You might recall that two or three years ago I was stuck in an elevator with him for several hours.

Why do you call him my enemy?

Then he is your friend?

Maybe a bit of both.

He told me about you, and it seemed to me he did so with little affection. He said that you had a fetish for the Stufflebeam girls. A rather unremarkable fetish, unless it was intended to sully your reputation. Tell me about these girls.

These are just nubile young women painted by some commercial artist. I heard somewhere that he's a Canadian. He did these girlie pictures mostly for outdoor magazines, you know? Fishing magazines and automotive calendars. The girl on the spark plug calendar laden with parcels. Her nickers fall down because of the vibrations from a man with a jackhammer. The girl wading a stream. She catches her—

Ah, I see. Techla writes something down in a small notebook.

Millions of girls will get these Barbies this Christmas, she says. Millions of young North American girls. They will love their Barbies to distraction. They will model their wardrobes, their bodies, their *lives* on these epicene monsters. Look at this hair. She's a dyed platinum blonde! Look at these clothes, this makeup. This is not a little doll; it's a little girl hooker, a pedophile's dream come true. Except, of course, she has no vagina or pubic hair. Mark my words, the young women of the next generation will have no pubic hair. It will atrophy with their brains.

Tim has never thought about dolls before. He nods so that Techla will continue. Her thesis is about the impact of dolls on contemporary attitudes. She is always at war with her supervisor, who has less radical notions than Techla on the subject of dolls.

This is not just a doll, Techla continues, it is a role model. Imagine all the little girls talking to these dolls in their most private moments, those times alone when the girl starts to become aware of things around her. Of herself, of all that she can be in her life. Those magic moments at play, hm? Think of the impact of this little hooker on her imagination.

Techla walks down the aisle to a big display rack. She picks up an 007 kit, pulls out the pistol. She holds Barbie in one hand and waves James Bond's pistol with the other.

Here is what the little boys will be carrying with them in those magic moments at play. At their times of greatest awareness they will be shooting foreign agents in dark alleys with their little guns or wanting to fuck Barbie. She pulls on a small black mask and aims her pistol at a row of dolls, squeezes off a round. She reminds Tim fleetingly of Cat Woman.

Techla picks up a talking mama doll and holds it to her body.

Oh, Schnickelputz, she croons. What do you want to be when you grow up?

Mommy? says the doll.

Techla's doll has several different responses, depending on how far you pull the string on her back.

Who is your favourite philosopher?

Daddy?

What are the chances for sexual equality in the next decade?

Time to do my hair!

They walk through the toy section and take the elevator up to Women's Lingerie. Techla points to a window display The Boys have made ready for tomorrow's big sale. They have arranged a group of young Twiggies in miniskirts and paisley cocktail dresses. They all stare dreamily off into space, also in a way that reminds Tim of

Stufflebeam girls. There is no eye contact between any of them.

The Boys always do this number on the women, says Techla. They never do this with the male mannequins.

They take the escalator down to Men's Wear. Sure enough, all the men have been arranged in such a way as to suggest an awareness of each other. An older man in an outdoor jacket and a pipe in his hand is eyeing a young man in casual slacks and an Irish knit sweater. The older man looks as though he too has just stepped out of a painting by R.J. Stufflebeam.

Techla totes the Mama Doll all through the store. I want to change your tape, she says to the doll. I want to give you a voice they will remember. A new voice for Christmas.

He likes this idea. He still isn't sure if he likes Techla. But he likes a lot of her ideas and he tells her so.

She stares at him for a moment. You are breaking through the consciousness barrier, says Techla. That's my diagnosis. All your depression and your confusion come from this fact. Like a blind man who has had a miracle operation to restore his eyesight, you want to see the world around you. Now you begin to see it. But you still haven't managed to accommodate yourself to your newfound vision. It is all too ugly for you. So you retreat into one form of blindness or another, one form of womb or another. Your search for the trout fishing stream, you know? It is merely the search for the birth canal. You dream to go back into your mother's womb.

I've gotta go, he says.

Techla Wahrsager throws up her hands.

He dials Joel Black's office number again, and still there is no answer. He sits at the little window in his old kitchenette on the third floor, looking out at the snowfall. He has worked himself more securely into his depression. His appetite has lapsed once more into nothing. Several times he has felt the whirlpool recede, the spook drift away. But as soon as he tries to return to his student routine or read anything that requires concentration, the whirlpool pulls him back into his endless cycle of inaction.

The cycle. If he wasn't a born doubter he wouldn't be in this state of mind. He'd be just like the happy Christians who recited the Apostle's Creed every Sunday in church. But the more he got to know these happy Christians from his part of town, he saw them not so much a community of the faithful as a bunch of nice well-fed rich people who wanted to stay that way. If he could be a believer like these people, he could move down along the stream of life and take his place as a productive citizen. He could get married and have a family. He could coach kids baseball or be a cub master or something. He could give up his fancy notions of being a writer in a garret. And why not? As far as he was concerned, the writer's life would breed even more gloom and confusion than grad school. He'd be spending the rest of his life wandering through the Hudson's Bay at three in the morning with Techla Wahrsager and her outcasts. Besides, who was he kidding? He could never write like James Joyce. So he does the next best thing and tries to get a Ph. D. in English. But he can't even bear to write another term paper. So he does the next best thing after that and teaches Basic English to New Canadians. But that's only part-time. And how do you meet a nice woman and settle down if all you've got is a part-time job? And how can you consider settling down if you don't even have a girlfriend? Well, this unfocussed way of life gives you a lot of spare time. You could write a book of poems or something. But what if you spent your entire life stuck in a gloomy attic trying to write a book of poems and there turned out to be a God and an afterlife and you had to justify your life to Him? Well, I spent my entire life *penning sonnets.* AND THESE SONNETS, ARE THEY ANY GOOD? Well, in the grand scheme of things, I guess not. AND ALL THIS TIME, TIMMY FISHER, DID YOU MANAGE TO LOVE ANYONE BESIDES YOURSELF? I didn't even manage to love myself. But I fell in love with Margo Godswine, and with Slimy, and with Nancy Fuller, and with— I DIDN'T SAY FALL IN LOVE WITH, I'M NOT TALKING ABOUT MERE WORSHIP. I SAID DID YOU *LOVE* ANYONE? Well, I guess not. AND DID YOU CAUSE HARM TO ANYONE? Well, I think I broke Ginny Culp's heart, and I know I've been a trial to my parents. BUT WHAT HAVE YOU *DONE* WITH YOUR LIFE? I have wandered into the woods and caught a few fish. I have sung a few songs, I have an M.A. in English. I have tried to be happy... SORRY, TIMMY FISHER, YOU WILL FLOAT OUT INTO THE COS-MOS IN A COLD GLASS CAGE FOR THE REST OF ETER-NITY. LOTS OF TIME TO ENJOY YOUR DESPAIR OUT THERE. But wait! Is there no forgiveness? NONE FOR THE IRRESO-LUTE. NEXT, PLEASE.

Sitting up in his bed he mumbles to God. *Please deliver me from the weight of my own thoughts. Please deliver me from all this nullity around me. Help me to remember how sweet my life was, how sweet it could be. Is there no such thing as salvation? Am I that far gone, Lord? Help me back to my innocence, Dear God. Help me to rediscover the pure springs of my life. Show me you're out there, God. Show me that I'm not alone.*

He wanders into the centre of his garrett just below the peak of the ceiling and paces back and forth. He could try and play his banjo, but the fifth string is broken. He could phone someone else, but he can't imagine anyone out there who would enjoy speaking with him. Gump? Elliott? He tries Black's number again.

The phone in the suite below his attic also begins to ring. And there too, no one is home to answer. An unanswered telephone, what a lonely sound. The same sound *his* call was making in Black's office. And somewhere in the city other phones are ringing. A city full of unanswered phones. A city full of people who are phoning other people, who are out somewhere trying to phone other people. Each phoner praying that someone else is out there.

On the old staircase three floors below, there is a footfall. Someone on the way up. Perhaps to see him? Perhaps Techla. Or Gump. He hasn't talked to Gump in over a month, and then they quarrelled all through supper about the war in Vietnam. Tim has become quite pious with Gump, who thinks of the war as a strategic rather than a moral problem.

The person on the staircase doesn't sound like Gump. The step is too brisk.

Perhaps it is Death. What would Death walk like? Like the Mad Russian, slouching up the stairs in his prison fatigues. This footfall is much lighter. It continues up the shrieking stairs past the second floor apartments. This means that the visitor will either knock on his door or on the door of the stewardess across the hall. He waits. The phone below him rings on persistently like a cat meeowing outside in a storm.

And then the knock. It doesn't sound like Death, or Salvation for that matter. It doesn't sound like anyone he knows. Techla would make a different sort of racket. She would knock abruptly and with great authority. He opens the door.

Hi.

Nancy Fuller with a crest of snow on the shoulders of her maxi and a wintry bloom on her face.

Hi.

She hunkers down on the carpet and seems to curl up like a cat among the chaos of books and crumpled papers. How does she do this? The most simple action, like walking across the campus or sitting down on a floor in a turtleneck and jeans, becomes a balletic gesture. No one he has ever met sits down as beautifully as Nancy. He's almost relieved to see her. He wonders why she is here, why she hasn't phoned first to warn him.

And how have you been? she says, just like her mother.

Up and down.

Are you eating? I take it your shrug means no.

Nancy leans her head on the palm of her hand and slowly uncurls before him.

Barb Viner keeps asking about you. She says she likes your Jewish nose.

Nancy yawns.

Barb says she likes the tortured ones best. How about a cup of coffee? I might just pass out on your rug.

Are you on valium again?

No, says Nancy. Her voice follows him into the little kitchenette. I've found something better. God, this place is a mess.

He brings her a mug of coffee.

Put it on the table, she says, holding a little brass pipe to her mouth, lighting it, sucking in great gulps of air. The pipe smoke smells like the basement of the Arts Building outside the Grad students' offices on Friday afternoon. Sweet. Willow twigs and poplar leaves burning in October.

Try some.

He knows he has to or she might walk out on him. Besides, he trusts Nancy. Her valium worked okay, so why not this stuff, which seemed to sustain all the other grad students? He takes the pipe and holds it like Nancy does. He sucks mightily on the pipestem, takes in a lungful, and breaks into a fit of coughing.

Go easy. I didn't come here to see you get stoned. I just came to see how you've been getting on. I've been thinking about you, she says, and takes the pipe back. There's some things you ought to...there's some things I—

You've been thinking about me?

Yes, says Nancy, and stops, closes her eyes. But I don't think you're ready to hear. Let sleeping dogs lie. You know what? Not to change the subject, but I think I'm beginning to understand. I mean about what you're going through? Some guys....

Nancy takes up the pipe again and draws slowly on it. She holds in the smoke and gazes past Tim at his frosted north window.

Some guys just don't want to, Nancy murmurs, and there's nothing wrong with that. If a guy doesn't want to, he doesn't want to.

Nancy takes out a little tinfoil ball from her handbag. Delicately she picks out a small resinous morsel, places it in the bowl of her pipe, and lights it.

Arthur Locke gets me the best stuff. He should probably go into the business. Here, she gasps, holding her breath, and hands Tim the pipe.

He has another go at it, and this time he manages to hold down some smoke. He breathes a small prayer that if he gets high, he won't lose his mind. Nancy is reassuring. She has taken a small plate from his shelves in the kitchenette and is munching on some seeds.

Have some.

Are they....

No, silly. You don't get high on these. They're just pumpkin seeds. I baked and salted them myself.

He tries a couple.

Do you want to talk about it?

He looks at her.

About your problem, she says.

Maybe it's like you say. I just caught your spook.

Not *that* problem.

What problem do you mean?

The let's not do it problem. Like I say, I can understand perfectly well. I grew up with Benny, right? Lots of his friends are my friends now and I get along very well with them. There's an advantage to going out with them, too. At least they keep their hands to themselves.

She gives Timmy the pipe.

You mean you think...you think—

Have a puff before it goes out. It goes out real easy.

He holds down the smoke and wonders why he hasn't gotten high. Maybe some people just didn't get high. Too uptight or something.

Yes, and there's nothing wrong with being...that way inclined. Like I say, all sorts—

I'm not a *homosexual!* Is that what you're getting at? That I go around yearning for guys to...to...*do it* with?

I have my spies, says Nancy, passing Tim the bowl of pumpkin seeds. Let's say a certain friend or two of Benny's. You shouldn't fight it. If you're queer, you're queer. When I found out that Benny was queer, I was shocked. I don't mind admitting this to you, Timmy. I got angry. I wouldn't even give him the time of day. If Mom and Dad ever found out, there's no telling who would have the first heart attack. But finally we *talked* about it, me and Benny. And now... Nancy shrugs. It's no big deal.

Have you been talking to Joel Black about me?

Not lately. No.

Well, who's been putting all these weird thoughts into your head?

Have some pumpkin seeds, Nancy says, unfazed by his anger. She smiles conspiratorially. And don't worry. You're among friends.

He isn't sure why Nancy pluralizes friends.

You know who you should talk to some time is Arthur. He knows a lot about it. I guess his being in the New York, Montreal art scene and all that, he runs into quite a lot of queers. He says it's no big deal. He figures a fifth of all the men in North America are potentially bent. Maybe even more. He says you should—

You've been talking to Arthur Locke about us?

Timmy, says Nancy, loading up her pipe again, there *is* no us. There never was. And I used to think it was because you were such an angel. So did Rita. Imagine that. Silly us.

For Christ's sake, Nancy, I am not a homosexual! I don't go out with guys on dates, I don't want to get buggered by some horny old sybarite, I don't lurk in parks looking for boys to corrupt, I don't...desire....

Your idea of gay men is, shall we say, somewhat *negative*?

He is tongue-tied. Why should his words resist his bidding of them? Could it be that he is some sort of a homosexual, and that he has *repressed* it? There was that erotic dream he'd had once about Alistair Vaughan, and of course the mother thing Techla was talking about, but....

He has forgotten what he was thinking about.

Nancy stands up and stretches. She smiles down on him. She places the bowl of pumpkin seeds on his lap and says, We will see. I'm getting hungry, are you getting hungry?

I've done the deed with all kinds of women.

So?

It's always been women with me.

Timmy, I am starved. I haven't eaten all day. Why not let's phone for a pizza? We could have a nice hot one. With red peppers and hot sausage and stuff. Do you like anchovies and smoked oysters?

He drifts into the kitchenette to clear his head.

Please? she calls from the phone stand in his bedroom. I'm *starving*.

Somehow Nancy has eaten most of the pizza, and somehow she has gotten things arranged so that they eat the whole thing on the bed. They are back on the topic of the day. What topic of the day? Oh, *that* topic of the day, and they are on his bed listening to jazz on CKUA and Nancy has unbuttoned her jeans to accommodate she claims the pizza.

You hardly ate a thing, she says. Talk to me.

He faces her in bed. What was the other thing you wanted to tell me?

It can wait. Tell me about your fantasies, she says. Tell me anything you want. Give me all the dirt.

Have you ever viewed, he says, stretching out the vowel, the paintings of the great Stufflebeam?

Nancy shakes her head as though to clear it. Is he like an artist?

He celebrates the human body, you might say.

Is this a fantasy?

From the heart, he says. One of Stufflebeam's fine women had a certain resonance, as our friend *Locke* the *gallery chap* might say.

Tell me about her.

In one memorable exhibition she was *rendered*, she was *rendered* lying in a pup tent in a state of semi-undress, while *outside* the tent her *consort* was beckoning. Am I talking funny?

No.

The man in question held a pipe like this one in his teeth it made him grimace in an outdoorish guy sort of way and he was wearing a string of pickerels and this is the motif that *deflected* the history of modern realism as we know it.

He was wearing a string of pickerels?

He was *holding* a string of pickerel.

What did *she* look like? Nancy whispers breathlessly.

(Could you whisper breathlessly could anyone whisper breathlessly?) What?

I *said*, What did *she* look like?

She had her hair done up in a scarf? She was young? And full of juicy gestures? She smiled? She was a redhead? She seemed not indifferent to pickerel?

What are juicy gestures?

They are *tumescent* as the spring. *Saturnalian* as the summer.

Nancy cackles away in her cartoon witch's laugh. Close your eyes, she whispers. No peeking.

He is obedient to Nancy's no peeking in spite of the difficulty implicit in the absence of peeking because if there was no peeking there was also possibly no china she wrestles open a bureau drawer she is definitely no peeking she is about to do something saturnalian he wonders if he should take off his arduroys—his *arduroys*? That would be so that his ardur could get out for if indeed there were no china there will at least be orgies till at last serenity will flow over their bodies and their souls swimming upstream from the fetid *suck* of the whirlpool the narcolepsy of the soul and what God provideth let no man set asunder as up the shrieking star case comes the footfall of Death himself for whomsoever transcendeth the waters to reach the purest of springs yea though the trout do not bite today even then will you seek salivation in that perfect synthesis of moral action and religious belief no mystical no aesthetic intent no between between between

Tim, now. Open your eyes.

Nancy but for her *knickers* is naked as a jaybird, except she has bound her hair with a red handkerchief. She stands at the foot of his bed with one hand on her hip holding a fishing rod *his fishing rod* and my how her breasts are perky he feels the long somnolence of Stufflebeam unfurling like a canvas immortal. He looks at her and looks at her. She has fresh lipstick on, she smiles like an ad in...like an ad in....

I want you, he says.

But what will the mothers think? says Nancy. Who now is pulling off his arduroys as fast as she can go and who is now on top of him yea though even at this moment he is not yet in a state of total undress in a state of—

What about your vows of celibacy, you naughty boy?

What vows of

Up the shrieking stairway comes the footfall of Death he goes knock knock knock and singeth Nancy who's that kno-o-o-ocking at my door I'll scare him off I will I will I will she laughs and laughs he laughs and laughs the big bald man he doesn't laugh he just stands there at the entrance to the baudroom he says maybe I came at a bed time and Nancy laughs and laughs but (never at a loss for words) ol Timmy he says c-c-c-come an see us adam an *eve-ulate!* but the bald man he looks so *familiar* he doesn't want so much to witness eve-ulations, no he seems to be forming an anguished word or two he is probably not Death at all, he even *sounds* familiar....

Aha, says Timmy to the bald man's dome: did you know that Will invented the world? And that the irresolute are responsible for their own losses? Hm? Yes? Did you know that?

Timmy.

Hush, fair Nancy, I would speak with this learnèd Theban. Do you believe in original sin? And yet men deny original sin. And to whom does the child owe its first drubbings, whom other than the parents?

Nancy is balancing on one foot, she is trying to pull on her jeans. She calls to the bald man.

The bald man? What bald man? Oh, *that* bald man.

Have we just had our first loosination? he says. To no one.

Nancy would appear to be running down the stairs calling someone's name. Someone's name? Whose name? It echoes up the stairs in Nancy's lovely voice, Nancy's lovely *distressed* voice: Reverend Mountjoy? Reverend Mountjoy!

The door in the main hall it goes *whump!*

In February the sun's rays seep into the corners of old houses flooding the rooms with forgotten light. A good day in February can do imitations of March. That is February's chief virtue. The chief virtue of March is that on a good day it seems to be rehearsing for April. April with its muck and puddles flooding the streets. But April is a fickle month; just when you start to dream of wading your favourite stream in the foothills, you wake up to a blizzard and it may as well be February.

May. Now there's a month. The problem is how to get to May with all your faculties intact. Well, really the problem is how to trick yourself out of bed on a fine bright February morning that is *really* just an imitation of March, which is only a faint promise of April, itself a sham of May. Perhaps the trick is to have a shower in your sad little bathroom. Or better yet, open your garret window so that you can hear the tinkle of icicles shattering and the high-pitched wheezing of cedar waxwings. This, finally, is what gets Tim out of bed.

He moves toward his window and sees a soiled manuscript before him on the desk. It is thirty pages long and still going. The last sentence reads, "She dropped the doll and screamed loud enough to wake her mother." He forgets why he got out of bed, why he has crossed over to the window.

Oh, yes. He wants to hear the sounds of February. The waxwings. The falling icicles.

There is a commotion in the ravine directly below his wind man calling. Anger and authority in his voice. Children swearing large policeman wades downhill through the snow toward a girl in a red jacket. She tries to flee, but the snow is too deep for her short legs. Tim recognizes her, a native kid named Maria. She and her friends, including her older brother and a younger half-brother, spend a lot of time in the ravine. Playing, one could say. They are nine, thirteen and fourteen, and they play with tubes of airplane glue squeezed into plastic bags. They hold these bags over their faces and inhale.

Another policeman gives chase up the other side of the ravine, Nancy's side, but the kids have at least a hundred yards on him. This second officer stops, turns, and trudges back to his partner, who has caught up with Maria. They will take her in their squad car to Children's Aid and try to explain to her approximately the same things Tim attempted to explain in mid-January: how the fumes, if inhaled in any quantity, will dissolve the fatty layers around the brain and induce a kind of permanent dementia.

He cannot help thinking about Maria and her stoned little gang. He entertains fantasies of adopting the whole sad bunch of them and giving them a proper home. He knows he will never do this, but this fantasy is the only thing that makes his thoughts about their bleak lives seem bearable.

Alone every day, Tim tries to work on his last couple of term papers. He sits at his desk in bathrobe and pyjamas. There's a benign sense of rebellion in his morning attire. This is exactly how Elliott or Alistair, or Derek or his father, would *not* comport themselves. On his best days he dresses in the late afternoon and ventures out for supper. Once a week he goes to the university for his evening class on the Theatre of the Absurd.

Two evenings a week he tutors a small group of Polish immigrants on basic English. He calls them The Optimists because they are so intent on self-improvement. Every class he tries to teach them popular songs to sing in chorus. They do dazzling renditions of "Oh, Susanna" and "There's No Business Like Show Business." He hopes their positive attitude will rub off on him, hopes and doubts it. Until further notice all hope will be held in check by doubt.

A long story has been crawling around inside of him since Christmas time. It's looking a bit like a horror fantasy with opportunities for social commentary. He has decided to call his story *The Doll*. Perhaps inspired by his talks with Techla Wahrsager, the story begins with a girl of the streets, the sort of forlorn creature who, with luck, might some day become a bag lady. She is about seventeen, an alcoholic, drug user, part-time prostitute. Wherever she goes she is pursued by a pimp named Hunch.

Description of Hunch. Short and stocky like the Mad Russian? No. A tall gaunt man with a pronounced limp who lives off street girls.

This girl fears she will never be free of Hunch or free of the law, at least in this lifetime. For several years she was raised by a grandmother with fervent Christian beliefs and a grandfather preoccupied with tribal magic, and the residue of these religions has remained to haunt the girl. She has at last come to fear for her soul. She wants an innocent dwelling place for her soul, outside of the body she has defiled as a prostitute.

Her name. It will come.

One night in the bar, Hunch the Pimp spots the street girl, and for the first time ever, she openly defies him and runs away. All night she wanders through the streets of downtown Edmonton. Afraid to go home, she staggers past a department store. A cleaning woman recognizes her and lets her in. Exhausted, she drifts down to the bargain basement where the toys are and has a brief moment of communion with the baby dolls, so trusting and undefiled. This place, she realizes, is where she wishes to leave her soul. She must allow herself to die and be reborn inside the body of a baby doll. What purer shrine?

He scribbles his story in the latest green spiral notebook. Sometimes the story moves forward; sometimes he merely makes notes. How does a girl die and get reborn within the body of a doll?

Aha. This waif has a friend (like Techla's best friend Rona) who is a witch. Rona is not someone Tim wishes to spend a great deal of time with. She is not fond of men, and she does not have what most people would call an agreeable personality. What Tim needs for his story is an un-Ronalike witch, a healing witch. Rona has told Tim about a book she often refers to: *Ancient Rituals and Ceremonies of Wicca.* He finds this volume in a used bookstore. He discovers that there is no ceremony that might include the transmigration of souls into the bodies of dolls, so he borrows a bit from several ceremonies until the whole thing sounds plausible. He's determined not to get bogged down yet on the issue of authenticity. He is usually too depressed to worry about authenticity. When he reaches page twenty or so in his scribbled manuscript, he has managed to construct a ritual in which the girl dies in the company of some fellow outcasts, including her cousin, who like others in the neighbourhood, wants to escape the clutches of Hunch the Pimp.

But who, really, is this bedraggled girl? A gypsy? Who the hell ever saw a gypsy in Edmonton? An immigrant, then? A native kid? A rich white girl from a loveless family? And how in the first place does she slide into a life on the streets? Tim knows what he wants to happen in his story, but how to set it up and make it halfway plausible?

And something is wrong with the voice here. He has begun his story with an omniscient narrator who knows everything there is to know about street life. But how can that be? His narrator is just faking it, because regardless of how many nights he spends drinking in the Shamrock or the Coffee Cup Inn with Techla and her outcasts, Tim can never know enough about these people. Occasionally he believes he can *feel* their lives, and sometimes, oddly, that seems to be enough. Maybe his narrator could be one of the characters.

Yes, a well-meaning observer who first sees the street girl on Twenty-fourth with two drunken men. The tall one knocks down the smaller man, takes off after the street girl, and Tim's narrator tries to save her! (Description of street girl. Dumpy? Pretty but ragged?)

And then Tim remembers Maria. And his street girl becomes native, and bearing her first name. Last name, Culp. How long has he known that this would be her name?

Maria Culp is taken to her final reward. She dies in a blood ritual that allows for the passage of her soul into the body of a Christmas sale baby doll. Maria's cousin contrives to return the doll to its box and to its department store with the hope that Maria will at last find a loving home. Luck seems to be with Maria. The doll is purchased by a lovely, fashionable woman for her daughter.

Description of woman. Younger version of Reenie Fuller. She has the politics of Alistair's mum.

The woman orders the doll by phone and it is delivered on Christmas Eve. The little girl is given the choice of opening one present before she goes to bed, and of course she chooses the package containing the doll. At first, all the doll will say are things like *Mama* and *Comb my hair*. For the little girl, it is love at first sight.

The family: husband, wife, son, daughter. On some days they look like the cast of a soap commercial.

They all go to bed on Christmas Eve. But the little girl can't sleep.

Description of girl. Braids, like Rita Symington used to have. Perfect little nose, like Alistair Vaughan's mother's nose. A spoiled girl, but with an inquiring mind. Bosses her brother. For some reason, her brother has acquired all of the mother's fashionable neuroses and some of the father's shallow convictions. But the little girl is too courageous and inquisitive to take after her mother, and too honest about things to take after her father. Alone in the dark under the Christmas tree, she feels a sense of enchantment talking to her baby doll.

Suddenly, for the first time, the doll opens one eye. She says to her new owner, *Have you ever gotten high on airplane glue?*

No, silly! says the little girl.

Do the cops ever hassle you?

No!

Does your Daddy touch you here? Or here? Does he do this to you?

The little girl screams. She screams like an actor who studied under Antonin Artaud, and the mother awakens out of a dead sleep.

Outside Tim's window on this fine February morning, the real Maria screams as one of the policemen stuffs her into the patrol car.

Inside Tim's head, Maria is screaming with the little girl under the Christmas tree. Her mother screams herself awake and the real Maria screams ferociously at the policeman who stands by his squad car, his large hands dangling uselessly by his side. All the screamers within and without are feeding into this conspiracy of outrage and horror.

The whole spectacle frightens Tim. His story frightens him. He puts it aside, closes his window, and climbs back into bed.

Later, it might even be the same day, he imagines a conversation with Techla Wahrsager. He calls her for moral support. It was your idea, he says, and now it's driving me crazy. Well, it's become your idea now, she says, and I can't write it for you. If it's driving you crazy, she says, it's probably doing you some good. Good? I'm shaking in my bed in the middle of the day. How can that be good? I'm haunted by the thing. It's turning me weird. No, she says, I can't agree with you. This is merely your fear talking. The story is activating your conscience, and that can be a very meaningful process. Let the thing unfold in all its horror and despair.

She succeeds in calming him down, and finally he hangs up.

But how, he wonders later in bed, when the sun is beginning to set outside his garret, how can an imagined conversation with Techla Wahrsager or anyone else be comforting? Later still, and still in bed, he wonders if he didn't *really* have that conversation with Techla. It seemed utterly real. He wonders if he should phone Techla and ask her if he spoke with her earlier that day. He decides against it. If she suspects that he is as far gone as *he* suspects he is, she might start avoiding him.

He phones Nancy's place to find out if she saw the nat
the policemen, but Nancy is not home. Barb Viner tells him
is out with Joel Black.

What, like on a date?

Oh, our boy Joel never uses that word. A date is wh___ ___aight
people do. No, just a little dinner and wine, a little massage therapy,
and who knows, maybe a harmless bit of *boffing!*

Tim can't always tell when Barb is kidding. He changes the subject. He wonders out loud about the fate of the native kids on her side
of the ravine.

Wow, are you ever a full-time worrier or what? No, I didn't see the
big cop chase the little delinquent, and no, I don't know what'll happen to the poor little Indian dears and no, I don't know what's in store
for Nancy. Thank God I'm not her mother. Or your mother. Thank
God I'm not a mother to our glue sniffers in the ravine. Thank God
I'm just an apathetic hedonist trying to make her way in the world.

He tries again to change the subject but she interrupts him. If I
were Nancy's mother, I would wonder why she was going out with
that gold digger Joel Black and not with a certain brooding beak-
nosed banjo player. Are you listening I hope you're listening Timmy
because you could do worse than Nancy Fuller believe me.

There's nothing between us. She just told me that two months ago.

Nothing between you, eh? Well, I would beg to differ. You are connected to this lady in more ways than you could imagine in that vague
little brain of yours, like the song goes *She luffs you oivé* and if you weren't
such a woeful innocent she would *explain* this connection.

Connection? What do you mean? Explain what connection?

Like I say Timmy I'm only her roommate and mum's the word but
if I were you I'd be worrying a helluva lot more about your friends and
a helluva lot less about the fallen world around you. Cheerie bye.

The middle section of his story focuses on the dilemma of the fashionable mother. She is more angered than awed by the girl's doll. She
tries to return it to the woman at the complaints department in the
basement of Hudson's Bay, but when the mother describes the various
obscenities the doll has come up with, the doll clams up. The mother
thinks that she must either bring the doll home or face the accusations
of the store lady that she has gone insane. And so she takes it home.

Others come to the house to see the doll. To one of the mother's
friends, the wife of the chief of police, the doll says, "Check the parkade

off 103rd and Jasper, level five. Every Saturday night there's a drug smorgasbord." She tells her husband, he checks into it, and sure enough, some pushers are caught red-handed. To a sixteen-year-old boy the doll says that a certain school counsellor in his own high school is molesting girls and threatening them to gain their silence. The boy and his friends set a trap for the counsellor. They catch him in the act.

As the months go by, the doll tells more and more. She tells the mayor and his wife of an endless string of corruption in the highest levels of society, including some men in public office well known to the chief. The chief throws up his hands. How can I police all this? he cries. How do I know you're not just spreading dirty lies around?

The doll curses him in the vilest street language and remains defiant. She insults anyone who will not listen. Finally, an enterprising young TV talk show host puts her on television, and even though some of her more profane attacks are bleeped, some people are threatened and scandalized. Edmonton becomes notorious over night. A group of churchgoers and business people bands together to destroy the doll before the doll destroys the approaching Christmas season for all of them.

By the last week of February, the manuscript has been expanded to one hundred and thirteen pages in longhand, and it's still growing. Tim has become convinced that if he doesn't reproduce his first draft on a copy machine, it will be destroyed in a fire. And since the distressing retreat of Reverend Mountjoy, he has a fair idea where this fire might come from.

At last he decides to phone Nancy. He needs to talk to someone about his burgeoning story, and Nancy is the obvious candidate.

Perhaps she has always been the obvious candidate. Perhaps Barb Viner was telling the truth. If so, he has another reason to speak with Nancy. He will need something to impress Nancy with, something Joel Black or Alistair Vaughan or any other guy would be incapable of showing her. So he phones Nancy's number. He can almost see her through the window across the ravine as they speak. He imagines that she is just out of the bath wearing her terry towel robe and that she is flushed all over from the heat of the bath water.

Hi, it's me, he says.

Hi.

Nancy sounds wary.

Tim makes some desperately casual conversation. He learns that she has taken a job in her favourite bookstore. He lets her ramble on about her boss, whom she calls Napoleon, and then he describes his story to Nancy.

You say it's in *longhand?* You call yourself a writer and you can't type your own manuscript? Timmy, you are much too easy on yourself. Take a typing course. No writer worth his salt shows someone a manuscript in longhand!

If you came over here on Saturday, I could read it to you. In person like.

You don't understand. I want a typed manuscript so I can read it at my leisure, so I can re-read if necessary. I don't want it *dramatized* by the author's own loving voice, I want the real thing. And I don't want to fear criticizing it in front of you. You'll give me one of your suffering looks and I'll feel like a villain. If I'm going to read the thing, I want to do it in my own flat, thank you very much.

But Nancy, I think it's real good.

Good enough to type?

The typing course is pretty painless. The woman who teaches his group is so methodical that she makes everything seem easy, even to his muddled mind. He is the only man in the class. The students are women of all ages who need typing skills to apply for secretarial jobs. Some of the older women, the ones in their forties and fifties, tend to gravitate toward Tim, fuss over him at coffee, and help him along with the technical things. He tolerates this. In a few weeks he gets his speed up to thirty-five words a minute and quits the course.

At home he reads the funny papers, plays solitaire, pecks away at his long story. He does all this in his pyjamas and as much as possible in bed. Even typed, his story is going to be more than a hundred pages, and it's still unfolding in Tim's least gloomy periods.

He has just received a thick letter from his parents, who are having a holiday in Victoria. For some reason he can't bring himself to open the letter. He knows that it will contain advice, and the thought of receiving advice from his parents—and especially *cheerful* advice—is intolerable.

One night while watching *Batman* on television he fails to hear the tell-tale shrieking of his staircase and someone knocks on his door. An efficient little rap. He shuts off the set, adjusts his pyjamas, pauses for a guess (Nancy Fuller, to apologize), and opens the door.

Techla Wahrsager stands beneath the hall light in a full length military coat complete with epaulettes and brass buttons. She is wearing lipstick. Just a trace, but yes, lipstick.

Come in, he says. Pardon my—

She sails in like a diva, spins off her new coat, tosses it on a chair. It lands like a falling body and the chair crashes to the floor.

I have something for you, she says. Don't bother to get dressed. I can't stay long.

Techla picks up the chair, sits down, and with exaggerated precision places a small envelope on Tim's table.

What is it?

A plane ticket for Toronto. Don't worry, I didn't even have to pay for it. Someone else bought it and now she can't go. It could not be refunded, and so. If you decide to come to Toronto with me, we will stay for one week at the expense of my department and return on March third. I am doing a presentation at a conference. You can do what you want.

You mean fly with you to Toronto, stay for a week and fly back?

Even the hotel is free, she says. She closes her eyes and smiles at him. What do you think, oh gloomy one? Could you use a break from this ridiculous winter?

But it's also winter in Toronto.

Techla emits a scornful flurry of snorts, which is her way of laughing. She sits erect in her chair, stares down at the envelope. She has perfect posture.

Sure. I've never been there. I might as well go with you.

Afterwards he doesn't know why he's decided to go. He had heard that Rita Symington's group sings occasionally at the Bohemian Embassy in Toronto. Maybe he is hoping he will find her there. No, he is not looking for Slimy. Mainly because she has dropped off the face of the Earth. But Tim needs a change, some new air to breathe. He checks out Toronto on a map of North America, as though he has never seen it before. What impresses him is that it's so far south, it's just a stone's throw from Buffalo. At least the weather will be warmer.

The weather is snowy, windy, grey, ugly and damp. Glimmering through a dusky veil of clouds, the sun looks like the mere reflection of a sun on the grimy hood of someone's car. When the wind rises, the sun disappears entirely. The wind blasts off Lake Ontario laden with moisture and mayhem, races up Yonge Street, dismantling hairdos, and passes through Tim's army parka as though it always knew the way, the coldest bloody wind he has ever felt in his life. Soon, however, there is a streetcar. He climbs inside and collapses on a seat.

On purpose he has left his story manuscript back home in Edmonton, and he has very little to do except read for his last term paper. But he is determined not to stay in the hotel room all day long. At last it's time for his daily milkshake. He wants to find a nice place that serves them in winter time, an old-fashioned department store restaurant perhaps. A restaurant down from his hotel serves milkshakes, but only vanilla and chocolate. It has to be strawberry or nothing. Besides, he must get out and walk around once a day or he'll suffer a worse lapse into his long winter's gloom.

If his courage is up, he might bring himself to read the letter from his parents. It lies, still sealed and a little soggy, in the pocket of his army parka.

Tim and Techla are staying together at the Victoria, a small hotel on Yonge Street just up from King. This is the cheapest place Techla could locate that is reasonably close to her conference. As well, according to Techla, it seems to cater to a clientele that is anything but bourgeois. It even has permanent residents: mostly old people who look European, bookish, and vaguely aristocratic. She has another reason for staying at this hotel, she has confessed as much, and it has something to do with a creepy old man who lives down the hall from their room. Tim suspects that this old man has become one of her reclamation projects, but she remains quite secretive on the nature of her relationship with the fellow. Tim almost likes the Victoria, its shabby grandeur and musty smell, but he can only appreciate the Victoria's charms if he can escape from it while Techla attends her conference.

The ride in the streetcar is somehow fraught with possibilities. He has the feeling that right here or around any corner in Toronto he might just run into Rita Symington. He has had this feeling several times since arriving. He transfers west at Bloor Street, then spots a row of cozy shops and restaurants. He gets off at Bathurst and wanders down Bloor in search of the right place. At last he stops at an old Hungarian restaurant, and yes, it serves milkshakes. He takes a deuce in the darkest corner and orders his strawberry milkshake

A milkshake on a day like this? says the waitress.

Yeah.

You can have a nice big bowl of goulash for two bits more. That includes dumplings and everything.

I'll just have the milkshake, thanks.

The waitress disappears with his order. He forgets her, he forgets everything. He has gone dumbstruck again. Into his whirl-pool. The strangeness of this big city doesn't seem to faze him, the strangeness of the clientele at the Victoria Hotel. Nothing seems to surprise him. He decides to worry about the old man Techla keeps accosting. He looks like a villain from an old movie.

He'll be company for you. For God's sake, just go up to his room. Talk to him, says Techla.

He asks her why he should meet this creepy old fart, but she is evasive. He assumes that this man is some sort of Marxist subversive. Perhaps he is destined to be the instrument that will liberate Tim into some new and revolutionary understanding of the world. In which case, this old fart is not Techla's reclamation project. Tim is.

I prefer not to.

You prefer not to?

Yes.

The world is bustling all around you, a new age is being born, and you prefer not to.

Yes, I prefer not to.

Much to Techla's annoyance he says that a lot these days. He has begun to identify with Bartleby the Scrivener. He is honing his depression into such a fine art that people keep mistaking his ex-tended funk for worldly wisdom. It's becoming part of him, like the cloud over Joe Btfsplk's head. Ah, well, nothing to be done.

He says that a lot too.

The waitress sets down his milkshake. She moves back from his table and leans on the counter. She is pale and plump with dark hair and troubled grey eyes. As she stares out at Bloor Street, holding her elbows, folding them into her chest, her face takes on the brooding expression of a Hollywood heroine. She seems to be waiting for her hero or for spring. A yearning look.

Tim extracts his parents' letter from his coat pocket. He looks at the address. It has become blurred so as to be unrecognizeable. He stares at the soggy envelope.

Excuse me? Are you okay?

The waitress is looking down at him as though he were someone's lost mongrel. He suspects that she is merely curious, prying. But her question is so forthright he can't help but be touched by her concern. It's like the return of the Café Madonna. New body and new uniform, but the same look on her face. He feels compelled to answer her, to say anything.

I'm trying to make up my mind about this letter, he says. Whether to read it like.

Girlfriend?

Parents.

Heavy.

Yeah.

You looked a bit down, that's all.

Tim shrugs. Yeah, well. Thanks for....

The waitress pulls up the other chair and sits across the table from Tim. She leans forward. I think you should read it, I mean I really think you should read it.

Why?

I'm a Scorpio and Scorpios tend to avoid knowing the worst. You're probably an Aquarius, right, you wouldn't understand this avoidance thing unless you're a Scorpio, but believe me, my intuition tells me you should read that letter.

I *am* a Scorpio.

You *are?* She peers at him for a moment. You know, deep inside, I just knew that? A Scorpio. Wow. Yes. Definitely. You should read that letter.

She rises to serve some customers.

The envelope doesn't tear; it draws apart without a sound, like wet kleenex. Inside is a stack of clippings on the rewards of regular exercise, cooking for bachelors, the value of a university education, investing while you're young, jobs in the education field, diet, dressing for job interviews, and a particularly long article on the dangers of driving a Beetle. There is a note from his mother which she has apparently slipped into the envelope without his father's knowledge. She wishes Tim health and happiness and the wish that 1966 will bring less despair and a lot more opportunities for their youngest. Then she gives a summary of Pug Fisher's latest decision, to leave his job with Hatch, Cooper and Strang. "A sort of early retirement," she calls it.

"Your father has decided that life is too short and his health too important to go on selling stocks and bonds for ever and ever. I think the tension of his job, trying to keep up with younger men in a competitive field, etc was more trouble than it's worth. He's been looking pretty grey of late, and I think he's made a wise decision. Who knows? Maybe we'll move out here and turn into beach bums? Anyway, he has been thinking a lot lately, about your depression, Timmy, and here's his final word on the subject. Not a whisper about this retirement business to anyone, do you hear? Pug's decision won't be final until we get back from Victoria. Love, Mum."

Tim turns to his father's note, which is at the bottom of the stack. The letter is folded in two. The top fold is legible and dry, but the bottom fold is pretty soggy. The letter begins, "Dear Tim, Just a note to see how things are going hope you are feeling a bit *less depressed* (underlined). Enclosed is a word or two for you, the sum total of my wisdom on life, etc. *Yours to read and do as you wish* (underlined). I'm telling this to you because I'm worried you might be having a rocky season as we used to say on the gridiron. Too many books, too little fun, whatever. This is the doctor speaking I've thought about your "problem" for a long time and *number one* (underlined) your mother and I think you need to take a serious look at—

The second page is almost entirely smudged into oblivion. This comes as a relief to Tim. However, there is one phrase that remains unsmudged by the Toronto sleet: "...need a girl just like the girl that married your dad..." He is puzzling over this phrase when a shadow falls over the letter.

Tim looks up.

Well? says the waitress.

You were right.

Didn't I tell you? she replies with a sad and wistful smile. She goes over to her customers, takes their orders, and disappears into the kitchen.

He really ought to get back to the hotel. He should go home and do some more reading. Maybe he could make some notes for his story, for when he gets back. Maybe Techla will be there, waiting for him. In bed at night with her, she talks while they do it, she can't seem to stop. What does she talk about? Ideas. But he can't seem to respond to them, he can't even remember them the next morning. She is boney to the touch, even bonier than he is, and surprisingly eager and agile. She chatters away during her climax, which is fast and brief and unremarkable, and when they are finished, she clings to him so tightly he feels like a life raft. He wonders what she's trying to hold on to. In the daytime she seems to be disdainful of him. In fact, he almost likes it that she is disdainful of him in the daytime. This must mean that she's not getting serious about him and that they are connected by a casual symbiosis. Her daytime wisdom for his body at night. Both are renting. One of them, likely Techla, is the host animal, an alligator perhaps; the other is the bird that picks her teeth. Carefully.

Where have *you* been, says Techla from the shower.

Having a nibble at a place on Bloor.

So. Well, I was dazzling today, ferocious. Have you forgotten? I presented my dolls paper. It was great. The question period lasted so long they had to delay one of the other presentations. Some silver-haired old tyrant from Montreal kept challenging me on theoretical grounds and I really sucked it to him.

You wouldn't mean socked it to him, would you?

Whatever. Are you ready?

He examines his scruffy little beard in the mirror, pulls his killer turtleneck on over his head and begins to wrestle with the sleeves.

I still don't see why we have to meet this old guy.

But you will see, she says, adjusting his turtleneck, picking out the pills, letting them drop to the floor.

Techla's old guy is waiting downstairs in the lobby. It's crowded, and he is watching a group of young women with particular interest, moving his tongue absent-mindedly in and out, the way a lizard does watching flies on a hot day.

Ah, Techla, he says, liquidly, through stuffy adenoids. He is breathing heavily from having been outside in the cold. Either that or too much ogling.

I've brought one of your devotees to see you.

One of my devotees? Dear me, I didn't know I had any *male* devotees.

The man wears a heavy black overcoat lined with black persian lamb and a black hat with an enormous brim. He has a full grey stormy beard and leans on a silver-handled cane. The skin of his face is wrinkled and pale but flushed and varicose at the cheekbones.

Tim Fisher, I want you to meet the one and only R.J. Stufflebeam.

I beg your pardon?

R.J., this is Tim Fisher.

At first he thinks that Techla is having a little joke, but no one is smiling. The old man extends his hand. It is warm, moist, red and puffy.

Stufflebeam leads them into the bar and over to a table where an elderly lady is sipping a drink. She's a small woman, with cheeks so thoroughly rouged and lips so freshly painted, that in the darkened ambience of the bar she seems somehow unreal, a ventriloquist's perfect doll.

This, says Stufflebeam, is my pussy.

Tim waits to see if this last word will acquire a capital letter.

The lady looks up demurely and gives a pink little smile. In a few seconds she has gone from lady to woman to girl.

How are you, says Techla, extending her hand.

Pussy, are you pissed? says Stufflebeam.

Roger, says Pussy, in a voice as soft as a kitten's fur.

They all sit down, and Techla turns to Tim. Apparently, as the designated devotee, he is expected to begin the conversation. But he is tongue-tied, a familiar condition since his long depression began.

This young man is familiar with my work, I can assume? Stufflebeam says to Techla. He extracts some snuff from a tiny silver box.

He thrives on it, says Techla. Or is that past tense? Fisher, enlighten us.

Yes, Mr. Fisher, when did you first encounter my little atrocities?

In *Fin & Feather*, I believe.

Those loathesome, tightfisted, you should excuse my vulgarity cocksuckers. They still owe me money from work I did in the fifties.

I was his model back then, says Pussy, a bit louder than necessary.

You *are* pissed.

I am not.

You're pissed and I can prove it. You weren't my model in the fifties. You were too bloody old in the fifties. You had flabby arm pits and you sagged.

Oh, Pussy sighs. You two musn't take Roger seriously. He gets like this whenever a young woman shows him any interest at all.

Oh, shut up you old slut. No one wants to hear your pathetic attempts to get attention.

Maybe we should come back at a better—

So, Pussy, says Techla, do you mean to say that you modelled for Stufflebeam?

Pussy turns from the enraged face of her husband.

Yes, dear. I was his first model. I was on all of the early calendars.

The calendars? Tim blurts. Including the Autolite Sparkplug calendars?

Why, yes. You remember them?

There's this girl stepping out of a bubble bath? That one?

Indeed yes, Mr. Fisher, she purrs with a dreamy smile.

And that one with the guy with the jackhammer?

Oh, that one. That was so silly. I nearly *died* of embarrassment. And that man, that awful man Roger convinced to pose as the construction worker. He was our next-door neighbour. Oh, he was quite impossible.

You didn't complain too much when he started drooling all over your tits.

Oh, Roger, you are such a *bear* today. He did no such thing. I think he was just a very lonely man.

That money-grubbing bohunk hounded us for months—as though he were some sort of professional!

Why? says Techla, her face a mask of academic curiosity.

He insisted on being paid, dear.

Paid, grunts Stufflebeam. Back then, you didn't go paying models a fortune. You couldn't afford to. You had em sit for you and you gave em a couple of sketches of themselves. The girls were easy. They were pleased just to see all that attention paid to them. Vain little vixens. Ha! Delightful little—

What kind of attention were you referring to, Roger? says Pussy.

Well that's another matter entirely. A man has his needs, hey, Tim? He's never so foolish as to turn down little a gift from Cupid, hey? *This* man understands what I'm talking about, says Stufflebeam with a gummy smile. You don't understand me. You never have and you never will.

Well, says Techla, I think we've presumed enough on your time.

Pussy would rather suck on a bottle of gin all day long. That's *her* idea of a good time.

It beats sucking on that thing of yours all day long, cries Pussy. Oh, Techla. Tim. Please, don't take all this so seriously. You must come and dine with us soon. We'll have a *wonderful* time.

She lowers her head to flash a shy smile at Tim as he rises from the table.

Well, says Techla to Tim back in the lobby.

She is attempting to suppress a smile. She looks almost radiant.

Don't say it, he says.

Say what?

She laughs all the way up on the elevator, all the way into their room. It is the closest thing to a normal laugh he has ever heard from her.

Much later, after their nightly *Unzucht* (Techla's word), Tim asks, Does this mean we're a...we're a....

Couple? she says.

Yeah.

Roger and Pussy?

Well—

We'll talk about it in the morning.

At breakfast, at the Toronto airport, Techla says, With regard to your question of the night before, hm? The woman whose ticket you inherited, well, she asked me the same question. It was Rona, actually. And I must answer you as I did her.

Yes?

As your friend Bartleby might say....

Ah, yes.

I prefer not to, they say in unison.

IN EARLY MARCH THE MERCURY PLUNGES DOWN, and day after day snowless slate-grey clouds drift through the Edmonton skies. On one of these desolate days, Tim finishes typing his first draft of *Maria's Doll*. He has worked all day on it because he has finally persuaded Nancy to compromise and come over that night to read the typed manuscript. All his typing and revising have got the juices going. He manages to wash down a hotdog with a bottle of beer for lunch at four o'clock, and he eats a couple of donuts for supper at seven.

He has an idea for his final paper of the year in the Theatre of the Absurd course, an interpretation of *Waiting for Godot* that everyone in the seminar is likely to find acceptable. He finds time to clean up some of the stickier messes in his kitchen and the grottier ones in the bathroom. He washes his dishes. He is far from happy, but he is one full step above his nothing-to-be-done mode and he isn't shitting five times a day with existential dread. And Nancy is coming over. Soon he will hear her swift, careful step on the old staircase.

Around two thirty in the morning, after too many cups of coffee and an exasperating silence, Nancy summons Tim from his seventeenth or eighteenth game of solitaire in the bedroom. She sits on the chesterfield with his manuscript pages neatly stacked on the coffee table. He has provided her with pencils, pens, erasers, bookmarks—anything for her convenience. But these have been shoved to the side of the coffee table, so the manuscript remains unmarked.

Well?

Timmy, this is so weird. You know what? The mother, she reminds me of *my* mum. This story...this long depression of yours...this new physique...it's....

New physique?

You have lost so much weight, I scarcely recognize you. I think what's happening is growing pains. I think you're gonna be a writer when you grow up.

But did you like it?

She shrugs, then yawns. Yeah, I guess so. I mean I know so. But if my mum ever gets hold of this thing, you're in deep shit.

Can we put your mum on hold for a bit? Did you like it?

Yes. I told you I did.

You seem kind of unsure.

No, really, I liked it. In fact I loved it. Yes. Loved it.

You loved it, you really loved it?

Well, it's not like you're an expert on native people or abandoned kids. There's something kind of Hollywood about these kids. And the baby doll, I think she'd be better if she was a boy doll. You know, to go with the Christmas thing?

The Christmas thing. You didn't like it, did you.

Don't look so depressed. Yes. Look, I really love your story, she says, measuring her phrases, but....

But what? You didn't like the kids.

Oh, nothing. Forget it.

No, really, I want the truth. I can take it.

It's nothing. It's just that....

Tell me!

I think it might make a better movie. That's all.

Nancy's lips are quivering.

You mean if I made the kids more realistic—

You can't just make your kids more realistic. You have to know something about kids. And you can't possibly know anything about kids if you haven't raised any.

That's crazy, Nancy. You mean before I can become a writer I've got to become a father?

Before any man can presume to write about kids he should know something about them. That's all I'm saying. And most guys are scared silly over the possibility of having kids.

I hope you're not putting me in the same boat as Alistair Vaughan.

Nancy doesn't answer. She just looks at Tim. She looks at him for so long that he finally has to look away.

The sound of someone climbing the old staircase. Tim monitors the steps up to the second-floor landing, hoping they will stop at either of

low him. But the footsteps move slowly upward. The feet
and quite possibly masculine. They labour up the stairs and
a halt in front of Tim's door. The owner of these feet breathes
. He waits until he catches his breath. Then he knocks. A mod-
erately heavy man. Therefore not Tim's dad, back from Victoria with
more advice. And definitely not Techla Wahrsager.

The visitor knocks again. Each knock is a hamfisted thump that
seems to shake the garret. A policeman?

Tim! someone roars, perhaps through a scarf. Open up!

Tim slouches out of his bedroom in his bare feet. He steps into a
sticky puddle of spilled orange juice. He fumbles open the door. Brother
Derek. He looks immensely pleased with himself, his bronchial cords
already heaving themselves into a laugh. But Derek doesn't laugh.

Tim. Jesus. You look awful.

Come in.

Tim's big brother wears his old convoy coat with the wooden pegs
for buttons, heavy green corduroys, and an alpine toque. His beefy
complexion has reddened in the wind. He looks around the garret,
squinting disapproval. So this is where the tortured genius spends his
time. God, your place is a mess. You were never this bad at home.

Nothing to be done, Tim sighs, inspecting his foot. He hates it
when his feet get sticky. Orange juice is absolutely the worst.

Derek turns to face Tim. Are you sick or something?

I dunno, says Tim, crawling back into bed.

Can I make us some coffee?

Yeah.

Tim nods toward the kitchenette. He will let Derek make coffee.
Maybe he will go along with the sickness thing. Watch your step, he
calls to his brother. I spilled some orange juice on the floor.

Derek swears.

He returns to the bedroom, inspecting his boot. He has taken off
his coat to reveal a Scandinavian ski sweater. Two or three years of
dramatic change in men's fashions and marriage to a stylish woman
have made no impression on Derek Fisher. He still sports a brushcut.
He has acquired more flesh, which seems to round off his body without slumping over his belt. He looks healthy and prosperous.

So, give me the lowdown. Why are you in the sack?

I have no reason to get out of bed.

Tim, it's a beautiful day.

What's so beautiful about it?

The sun's out. The birds are crapping on the cars.

I repeat: I have no reason to get out of bed.

When did you ever need a reason to get out of bed?

Very well, I've lost my reasons for getting out of bed in the morning. I'm going through a...a phase or something. The world can't seem to let me alone. Why didn't you phone before you came over?

Nancy told me not to. She said you'd find an excuse not to have visitors. Was she right?

Partly. I talk to some people.

What people?

People who are as fed up as I am.

Fed up with what?

All the bullshit. You know.

Derek looks bewildered. He goes out to the kitchen and returns with two mugs of coffee.

What bullshit are you talking about, Tim?

Everywhere.

Yeah, but can we narrow it down a bit?

Seven thousand Americans have died in Vietnam. God knows how many South Vietnamese. God knows how many North Vietnamese or how many civilians. Does anybody besides me ever ask why?

I don't know anyone, besides Alistair Vaughan, of course, who thinks it's a real *good* war, says Derek, sipping his coffee. But why should a war halfway around the world keep you from getting up in the morning? I mean if it's bullshit that's getting you down, surely you could at least come up with some *local* bullshit.

Okay, here's some local bullshit. This ravine behind the house. You can see it out my west window. Nice view, right? You can even see Nancy's house on Villa Avenue. I've got a beautiful view. She's got a beautiful view, and all because of the ravine. Nancy says that's why the property is so expensive in this part of town. There's goddam *pheasants* down there. So here we are, all of us happy Wasps, we live in this lovely neighbourhood and we look at this lovely view. Do you have any idea what goes on *in* the ravine?

Don't tell me the pheasants are copulating.

Tim doesn't laugh.

There's a group of native kids, he continues. They go down that ravine time after time, and they sniff glue. They've all been taken out of their homes up north because their parents can't take care of them. They hate the foster homes they've been assigned to. Some of them

their real parents are or where they are. They don't
town, the Indian kids no longer belong on the reser-
ed kids have lost track of their people. So they all
in our beautiful ravine, blitzed out of their minds on
...ie glue. Who's taking care of those kids? Who's loving them
when they need to be loved? Who is responsible for these kids?

Since when have you ever worried about kids? You don't even
have kids.

I talk to them. I try to tell them they're hurting themselves. But as
far as they're concerned, I'm just another white guy telling them they're
no good.

So why do you bother? says Derek. I mean, if they're hopeless
cases.

There is an impatient edge to Derek's voice.

I don't bother, Tim says. Not any more. I'm sick and tired of the
whole Godforsaken mess of humanity. I figure if I stay in bed I won't
meet up with any of this bullshit. Either that or move to Victoria. I
dunno, he sighs. Nothing to be done.

Somehow you never struck me as the social worker type, Tim. Derek
stares down at his mug. I think you're just depressed. And you know
what? I think you're depressed because there's nothing *happening* in your
life. Nancy tells me you're taking this course in the literature of the absurd? She says you've gotta read this guy Thomas de Beckett?

Samuel Beckett.

I went to a play of his once. Sara's folks had tickets, so we all went.
Talk about bullshit. Talk about twenty-four carat bullshit. These two
guys, all they do all night long is sit on their asses like a couple of
welfare bums waiting for some guy who never shows up. This guy
Beckett, he's a Frenchman, right?

He's an Irishman.

Well, Irish then. My point is, maybe life is absurd in Ireland. Maybe
life is absurd in Vietnam or whatever. But life here in Alberta....

Derek tosses down the last of his coffee and stands up. He begins
to pace at the foot of Tim's bed.

Life here in Alberta—if you're not an Indian orphan or whatever—
is just not all that absurd. There's building in the building sector, there's
oil in the oil patch, there's growth in the chemical industry, they're
logging the north again, there's money to be made in the beef industry. Even the farmers don't seem to bitch any more. You and me, Tim,
we were born at a very good time. We were born in a lucky place. Sure,

we have the odd bit of bad luck, but we bounce back and get out there and continue the battle. It's like we were…appointed by the Big Guy to go out there and do something with our lives, and have a good time doing it. I mean, try to help our neighbours if they're not a hopeless bunch of losers. Try to be a boy scout once in a while. I've taken my share of old ladies across the street. But Tim, life is short and the world is not a leper colony. And even if half the world is a leper colony, you don't belong with the lepers. Lepers don't play those things, he says, pointing at Tim's banjo case. Lepers don't make people laugh, they don't love to go fishing. Come on, Tim, snap out of it.

Derek approaches Tim's bed and throws his patented slow-motion left hook. It lands on Tim's shoulder.

If I snap out of it, as you suggest, I'm not sure I have a better place to snap in to.

That's my point, Tim. There *is* no better place than here. You're living in paradise and you don't know it. Get up. Smell the flowers. Get laid. Get drunk. Get a job. Anything but lie around and feel sorry for the world's losers.

Derek wraps his scarf around his neck. Then he gets his old convoy coat and hesitates. Should he pull on his boots first or should he put on his coat? He is rarely confused about such things, rarely flustered. Rarely angry enough so that the nerves seem to twitch beneath the skin of his hearty face.

The snowless clouds of early March arrive with a dry wind and slow bouts of melting and freezing. The snowbanks blacken into grimy crystals. The streets are streaked with black ice. The road crews continue to pile on the sand and the salt, and the avenues and boulevards turn by degrees a darker grey. Tim gazes at the street below, at the ravine, at Nancy's converted mansion on Villa Avenue, all of which seem to have emerged from the great nullity in his brain. He begins his morning with a game of solitaire. He will go ten games and then he will quit. He is capable of going twenty or thirty games until he wins, but after the first ten or so, the pleasure seems to be replaced by a momentum that keeps him blinky-eyed and dealing his cards for no apparent reason.

He knows this is not healthy. He knows there is nothing to be done. But hark. The sound of footsteps on the old staircase. Up past the second floor. Once more, a man's walk.

Doesn't anyone use the goddam phone any more?

This walker pauses even more than Derek did to catch his breath. This one's breath has a little familiar squeak to it. By their breathing shall ye know them.

Before Gump Lowney can knock, Tim opens the door. Gump looks stupefied by the exertion of climbing to the third floor in his heavy parka and boots. He stands in Tim's doorway with the tiniest stub of a cigarette, ambushed, caught smoking perhaps, facing disciplinary action.

Gump, come in.

He lumbers in shyly, humbly, following his great red nose. He is not sure what to expect.

So, he says. So. This is where you hang your hat, eh?

He grinds his cigarette into a dirty saucer on the coffee table, gazes around the flat. He gives Tim a side glance.

You under the weather or something?

Not feeling my oats these days.

Kinda punk?

Not much get up and go.

Hm.

Gump saunters around beneath the spine of the attic ceiling where he can straighten up without fear of bumping his head: gawking.

You've gotten as messy as I am, he mutters. His words always seem to come from the nose. Like a large dog he seems to filter all data through his nose. It's the key to his character. You couldn't put Gump on paper without learning about his nose in all its red and bony glory.

You like my digs?

Seen worse.

Gump hesitates over an unlit cigarette. He stares at the cigarette then sticks it up above his large left ear.

Well, I was in the neighbourhood. Thought I'd stop in. See how yiz are getting on. You haven't exactly been what I'd call sociable these days.

Tim wonders if word has gotten out. Who would have told Gump? His parents? Nancy? Derek? He could have run into one of them.

What does an old friend have to do to get a cup of coffee around here?

Tim gets out the coffee pot. Eyes focussed on the chore at hand, he tells Gump about his fallen state.

I guess I've come down in the world, he says. Temporary setback. I've run out of things to do. Don't know what to do. Don't want to teach. Don't want to be a grad student any more. Don't like the world out there, but it won't leave me alone. Don't much like the world in here. Don't even like getting dressed in the morning.

It's Saturday. What the hell.

Any morning.

Gump warms his hands on the mug of scalding coffee. He blows on it, settles his rump on the radiator by the west window.

Remember when you were in the States getting all edge-mucated? Remember what I was doing up here?

Teaching.

Well, sort of. I was only a sub. Some days I had to do army stuff because I was on the last year of my R.O.T.P. warrant. So when I wasn't down at the armories or out on parade or something, I had to walk into a new class of adolescent psychopaths. I'd get the kids some poor slob had abandoned for a day because he'd lost control of them.

Disciplinary cases?

Yahoos. Thugs with no respect for anybody. One was a fourteen-year-old girl who weighed two hundred pounds and beat the shit out of anyone who got in her way.

Yeah, says Tim, I remember now.

Well, do you remember the time I didn't write?

No.

For the longest time I didn't answer your letters, Gump says.

I guess it slipped my mind. I guess I never thought about it very much.

Well sir, Gump continues, I will never forget that time. Those yahoos. It was like they were lying in wait for a sub so they could try out their guerilla tactics. And it got to me. Early on, it really got to me. I was a goddam moving target. Not every day. Sometimes I got some nice kids. The regular teacher was maybe not faking it, not running away from his class. And the kids were half decent. I'd get to thinking maybe this wasn't going to be a bad year after all, then *whamo!* I'd get thrown in with a swimming pool full of sharks. One day some kid tossed one of those jumbo firecrackers at me when I was writing an assignment on the board. The kind that's illegal now? Well sir, I found out why they made them illegal.

Gump retrieves his cigarette from his left ear perch and stares at it.

Yahoos like that. Jesus. Anyway. I'm getting side-tracked. It got so bad by the winter of that year. Sixty-four? Same year you were breaking hearts in Oregon.

Yeah.

It got so bad I couldn't—Gump gestures with his mug at Tim's robe and pyjamas—get up in the morning. The office'd phone me and I'd say I was sick as a dog! Lucky my voice is so nasal, they'd always believe me when I said I had a cold. But when you say no a few times, they stop phoning you.

Gump lights up and takes a long thoughtful drag.

So I tells this major, this guy from down at the armories. Real good guy. Old guy, pensioned off. Always hanging around the legion. I tells him, "George," I says, "these yahoos at school have got me down so bad I can't goddam rouse myself to get up in the morning." "You can't get up in the morning?" old George says. "Well," he says, "do what I do."

Gump puts down his coffee mug and his cigarette and he waves Tim into the bedroom. Gump sits down on the side of Tim's bed, chortling nervously, then he lies back on the bed.

This major, he says, "Look! If you can't get outa bed in the morning, do this. Put one foot on the floor. Won't kill ya." So there you are, nice and warm in bed, one foot on the floor, right? Then this old major, he says, "Put your *other* foot on the floor." Like this. Gump remains stretched out diagonally on Tim's bed, his stocking feet now touching the throw rug by the bed. "You sit up," he says, "and you rock back and forth, like this. If it's a ballbreaker of a cold morning, you keep the quilt around your body, but you rock back and forth, back and forth. Now here's the only part that takes will power," this major says. "But it only takes a small bit of will power. You give your body just a tiny little shove, just enough to rock forward."

Gump rocks himself from a sitting position on the edge of the bed to a hunched but standing position. With the quilt draped like a shawl over his shoulders, he looks like Granny Mullen on a bad morning.

See? Now that you're up you have *another* choice. Do you keep on going all the way to the pisser or do you go back to bed? It takes about the same amount of energy to stay up as it does to get back into bed, eh? You may as well get up!

Gump wears a huge smile. Even his nose is smiling.

Every fever, except for the last one, breaks. Every winter, except for the last one, turns to spring. For the lucky ones perhaps the season in Hell is a limited sentence. For Tim, it has something to do with not being able to get out of bed in the morning. But after a while even Hell is boring. You don't beg your keeper to let you out. You don't beg God on your knees. By this time, if a vestige of belief remains in you,

you are all prayed out anyway. There are no stocks, no chains. If you're bored with this version of Hell, you just walk out.

The exit from this prosaic Hell begins with a certain kind of honesty. You begin to admit things to yourself. If the world and much of the universe is black, there must also be at least the occasional splash of white. Black depends for its existence on the omnipresence of white. And despair could not thrive without the possibility of exultation. Evil would have nowhere to go without something we have come to call goodness. In Tim's case, this quality showed itself most recently in Gump. The world can be half-full of shit but it cannot be completely full of shit. This is biologically improbable.

You mutter clichés about the flux of interdependent opposites everywhere in the cosmos. *For evere the latter ende of joye is wo.* Geoffrey Chaucer. *Every cloud has a silver lining.* Granny Mullen. You are led around once more by the clamours of your body. You start to think about food. Or Rita. Or Nancy. You walk long distances willingly because your body's wisdom, long dormant, enslaved to the vagaries of your zombie mind, insists on being heard. You pull on your rubber boots and you walk downtown or across the river. You go for the quiet neighbourhood roads, the alleys. You go where the puddles are deepest and flow like brownish grey rivers. God's bloodveins in a mucky world. In your rubber boots you're a giant in a land of new rivers. You are Thoreau. You're a child. Everywhere you go, the ice feels exhausted and turns to slush beneath your boots. The chinook brings a new wind across the city and past the brewery so that a warm and yeasty emanation blows into your nostrils like the breath of God. All the unanswered prayers for sanity, for *meaning*, for *hope*, are suddenly answered without the least syllable of a prayer as you wander all the way back home smelling and smelling with boundless surprise the squalid leavings of winter. The smell of melting mud. Isn't that your mother's flower garden? Smell those wonderful excavations down the old street, the ones the bulldozers used to dig for the basements of new houses? And then the smell of melting dogshit. Attar of returning life.

You are in love with no one, but try to tell your body that. It has its own ideas. It feels a warm sort of magnetism in the direction of Nancy's flat in the converted mansion. Last night he dreamed he was dancing a slow one with Techla Wahrsager of all people. Let's bring her in on this. The song was "Blue Skies," sung by Frank Sinatra. And what about Slimy? Where on earth have you gone to, Slimy?

Gump's getting up method. Perhaps it all began there, the morning after he had talked to Gump, April 15, 1966. Eleven fifteen A.M. The foot on the floor, then the other foot, then the rocking, that little push forward, and you are standing. Not happy, not even hopeful, but up in the Granny Mullen crouch. Up and standing. Then you get dressed. No appetite, but at least you are vertical, radio on. And it's not even nine o'clock. Bessie Smith is singing so loud that you don't hear the footfalls on the old staircase. Dressed, coherent, you open your door to the sound of a terse knock.

Good morning, says Barb Viner.

She has an expressive round face alive with stage grimaces and cocking eyebrows, a face rich with irony. Today she is offering a static smile, Groucho Marx on a marquee poster. She wears an open trenchcoat. Underneath, a bright red and white pant suit with huge drooping collars and an impressive brass ring attached to the zipper on her collar. She looks you over.

Jesus, are you sick or something?

Ah.

Your hair, it's all over the place, your beard, you've lost weight, you look like an old rubbydub, Timmy, are you going to ask me in or what, no, I haven't got time to seduce you, you look too terrible for sex, I just came to say hi.

Maybe I could get cleaned up a bit.

Now you're talkin.

And we could meet for coffee?

Right now but.

I'd ask you in but my place is uh sort of—

I'll wait out here in the hall. Sheesh.

He not only shaves, but he undresses to take a fast shower, combs his hair and resolves to get a haircut real soon. He feels the need for what some people call spring cleaning. Barb leads the way into a restaurant on 124th. She ducks down behind a menu, reappears.

I'm famished. Let's have lunch instead.

He orders a big lunch at Barb's urging, but when the waiter brings his steak sandwich, he recognizes what might be the beginnings of hunger. He cuts off a small morsel of sirloin. Done rare. The juice pours out around the tines of the fork. Very tentatively he puts the small piece of meat into his mouth. Not bad, actually.

So. Our mutual friend, Madame Bookstore, read your manuscript. Pretty impressed she was.

I don't know what she told you, but she told me it needed a lot of work. It's about a female doll, but she thinks the doll should be a baby boy. And that's just for starters. Maybe she's right. Maybe the kid should be a baby boy.

The kid?

I mean the doll. The doll in the story.

Barb Viner eats in thoughtful silence. Tim carves another piece of steak, a larger one this time. This piece tastes as good as the first. He tries a third piece. He tries a bit of salad. He tries his hot roll slathered with butter.

Like your lunch? Barb says.

Zhgood.

You look like you haven't eaten since the Brooklyn Dodgers won the pennant.

Ym. Tell me about it. I've been turning my vast talents to a term paper on *Waiting for Godot*. In case you haven't seen it, it's about a guy who doesn't show up. I think I've been waiting for the bugger all winter. That kind of stuff is hard on the old appetite.

Could brother Derek be right? he wonders. *Law Student discovers Real Meaning of Beckett's Godot.*

Barb shrugs. She pours herself a cup of tea, stirs in a double sugar, adds some milk. She dislodges something from her gums with her index finger.

Yeah, she says, and stifles a yawn. If our mutual friend knew I was about to tell you something, she would sentence me to a fast slide down the razor blade of life. Sorry, you're still eating.

Continue, he says.

A steak belch bursts into his adenoids.

Our mutual friend, do you like her these days? Excuse me but I have to ask. Do you sometimes want to get together with her?

He shrugs. Like her? Yeah, I like her. Okay, nosey, I sometimes have these...thoughts about her. I still—I was even in love with her once. But she went and got knocked up. For her it was always Alistair fucking Vaughan. Why?

Alistair Vaughan is ancient history.

It doesn't matter. A long time ago, she could have chosen me and she chose him.

Oh, poor baby. So like you'd rather sit around and brood and feel sorry for yourself? Gimme a break. Would you believe me if I told you that Alistair fucking Vaughan has like a *problem* ? Would you believe me if I told you that she felt like sorry for Alistair fucking Vaughan?

No. I wouldn't. Besides, now it's Joel fucking Black and tomorrow it'll be Someone fucking Else. She likes guys who are bad for her. I'm her little court jester.

Maybe these guys are just a substitute for the real thing. Funny. I just had this little thought. Do you believe in Fate? Forgive the two-bit psychoanalysis, okay? You're writing this story about abandoned kids, right? Nancy thinks your doll should be a boy. You think she might be right etcetera etcetera. Did it ever occur to you that the two of you are both thinking somewhat obsessively about abandoned kids?

Get to the point, Sigmund.

Well, it seems she has her reasons. You have your reasons.

Nancy gave her own baby up for adoption. I'm writing a story that has kids in it. In fact, yes, I think the doll should be a boy. There's this Christmas motif. Where is all this deep stuff heading?

Can you keep a secret?

Yes, he says, and a huge fear like a cloud begins to loom over him.

This comes from the mothers' network, which means as well....

Barb pauses, throws her hair back out of her face.

...the doctors' network. And let's say that, according to my information, medical information, there's no way in hell that Nancy's—

Oh, my God, he says, and Barb Viner nods, and this time there is no irony anywhere to be found in her face.

Oh, shit. Oh, no. You've got to be. You've just got. Oh, shit. Oh, Barb. Oh, shit.

Let me guess. You've been talking to Barb.

She didn't tell me, I mean technically speaking. I figured it out myself.

She absolutely promised she wouldn't tell.

Like I say—

Sh! Napoleon's doing his rounds. Whisper.

Like I say, Barb did not tell me. I figured it out on my own.

With Barb's help.

Some.

She promised me. She swore.

Nancy, who else knows about this?

None of your business.

Did you tell Joel Black?

Look, Timmy, you are so behind on the news, I scarcely know where to begin. Here, hold this. Pretend you're a customer.

Did you tell Alistair?

I happen to be on shift here, in case you thought I had nothing better to do than exchange pleasantries with you.

I can't believe you'd tell those assholes and you wouldn't tell me.

Did I say I told them?

Go ahead, deny it.

He's coming back. Keep your voice down.

I've been some kid's father for four years and every guy in town knows it except me.

Three years.

Nancy, Jesus.

If we're going to slug it out, with Napoleon on the warpath, we may as well do it in the alley.

Where are you going?

The same place you're going. Come on. I have a little surprise for you.

Charming. Garbage cans and rubble. A perfect place for a fight. So, what's the big surprise?

In due course. You say why did I tell Alistair? Because he thought it was his and I didn't want him to think we were connected in any way. I wanted a clean break. For the record. You say why did I tell Joel? Because I was in therapy and I had to talk to someone.

I dare say you're doing a lot more than talk to our friend Joel.

More of Barb's information?

No. Five minutes with that opportunist weasel and I just knew you'd be on his dance card.

What is that supposed to mean?

You have a built-in thing for Canada Fancy Blue Ribbon bastards. Evidently.

Don't include me in that smarmy company. I never used you. Nancy, I don't get it, I just don't get it. Why would you tell those assholes and not tell me?

You wouldn't understand.

Well, try me. Just...would you try me?

Timmy, there's just some things you don't tell someone because they aren't ready to hear them. You know yourself, when you want to reveal something, you choose who to reveal it to. You were just not ready to know that you had fathered a child. I doubt if you're even ready to hear it now. I wanted to tell you, sure. Lots of times. Sometimes I'd make up my mind to tell you and then I'd figure no, wait, he's having a huge crisis and he's too depressed. I'd give the poor guy another nervous breakdown. Other times I'd think, no, he's happy in his innocence. Why bring him down to earth? He's too too...you're too....

I'm too what?

You never want to hear bad news. You're too involved in your own world to find out you've fathered another human being. Most of the time you're lost in the past, remembering your childhood or something, and life isn't lived in the innocent past. It's here. In the alley with the garbage cans. You're the only twenty-four year old guy I can actually shock, do you know that? You are the only twenty-four year old guy I know who sees these entanglements strictly in moral terms. Remember that awful day when I told you I'd given him away? My baby?

How could I forget it?

I was so terrified you'd judge me, and yet I had to tell you I'd done it, and when you didn't judge me and you gave me that hug, I felt so....I don't know, *restored* again. I thought, Yes, I can tell him, I *will* tell him. He's ready. And what did you go and do?

I road off into the sunset.

You tried to cut me out of your life. And you did. I was suddenly unclean, wasn't I. I was tainted goods.

No!

Oh, yes I was. Except you thought you had no part in it. Isn't that a riot? And Joel Black may be as big a womanizer as Alistair ever was, but at least I could talk to him about the seamy side of things without any fear that he'd judge me for it. You see what I mean? You think sexual entanglements are all a matter of right or wrong. Well, for those of us who live, actually live, in this vale of tears, they're more complicated than that. Desire has bugger all to do with right or wrong.

Nancy, these affairs are only as complicated as you want to make them. And spending all your sack time with counsellors who prey on their clients when they're at their most vulnerable, or with Don Juans like Alistair, only makes you more cynical about love. Sure, I've been the innocent all these years, and I tend to prefer trout streams to alleys and garbage, human or otherwise. But don't tell me your cynicism isn't just as blind as my romantic notions about things. You court cynicism. And surprise! You find it around every corner.

You know, it's very odd. You haven't once asked me about William.

Boy oh boy. Not another one.... That's a very cynical cackle you have. What's so funny?

Yes, I suppose I do have a cynical laugh.

Who's William?

William is our son.

Oh, my God. How did you find that out? I mean I thought you weren't supposed to know anything—

I have my spies.

Well, tell me. I want to know. I mean, yes, sure, of course I'm interested in William. Tell me about William.

When I think you're ready to hear about William, I'll tell you, and not one second sooner. Now, just don't interrupt. That night, almost four years ago, I had sex with you—

Because you were pissed off with Alistair.

No. I did it because I thought you really loved me. I thought this wonderful poet, this guy I'd known all my life, this guy who was just starting to bloom, he is just gaga over me.

And you were pissed off with Alistair.

Yes. And drunk too, I might add.

And you were right about me. This wonderful blooming poet was gaga over you. But in your typically self-immolating way, you chose Alistair. Right?

He hates you. To this day he hates you.

I find that a little hard to believe.

He's jealous of you.

Alistair fucking Vaughan is jealous of me?

Want to know why? It goes back to that time when we were all little actors and actresses in high school. Remember when all that flu was going around?

Yeah. *A Midsummer's Night's Dream.*

Well, everyone was getting some exotic flu, but Alistair, being Alistair, had mumps. He was the star of the show, but he went and got mumps. I guess the rest of us had it when we were tots, but not Alistair. And from mumps, he got an infection. Do you see where this is heading?

What, he's impotent?

Don't you wish it. No, but he's sterile. He found out maybe three years ago. And then I told him about our little night at the Crop. I'd known it was you right from the start. I think it must eat away at him to this day, that it was you and not him. And do you know what? Sometimes I really feel for him. I don't mean I'm in love with him. That ended ages ago. But I feel really bad that I hurt him by telling him, and I feel bad for what this condition has done to him.

Holy shit. Is this your big surprise?

No. Is this too much reality for you? You see, you've got your little moral categories for people. I am plainly promiscuous.

I didn't—

Don't interrupt. Joel Black is unprofessional. Alistair is an exploiter of female virtue. And you can't see beyond your precious little categories because you want to be aloof from what you see as the garbage. You want to cling to your innocence as though it were some sort of priceless pearl. And you ask me why I tried to spare you the news that you were part of the whole mess? Give, me, a, break.

You must really despise me. How long have you—

I don't despise you. But you do tend to piss me off. Of late. I started to get pissed off when I read that long thing you wrote. I kept thinking, he is so smug.

Smug?

So sure you occupy the moral high ground. It made me want to...well...rattle you a bit. I have to go back.

Nancy, wait. When can I see you again? We need to talk about this.

I don't know, Timmy. I'll have to think about that. Your timing is not terrific. When I needed you to care for me, you fled. Now that I'm moving forward with my life—

You want me to show you that I care? You already know what happens to guys who care for you. You wrote the book on how to handle them. You let them get all mushy over you and then you pull the carpet out. You know your problem, you're afraid of intimacy.

You can't possibly mean that.

You know what appeals to you about Joel Black? He's virtually incapable of returning love. You chose him because he has this *sign* over his brow: I am too cool for lasting love. Then you're perfectly safe. You don't have to fear intimacy, right? Am I reading this one right? When Big Joel gives you the slip you can blame it all on him and go on back to feeling like the injured party. How utterly safe.

So. So so so. We're back to that theme again, are we? You think you've got me figured out, eh? Well, I'm glad you brought up the subject of Joel because he and I happen to be moving in together. In fact, we do the big move at the end of the month.

Moving in together? Is that the surprise you had in store for me? Well....

You can't do this. We'll never see each other again.

What's this renewed enthusiasm all about? Are you bo. being Timmy Fisher? Do you want to get things going with cause you're bored? Or do you just crave the experience of havi affair with the girl next door?

No, none of that. I've never been bored like that, at least not with you. That would never happen. Maybe I'm a bit bored with teaching night school. I'd like to spend more time writing, especially since I'm out of my big funk. I've been having these thoughts and I can't wait to get to some place where I can write. It's hard to explain.

You see, Tim, this is what bothers me about you. You have this sort of idea that you want to be a writer, but no books to show for it. Now that you have this job you say that you ought to be writing. If you wrote full-time and found out how hard that was, you'd wish you had a good paying job again. You have this sort of idea you want to be with me, but not really, because you never stick with anything. If we became lovers, I can see you a week or two down the line, absolutely dying of post-coital sadness, and saying to me why don't we go back to being friends.

That wouldn't happen, Nancy. Nancy?

Don't you see? I don't need another lover. I'm tired of the parade. If I need anything at all it's a....

What? Say it.

It's a life's companion.

Where I come from, those are called husbands.

Yes, I suppose they are. It's a frightening word.

Is that why you're moving in with Joel Black?

Let's just for the sake of argument say, Why not.

And I'm what? Dangerous?

In a way you are. You still have this appearance of innocence. And some women might think you're a great catch and fall for you for the wrong reasons and then wake up one morning to discover you're off to find yourself in Katmandu. Until you find something, you're a rather likeable disaster waiting to happen. Don't look at me like that. You know it's true. You've got to get your teeth into something and stick with it. You have to become passionate about something before you can...you can...You've got to *believe* in something.

But I'm an artist. That's what artists are supposed to be like.

And what is your art?

I'm a writer for God's sake!

Timmy, writers write things.

I write things all the time. You just read my doll story not that long ago.

You told me that got rejected.

So?

Writers sit down and *finish* things, and then they send them off and they get published. These things are called books. Then they get money for these books because some people out there somewhere have bought them and read them. Willingly! Then they write another one and another one. They do it because they *want* to. Maybe this isn't fair to say, but the only published thing of yours I've ever liked—besides your letters—is that poem you wrote for me.

Well, I've got some bad news for you.

Don't tell me you plagiarized it.

No. I really wrote it. I don't think it's much good, but I really wrote it. But...I didn't really write it for you.

You mean to say you wrote this thing for someone else?

Well, sort of.

You bugger. That was the only poem any guy ever wrote for me, and I was really proud of it. I've kept a copy of the published version. I showed it to Joel once and it made him jealous. Who'd you write it for?

Rita Symington.

Her!

Look, just promise me one thing.

What?

Just one thing. Promise!

What!

That this isn't just some terminal conversation. A way of dismissing someone who's been a pain in the ass. That it's just the first round, okay? That we'll talk again?

I have to get back to work.

And wait wait wait. Promise me that you won't move in together without thinking about it. I mean, who else would I talk with—willingly —in an alley full of garbage?

You're so poetic.

I'm serious.

We're not just moving in. We're getting married.

My God.

Are you happy for me?

This is probably not the best time to ask.

I've wanted this for a long time now. That some day I'd have a kid or two and do it right. If I got a second chance.

You never once told me you wanted to be married and have a kid.

Maybe you never asked. You're not getting depressed, are you?

No.

Your lip is quivering.

I was thinking about the other thing.

The other thing? You mean the let's-keep-the-dialogue-going thing? Timmy, long after you've gone to your final trout stream in the sky, I'll be having conversations with you.

Me too.

Can we at least shake hands on that?

I guess so.

Goodbye, Tim.

Bye.

4 *the* FIRST TROUT

At night on the Banff-Jasper highway there is almost no traffic. He slouches on the shoulder of the road, hoping for a late-running tourist bound for Lake Louise. He wonders if twenty-five isn't a bit old for this sort of thing.

Tim has been fishing with Gump Lowney, a strange trip, this one. Alone now, he's on his way south from Jasper. To make a visit to a very special place. If you were searching for a word to describe his emotional state, excited would be that word: the excitement of slow-burning fuses; what Reverend Mountjoy used to refer to as the stirrings of youth.

The stars are coming out. Venus first, then the North Star, which at this moment will rise above the mountains that surround Lake Louise. On the phone a certain young woman said, If you promise to do some work around here and do something with all your junk, I promise to put you up for the next while. His junk, as she calls it, is mostly his files, letters, photos and keepsakes from a life dedicated to preserving his past. When his parents moved to an apartment, he had to box this junk and take it to his garret. But now he has sold his ailing Beetle and lost his garret to a new owner. This certain someone said that she would let him store the junk and his banjo for a while, but soon it has to be gone. Without a car, he can think of only one way to deliver on his promise.

Burn it all. Except for the banjo, of course. Burn it all. It feels a bit like burning bridges, but what the hell. He has a few hours left to think about it. Right now it sits in a corner of her little cabin. This certain someone. He knows her name, but to speak it would be a bit like telling his mantra. She and Tim have not become lovers, not yet, but they are beginning to drift like milt and roe together, beneath the same riffle.

The night is fragrant with larch and juniper, and the constellations are on display like a cosmic jewelry store. Orion. Ursa major, the Great Bear, his ass end in the Big Dipper. Tim can't keep his eyes off the constellations. He wanders like a drunk over the median line. Each little galaxy grows brighter. He spins around and glides tapping up the highway like Gene Kelly, da da daddin dada da da daddin, while the stars swarm like a million fireflies. He calls the Great Dog Albert, and the Little Dog Pepper. He calls the Serpent Ouroboros. Da da daddin da da....

He informs the cosmos,

I'm singin in the rain...

then from the foot of Orion, humming and wheeling into the southern horizon, let's see, yes, perhaps Eridanus? The Great River. Where Phaeton crashed in his flaming chariot. No doubt Phaeton's dad found out about the child Phaeton had fathered and grounded him.

I'm free! he shouts. I ain't got no car! I ain't got no 'partment! I ain't got no worries from no woman!

O woman, cries a voice in the night.

At first the sheer immensity of all these galaxies is too much, the stellar distances too daunting. His gaze retreats to the horizon and the aurora borealis pulses low on the northern sky. Academy award time. The farther along he walks beneath the stars, the more they seem to dance. Da da daddin dada da...Almost as though they were dancing *him.*

Just singin in the rain...

A comet sweeps through his line of vision. The aurora borealis pulses brighter and more massive to the north, but comets and northern lights are only the sideshow. They can only lead him back to the stars' feature event, the Dance of the Universe.

My God!

Drunk with exultation he staggers along the road and his soul is dancing. It dances all the way up the estuary of the Great River. Something out there, something everywhere, is humming. A great orchestra tuning for the big overture. Or in here? Yes, of course, inside too. The string section hums in his chest cavity and the coils of his small intestine are a French horn warming up for a fanfare. For this humming moment, he is star-struck, un-Timmed, less a man than a constellation. The Fisherman? Oberon? A being omnipotent and all-loving. He knows nothing but seems to encompass everything and dances and shudders in his soul...a force mighty as sex moves through him, mightier than sex, a thing he has only dreamed of to rattle and pound at the gates of his heart. For a dizzy moment he ascends.

Later, many times, he will wonder about this, believing, in an arcane recess of his mind, that he had reached the edge of something vast and unknowable for which *Mysterium Tremendum* is only the faintest glyph, but not now, because now is what time it is, and already he is on his way down. Coming down the great spangled way from the source of the diamond-studded river and once more to the foot of Orion, not fleeing Phaeton's corpse or fleeing anything, but calm. Calm, but ready to burst with the song of a thousand courting chickadees.

No, Fisher, you're not even close.

The only language he can invoke is one he learned on his mother's lap and his father's knee, a thumb-sucking dialect perfected in bed while talking beneath the covers to God, and that voice is lost forever....

Thank you, he says, nevertheless. Thank you! he cries, like David praising God in the firmament of His power with psalm after psalm. Thank you for this...for this...but now there is altogether too much to be thankful for.

From a long way off comes the drone of an approaching vehicle. He resents the sound of the car.

Thank you for this...time up there. Thank you, God, for the constellations, for Nancy, for little William wherever he is, for the fishing trip with Gump, for all the fish I ever caught, for puddle walks in the spring, for chickadees calling in May, for a decent mum and dad, for the old walnut radio, for the Milky Way, for Ginny Culp, for my big brother Derek, for being Bottom, for Jarvis Larsen not shooting me, for trout streams, the ones we haven't ruined, for Bolski and Slimy and fun at the lake, for sending down the Café Madonna, for Barb Viner, for Alistair Sim in *The Christmas Carol* and Jimmy Stewart in *It's a Wonderful Life* and Ethel Wilson and James Joyce, for robins who sing in my sleep, for the smell of larches and juniper, for Gump and Elliott if I haven't mentioned them already, for D.H. Lawrence and all the books I've read and all the ones to come....

The vehicle comes closer, headlights bearing down. He'll have to hurry.

...for all my boyhood adventures and for Walt Whitman, for all the banjo tunes in the world, and for Rita my banjo teacher, for waking up at the lake with the smell of coffee and bacon and the sound of the CNR steam engine chugging across the trestle, for Joan Baez, for *Blue Skies* and a million beautiful songs that make my heart swell, like right now, for the Nanaconda, for a thousand trips up the Amazon, for Tom Lehrer, for the cashews in the bowl of mixed nuts....

The driver slows his vehicle, a rusty old Meteor. He's a short stocky man as bald as Reverend Mountjoy.

You wandit ride?

The Meteor's interior smells of bad meat. Tim clears a space for his pack among the rubble in the back seat: soiled garments, oily rags, empty pop bottles, an open tool box, a hatchet. He climbs into the front seat. In no time they are clunking along past the Crowfoot glacier, its long glacial toes aglow in the moonlight.

How far you going? says Tim.

I go sout, the man says, shrugging. Maybe I go to Great Divide yet.

Silence. A moody silence? Doleful? Inchoate, Tim thinks, relishing the word. Rita used inchoate in a letter once. He would love to read or write a story full of inchoate silences. But how could silence be inchoate? Good question.

Mountains in shadow, mountains in moonlight, mountains in memory. It was supposed to be a farewell fishing trip into the mountains. Farewell to Edmonton, farewell to Gump, farewell to life this side of the Rockies. He and Gump had started at Mountie Lake this time so they could try Ochi Creek. But the best stretch was now in the hands of a nearby realtor, fenced and subdivided. Around the source of the creek where he'd landed his first brown trout, all the cover was gone, the beaver dams blasted out, and where the Ochi Campground used to be, there was a new summer camp for Jesus freaks. They'd put in *lawns*, for God's sake, right up to the edge of the creek. And worse. A gas pipeline had been gouged across and under the stream. The stretch above the pipeline had been subdivided into a bunch of little acreages and settled by people who thought you could buy a stream and improve it by diverting the water supply to grow gardens or raise a few cattle.

These people! he declared to Gump. They destroy their reasons for coming here by their own presence!

Aw, I dunno.

They drove west over the David Thompson Highway to Banff and camped in the mountains at Two Jack Lake. The next morning they headed for Johnson Lake. Tim had not been there since his melancholy fall and winter with Altrogge. But Gump knew it had some big brookies and even bigger rainbows, which was amazing for such a small lake—he'd taken his limit there the previous summer—so they drove out through the early morning mist with high hopes and arrived at the lakeside parking lot. Tim took the old path to the first rise overlooking the lake. He looked at the water.

More accurately, he looked *for* the water. In the misty light, it appeared to have vanished.

Gump, look!

Jesus!

The lake was gone. The dam at the outlet had somehow been destroyed, and almost the entire body of water had been drained. Left behind was an ugly grey cavity. They raced down to what had been the shore and leapt into the muddy crater. Gump wanted to see if the remaining stream had any fish. They walked all the way to the middle trench of the lake to what would have been one of the deepest holes. All they could find was a trickle from the feeder stream. First Ochi Creek and now this.

It was like wading through a sad dream, a very persistent dream. *He is in a car, perhaps the old family Chev. They are going fishing. They will go up Ochi Creek or one like it. As the day unfolds they see purple mountains, bucolic foothills, lush meadows, and then at last the stream. They glimpse it a half-mile off, perfect, murmuring and bubbling through a grassy meadow. But the road turns the wrong way. Don't worry, says Mum or Dad, we'll get there. The road winds through little towns and finally through a city, and they know the stream is right there somewhere, but time is passing and they still can't find it. Well, let's turn around! cries Tim. We saw it back there several hours ago! Don't you yell at your parents, says Mum. We can't go back, says Dad. You'd only have to walk all the way across that old meadow and then you'd get yourself tired. Tired? I wouldn't get tired! Don't yell. I'm not yelling! And the sun sinks into the hills and try as they might, they never ever reach the stream...*

All Gump could do was swear. They slogged back up from the deepest part of the crater and walked through the clay gumbo and dried weedbeds where lunker rainbow and brook trout used to hunt for nymphs. Gump was almost back to the former shoreline. Swearing, incredulous. Tim stopped to look at an object at his feet.

Y'comin? Fishy?

Tim reached down among the dried weeds and the mud and

picked up a wine bottle. The label was long gone, but the telltale shape...he was sure. Crackling Rosé. Perhaps it might have been the bottle of some other banjoist, equally heedless, but Tim was sure that it was his. He stood there in the crater as the lake poured out its memories like a great sad tired brain. *I will never be happier than I am right now. I am nineteen years old and I will never be happier.*

What collossal twenty-two karat horseshit. You just wait.

Gump was beside him. What's that you got there?

Crackling Rosé, he replied. I'd say about 1960 vintage.

How can you tell?

I'd know this bottle anywhere. It was the wine of the gods.

Tim stood there in the gumbo and listened to the wind.

You can have that stuff, Fishy. So can the gods. Gives me a hell of a head the next mornin.

Yeah.

C'mon, let's get back to the car.

The wind was whispering *Rita*.

Too bad I can't hang around for a bit. Maybe I could teach you a thing or two.

Somewhere upwind, a banjo was frailing in C minor. It was the saddest sound in all the world.

The man at the wheel swears at something. Deep down in his throat he hockles for phlegm. Damn buncha deers, he says.

Tim sees them on the shoulder. White shadows at the corona of the headlights' blaze. Elk, not deer. He doesn't bother to correct his driver.

You could easy hevit the excident, the man says.

All at once Tim wonders if he has hitched the wrong ride. Things happen on this highway. He glances at the man, hunched down low in the driver's seat, squinting.

Damn buncha deers, he says again.

So on they went, undaunted, Gump and Fishy. All the way up the Banff-Jasper Highway into the alpine country to Morraine Lake where the splake used to be so hot. And the man at the lodge said, Hell, they haven't stocked this lake for years. They shut down the hatchery up in Jasper. Fungus or somethin. None of these mothers has been stocked for a dog's age, eh? You should try hikin into one a them high country lakes.

What the hell is comin off? Gump kept saying. We used to do great here.

But they didn't give up. They unloaded Tim's boxes and trunk at the bus depot at Lake Louise, left them in storage for Tim to pick up on his bus trip west. Then they headed over to Lake Louise and climbed the trail to the teahouse at Lake Agnes. Former home of the Teahouse Maid.

This is how it happened. Lowney parks the car at the public lot, and when he looks up and sees the Victoria Glacier, dazzling in the intense shock of light, he goes giddy. After a moment of awe, he breaks out into his favoured falsetto.

When I was seventeen, it was a very good year.

They throw on their hiking gear and begin the trek by crossing the bridge over Louise Creek. Tim pays a brief homage to Alistair Vaughan and Sandy MacDonald for having rescued him from a drunkard's death in this creek, and Gump's falsetto goes into a discreet whisper.

It was a very good year for small town girls.

They continue past the poppy beds and the great European dream that is the Chateau, then move quickly through a narcoleptic brigade of tourists who wander to this day among the poppy beds in a perpetual ad for sleepy rich people. They find the trail that leads back towards Victoria Glacier, reclining above them like Odalisque on the mountains that rise to the west above Lake Louise. The path goes steeply upward, winding back and forth through the forest until at last the trees begin to grow smaller and the alpine meadows begin to reach down into the sunny glades. Gump is puffing too much to continue his song, and finally it dies as he gawks down the slope they have just climbed.

See what you're leavin behind, Fishy?

Yeah.

Sure you want to go to Vancouver?

Vancouver. Steelhead rivers. A multitude of ethnic restaurants. Salmon fishing in Horseshoe Bay. Old bookstores. A multitude of well-read women. Lotusland.

You bet, Gumper. I wish I didn't have so much junk to drag out there.

Ditto. Jeez. What's in those boxes?

My past.

The idea is to go fishing with Gump and then for Gump to put Tim and all his boxes on the bus for Vancouver. Derek moved back there, so Tim can at least store his junk until he finds a place of his own. Best laid plans.

The chateau and its chalets are dwarfed now by the mountains ranging on three sides of the valley. The buildings look like clever miniatures modelled from a Swiss village. Up they go, Tim and Gump, past lines of exhausted walkers who are wishing they had worn sensible shoes instead of the little pumps they have brought all the way from London, Berlin, Tokyo, the World. The farther up they go towards the end of the treeline, the fewer the tourists. Hairpin turns begin to proliferate, oxygen seems to grow thin, high country hikers on their way down include Tim and Gump in their knowing glances. *You are no longer a tourist. You are one of us, o brethren of the healthy lungs.* At last they tramp around Mirror Lake, and move uphill again as far as the sturdy wooden stairs bolted to the sheer rocks by the waterfalls that feed Mirror Lake. They stop to dip their cups into the icy water.

Amazing taste, eh Gumper? We're practically at the source of all water. The mother stream of the old Saskatchewan. One of the fallopian tubes of the nation.

Fuckin A.

They trudge up the last hundred steps or so. Behold, the chalet on the shores of Lake Agnes, host to a svelte couple sipping tea. At first Tim thinks it's Nancy and Joel, but as he approaches them he realizes they bear not the slightest resemblance to anyone he knows. The woman speaks with some kind of a New York accent and the man has a Dutch flag on his pack. Tim has the feeling that he is going to meet Nancy just around the next corner, but he blinks the thought out of his mind and the thought hovers with the mosquitoes at the edge of Lake Agnes. The lake is sheltered from the breezes by the peaks to the north and west, so the surface is calm. Calm enough for....

Yes!

Gump spots them rising close to shore, halfway down the lake. They break out their rods, tie on dry flies, and hike up the path past the teahouse. It leads through a scree, past some huge boulders, and out onto a ledge about ten feet above the lake. A sudden scud over the water beneath some encroaching clouds makes it hard to spot anything. For several minutes the world goes pallid and grey and the water holds no promise. Then, just as quickly, the clouds roll ba breeze drops, and every rock and ripple is drenched in pure light shades explode into primary colours, lush and organic. A sch trout comes drifting past the boulders, the occasional one rising for midges, then drifting on, circling back. And then, as though a new meal was being served ahead of them, with one synchronized shudder they all dive into the deep water.

Tim hangs his packsack and jacket on a sign, clambers down from the ledge to the shoreline, and leaps out over the water from rock to rock until he finds himself straddling a flat boulder about ten yards from shore. The trout have gone deeper. He waits. He thinks he might have seen a swirl no more than forty feet beyond his rock.

Because he works with reflective surfaces, he is a bit like Alice dreaming up a passage through her looking glass. When the water is unruffled by any rises, the trout are only hypothetical, a happy construct of the imagination. And then the magic swirl: one swirl means one fish, but it could also mean an entire school. He can't see them, but he knows they are there. The monsters he dreams of, the ones he must come to terms with. Tremulously, like a tiny male spider gone a-courting for Grunty, he tries to seduce these perfect monsters up from the depths and into the dazzling light. It takes a smooth line. It takes a fly subtly made, like any other imitation of nature. It takes a certain faith that is closer to religion than scientific certitude. *I have seen a rise; I believe they are there waiting, the silver multitudes. They sulk in the shadows of the boulders. They hunt for nymphs in the littoral zones. They are fated to rise for my lines. It is part of the big plan.*

He pulls out ten or fifteen feet of line. He lets it hang in the breeze. At the end of his leader is a tiny mosquito imitation. Or a moth or an emerging nymph. Now he flicks the fly behind him and pauses, flicks it in front of him. Back and forth. Feeds the line so it gets longer and longer, a winged umbilicus, a lariat with ballet lessons. He lets his line soar out to where the last rise dimpled the water, drives the rod forward and down until the line falls straight onto the surface, delicate and deadly as a spider web.

There is a new twist in his line. It uncurls back upon itself, unobtrusively, the art that conceals art; it flips his fly over in the water like a struggling gnat. This is the moment of *Verbindung* for the artist, for if the art is true, Nature itself is taken in by this ultimate illusion. This is the moment after foreplay, the moment before the onset of prophecy, the moment he has been waiting for all winter. A silver *glurp*, his fly is gone, and Nature beguiled. His rod comes up erect and unapologetic as mushrooms, his line plunges down into the deepest part of his lake, he is fast to a fish. It might be his nine hundred and ninty-ninth trout, but it is his first; it is always his first.

How long has he known that this fish was destined for his creel? How long has he studied and plotted and rehearsed and read and practised and dreamed of its perfect flesh? How many copies of *Fin & Feather*? How many botched flies torn open in his vise? The water is clear as a postcard lake, worthy of the waters of the great Stufflebeam. The only thing missing is the immortal Pussy, barebreasted in hip waders, and the banners above her head, heralding ecstatic news about spark plugs or tubeless tires. The ultimate nymph emerging, the muse you use for your musings, the—

Excuse me? Mister? Excuse me!

A strident voice. She seems to know something he does not.

Yes? he says without turning around. Any fool can see he has bigger fish to fry.

There is a sign that says No Fishing and that's exactly what it means. Mister?

A chunky rainbow cartwheels over the water in slow motion, dives for the bottom, and Tim's reel whines. This is going to be a tussle.

Did you hear me?

Yes, I heard you.

And?

I didn't see any sign.

Well, you just happened to hang your packsack on it, that's why.

The woman's voice is familiar, but the rainbow makes another leap and Tim brings in more line. It begins to thrash on the surface; it is tiring. And that voice, yes, that voice—

Did you hear me?

I heard you.

Well?

Sorry.

Sorry isn't good enough. You'd better let that fish go and dangle your worm somewhere else.

Dangle his worm indeed. The fish is spent, seventeen inches of silver, steel blue on the back, a rainbow stripe of greenish blue, purple and pink on the side. A meal of memorable proportions.

Are you sure I—

Your damn rights I'm sure. Jeez, what do you need, a picture?

He reaches into the mouth of the rainbow, plucks out the fly, and releases the fish. It swims slowly away and seems to grow larger as it fades into the deep water. His hands are slimy. He washes them in the gravel and turns around to—

Oh, shit, she says. I don't believe this.

With her hand over her face, the anguished young woman sits down on the ledge above him. When she takes her hand away, the same thin hand that has frailed so many banjo tunes, all he can say is, Oh, my God, because he knows even before the thought begins to form that he just might not make it out to Vancouver.

The logistics are tricky, but he manages to bring it off with Rita's blessing and Gump's assistance, and because Johnny Aubichon, the head wrangler at the corral, remembers him from the summer of 1960. Tim and Gump haul the five boxes up to the corral and help the wranglers to tie them onto the horses. They ride with the pack train all the way back to the teahouse.

Fishy, what the hell did she *say* to you?

What do you mean?

One minute you're on your way out to Vancouver to find a job, the next minute you're gonna be a dishwasher at Lake Agnes.

She said I might be able to stay with her.

Just like that?

Just like that.

They sit on their nags and gaze around them at the lake, the scree, the alpine meadow. Johnny is untying Tim's boxes. He is humming an old song.

Sure you want to come to Jasper?

I said I'd come fishing with you, Gumper, and I meant it.

But what about—

She knows that I'll be back in a couple of days. We can part company up in Jasper after we've caught some fish. You can drive back to Edmonton and I'll hitch back here from Jasper.

Is this true love, Fishy?

It's something.

Well then. Is this the last of Tim Fisher?

Nope. You an me, Gumper. We'll fish together into the next millenium.

Well, Fishy, she's gonna be a good spring.

he man at the wheel is almost yelling.

s Tim.

ι doing for work like?

ι up here in the mountains?

ιu doing for job like? You one of these guys on the pogy, yassr ιᵤ me kinds heepy? Or no maybe you godit the job.

I've always had a job, says Tim.

He speaks cautiously. He remembers the hatchet in the back seat.

Whad you do for job? says the man.

I've been teaching basic English to new...to...I teach night school.

Young guys. Avrywhere. Young guys they go roun look like bum, no work no good for nothing.

Tim grunts in reply. He hopes his grunt will sound noncommittal. But the man wants more. An argument perhaps, or a denial.

Actually, when I can find the time....

Yass?

Tim has second thoughts. He casts around for an avenue of retreat. You don't give true confessions to a fellow like this. Or maybe he isn't a psychopath. Maybe he's just an unappreciated guy on a rant.

In my spare time, he says, I'm a writer.

A rider?

No, a writer.

The man snorts, winds down his window, gobs out into the night.

The stars are still unusually clear, profuse. Bright bugs suspended in the web of night. Why weren't there any constellations named after spiders? In the ideal car and on the right night, he would be able to discuss this stellar insight with his host. A constellation named after Grunty, perhaps. But the man behind the wheel is dumb to the dance of the universe.

A rider, he says. Like Dostoevsky, yass?

Mouth open, Tim stares at the man.

You readit that guy? Dostoevsky? You readit him?

Yeah, he's great.

Holy sonombeach.

Tim could not have put it better himself.

Whad you rideit about? Canadian Mouny police? Hey, you Canadian Dostoevsky? The man at the wheel errupts in a throaty explosion something like a laugh. You rideit about the heckey player? I just asking.

You can keep on asking.

The bald man is undaunted. Hey, I rideit things in new-spaber. In

Sowiet Union. No Dostoevsky, okay? Just rideit in new-spaber, I say this thing that thing they throw me in Siberia. You know Siberia?

I've heard of it. Everybody's heard about it.

So what you rideit about in the Canada, hey?

What do you think we write about? The same things Soviets write about.

Like what? You tal me.

Suddenly it's like talking to Techla Wahrsager when she's out for blood. Preposterously highfallutin expressions twinkle like sequins in the night: The Eternal Verities, The Perilous Issues Confronting Us All, The Universal Themes of Great Literature. Tim turns to his driver. He is thinking about his most recently abandoned story, one of those gee-it's-tough-to-be-in-love-when-you're-as-sensitive-as-I-am sort of narratives.

Love, he says. Do you have love stories in the Soviet Union? You know, man meets woman, they fall in love, woman disappears?

The driver laughs again. This abrasive approach to conversation seems to suit him.

I try once to rideit the novel. You see? I knowit guys they tal me maybe I can pobbly-shed this stuff. No bloddy way I tal you. Work like hell. No way I could make to *finishing* this stuff, hey?

The man turns his attention to Tim. I try to rideit the love story, man meet woman like that. I try.

Maybe you'll go back to it. Try again.

The driver groans. He swears.

One day I look at this stuff I say today I rideit shit, avry day I rideit shit. Byebye Dostoevsky.

At Peyto Lake the old Meteor pulls over to the shoulder.

How far you are going?

I want to make Lake Louise before too long. There's a station bus I can catch up the hill.

The man takes out a thermos and pours some coffee into the cup. He takes a sip, turns to Tim. You want coffee?

Tim doesn't want any coffee. He has things to do. Like get reacquainted with Rita. Like burn five boxes full of junk. Like get some sleep. He looks at the man. The bald head, the stocky build, and something lurches in Tim's belly. *I do not believe this is happening!* He can't be sure, he can't be absolutely sure. He holds the cup in his hand.

You try.

He sips the coffee. And yes, it has to be him.

Good, yass?

Yes, Tim replies. It's okay cowboy.

Okay cowboy, the man says, nodding. Okay cowboy, h

They drive on and he tells Tim a story. Once upon a tim
cow there was a journalist who told the truth once too ofte
was sent to Siberia. On winter days he and the other prison
march out to work in double columns through the snow. Th
march in silence and never break out of their columns or th
would shoot them. For years the man followed this routine.

One evening on the march back from his shift this man s
tiny red object on the snow. Risking death, he broke from his
grabbed the object, and lurched back into line. By some small
the guards did not notice. He waited until after they'd eat
evening meal to identify the object. He took it into a dark c
the compound, and all by himself he examined it by the light of a
match. It was a cigarette butt stained with bright red lipstick.

Night after night he gazed at his little treasure. He spoke to it. He
chastised it as though it were an unfaithful mistress. You never loved
me, he would mutter. You flew over this miserable camp without a
thought for me down here dying. You flushed this cigarette butt from
60,000 feet to show your indifference. Some love letter!

Many times he chastised the cigarette butt, yet still he loved it.
And then one of the prisoners saw him with it, and he too acquired a
strange obsession for the cigarette butt. More and more of the men
heard about it and stole glimpses of it. It became a sort of camp icon.
At last, with his sugar rations running low, the man gambled for sugar
with the cigarette butt. Eventually he lost it. In dozens of card games
it went from hand to hand, and at last became unravelled, disinte-
grated, and disappeared.

The man missed his cigarette butt. He also missed the power
and prestige it had given him. One night in his bed he rolled a
cigarette and smoked it down to the butt. Then he crept into the
latrine, cut his lip with an old razor blade, and bled onto this butt.
A few days later he showed it to the men, claiming he had found
another one. This too he gambled away, and once more, like an
aging hussy, it did the rounds of the camp.

Isn't that an amazing story?

Yes, says Rita. It was worth getting woken up for that one.

She is poking around in the corner between the stove and the mantel
for more firewood. Her back is to him. Outside the air has turned cold

272 DAVID CARPENTER

and the wind is bringing down a storm from the glacier.

Talk about the vanity of profane love, eh?

Talk about the *need* for love, says Rita.

She looks down at him as he stretches out by the stove.

Yeah, that too.

He wishes he'd said that. He is inspired and jumpy. It's almost two o'clock in the morning. He has rediscovered the Mad Russian, heard his story, and now he is all alone with Rita in her little cabin up the slope from the Lake Agnes teahouse. There is a two-inch scar on her lower lip, and her face is peeling from too much sun, but she has the same smile she has always had, even when she was fifteen. (*What are the elements of this smile?* Mischief. *Check.* Playfulness. *Check.* Irony. *What kind of irony?* Like she gets the joke and we don't. *Too vague, try again.* The irony of cunning women. *What the hell does that mean?* Her smile is formed by gal wisdom, as though she knows the next step and I'm still trying to figure it out? *What's the next step?* Bed. *Check.*)

What are you smiling at? he says.

I'm not smiling.

So, what are the rules? What are my duties besides washing dishes? Who are we working for?

You are working for me. I'm not just a waitress any longer. I bought the concession up here.

Wow. What happened to your band?

We broke up. I used the money from my share to buy this concession. I even sold my instruments.

Your banjo and everything?

Yep. I could have gotten some gigs singing work songs for various unions, or a slot at Expo, or more bars, but who needs that kind of work? No one wants to hear me warbling about those things any more. Besides, I seem to have acquired a new banjo.

So. You're out of the business.

Not really. But I want to write songs. Concentrate on that. And I want to do other things too. I want a real life for a change.

Rita throws some scraps and twigs into the fire and they are consumed in seconds. She lights a cigarette, inhales, breathes out, and still she is smiling. She is definitely smiling.

I burned up all the good wood. You're going to have to take an axe to that big stuff out there.

In the dark? In the cold? Do you have a flashlight?

.tteries are buggered. All I have is candles and the lantern.

couldn't see a foot in front of me to do the chopping. I'd chop nger off.

Yuck.

Tell you what. We can burn all my junk. We can roll the papers up into thick scrolls and burn them like logs in the stove. We've got enough to last for hours.

She crouches by the mantel with a blanket over her nightie.

Tim, you can't just *burn* this stuff. For all I know one of my own letters is in these boxes. Besides, your whole past is in here. You might need them some day for your writing.

Didn't you once say that I had an unhealthy tendency to dwell on the past?

I was probably exasperated with you.

Exasperated. Rita is probably the only friend he has who would prefer exasperated to mad.

This is like a museum of your whole past. Tim?

My whole past is a monument to insular boredom and comfortable assertions. You could never write a novel about that.

He stares at his banjo wondering if this is true. The banjo leans against an easy chair as though waiting to be played.

I am free, he thinks.

Are you now? says the banjo.

Let's burn the stuff, he says. Most of it anyway. It would feel like a new beginning.

He glances up and sees Rita's look of disapproval.

We can save *your* letters.

Five big cardboard boxes. If they were stacked one on top of the other, they would make an impressive totem pole. A column of tedium, a tower of babble.

Okay, he says, if we find some photographs or something too precious to throw out, we can put them here on the chesterfield, right?

Okay, says Rita. She sounds unconvinced.

They begin with the nearest box. It has mostly recent stuff, letters from Tim's parents (retired, adjusting to apartment life, yearning for Victoria), from Mahler (in San Diego, remarried and happier), from Janey Bream (pregnant), from Elliott Crystal (in his first articling job, an owl among vultures), from Tim's old math teacher Mr. Huculak (back in graduate school, still jogging long distances), from Sandy MacDonald (moved to Atlanta, now travelling secretary for his fraternity), from Techla Wahrsager (living in a Montreal commune, teaching at Concordia, considering the big leap back to Europe, expanding her thesis into a book "that will revolutionize the entire fucking toy industry," closing her letter with solidarity, which Tim willfully reinterprets as love). These and many more.

They stack the letters and roll them up into tubes, twisting and bending the tubes in the middle. These hang together enough to make reasonable faggots. The fire blazes in the little potbellied stove with the first few offerings. They work quickly, and at last they come to the end of the first lot. They get ahead of themselves and toss the faggots into the empty wood box. Rita is *still* smiling.

When we run out of letters, she says, we can burn the cardboard boxes. This is fun.

Are you warm?

As long as these things last.

The next lot has stacks of old newspaper clippings and some drawings from when Tim was in elementary school. Pages of cowboys shooting guns, several Nanacondas devouring things, some adolescent cartoons reminiscent of *Mad Magazine* (a few tries at Alfred E. Newman, a woman out walking her pet tarantula on a leash), some girls and some trout in the Stufflebeam tradition.

You're not going to throw those *drawings* into the fire.

Just watch me.

You'll be sorry.

They burn the drawings and the newspaper clippings, and the fire roars. When they get to the photographs, they burn most of them too. What the hell. Tim's mum probably has copies in the family album. He gives another photo to Rita.

Oh, my God. We're holding hands! I was only fifteen years old. Look at my Titania dress, I just hated it. It was made for Nancy Fuller.

Lotta leg there.

By the time they finish the third box the little cabin is warming up. Rita lets her blanket slip from her shoulders and sits there in her flanelette nighty and ski socks. Her nightie is full-length and it clings to her body like a bedsheet. She is older, she looks older. She is no longer the perfect beauty he used to think of as the Teahouse Maid. Maybe she never was. He wants to ask her how she got the scar on her lip. She butts out her cigarette, yawns, and squints at the picture of her and Tim on stage, *circa* 1957. Her voice makes vibrations on the strings of his banjo.

Here's a poem, she says.

Let me see that.

I think it might be a love poem. Surely you're not going to burn it too.

He holds the sheet of paper in front of a kerosene lamp on a small table so that he can read.

Let us arise, you and I
In the grey dark hours of the morning
When the robin's gurgle is heavy with sleep.

Robin's gurgle? Ouch. Surely I changed that.

Just read it.

Slimy, you won't believe this, but I wrote this thing for you.

You wrote it for me and you never *showed* it to me?

I considered it. But I could never find you.

Read it. Read the whole thing.

Naw.

Come on, please? It might be the only decent poem I've ever inspired. Her face softens, relaxes into a tender look. A yearning look? Was it Slimy who inspired that poem or some remote idea of Slimy?

Read my poem, she says. Please?

He holds the poem up to the light and reads as solemnly as he can. At the end of each stanza he pauses to send off silent voodoo incantations directed straight at Rita's heart: *You are strangely attracted to me... You would die to be held by me... You are losing your will to resist... Besides, it's a cold night. Alone in bed you might freeze to death....*

Well? he says, when he has finished the poem.

Well what?

Do you feel like a muse now?

I feel amused, she says, throws her head back and breaks into a vaudevillean laugh. Her throat seems to glow in the lamplight, and again comes the hum of the banjo strings. There is a certain roundness to her chin and to one shoulder that begins to emerge from the collar of her nightie.

What are you looking at? she says.

I'm not looking.

You are so.

How did you like my poem?

It's touching. It's....

What?

Innocent. You don't have to groan like that. I like it. Sort of. What's wrong?

Innocence is becoming in children but I have no use for it in adults.

Well, whatever. I'm going to keep your poem. I could even make it into a song.

On all fours he pads across the floor and puts his arms around her, draws her to him, and kisses her. Nothing. She smiles at him from a long time back or a long way away.

What's wrong? he says.

Nothing's wrong. I was just remembering. How we lay down in that little cot in your garret at the Garage. How your head was down there and mine was up here.

But something's wrong.

I got out of singing for several reasons. That guy you saw me with at Gump's engagement party was one of them, but another reason was to get away from a life where love was quick and deadly without much staying power. One of the things I liked about you was that you never came on like King Kong, you never had these...expectations.

Sorry.

Just go slow. Slow is fast enough for me. For the time being. Come on, it's getting chilly again.

They go at the fourth and fifth boxes together, term papers, report cards, classroom assignments and exams. From time to time he peruses them. The fire in the little stove keeps blazing. As long as they feed it regularly, the room stays warm, but as soon as they start to nod off, the chill returns and one of them has to open the stove lid, stir the ashes, and feed the fire again.

Around four-thirty in the morning the full force of the storm descends on Lake Agnes. The wind roars down from the glacier like a great dog in pain; the rain blasts the north side of the cabin. Rita stares out the window. She seems concerned.

You know, Recently-Hired-Jack-Of-All-Trades, we are going to need some dry wood. Those big logs outside, they're going to be hard to burn.

I don't think so, he sighs. All we have to do is stay warm tonight. Your cot will be real cold. We could drag sleeping bags out here and stay by the stove. We could even—

Look, she says, there's only one bag in the cabin. I'll lay it down here for you and I'll get some blankets for me over here. If I fall asleep, you throw on the paper logs. If you fall asleep, it's up to me. We could even do shifts. What are you thinking about?

I was thinking about that trip where I first saw the Mad Russian. Gump and I had to feed the fire at the campground on Ochi Creek. I bet if we hadn't done shifts at the fire all night we could actually have died from the snow and the cold.

Boy, are we getting your whole past tonight, or what?

It's true. His entire life seems to rise and ambush him around every corner. He can hardly say or think anything that doesn't remind him of something else. Perhaps it was that walk under the stars.

Look, he says at last, we could put the blankets on the bottom, unzip the bag, and put it on top like a quilt. Then we could sleep together and keep warm from body warmth. Let's be practical.

No. You sleep there and I sleep here. We are not going to freeze to death. It's June, not January.

As she speaks, there is a new sound pattering on the window, the sound of sleet turning to snow.

Look, he says. A blizzard.

So?

I was just thinking about hypothermia, that's all.

Hypo what?

Hypothermia.

Never heard of it.

Tim sighs. He kneels by the stove, feeding it a pile of term papers: a thirty pager on Chaucer's *Troilus*, an even bigger one on *Anthony and Cleopatra*, an annotated bibliography of D.H. Lawrence criticism. The fire blazes away. Rita kneels with her back to the stove and faces him. She begins to fiddle with a long strand of her hair. She winds the strand around her wrist.

Remember that party for Gump and Sherry's engagement, and we saw each other?

Yes.

You just stood there.

I didn't have time for much else. You disappeared. I looked everywhere for you.

I guess I must have thought you weren't interested. Or else you weren't ready or something.

And you were with your gypsy musician.

Well, yeah.

She is not smiling now.

Nay, I can gleek upon occasion.

Rita smiles and yawns.

Anyway, you've changed. Something's happened to you. You're not so vulnerable any more, right? And I expected you'd be the last word in stability, but instead there's this new rootlessness of yours, selling your car, moving out of your flat, burning up everything. I can't keep up with all these changes.

Neither can I.

Well?

Well what?

Will the real Tim Fisher please step forward?

He will, I promise. But too much has happened too fast. You and me in the same room together. Meeting you at Lake Agnes again. All that and the Mad Russian. He was probably the first writer I ever met. And then the thing that happened before that. I haven't even told you what happened before that.

All right, what happened before that?

It was sort of mystical.

She ducks into the tiny bedroom at the cold end of the cabin and returns wearing a thick wool sweater over her nightie. The chill has returned, so they go at the last box and build up the fire in the stove again. They toss the extra faggots into the wood box. Rita spreads her blanket over the rug and lies down on her side, facing the stove.

He unzips the sleeping bag completely and it becomes a large quilt. He throws half of it over her, nestling under it next to her back. He puts his arm over her body and closes his eyes.

So what happened to you that was all so mystical?

It's hard to explain, he says. I was hitching south to Lake Louise. And the stars were out. And I just felt...this terrific...thing. It's like I could see my place in the universe or something. All those mountains. Maybe it's what you call a peak experience, eh?

Hardy-har.

Okay, seriously. It was like this thing that made the stars dance was making me dance too. And you know what I did? You're not falling asleep, are you?

I've got to warm up. I think I'll see if the hot water is still working and get a hot water bottle. Keep on talking.

She runs the water in the sink at the far side of the room and fills the hot water bottle.

It was just like I was a little kid with a new fly rod or something. I started to pray!

No kidding.

Yeah. That's all. That's it. I guess you had to be there.

That's neat.

She stands by his banjo holding the hot water bottle to her stomach and turns to face him. He rolls back underneath the sleeping bag. Rita slumps by her chair drawing the hot water bottle up against her breasts. She gazes down at him as though she wanted to mention something. His mind is off again, dipping down into his dreams and up again to feed on the surface....

Tim, what did you *say?*

When?

On the road, grooving under the stars.

Tim shifts his weight beneath the sleeping bag, yawns, and thinks for a moment. I said something like...thank you for the stars and for the fishing trips I've had, and for all my friends, and for...you really want to hear this?

Yes.

Well, it's embarrassing, but I felt so *blessed* all of a sudden. I felt so full. All I could do was extol all the things I've ever loved in some way or another. I thanked God, for godsake!

What else for?

Smiling, she comes toward him. As she steps over the banjo, the edge of her nighty brushes across the strings, faintly strumming a chord in G major.

What else did you say?

He wants to tell her, but he senses that a forgotten idea, some magic, is somewhere close by, tailing in the current. He can't both tell her about his experience and cast around for the idea.

I *think* I thanked Him for the Nanaconda. You remember the—

The Nanaconda, oh yes, she says, and nestles in next to him, yawning. The Nanacondaconda.

And for the banjo.

The banjobanjo, she sighs, her voice drowsing more than talking.

And of course the Café Madonna. Did I ever tell you about her?

The Madonnadonna.

Yes, he yawns, the Mad—

He sits up. He struggles to his feet. Where did I put my my my—

What are you doing?

I'm looking for my—found it.

His green spiral notebook. Then a pen. He sits in a cha
stove where the lantern sheds just enough light for Tim to
down three words: Onna donna tine.

What are you *doing?*

The first trout is in the creel, he replies.

A note of triumph in his voice.

Rita yawns. Right.

ACKNOWLEDGEMENTS

The author wishes to acknowledge some help from a lot of friends, but especially from the following people: Bob Derksen, Elena Glazov-Corrigan, Guy Vanderhaeghe, Louise Halfe, Yuz Aleshkovsky, Robert Minhinnick and (for countless bits of advice), Honor Kever. I would also like to thank Geoffrey Ursell, whose editorial skills kept me on track during the final year of re-writes; my writing group on Connaught Drive, who waded beside me through the stormy waters of the early drafts; the SWAC Committee, for all those colonies at the Abbey; the holy men of St. Pete's, for hosting me so many times; the Saskatchewan Arts Board and the Canada Council, for two grants that allowed me to leave my job and write.

DAVID CARPENTER was born and raised in Edmonton, and has spent most of the last 20 years in Saskatoon, teaching at the University of Saskatchewan, and forging his writing career. His previous books include the fiction titles *Jewels, Jokes for the Apocalypse,* and *God's Bedfellows*, and the non-fiction works, *Courting Saskatchewan, Writing Home,* and a how-to guide, *Fishing In the West.* He has also lived in Oregon, Winnipeg, Toronto, and Victoria, and spent many summers living and working in Banff.

He won the Canadian Novella Contest sponsored by Descant magazine in 1988, and has received several Western Magazine awards for stories and articles. His work has also appeared in a great many periodicals and anthologies.